FORGOTTEN TRAIL

Steven D. McKain

T. Rover Press—Richmond Hill, GA
Paperback ISBN: 979-8-9985647-2-7
eBook ISBN: 979-8-9985647-3-4
Library of Congress Control Number: 2026909658
Title: *Forgotten Trail*
Author: Steven D. McKain
Digital distribution | 2026
Paperback | 2026

Published in the United States by New Book Authors Publishing

DEDICATION

To the folks of The Texas Hill Country

"The Lord is close to the brokenhearted and saves those who are crushed in spirit."
Psalm 34:18

CHAPTER ONE

The grass smelled fresh as the afternoon sun warmed my tired body. In the distance I could hear the cannon and musket fire as the battle raged on. All morning shots were traded between the two belligerents, ground was given, and ground was taken yet we had not been committed to the fight.

So, I lay on my back, hat covering my face, trying to catch up on some much-needed rest. We had been on the move night and day with the Army of the Shenandoah to reach this place, this time, this moment on the battlefield. Yet, here we sit, waiting for the order. The order to attack, to scout or move again. Here we sit, anxiously awaiting the order from those with the knowledge of the battle, the knowledge of the enemy and the army. That is how it was for the soldier in every army I suppose. The lower down the chain you are the less information you are privy to, and the more waiting you must endure.

I was thinking of my home and trying to quell my growing anticipation of the coming fight. The crops would be coming in about now. The weather in July would be hot and humid in Southern Georgia. August, now there was a humid month of the year. The humidity so thick at times you could almost see it hanging, hovering in the air. Not unlike this day in Northern Virginia.

I often sympathized with my soldiers having to endure this God-Awful humidity, especially since most hailed from parts immune to such weather. I suppose they had other miseries to deal with that we in the Deep South did not. The cold for one, deep and often penetrating no matter how you try to ward it off with layers upon layers of clothing, and an experience I hate to repeat. I had my fill of it while attending the Virginia Military Institute not so long ago. The cold and the snow that so often blankets this region is a misery I can do without. So, I lay here in the sun, hat over my face, hands folded across my chest, trying to catch up on some much needed and desired sleep, grateful for the warming sun.

But it was not to be.

I heard his approaching footfalls, heavy through the grass, though he himself was not a large man. I knew who it was without looking. He was always there, always within sight if not within reach. He came with me from the Federal Army when the Southern States seceded, and we had returned to Georgia. I, a newly commissioned lieutenant in the Federal Army, and he a corporal in the Federal Cavalry, my first assignment upon graduation from VMI. Barely a year being a lieutenant, I decided to resign my commission and return home.

We both knew that it would be wrong to take up arms against our home, our kin folk, so we began the long journey south to offer our services to 'The Cause'. We traveled on horseback, still dressed in our Federal blue uniforms, through the southern states from Washington City. We quickly became friends and decided we would join up together in the same regiment, hopefully a cavalry outfit and stand with our brethren from Georgia. That is what brought us here, this tiny place on the map, Manassas Junction, Northern Virginia.

He stopped next to my resting figure. I knew he was looking down at me, so feigning sleep was not going to fool him. Cleet knew me too well. He knew I was awake, alert, and ready to go into battle.

"Captain," he said. "There is an awful lot of activity at headquarters. Reckon it is near time."

I moaned to hide my growing anxiety. This will be our first major engagement, and I cannot lie, I was excited. "Oh, go away Corporal," I mumbled.

He chuckled. "Now Captain, you know that ain't gonna happen."

I lifted my hat and looked at him. "Where is the First Sergeant," I asked.

"You mean our drunk Napoleon," he answered.

I sat up and cast a disapproving look his way. "Corporal Haines. I told you about that."

He pushed his kepi further back on his head exposing a lock of unruly blonde hair. He squatted down next to me and lowered his voice. "Shit Wyatt. I know. He is gonna get somebody kilt, the drunken fool."

I took in his boyish features. Even though he was a year older than me he looked no more than sixteen years. I sympathized with his plight of being a non-commissioned officer under a drunken First Sergeant. "I know Cleet," I said, "I will take care of him in due time. You just take care of the troopers under your charge."

Cleet nodded his head. "Reckon so Wyatt." Yet he continued his protest. "I do not know how it is you will take care of him, seein' how the Major is his uncle."

I looked at Cleet once more and said, "When are you going to get a proper cavalry hat and get rid of that kepi?"

He took his hat off and looked at it. "When I find one as fancy as yours Captain Chambers." He put his hat on his small head and laughed, looked up and quickly stood. "Here comes the Major with the First Sergeant, Wyatt," he said quickly.

I stood, brushed the grass off my uniform, and put on my pistol belt, complete with saber. In the few skirmishes we had been involved in I hated wearing my cavalry saber. It made too much noise and often got in the way. At night, while doing scouting missions of the enemy positions, I would leave it behind. The damn thing sounded as if I were kicking a tin can down the road, clank, clank, and clatty clank. I doubt I would use it other than to rally the troopers, but it was part of my uniform, and I obediently wore it.

"Captain Chambers," barked Major Bronson. "Gather your men."

I saluted smartly and said, "Yes sir. First Sergeant Bronson have the bugler sound assembly."

The First Sergeant and Cleet went to assemble the men while I stayed with the Major to receive my orders.

Major Bronson, tall and lean with one of the most well-groomed mustaches I had ever seen, was a proud career soldier, who also came from the Federal Army before the war. I respected him as both a man and a soldier and while doing so I was, admittedly conflicted as to why he would tolerate the drunken antics of his nephew, my First Sergeant. I suppose there was something to be said about kin.

He pulled a map from the inside of his jacket and unfolded it. He pointed and said, "Captain, these are our current positions."

I studied the hand drawn military symbols denoting both our positions as well as the Yankee Army facing us. His finger rested just below Henry Hill near the Manassas-Sudley Road.

He continued. "We are to the left of the 49th Virginians. We sir are the far left of the army. I want you to take your company of troopers and scout along the Manassas-Sudley Road. Colonel Stuart and I will bring up the rest of the cavalry and a contingent of 6-pounder guns. We must know what is ahead of us. The Yankees may be trying to out flank us, Captain."

I studied the map, committing it all to memory. The roads, terrain, woods, and streams. I had the ability to recall with the greatest of detail all that I read and saw which made me an effective cavalry officer. I looked at my gold time piece, near ten in the morning. The day is still young.

I pulled out my map, made a few notations and said, "When do you want us to leave Major?"

"Immediately Captain. I will bring up the remainder of the cavalry with Colonel Stuart. Time is of the essence."

I saluted smartly and turned to leave.

Major Bronson stopped me and said, "Good luck Wyatt. This is our first major engagement, and the outcome of the battle may be decided this afternoon." He smiled. "No pressure son." He offered his hand.

I returned his smile, shook his hand, and excitedly went in search of my horse. We were finally going to prove our worth on the battlefield.

The First Sergeant and Corporal Haines had the men assembled in good order, although I knew it was Cleet who had motivated the men to form up so quickly. My troopers stood next to their horses waiting for the order from me to mount up. I looked them over with a practiced eye. I was proud of these boys and prouder still to be the one to lead them into battle. I joined the First Sergeant and Cleet at the head of the formation.

I stood next to my mount and cleared my throat, my mouth suddenly dry, and addressed my troopers. "Men. It is our turn. We are to move on the Yankees and scout the left flank for the rest of the army." I looked at their faces and saw the eagerness in each one as they hung on my words. "We are going to lead the rest of the cavalry into battle, us, this company of cavalry troopers is going to take the fight to the Yankees! Colonel Stuart expects the best of us men and we will give it our best. Anything less is unacceptable!"

The men grabbed their hats and held them up high, cheering, yelling, celebrating the mission that was given to us.

I mounted up, drew my saber, held it high and shouted, "Troopers mount up!"

As one, the soldiers mounted their horses and maintained the disciplined formation while awaiting my next command.

I looked them over one last time, intentionally allowing the anticipation to build until I could no longer hold back my own excitement.

A bit taller in the saddle I yelled, "Column of twos, by the left...," I paused. "March!"

I turned my horse to the right and moved to the head of the formation as the troopers began to fall in behind me. As I passed Major Bronson, I held my saber in salute calling out the command, “Eyes... right!”

The Major stood smartly and held his salute until the last trooper passed. We were off to the battlefield and glory.

As we rode out of the camp the sounds of the battle ahead of us continued. I turned the troop in a more southerly direction giving a wide arc behind the 49th Virginians with the intention of turning north on the Manassas-Sudley Road, putting us on the extreme left of our army.

I looked over my shoulder at the tight formation of cavalry soldiers behind me. I called out, “First Sergeant...forward!”

First Sergeant Bronson kicked his mare and fell in beside me. I could smell the liquor on his breath even over the stench of his body. I shook my head in disgust as I looked over his disheveled appearance, filthy uniform, and unshaven face, but held my tongue for the moment.

He saluted and said, “Yes sir.”

I returned his salute and looked at him. “First Sergeant. I want you to put out flankers. Make sure they stay along with our formation; I do not want them falling behind or getting too far forward of our position.”

He saluted and said, “Will do sir,” and turned to carry out my orders.

I yelled, “Hold on First Sergeant! I ain’t done yet! After you do that, I want you on the rear of the formation and watch for stragglers.” I lowered my voice. “One more thing First Sergeant. I catch you taking a drink between now and the conclusion of this battle I will personally put a bullet in your head. Do you understand me?”

A look of shock and surprise spread over his face.

“I will not tolerate a drunkard in my company. Especially when it jeopardizes the troop.”

He saluted weakly and turned his horse away to carry out my orders.

I was not alone for long when Cleet joined me at the head of the column. He slid in next to me and remained silent, respecting my revery while we rode along. I had already made my decision to relive the First Sergeant upon our return and give control of the company to Cleet. Major Bronson be damned.

I broke the silence. “Cleet, I need you to scout out ahead of the formation. I do not want to lead the company into a Yankee ambush.”

Cleet smiled and pulled his pistol out of the holster, half-cocking it and rotated the cylinder. “With pleasure Captain,” he said.

I looked at the massive pistol in his small hand. "Been meaning to ask. Why the hell do you carry that Walker Colt Cleet? Damn thing weighs near six pounds."

He looked at it with admiration and said, "I ever tell you my Daddy rode with Captain Samuel Walker in the Mexican War?"

Having learned and studied tactics at VMI, the battles of the Mexican War were very familiar to me as was Captain Walker and his Texas Rangers, as well as the pistol that bears his name.

I said, "You never talked much about your Daddy, other that he passed on. I did not know that Cleet."

Cleet holstered the weapon and said, "Yea my Daddy was with him when he was kilt. My Daddy did not talk much about the war but when I joined up, he gave me his pistol, said it was more powerful than any rifle the army would give me. So, I keep it."

I looked at my friend. "Well Corporal. I suspect the Yankees will not appreciate the power of that pistol, seeing as they are the ones you aim to use it on."

Cleet said, "Tis a fact Captain Chambers," as he kicked his horse and rode out ahead of the company.

We were on the road soon enough, and I turned our element north. Ahead of us the battle raged, and the smell of spent powder drifted on the wind. We were close and I watched our front, leaving the flankers out to do their job and protect our sides. The rear, I was not so concerned knowing that the remainder of the cavalry was close behind.

Suddenly to our front came a rider. It was Cleet and he was moving fast, low in the saddle only stopping when he was along side of me. I signaled the troop to halt.

Out of breath Cleet reported, "Yankees Captain. Whole bunch of 'em. At least one regiment. New York boys for sure. Some other units I could not rightly see. Theys all headin' this way looking for trouble."

"How far," I asked.

He looked over his shoulder. "Half a mile, no more."

"Any cavalry Cleet?"

He caught his breath and said, "No sir. Couple of mounted scouts but I done shot them off their horses." He smiled.

I smiled back. This was it, our moment. I looked over my shoulder and shouted, "Colors forward!" I looked at Cleet. "Go back and tell the First Sergeant to ride back, marry up with the main element and tell them that we are moving into the line and will try to slow the Yankee advance. They are to double-time it up here." I thought of my orders from Major Bronson and the fear that the Yankees were trying to out flank us on our left. "Also tell the First Sergeant to inform the Major to prepare to push out to the left when they come up."

Cleet saluted and said, "Yes sir." Then he kicked his mare and took off like a shot.

The color guard and bugler joined me at the head of the column. "I want all Non-Commissioned Officers on me now!"

The NCO's joined me at the front. I said, "We have a Yankee regiment headed right at us. We ride straight into them. First platoon I want you to go right and anchor in with the 49th Virginians while second platoon stays on the road. Third, comes with me out to the left. Major Bronson and Colonel Stuart will be coming up the rear with more cavalry and 6-pounders so prepare to move left. The Yankees are going to try and out flank us. We move at the double."

All the non-coms saluted smartly and returned to the formation. I looked at the bugler and said, "Are you ready son?"

He nodded.

I looked forward and said, "Blow the charge trooper."

He raised the brass bugle to his lips, took in a lung full of air. Nothing sounded sweeter to me than that bugle. I drew my saber, held it high and yelled at the top of my voice, "Charge!"

I held my saber up high and stayed at the head of the formation. I did not look left nor right but only straight ahead as I saw the trees of the forest, the hillside of Bald Hill, the dirt road leading me to the fight, and the blue jackets of Yankee infantry taking up positions determined to fight. I rode straight at them.

I signaled with my saber that the company should break and spread out to form the line. The sight of our charging horse soldiers put the fear of God into the Yankees, and they quickly broke formation and ran to their rear. We spread out and pursued them until they took up defensive positions at which time I ordered a dismount, and the fighting began in earnest.

Blue and grey uniforms were mixed in with the smoke of spent powder. My troopers quickly moved about, pistols and rifles in hand and won the ground to which they fought over, again routing the New York boys from their positions pushing them back further still.

I moved up and down the line encouraging my men. Only stopping to fire or observe the enemy movement through the haze. I watched, I yelled, I directed fire, I motivated my men and kept the fight moving.

Sometime during the battle Cleet rode up, jumped off his horse and knelt beside me. He was out of breath and sweating.

I yelled above the gunfire, "You okay Cleet?"

"I am Captain. Sorry it took so long to return. I could not find the First Sergeant and took your message back to the Major myself."

I took my attention away from the fight for a moment. "What do you mean you could not find the First Sergeant?"

Cleet yelled, "I believe he skedaddled Captain."

I shook my head. "Lord Almighty Damn!"

My anger was quickly replaced with relief as I saw the lead elements of Major Bronson ride up and join the fight. I waved the Major over.

He joined us, knelt beside me, and asked, "How goes it Captain Chambers?"

I looked out ahead of me and quickly assessed the battle. I pointed to the left and said, "I think they are going to try and move left Major. We are spread thin here. We need more troops to the left sir."

Major Bronson looked around and said, "I will make the recommendations to Colonel Stuart. We have heard from General Kirby Smith. This entire army will push left. You leave your First Sergeant here and you and the Corporal will lead the arriving elements to the left. We are going to push back at them. We will set up the six-pounders here."

I said, "I will have to leave it to one of my other Sergeants sir. The First Sergeant is gone."

The Major looked shocked. "What do you mean he is gone?"

Cleet said, "He skedaddled Major."

The Major's face turned red with anger. He said through clinched teeth, "I find that drunken sod I will personally shoot him!" He quickly composed himself. "Never mind that right now Captain. Find the rest of the cavalry. This entire army is moving left."

I left the Second Platoon Sergeant in charge and went out in search of my mount. A well-disciplined horse, he was not too far away from the line, and I quickly joined Cleet.

I took a drink from my canteen and handed to him. "You okay Corporal?"

He took a drink. "Oh, fine sir. Just fine."

We joined up with the rest of the cavalry and set out to the left, Cleet leading the way. He was a natural in the saddle as he picked his way through the woods and hills. He and the horse were one as they moved about. The battle still raging, he led us further out to the left as both the day and the fight wore on. Behind us, the Army of the Shenandoah followed.

It was late in the day when Cleet stopped and looked around. I pulled up next to him and asked, "Something wrong Corporal?"

"I am not sure Captain. Thought I saw something in that brush up ahead."

I looked. "Well hold here and we will send some troops forward."

Cleet scoffed. "Ah hell Captain. I can have a look see."

Before I could stop him, he rode off towards the thick brush. "Damnation," I uttered. He knew better. I called to him, but he kept going.

Cleet was just a few yards from the brush when a blue jacketed soldier stepped out, leveled his rifle at Cleet, and fired.

Corporal Haines had seen the soldier and was trying to pull his revolver when the Yankee ball hit him in the chest, throwing him out of the saddle. I yelled, drew my saber, and charged at the Yankee as he was trying to reload. Another soldier stepped out of the brush and fired off a shot at me, hitting my right arm, but I kept at him.

I jumped off my horse, pulled my revolver with my left hand, fired at the first Yankee, ran forward, and ran my sword into the chest of the soldier that shot me. Before I pulled the sword from his body I shot him in the chest. They both fell to the ground, dead.

I holstered my pistol, dropped my bloodied saber, and ran to Cleet who was still moving. I rolled him over and held him in my arms.

He looked up at me, his face pale, eyes wide. "Reckon they got me Captain."

I grabbed his hand and said, "You will be fine Cleet. No worries my friend, we will get you fixed up fine. You will be back in the saddle in no time."

Soldiers gathered around us. Cleet looked at them. "Keep the fight goin' boys. Carry the day." He looked at me and said, "Damn proud to ride with you Wyatt. You the best Captain I ever did have."

One of the troopers knelt beside us and said, "Do not worry Corporal. We will carry the day. You just rest easy now."

Cleet reached down to his pistol, struggling as his strength was leaving him, he grabbed his Walker Colt, unholstered it and handed it up to me. "It is yours now Wyatt. Take care of it. My Daddy would be proud to know you have it now."

I took the pistol just as Cleet's eyes closed, and his last breath left his body.

That night, my arm bandaged, I rejoined my company and learned that we had one soldier killed in the action, ten wounded and one missing. Cleet was our only loss, but it was a great one. He was well liked and respected.

Our company was now a battle-hardened fighting unit. We learned that it was a great victory for the South. A victory that will be short-lived in a war that will take more lives as battle after battle will be fought. We now knew this war would not soon be over. But those days were yet ahead of us. This day we lost so much. We lost a friend and comrade. We also lost the innocence we brought into this war. We had shed our ignorance of some romantic notion of how wars were fought. There was little glory in what we had taken part in, little for us to celebrate. We were forever changed men, and some did not like what we had become.

For me, the rest of the evening was shrouded in darkness. No memory, no other event, no conversation, or concern comes through. The only thing that happened on the twenty first day of July, eighteen hundred and sixty-one, I lost my friend, Corporal Cletus Wilberforce Haines.

That night I lay on my bedroll still wearing my bloodied saber, Cleet's pistol and holster on my belt. I pulled my hat over my eyes, crossed my hands on my chest, and slept.

CHAPTER TWO

The sound of wood cracking on a fire brought me out of my slumber. My eyes still closed under my hat I listened to the sounds surrounding me, or the lack of them. I was confused as to the lack of noise, and the sounds of a fire that was close by. I felt the warmth, smelled the smoke. This should not be. Where were the normal sounds of camp-life, soldiers moving about, making ready, talking and laughter? I forced my thoughts to come clear of the fog that hung on after waking. I lifted my hat and looked out.

I was alone.

I threw my hat aside and sat up. I was looking at a different environment, a different landscape. This was not Northern Virginia, this was...Texas?

Then it all came back to me. I was in the wilderness of West Texas. I was a Deputy United States Marshal for the Western District with my friend Robert Barton under Judge Johnathan Hayward DuBose, the District Judge. My posting was Fredericksburg Texas, as was my home. I was not at Manassas Junction but here in Texas doing...what? I could not remember. I looked at my clothes, my pistol belt. My pistol was there but where was my saber? Was I really in Texas?

"Good morning my friend," came a voice behind me.

Startled I turned and looked at the smiling face of my Indian friend, Long Buffalo. I turned back to the fire and saw Robert on the opposite side of the blaze stirring on his bedroll.

"What the hell is going on here Long Buffalo," I asked.

He walked around me and dropped an arm load of tree limbs by the fire, took up a position to observe both Robert and me and sat down. His top hat bedecked with colorful feathers sat atop his head. His long black hair spilled out over his shoulders and sitting on the bridge of his nose he wore blue spectacles against the morning sun. He was as I knew him. He was a sight to behold that was for certain, but it told me nothing about our current position in the middle of nowhere.

I asked him again. "What in the hell is goin' on here Long Buffalo?"

He said, “Do not worry my friends. The confusion will pass in a short time. Try not to think about anything for the moment. Let your mind go free. I will make coffee.”

I looked over the fire and saw Robert sitting up with a look of confusion on his face. He too was trying to decipher the events of the previous night and what brought us here. He looked over at me and nodded, choosing not to speak now, which was probably the better decision. I looked at Long Buffalo who was more intent on making coffee than explaining the occurrences of the evening to us. I had no choice but to live on his timetable and wait.

Was it a dream?

I stood, stretched my legs, and walked around our small camp, taking in the sights thinking that there was an explanation out there. Something that will tell me, tell us what we had just endured. Something, anything out in the vast open space before us to shed some light on the confused state we found ourselves in.

Long Buffalo said, “The answers are not out there Wyatt. They are here, with us and will be made clear soon.”

I turned back to him and said, “Hurry with that coffee. Tastes like a buffalo shit in my mouth.” I spit on the fire. “What the hell was that stuff you gave us last night?”

He put the coffee pot on the fire and said, “Peyote.”

He said it as if it alone would answer the multitude of questions circling through my head. I looked at Robert who shrugged his shoulders. He too was ignorant of the concoction we drank but, it obviously had some sort of effect on us. Long Buffalo had only said it will help us in our journey, wherever that was.

I looked up at the cloudless sky. It was going to be another sweltering day. Out here the heat of the wilderness was a dry one, unlike the heat of my younger days in Southern Georgia. Hot and humid and mostly without a breeze to cool things off. But, like most things, one can get used to it and adjust their daily routines to compensate for the uncomfortable climate. Out here though, it was hard to make adjustments. The heat was brutal and unforgiving. One had to prepare and take precautions or end up dead on the dusty ground, unidentifiable sun-bleached bones among the rocks, dirt, and mesquite.

I went back to my bedroll and retrieved my tobacco and pipe. Holding my pouch up to Robert he nodded, grabbed his pipe, and joined me.

I packed my pipe and handed the pouch to Robert. "What in the hell happened to us last night," I asked him.

He packed his pipe, cleared his throat and spit on the ground. "I have no idea," he began, "but the buffalo that shit in your mouth also marked mine."

I grabbed a burning twig from the fire and lit my pipe. Softly I said to Robert as I drew in the welcoming smoke, "I am not ashamed to tell you my friend, but I am a bit un-nerved as to what I experienced last night."

Robert took the burning twig and lit his pipe. "Hell Wyatt. It scared the hell out of me. I thought I was there again. I lived it all over last night."

I looked at him. "Where?"

His face showed a sadness I had seen before. "Stony Ridge," he said in a whisper.

"Lord Almighty Damn," I said. Robert had relived his nightmare experience from the war as I had. He, a Union soldier, had his Stoney Ridge where I had my Manassas Junction as a Confederate officer. Both events separated by time and distance had left dark stains on our very souls. Yet, here in the wilderness of Texas with our Indian friend, we had somehow traveled to that dark place in our history and lived those two select days over once more.

It had been more than a dream to me as it seems to have been the same with Robert. The sights, the sounds, hell, even the smells all came back. The conversations, the faces, and the gunfire, it was all there. The feelings and emotions, both good and bad had been felt. That was the journey Long Buffalo spoke of. We had journeyed to some unknown place to live through the torment once again for a reason not yet known to us. But how, and for what purpose had he brought us here?

Long Buffalo joined us, holding his decorated long-stemmed pipe. I handed him my tobacco pouch and asked, "Coffee ready yet?"

He grinned behind his blue spectacles that once belonged to Robert. "It is and I have some whiskey as well. Someone forgot to pack the sugar." He cast an accusing look at me.

The look on his face, the blue spectacles perched on his long thin nose all under his colorful top hat suddenly relieved me of all the stress and fear I harbored at the moment. Where I was fearful and confused, if not angry, I was now relaxed if not cheerful. His was a pleasant and comfortable presence. Long Buffalo had that way about him.

I smiled and said, “I still cannot see the Irish in you, my friend.”

Robert laughed heartily recalling the first time he met Long Buffalo and saying the same thing about him having an Irish mother, Indian father.

Long Buffalo laughed. “My mother did have the red hair.”

“To the coffee my friends,” I said. “This tobacco is doing nothing for this foul taste in my mouth.”

Coffee cups filled and topped off with a shot of whiskey we sat around the fire enjoying our tobacco. We remained silent, our desire for answers, our fears and confusion cast aside for the moment as we enjoyed each other's company and the coffee in our hands.

Long Buffalo spoke first. He said, “My friends I believe it best if I explain to you what has happened before you ask questions of me.” He looked at me then Robert for agreement. We both nodded.

He said, “I brought you out here to find the place and time that has tormented you for so long. You both have different demons that have plagued you and would soon claim you if something was not done to stop it. That is why we are here.”

I looked around thinking that perhaps this spot in the wilderness had some sort of significance to the Medicine Man.

Long Buffalo smiled at me and said, “No my friend. This is not a special place. I chose it because we are alone and not to be disturbed. The journey you took was to the spirit world where these terrible events in time live. They will go on and on for all of time to come. I only gave you the chance to rejoin them and see for yourself how it truly happened, not how you think they happened.”

Robert asked, “You mean we are not remembering it, what... correctly?”

Long Buffalo nodded his head. “That is how it is with you. You have not remembered these terrible moments as they truly happened. I have opened the door for you to see how they really were, not how you remember them. Time can change the way we remember things.”

I asked, “Then what we saw, or lived last night was the true happenings?”

Again, he nodded. “You have lived through this as if it has just happened and only now you can decide your part in it. I can no longer help you as I do not know what it is that tortures you. You, my friends, must rethink what your part in it was and if you are to blame for any wrongdoings.”

I sat back against my saddle and looked into the dying fire. Had I remembered it wrong? Me, with a knack to recall everything? The written word, a picture, or a face? Had I been punishing myself all this time for...what?

Long Buffalo said, "Do not think hard on it now my friends. It will come to you. Perhaps not today, or tomorrow but it will come, and you will see."

I stood and looked at Long Buffalo. "My friend," I began, "I will not pretend with you that I understand any of what has transpired. Ever since that night when you found us in the wilderness in the company of my dead troopers, I learned to trust your ways. You saved our lives, twice. I will take what you have told us and see where it leads me."

Robert stood and said, "I too am confused by all of this. What happened last night was, is real to me. The fear, the pain and suffering returned last night." Robert paused and took in a deep breath. "I will take what I saw and learn from it, though I do not understand how this has come to pass. It is beyond my thinking. Damn strangest thing it was."

Long Buffalo stood, stepped up to us and rested his arms across our shoulders, pulling us close and said, "You are both true warriors and I am proud to say you are my friends."

We separated and quietly went about breaking down our camp. It was time to go and return to Fredericksburg and our jobs as Marshals. Long Buffalo brought us out here to again, save our lives. This time from an all-consuming burden that was slowly destroying us from within. His skill as a healer was beyond our understanding though it was something we would and must accept. There were some questions better left unanswered, and this was one of them I suppose. The rest, as he said, was now up to us.

In no time we had packed out and had the horses saddled and ready to go. I stroked Caliban's neck and admired his strength. He pushed against my hand accepting the affection I showed him. We were as one now. It was another prophecy that came to be. Long Buffalo had said from our first meeting that Caliban and I were of the same spirit. He was right about that. Ever since that night, not so long ago, when Caliban carried my broken body out of the wilderness to safety and near lost his life in so doing. He was a fighter, just as I was.

"Never give up the fight," I whispered in his ear.

Robert had mounted his horse Cillian, another strong animal, and came up behind me. "Whispering sweet nothings in your horse's ear again Wyatt," he said with a grin.

I turned to him and asked, "Are you jealous Sergeant Major Barton?"

He laughed and said, "I believe I am."

I mounted up. "Then allow me to whisper in your ear." I leaned closer to him. "It is time to get back to work. We cannot leave Julius alone forever with that mean bastard of a prisoner we have locked up."

Robert sighed. "Then work we must pursue. Julius could also use our assistance with the new building."

The thought of Julius being left to guard our one prisoner did not give me too much pause. Even if the prisoner was one mean tempered son of a bitch. But he also had to deal with the building expansion the Judge had authorized giving us more jail cell space. An observation he had made when last he came to town, noting that we had space for eight prisoners and, at the time, were housing thirteen. Or perhaps it was fourteen, I cannot recall. Regardless, the Judge wanted more cells constructed as if he were expecting more guests at our fine establishment.

Be that as it may we were having a difficult time procuring enough lumber and supplies to build those extra cells, not to mention our carpenter. Nice enough fella when sober, mean as a snake when drunk, which was becoming the norm with our German handyman.

"Damnation," I said. "You had to remind me. I am gonna shoot that miserable drunk of a carpenter when I get back."

Long Buffalo joined us on his pony. "Pale face problems," he said and laughed. "You two did not have such problems when you lived out in the wilderness, like me."

Robert said, "That is true, but we also did not have money, food or a means to get them."

"Speak for yourself," I said. "I could always play cards to get my money."

Long Buffalo waved his hand at us and said, "More pale face problems my friends. All of what you say will make you old before your time."

I reached in my saddle bag and pulled out a bottle of whiskey. Holding it up I said, "Here is to getting old before my time." I took a drink and passed the bottle to Long Buffalo who took a drink and passed it to Robert.

I looked at our Indian friend and asked, "Will you ride back with us?"

Long Buffalo looked out over the vast expanse of wilderness and said, "Not this time my friends. I too seek peace. My trail takes me elsewhere."

I extended my hand. “Until the next time my friend. I thank you for all you have done for us.”

He took my hand firmly in his. “Look well to the future my friends.”

Robert shook his hand and said, “Thank you Long Buffalo. I value our friendship.”

“As do I,” he said as he turned his pony around and rode off.

I watched him ride away. “Well Robert. I suppose we best be gettin’ back. We still have a job to do.”

“That we do Wyatt.”

Not hurrying but not dilly-dallying we started our journey to the place that had become our home. It felt good to be a man of means and responsibility once more, even if it meant growing old before our time.

CHAPTER THREE

We were less than a day's ride from town. Long Buffalo had chosen a spot off the trail, secluded but not too far removed from civilization. At first, upon our arrival the day before we had not understood his insistence to join him in the wilderness. But we obediently followed him, trusting his judgement and heeding his concerns we established our camp. He had been there for us in the past, having saved our lives not once but twice.

The second time was when he killed the buck-toothed bandit that threatened to shoot us by sending an arrow into the man's chest before he could kill me, Robert, Gwen, and Arabella. Julius, with his trusty shotgun had finished the man off sending him to hell to face Satan and all his demons. We were forever in Long Buffalo's debt, and we surrendered ourselves to him.

The rest of last evening remains in a shroud, a fog, with only bits and pieces coming through. I recall sitting by the fire opposite Robert as the sun went down. Long Buffalo was signing, no... he was chanting something while we passively watched, unaware of where this ceremony of sorts was going and what part we were to play in it. Again, we put our trust in him and his powerful medicine.

The last moment I can recall, before I left this world if you will, was when he handed me a clay cup and told me to drink, lay back and begin my journey. When I awoke, I felt as though I had lived through a lost time, unaccounted for moments. A gap in my life that left both me and Robert confused, bewildered and un-nerved.

We rode on through the day, lacking in any meaningful conversation as, I am sure, we were both trying to apply some logical explanation to what we had been part of. Perhaps, as I had stated before, some questions deserve answers while others do not. What happened to us may never be explained to any satisfaction. Only the unseen results will bear that out.

I reached into my saddle bag and pulled out some jerky, leaving the hardtack alone. It was hot and eating the dry biscuit would do nothing but accelerate our thirst. Water was precious out here even when we were so close to town. A self-imposed rationing was in keeping with good order and discipline.

I handed Robert a strip of jerky. "Have some lunch, Robert."

Robert took the offering and said, "Why Captain. You did not need to cook on my account."

I laughed and said, "Keep ridin' me and I will put you on hardtack rations."

"I will mind my manners," he said with a grin.

"I do not know about you," I began, "but I could do with a decent meal when we get back. We did not get enough time when we brought this Mack whatever the hell his name is, in and locked him up."

"Mack the Knife he calls himself," Robert said.

"Yea, Mack the Knife." I was thoughtful for a moment. "How is it these bad guys always adopt some ridiculous name."

Robert said, "Not all of them. Just the dumb ones I suppose, or those that do not think their given name is mean enough."

"That is for sure and for certain," I said. Still, I continued my pursuit of a decent meal upon our return and cast aside this Mack the Knife nonsense. "So, whatcha think? Steaks at the cafe tonight?"

Robert looked distastefully at the jerky in his hand. "That sounds delicious right now. Steak it is Wyatt." He turned in his saddle and smiled. "You are buying."

I feigned shock and said, "Me? Now why would I do that? Tell you what." I grinned. "When we get back, I will cut you for it."

"Fine by me as long as I shuffle the cards this time. Every time you shuffle the cards I get the shit end of the stick."

I laughed and said nothing. He was not wrong. The last time we drew for high card the loser had to draw out Mack the Knife from the saloon he was hiding in. A fight ensued and Robert lost a tooth.

I looked over at Robert and saw that he was rubbing the side of his jaw where he took the punch from the drunken desperado. I smiled but kept the laughter to myself.

We rode at an easy pace content with our estimation of arrival. For some reason we both felt at ease, more so than I suspect either of us had felt in a long time. Whatever the reason, the revelations of our strange journey, how our lives had taken such a drastic turn for the better, or how the future looked promising not only for us but the people of the land we were sworn to protect. Whatever the reason, we felt good.

Off in the distance we saw the town of Fredericksburg, and we quickened our pace. Familiar surroundings, friendly faces, and a roof over our heads for the night, not to mention the prospect of a decent meal motivated us further and in short order we pulled up in front of our building, our place of business, our home.

The door opened and out stepped our jailer, our fellow lawman, our friend Julius. Bedecked in his new store-bought clothes and boots, his jailer badge pinned to his vest shinning in the sun, he looked the part of a professional officer of the Judge's court. He stood at the top of the stairs and said, "Welcome back Cap'n, Sergeant Major Robert." He looked around. "Where be Mister Long Buffalo?"

I dismounted, rubbed my legs to get the feeling back into them and said, "He went his own way, Julius. For a time anyway."

Robert said, "Hello Julius. How goes everything?"

Julius put his hands in his pockets and looked up at the sky. "Well sir, I tell you it has not been boring."

I did not become unduly alarmed by his statement. I knew Julius well enough to know that by his demeanor he was going to impart a tale that we would find interesting if not entertaining.

"Do tell," I said.

He looked down from the porch and said, "Well sir. To start Mister Mack the Knife tried to grab my shotgun when he came out the privy. He jus would not let go so I had to beat him to let go of the gun."

Robert asked, "How many times did you hit him?"

"Oh. Only the one time. He went down right enough but he left three teeth in the dirt when I picked him up." Julius smiled and pointed to his teeth. "Three in the front."

I laughed and said, "Oh that is fine. Lucky for him you only hit him the one time." Then I asked, "Any other concerns?"

Again, he looked up at the sky. "Well sir, the carpenter kinda got a bit uppity. Mister Schneider"

Robert dismounted and stepped closer. "Oh Lord. What did he do now?"

Julius stepped down off the porch. For his massive size he moved with a certain grace and ease. Muscular and powerful the former slave had endured much in his life, and it took much to get him riled. Something only a fool would attempt.

“Well Sergeant Major Robert, it was like this. We was waitin’ for a load of cut timber to come in yesterday and I reckon he got to drinkin’ again.”

Robert added, “He seems to take up the bottle when his hammer is dormant.”

Julius nodded. “That he does. Well, he started in on me. Yellin’ in German and carrying on and such. Well then, he throws his hammer at me. I ducked out the way then he comes at me with a saw.”

I said, “So you hit him.”

Julius shook his head. “Oh no Cap’n. I picks him up and tossed him in the horse trough.”

A huge smile began to spread across my face. “You tossed him in...” I burst out laughing.

Robert too began to laugh, and Julius joined in. Our little German craftsman had a lot of gumption to go up against Julius who was near three times his size.

I sat on the steps while I caught my breath. I took off my hat and looked at Robert. “Tell me again Robert, why we keep that angry drunk around here.”

Robert shrugged and said, “He is the best builder this side of San Antonio. Problem being he falls into boredom if he is not working, which leads to drinking.”

I stood and slapped my hat against my leg knocking the dust off. “Well, we best get some timber delivered soon our he is gonna end up in the jail, not building it.”

Robert said, “True enough.”

I said, “I am gonna take Caliban around the back then hit the pump and wash the trail off my face.”

“I will join you Wyatt,” Robert said.

Julius asked, “Near supper time. Was not expecting you back so soon. I can have somethin’ fixed up soon enough.”

“Thank you, Julius,” I said, “but we are going to get a steak and potatoes at the cafe tonight. It has been a trying couple of days. No offense to your cooking.”

Robert asked, “Can we bring anything back for you Julius?”

“Oh no Sergeant Major Robert. Reckon I will get some supplies tomorrow now that you two are back.”

We led our animals behind the building to the stables and began the task of brushing them down, inspecting their hooves, and feeding them.

As former cavalry soldiers we knew that we were nothing without our mounts, so we saw to the needs of our horses before our own.

Once that task was complete, we went to the pump and washed the dust off from the trail. Robert, more civilized in his methods had taken a small towel from his saddle bag and scrubbed the dirt away. Me, well I just stuck my head under the running water and let the dirt wash away as I worked the hand-pump up and down.

I was wiping the water off my face when I heard my name being called.

"Marshal Chambers, are you out here?"

I looked at the back of the building and called out. "I am. Who is there?"

A small man wearing a black conductor's hat with the word 'Telegraph' on the front and a starched white shirt with string tie stepped through the back door. It was our telegraph operator Jeremiah. He held a slip of paper in his hand.

"Hello Marshals," he said, looking over his oval glasses.

Robert said, "How have you been Jeremiah?"

He smiled and said, "Very well Marshal Barton. Yes sir, very well indeed." He looked at the paper in his hand, then offered it to us. "I have an urgent telegram for you."

Something told me I was not going to get my steak dinner. I took the slip of paper and nodded to Jeremiah. I read it and sighed heavily.

Robert asked, "What is it, Wyatt? What does it say?"

I said, "It is from the Judge and Marshal Sweeny in Castroville." I looked at the message again then read it aloud to Robert. "Bank of Castroville robbed of Federal payroll while in transit to the Western District. Come at once, Marshal Sweeny awaits." I dropped my arms to my side and looked at Robert.

Robert said, "You know what this means."

Again, I sighed. "It means no steak dinner."

Robert looked at Jeremiah and said, "Wire the Marshal back and tell him we will be there as quickly as we can."

Jeremiah nodded and said, "Right away Marshal Barton. Right away."

As I watched Jeremiah retreat, I sat on the lip of the horse trough and cursed our luck. Even though it was my job, our job, it would seem that every time we made plans for a decent meal duty pulled us away and forced yet another hardtack biscuit in our mouths.

Robert sat next to me and said, "I suppose we should start packing out for the trip."

I looked over at him, drops of water cascading down my face, my hair wet and unruly. I sighed and resigned myself to our fate as lawmen destined to live life on the dusty trail, living on hardtack, salt pork and beans. "Reckon so. We still have enough daylight to get some good trail time in, and I reckon we can make Castroville by tomorrow night."

Robert said, "Well. It is about sixty-five miles so depending on what we do today it will be late when we get there tomorrow."

I looked at the telegram and thought of Marshal Sweeny. It has been sometime since we had seen him, not since our shootout in the saloon that night with Long Buffalo and the Under-Sheriff of Karnes County, Clinton Baker at our side. The four of us against five of the meanest, murderous desperadoes to walk the ground of Texas. When it was over, the villainess desperadoes lay dead, and we met Marshal Sweeny.

Marshal James Sweeny, town lawman, standing there dressed in his red nightshirt, boots, pistol belt and star pinned on his chest. He was a sight to behold that night and one that still brings a smile to my face. But he was a lawman to his very core and not one to take any guff nor shenanigans from any man. Fast on the draw and ready to bash the head of those that required it, he was a fair Town Marshal, always ready to protect the citizenry that elected him to the post. For him to ask our assistance, with the endorsement from Judge DuBose, meant it was serious business, and the steak dinner will have to wait.

As I sat there reminiscing and perhaps feeling a bit sorry for myself Julius stepped out and came over.

I looked up at his massive frame and said, "Reckon you heard?"

He nodded. "I did Cap'n. I will get the grub ready and pack the panniers if you and the Sergeant Major want to pack out your clothes for the journey."

Robert stood and said, "That will be fine Julius. Pack us out for five days just in case."

"Will do Sergeant Major," he said.

I added, "You might want to pack some extra powder and ball Julius. I think I will take one of the shotguns as well."

He looked at me with concern. "You expecting trouble Cap'n?"

I stood and looked at the telegram once again. "May just be a feeling, Julius. Just a feeling."

As I walked back inside, I could not help but reflect on both mine and Robert's situation. Not so long ago we were both drifters, just short of being saddle tramps in the wilderness of South Texas, content to live our lives in obscurity through our self-imposed exile. Two soldiers from opposite sides of the battlefield moving from town to town alone, consumed with the guilt that so accompanies those that survived. Living the life of the self-pitied, drifting through the destruction left behind at wars end. Until fate brought us together.

Now, we were men of means and responsibility. Lawmen with a promising future, a roof over our heads, clothing that was not always a remnant of our old uniform. We also had friends; good friends born of sharing the burden of Reconstruction. Friends that looked out for us as we did for them with future promises of love and a family of our own.

I stopped in the center of the office and thought, yes, we were extremely fortunate to have come to this place in time. I looked around the spacious room and settled on the stacks of cut timber and wood working tools piled at the far side of the room.

Shit!

"Julius," I called out.

He came into the room. "Yes Cap'n?"

I turned to him and said, "While we are gone see if you can get that little bastard of a carpenter to do something other than drink his lunch."

"I will Cap'n," he said.

I smiled. "I know you will Julius. If you must dunk him in the horse trough, give him one for me and Robert."

Julius smiled. "With pleasure," he said.

Just then a voice called out from behind the thick door leading to the cells.

"Marshal! I wanna talk to you! Damnation Marshal!"

It was our prisoner, Mack the Knife. I shook my head as I made my way to the door and pushed it open.

The extension work that our German friend was supposed to be doing had been stalled awaiting materials. A thick dark tarpaulin covered the back wall, or the hole that now represented the back wall leaving the third cell unusable. Our guest was in the first cell, and none too happy I could tell.

I looked at him. Tall and lean he looked as if he were bred for the saddle and one that lived out of a saddle bag. I had many a trooper in my cavalry days that looked as if they belonged on a horse and nowhere else, and this fella was one of them. His face reflected days of growth as did his hair, only because his reputation told us it would be unwise to put a cutting tool in his hand much less a razor. Even though he chose to be called Mack the Knife I suppose there was some truth to his knife wielding skills, and we were not going to find out to the contrary.

I stepped up to the bars and asked in a neutral tone, “What do you want?”

He stepped closer and pointed to his mouth. “Look what that sumbitch did to me,” he said with a lisp.

I looked at the gap in his smile, his swollen lip and whistled. “I bet that hurt some when he hit you.”

He was getting angry. “You gonna let that nigger get away with that?”

I stepped a bit closer. “Boy, you best watch what you say, or I am gonna give you a busted nose to go with your busted lip.”

He stepped right up to the bars, spit on the floor and said, “I says, you gonna let that nigger...”

He never finished his sentence as I swiftly threw a punch between the bars and landed my balled-up fist right between his eyes. His head snapped back as he took the punch, his eyes crossed then he fell over backwards, bounced off the bunk and hit the floor, unconscious.

I looked down and the prostrate form and said, “I told you boy,” as I turned to leave.

Julius asked as I returned to the office, “Everything okay Cap’n?”

I nodded and said, “Ol’ Mack was tired, so I told him to take a nap.”

Julius grinned. “I will tend to the grub,” he said as he walked away.

I massaged my hand as I went to our sleeping quarters in the back to pack my clothes for the trip. Robert was finishing up.

He asked, “How is our prisoner?”

I scratched my head and suppressed a yawn. “Sleeping,” I said.

Robert grabbed his bundle of clothes, looked at me and grinned knowingly. “Good. I will see if Julius needs a hand.”

I sat on my bed and watched him leave. I smiled, took in a deep breath, and began my task of grabbing a change of clothes for the journey. As I was doing so, I caught sight of myself in the wash mirror.

I uttered aloud, “Oh, this will not do. I look like hell.”

I tossed my clothes back on the bed and decided a few more minutes delay would be of no consequence. I poured water into the basin and proceeded to shave and make myself a bit more presentable. Not for anyone in particular mind you, but there are times when a clean face and appearance can raise one's own moral.

Having accomplished shaving and currying my hair I looked at the dust caked on my clothing and decided that it too could do with a change, two days on the trail in the summer was telling. So, I pulled off my dirty duds, quickly wiped down with a wash rag and put on some clean clothes. Looking at myself in the mirror once more I was satisfied at my appearance, remembering that Judge DuBose once said he could not have his Officers of the Court dressed as a couple of saddle tramps.

I gathered up another change of clothes, took one last look around the room stopping at the picture of Arabella on my night table. I smiled, winked, and went out the door.

Outside I took my bundle of clothes and put them in one of the panniers strapped to Robert's pack horse. Buster, my mule, had been granted a reprieve as his duties will be used in hauling the building materials to the jail. Whenever they become available.

Robert came over with some food stuffs and took in my appearance. "Oh, what the hell," he uttered. He looked me over head to toe. "You go and get cleaned up and I look like a tramp." He turned abruptly and returned inside.

Julius came over and said, "Reckon Sergeant Major Robert is gonna get gussied up too Cap'n." He laughed.

"Reckon so," I said as I looked over my shoulder.

CHAPTER FOUR

Finally, we were packed out, mounted up and were ready to go. Robert had cleaned himself up and changed into fresh clothes and now the immediate plan was simple. We were going to ride south until we lost daylight then set up our first camp, rise before the sun and continue to Castroville. Time and distance were our immediate adversary, and we approached the circumstances with the notion that we would overcome both.

We rode out front of the jail where Julius waited for us on the porch. He stepped down and came over to us.

I said as I offered my hand, "If we can, we will send word if we get sidetracked any longer than four or five days. Do not rightly know what we will find when we get there."

He took my hand. "Be safe Cap'n. I got the store."

Robert took Julius's hand and said, "Do not take too much from Mister Schneider or our prisoner. Hopefully, the Marshal will send some men to pick him up soon."

"Will do Sergeant Major Robert," Julius answered.

As we turned our mounts to leave, I looked across the street at the construction of a new building that was slowly progressing. Where once before stood the wood and canvas saloon, The Heart of Dixie, now a more permanent structure was being built. It too was a saloon, two stories, made of wood and stone. A venture backed by the more affluent members of the town and one Miss Pepper Leeds, the former barmaid of The Heart of Dixie.

It only seemed fitting since it was I that burned The Heart of Dixie to the ground, thus putting Pepper out of work, that I should back Pepper in the rebuilding of the new saloon. With my backing and that of Robert, Mark and Chelsea Lauderback, Pepper had the controlling interest in the saloon and so it will be aptly named, Pepper's Place.

I said, "Pepper's Place is hurrying along. Be up and runnin' in no time."

"Probably why we cannot get materials for our little addition," Robert pointed out.

I led Caliban down the street. "Maybe so, maybe so Robert. But I for one am looking forward to a beer instead of that rotgut we have been drinking." I looked down the street. "Reckon we should stop at the Lauderback's and let them know we are headin' out again. Ask them to keep an eye on Julius."

Robert said, "Maybe ask them to have Doc Averbeck check on the prisoner."

I cast a look at Robert, attempting to feign innocence.

He smiled, shook his head, and said, "You are predictable if anything else Wyatt."

We pulled up to a store front that proclaimed in bright colors above the porch roof, Lauderback's Guns, and Inventions. Tying off we went inside.

As I opened the door a small bell rang over my head as the door banged against the bell spring, announcing our presence.

She came from the back room and stepped around one of the many glass display cabinets. Dressed in a floor length hooped dress of greens and browns with a matching bow in her blonde hair, she was beautiful and elegant as always. Chelsea smiled and came forward.

She hugged both Robert and me and stepped back, taking us in. "Well," she said with her slight Southern drawl, "where have you two been and where are you off to now?"

Robert removed his hat and said, "We were out on the range for some business with Long Buffalo. We just returned only to have to hit the trail again."

She shook her head, "Oh dear. No rest for the weary I suppose."

I said, "There was some trouble down Castroville way, and we must get down there as quick as we can."

Just then Chelsea's husband, Mark, came from the back. Tall and thin, dressed in black pants and white shirt he wore a leather apron to protect his clothing while pursuing his vocation as a gunsmith and inventor. He was wiping his hands with a rag, smiling as he saw us.

He stepped forward and extended his hand. "Glad to see you fellas back. What is this about Castroville?"

Robert said, "They had some trouble and asked for our help."

Mark nodded thoughtfully. Even if he was curious, he understood that somethings were better left unsaid, questions unasked, especially if it was not of his concern. He did not press us for any more information on the matter.

I said, "We were hoping that you could check on Julius from time to time till we get back."

We all remembered our earlier troubles and both Mark and Chelsea had pitched in to help us and Julius. Not only lending assistance but a helping gun hand as well. Both had been invaluable to us, so much so that we had made Mark a Special Deputy to be called on if the need arose. They were also our friends.

Chelsea asked, "Are you expecting trouble?"

"No," I said. "I do not believe that is the case. We just have an ornery prisoner locked up and we may be gone four or five days this trip."

"At least," Robert added.

"Be glad to help out," Mark said. "Anything we can do."

I said, "Thanks. Oh, could you have Doc Averbeck check on the prisoner. Seems he fell down a couple of times and knocked a few teeth out in the process."

Chelsea smiled and nodded knowingly. "Oh, I am sure he did. These things happen."

Mark, not so reserved in his reaction laughed aloud.

Chelsea cast a scolding look Mark's way and said, "Now Mark dear. You know these things happen. The man is probably something of a clumsy sort."

Now I laughed. "Clumsy," I repeated. "I suppose he is that seein' how he met the floor more than once."

The four of us laughed, bid our farewells, and retreated to the porch.

Chelsea again hugged us. "Be safe now and come home."

We mounted up and resumed our exit from the town of Fredericksburg Texas. We had a few more hours of daylight, and we needed to put some miles in on the trail before we called it a day.

So began our trek south.

The trick to traveling long distances, be it on horseback, wagon or even on a train was not to think about the greater distance one had to travel but the shorter distance. That being the distance to your next stopping point. The distance to the moment when you dismount and walk the horses, stretch your legs, or even pause by a stream of cool water. A place to make a pot of coffee or just to set up camp for the night. Thinking about the greater distance, the total distance to travel can easily bring your mental state down and add to the stresses of an already difficult journey. So, you divide the journey into segments if you will. Think more of the shorter distance to travel.

This is what we learned in our travels through the years. It made the journey easier on both mind and body. Either alone or with others, it put the sometimes-daunting task of traveling great distances in a better frame of mind.

Robert was a good traveling companion as he did not feel the need to gab the hours away. I, and Robert had as well, found it annoying when a traveling companion felt compelled to talk and talk and talk some more to pass the time. There was no need to talk. Silence had its values as did conversation. There was a time and place for everything and sometimes silence was more coveted than the spoken word.

The sun was going down and Robert broke the silence. "Think we should start looking for a place to camp for the night Wyatt. No need to press on too hard."

"I spect you are right." I looked towards the southwest and saw some mesquite trees around a small rock formation. I pointed and said, "Over there looks to be as good a place as any."

Robert looked at where I was pointing. "Fine with me. Looks good for wood for a fire too."

We headed in the direction of the rock formation.

Robert asked, "You give any thought to the other night out there with Long Buffalo Wyatt?"

I thought before I answered. Should I tell him the truth that it had rattled me to my core to have relived that day? Or that my lack of understanding how Long Buffalo had accomplished this had un-nerved me? It seemed that our Indian friend had a habit of showing up to help, only casting us deeper in the shadows of reasoning and understanding.

I fought the urge to retreat to my blissful ignorance and lie, but my Daddy always told me that hiding from your problems only worsens them and to address them head on as you would anything else.

I sighed. "I reckon I am at the point where I am trying to figure out how it happened. I suppose I should do like Long Buffalo said and think about that day, not so much as to how he got us there." I looked at Robert as I had said it with all sincerity. "Does that make any sense Robert?"

He nodded and looked at the ground with unseeing eyes. Lost in his thoughts for a moment then he said, "I suppose I have been doing the same thing. But I also remember that night when we were bleeding out and those men showed up. They helped us, Wyatt. Your men took us to Long Buffalo."

That was yet another topic that neither Robert nor myself had addressed. There we were, on Death's doorstep, shot to pieces the both of us, wandering through the wilderness when out of the darkness they came to protect us, escort us. I had asked Long Buffalo what had happened, how this could be, and he just told me it was the spirit world protecting us. Just like that. No further explanation. No rationale or logic, it just was, and that was that. He could be a bothersome horse's ass at times with his cryptic answers.

I saw that Robert was carrying the weight of what had transpired, as I was. Perhaps now was not the time. Perhaps the answers will come later, if at all. What I did know was that we had a job to do and that took priority over our confusion and ill feelings about issues passed. Especially when the outcome had already been decided.

Or had it?

"Ah, hell Robert," I began, "we can go on and on about this till the cows come home and we will be right back here none the wiser. Somethings have no explanation, I reckon. We have both seen things in the war that we cannot understand. Maybe Long Buffalo is right, and we should think about what happened and not how it happened."

Robert took in a deep breath, forcing away his melancholy. "I suppose you are right. What the hell. I could use a cup of coffee and some of that fine Virginian shag of yours."

I smiled, pleased that my friend was back with the here and now. "You supply the coffee, and I will supply the tobacco my friend."

We reached the rock formation and settled in for the night. I tended the animals while Robert got the fire going and prepared the coffee and dinner. It was not the steaks we were so looking forward to, just beans and salt pork, but it went down well and filled our bellies. We were grateful for what we had, and we both realized that though we had grown accustomed to living in a town, with a roof over our heads and decent food cooked in a kitchen, we still felt comfortable out on the range.

Life on the trail was not that bad after all. It just took a bit of self-motivation to bring us out here this time. But once we had hit the trail, we welcomed it once again as a life we truly accepted and enjoyed. We just had to get away from our comfortable surroundings to, once more, appreciate the wilderness and the openness it offered.

I suppose we had become complacent.

We were sitting by the fire, backs resting on our saddles, coffee in hand smoking my fine Virginian tobacco.

I said, "I do not know about you Sergeant Major, but I had not realized how I missed the open space of the wilderness."

Robert pulled on his pipe, exhaled and watched the smoke drift over the fire. "I believe Captain, we have gotten lazy in our current situation." He laughed.

"Lord Almighty Damn! Who would have thought that becoming a responsible member of society came at such a cost," I said. "I for one do not like being lazy."

Robert asked, "What do you propose Wyatt? Do you want to tell the Judge if he needs us to send word out here in the wilderness and we will come running?"

I chuckled as I tapped the ashes from my pipe. "Oh, if it was that simple my friend. But I do not think the ladies in our lives would appreciate living out here."

"There is time enough for Gwen and Arabella later," Robert said referring to our lady friends. "Right now, the task before us is a bank robbery."

I nodded. "It must be serious if Marshal Sweeny wants our help." I looked over at Robert. "What do you reckon it is all about?"

He was thoughtful before he answered. "I cannot say. The telegram only said Federal Payroll. It only brings more questions. How much was it? Was anyone killed in the robbery? Who are we going after?"

I said, "I do not even remember a bank in town last time we were there."

Robert suddenly perked up and said, "Hey, what say we stay with Miss Helga when we get there."

I remembered the little German lady that ran the small tent city cabins where we stayed the last time we were there. Her generosity had touched us. How she took in four strangers and made us feel at home, never taking our money, feeding us, watching over us. It will be good to see her. It will be good to share her home cooking once again.

These were my thoughts as I drifted off to sleep by the fire, looking up at a star filled sky, thankful for this moment.

I awoke abruptly and took in my surroundings. The fire was still going, not strong but welcoming against the chill of the morning. I looked at my time piece, five in the morning. Robert began to stir under his blanket. I pushed myself up, rubbing my stiff legs and tossed another log on the fire to get it going for the breakfast cooking. It may not be the ham and eggs we had grown accustomed to, but I found myself looking forward to the salt pork and hardtack.

Robert mumbled from under his blanket. "Do you want me to make the coffee, or do you want to?"

I stretched the soreness out of my body and answered, "According to you and Julius I do not make good coffee so the duty falls to you, my friend. I will check on the animals."

I put my boots on and walked out to where I had hobbled the animals and found them together. Caliban came to me, and I removed his restraints and rubbed his neck. He too knew of our task, I felt that. The responsibility we had gave both of us meaning. No longer were we wandering around without direction or purpose. Without knowing it then it had made the both of us angry, frustrated. Now, where I went, he went. Long Buffalo was right when he said we were one, though in the beginning the two of us were at odds with each other.

I stroked his head and said, "Those days are gone my friend." He pushed against my hand.

I tended to the other animals while Robert made breakfast. The two of us were old hands at this and our individual jobs, working for the common conclusion went off without question, without argument, without indecision. We worked well together, and I occasionally questioned how it came to be. Never once had we discussed who was to do what, how it was to be done, or even why it needed to be done. We thought along the same direction and purpose.

As I was brushing his horse Cillian, I watched Robert working around the fire. Cooking, breaking down the camp, returning it to its original state before we had arrived. We thought alike he and I, so much so that his girl Gwendoline had said we could be brothers, born of the same mother only separated through early years of life. I grinned at the thought and found humor in such a notion. If that were true, my mother would have had some explaining to do. I let out a laugh.

Robert stood from the fire and said, "Something funny? My horse tell you a joke?"

"Just a thought struck me funny," I answered as I continued to brush his horse.

Breakfast done, fire extinguished, animals ready we decided it was time to continue our journey just as the sun began to rise. We had a long way to travel, and we both looked forward to the journey.

I took one last look around. “Ready when you are Robert.”

He nodded and said, “Then, let us be off.”

We headed south at an easy pace, me pulling the pack horse, there being no real sense of urgency yet. We were not going to dilly-dally, but we were not in a rush. The bank had been robbed, the town of Castroville was still there and if any poor soul had been killed in the commission of the robbery, they would still be dead when we arrived. The bandits, whoever they were, already had at least two days on us.

I said, “Figure at this pace we should be in town after midnight.”

Robert looked up at the sky. “Sounds about right with the heat of the day coming down on us. I do not think we should push the animals too hard yet Wyatt. What do you think?”

“I agree. Ain’t nothing gonna change with us coming in late tonight or early tomorrow morning.”

Robert said, “You know Wyatt, last night I was thinking about this robbery. These bandits, whoever they are, have a two day jump on us already. Why is it that Marshal Sweeny is asking for us? How come he is not out chasing these fellas down with a posse?”

I too had thought about these things. “Reckon we will find out when we get there. Still, I do find it odd that they want us. Hell, it will be three if not four days after the robbery when we get there. He must have a good reason for not chasing after them.”

“Well,” Robert began, “like you said. We will find out when we get there.”

CHAPTER FIVE

Why is it that Marshal Sweeny was not heading a posse in pursuit of the bandits, whoever they were? That was the question that ran through my mind as we rode along through the morning. It did not make sense to us, but he had requested our help, and we were in transit to assist him in any way we could, and we would get the answers when we arrived.

As the sun rose higher in the sky so did the temperature. It was that time of year which caused us to take precautions during our journey. Rationing water became a necessity during these hot months. A lack of water can kill you as much as a desperado's bullet, only more terrible to endure. Less of course you were gut shot. That was about the only thing worse. There was not much one could do to help the suffering any, and it could last for days, much like dying of thirst.

We found a small stream and dismounted, allowing the animals to drink and cool their hooves while we walked upstream and refilled our canteens.

I took a drink and poured some of the cool water on my neckerchief and wrapped it over the back of my neck.

"It is so hot the hens are laying hard boiled eggs," I said.

Robert laughed. "It is that."

I reached into my possibles bag and handed Robert a strip of jerky, taking one for myself. The hardtack will be forgotten for now as will the salt pork, whiskey, and our tobacco. Those will be saved for the cooler, darkened hours of the day when we and the animals were at rest. We did not need to add anything to our diet that may accelerate our thirst.

I watched our animals meander through the cool stream and asked, "You have any good memories of the war Robert?"

The question seemed to catch him off guard and he looked at me for a moment before he answered. "I suppose I do," he said. "Odd, I have not thought too much on those as I have the bad times. Why do you suppose that is Wyatt?"

I took another drink. "Be damned if I know Robert. Seems to me we been thinkin' on nothing else but the bad times."

Robert was thoughtful for a few moments before he said, "It was not all bad when you really think on it."

"To hear us tell it, we did nothing but fight each other every waking moment of everyday for four long years," I said.

"It was not like that," Robert said. "We had our good times too."

We gathered up our horses and mounted up, returning to the trail. Again, as in water rationing, we instinctively maintained a steady if not easy pace not wanting to wear our mounts down in the heat. These are what we had to manage during the summer months, things we needed to concern ourselves with in our travels through the unforgiving wilderness. The town of Castroville was not going anywhere and we would arrive soon enough.

As we rode along our mood seemed to brighten somewhat. We both became more talkative. I had memories of those good times running through my mind. The jokes we played on one another to pass the time. The card games, sharing of news from home, letters, the girls we left behind and what we were going to do at wars end.

Robert too recalled the good times he had with his troopers, and he shared them with me, as I shared mine with him. We had the same kinds of stories but from different sides of the battlefield, in different uniforms. Soldiers will be soldiers no matter the cause, the uniform or one's allegiance. We shared our stories and shared in the laughter of those memories. We compared the types of soldiers we had under our charge. The unit joker, the serious stern soldier, the self-proclaimed ladies' man, the soldier that knew it all and was not afraid to share that knowledge, right or wrong. The quiet soldier, the braggart, and the tough guy. We had them all but under different banners, different flags.

Our conversation progressed with the passing of the day and changed from sharing good memories to the philosophical. The causes of the war, what could have been done to avert such a tragedy, and of course we had the answers to such questions, such issues. We had the gift of hindsight. To look back and provide the alternative that could have or would have changed the direction the nation went. We felt we had the right to voice our remedies, even if it was just between ourselves. Our right to critique our leaders was born in blood, sweat and the misery of carrying out the dreadful task of making war.

Then we conversed on the present day, and the misery dealt the people of the Southern States, this damn Reconstruction. Here Robert was in agreement with me when the implementation of Reconstruction turned into punishment of the Southerners, it was wrong. It was being wielded like a weapon against the common folk. He stated that he had written home to his kin and the difference in the mindset of those in the North had put him at odds with his two brothers. They had written back that it was justified, though Robert attempted to explain otherwise. It appeared to have fallen on deaf ears as the anger ran deep, justifying their notion to inflict yet more misery on the South. He thought it best to cease further correspondence about the matter with his brothers.

He had seen what was going on, he was living it. Texas was not even considered a state much less a part of the Union. It was governed by a military leader and referred to as a military district before it was referred to as a state. Folks came home after the war to find their land had been taken from them, their rights as citizens removed, and as an added insult a failure to be represented at higher levels of government. They became nonpersons, a nobody. The injustice continued throughout the South and the people were made to suffer. That is what Reconstruction had become, punishment and with it came those either perpetrating it or fighting against it and the authority that accompanied it.

That was where we came in. Judge Dubose recognized this injustice and like a Bible, he held up the law for the citizenry and used us as his weapon. When first appointed, both Robert and myself thought of refusing the position. We had no knowledge of the law or its enforcement, but the Judge stood fast and pronounced us Deputy United States Marshals. He emphasized our ability to exercise common sense in our enforcement of the law saying if we find it wrong, then it most likely was and he would sort out the legal details in his court. The only time he felt the need to reprimand us for our actions was when we were recuperating at Doc Averbeck's makeshift hospital, the both of us having been shot multiple times. He asked us not to kill so many folks' next time.

So that is what we were aiming to do.We would enforce the law and not rely so heavily on our guns as we had in the past. I cannot say it was working out for the best, much to Robert's dismay. That is how we came to apprehend this Mack the Knife character currently a guest in our fine establishment. I was for shootin' the varmint and be done with it, but Robert wanted to capture him, reminding me what the Judge had admonished us for. So, we cut the deck for high card, Robert lost and went into the saloon to capture the drunken fool. Punches flew and Robert lost a tooth, but Mack the Knife was subdued, only after I bashed him over the head with my Walker Colt.

I looked at the sun and suddenly realized just how late in the day it had become. Here we were, gabbing like a couple of women at the clothesline about this and that and the day slipped away from us.

"How far yet you reckon Robert," I asked.

"Oh, I think we should be in there well past midnight. Our course took us directly south. We must be well past Bandera by now," he said referring to a small-town west of us.

I said, "I been thinking. Do not make much sense us arriving so late. Got no place to stay and we cannot wake folks up and start asking questions at that late hour."

Robert nodded his head in agreement. "That is true. What say we push on till dark and call it a day."

I looked around at the terrain. It had become more rugged, hills and small peaks, rocky with little vegetation. It was truly an unforgiving land.

I said, "I am for that but if we come across water between now and then it might be best for the horses to stop and set up camp."

We rode on for a few more hours and were fortunate to come across a stream wide enough to accommodate our needs and those of our horses, so we stopped to set up camp right on the water's edge.

I dismounted and took in the scenery. Rocky hills, mesquite trees here and there, scrub brush and Indian Grass near the water's edge. The small stream was enough to keep the vegetation plentiful within its meager reach.

Again, I tended the animals while Robert set up the camp and the cook fire. It was a routine we had established and felt comfortable with. My Daddy always said do not fix it if it ain't broke, and it ain't broke so we left it alone.

Robert asked while digging through the panniers for the grub. "What do you think Wyatt, salt pork and beans, some pickles?"

I looked around, noting our abundance of water and said, "Why not."

As I was setting the saddles and bedrolls down, I suddenly had a notion to remove both my shotgun and Robert's Spencer Carbine from the scabbards and place them nearby, within our reach.

Robert took notice of this and asked, "Something amiss Wyatt?"

I shook my head looking around. "Nah, just a feeling Robert. Just a feeling."

Robert too looked around and said, "Might be wise to sleep in shifts tonight, Wyatt."

I knew he trusted my feelings, and I found his suggestion sound. It may have been nothing, but folks always said I had a sense about these things. I just felt trouble was near and we could not afford to ignore it. Especially during these difficult times.

The sun dipped down below the horizon and the temperature finally surrendered to the nighttime and the wilderness around us cooled pleasantly. So much so that we both enjoyed a good smoke, coffee, and some whiskey.

I took a drink and said, "Wish it was beer."

Robert said, "I am sure we can get a beer when we reach Castroville." Robert sat up against his saddle. "You think that fella at the saloon is still there? What the devil was his name?"

I thought back to that night we took on the five gun slingers in the Castroville saloon. I could see the barman's face, his chubby frame, his look of utter shock when we shot the five men down, bleeding all over his floor. I also remembered the terrible cigars he kept on hand.

I chuckled as his name came to me. "Melvin was the fella's name. Think he will remember us?"

Robert said, "I hope he does only after he gets us a beer and not before. We may walk out empty handed."

We sat around the fire and smoked another pipe before I suggested that I take the first watch. Robert agreed and made himself comfortable as I decided to stretch my legs once more. Grabbing my shotgun, I walked around the fire to the water's edge and looked up at the stars. No where else in my travels had I seen a sky as vast and beautiful as I had here in Texas. It was the only time I had felt at peace in my wanderings. To look up at the stars, vast and endless, made one feel small and with it one's problems equally small and perhaps insignificant.

I found a large rock, surprisingly comfortable, sat and had another pipe. I just listened to the night as I kept my watch, shotgun across my lap scanning the darkness beyond the light of the fire.

Around midnight Robert relieved me on watch, and I lay on my bedroll, pulled my hat over my eyes, and lay my hands on my chest. Sleep came over me and in no time, Robert was quietly calling my name.

"Time to get up Wyatt," he said.

I sat up and looked around. It was still dark, the fire still going and the coffee pot steaming next to a bed of coals.

I yawned and said, "You sir are going to spoil me. Coffee and a fire. I cannot ask for anything more."

Robert rested his Spencer over his shoulder and said, "Really? I could make breakfast."

I stood and rubbed my legs and stretched. "That will be even better my good sir. Ham, eggs, fresh buttermilk biscuits will do nicely."

Robert chuckled and responded, "Would hardtack and beans, do you?"

I sighed. "Reckon so."

Once more we settled into our routine of breakfast and breaking down our camp as the sun slowly climbed above the horizon. I looked around the morning sky, cloudless and bright it was going to be another sweltering day in Southern Texas. Nothing new, nothing unexpected and yet, I found it comforting. I led the horses into the camp, saddled and ready to resume our journey.

I said, "Give me a minute Robert. I gotta relieve myself."

Robert raised a hand in acknowledgment as I retreated away from the camp, still carrying the shotgun and found a large rock to perform my necessaries of the morning in privacy.

It was when I was strapping on my gun belt that I heard them.

"Jus stays where you are mister. Do not be foolish or you gonna be shot dead," said the voice.

Then a second voice, nervous and stuttering said, "Now we...we ga...ga...got you covered mister."

I picked up the shotgun, removed my hat and dared a look around the large bolder I was behind. There was two of them. Their backs were to me as they held pistols on Robert who was standing motionless, staring at his two would-be assailants.

The taller of the two spoke again, "Now git yer hands up for I shoot you dead."

Robert had been holding the reins of the horses which he dropped. He said sternly, "I am not going to put my hands up boys, just get on with what you tend to do."

The tall one looked over to the shorter one. It was then that I saw they were wearing neckerchiefs for masks. I shook my head at their stupidity.

The tall one took a step forward and raised his pistol a bit higher. "I says put yer damn hands up!"

Robert shook his head, crossed his arms over his chest and said, "No."

The two robbers exchanged looks. I can tell right away that they were out of their element. They had no idea what they were doing, thinking that robbing someone on the trail would be easy and not taking into consideration that their prey might and would refuse their demands. They were frightened by this turn of events.

I slowly slid around the bolder and keeping low, came up behind them. I was grateful that I brought the shotgun on this trip instead of my Colt Revolving Rifle.

The short one, stuttering his way through his threats said, "My bro...bro...brother dun said, git yer hands up!"

I raised the shotgun to my shoulder and cocked both rabbit ears back and said, "I think it is you boys that need to get your hands up."

They both turned slowly and saw me, shotgun at the ready, not four feet from them.

The tall one uttered, "Oh Lord," and dropped his pistol.

I motioned with the shotgun to the other fella and said, "Put the gun down boy or I will kill the both of you."

He vigorously nodded his head, released his death-grip on the pistol, and let it fall to the ground.

CHAPTER SIX

Robert pulled his Remington and stepped up to the two men while I covered him. He did a quick search, pulled their masks away and pushed them towards the remnants of the fire while I circled around and picked up the tall bandit's pistol.

Robert said as he pointed to his gold badge on his shirt. "You boys know what you just did was awful stupid."

They both looked at the badge, traded looks and dropped their heads in shame.

I put the first pistol in my belt and bent over to pick up the second one and stared at it in disbelief. There were no percussion caps on the cylinder! I snatched it up and turned to the two men.

I held the pistol out to the short fella and yelled, "You stupid bastard! Your gun was empty! You damn fool!"

I threw the empty revolver at him; he dodged the gun but not my punch to the jaw. I looked angrily at the prone figure. My God, he was just a boy, a foolish boy.

I pointed at him as he rolled over and looked up at me rubbing his jaw, I said, "You stupid kid! I could have killed you!" I looked at the other man. "Boy, you two have got to be the dumbest robbers I ever did meet."

Robert asked, "You two got names?"

The tall one nodded and said, "I am Clem and this here," he pointed to the prone figure, "is my brother Pete."

"How about a last name," I asked, my anger subsiding.

Clem answered, "Hawkins. Clem and Pete Hawkins sir."

I looked at Robert and shook my head. The last name did not bring anything to mind as I always kept up with the wanted bills that were sent to us. This must be their first time at this or their first time getting caught. I was inclined to believe it was their first time at robbing as they were not too proficient at this vocation.

Robert asked, "Is Clem short for something?"

Clem looked puzzled and asked, "Short for what Marshal?"

Robert looked at me and smiled. "Never mind son," he said.

Pete, still on the ground looked up at his brother and said, "I dun tol you this ain't gonna work Clem. Damn stupid idea."

Clem looked down at his brother and quietly answered, "How else we gonna eat? We ain't got no money."

Robert looked at me and shrugged. He asked the two boys, "When was the last time you fellas had something to eat?"

Clem closed one eye as he looked up at the sky as if it held the answer to an obvious question. "Reckon it has been a couple of days sir."

Pete said, "If'n you had not come along we was talkin' bout killin' our mule and eatin' him." He hung his head. "That is why we tried to rob you. I dun used all my bullets up tryin' to shoot rabbits and Clem was down to his last bullet."

I could not help but grin. "Not too good with pistols, are you?"

He shook his head and said, "No sir. Not too good at robbery neither."

Now I had to laugh. "Son, it is good to know your strengths and weaknesses."

Robert also laughed. "I do not know why we are going to do this, but we have plenty of grub. We will feed you boys."

They both exchanged looks of disbelief. Pete picked himself up and stood next to his brother and I saw the resemblance in the two. They were both youngsters caught up in terrible times.

Robert got the fire going and prepared a meager meal for the two young men while I took to cleaning both their pistols while maintaining a watchful eye. I had an idea brewing in my head as I watched the Hawkins boys devour everything Robert gave them.

While they were eating Robert came over to me. He had noticed me cleaning both revolvers while he made them something to eat, I was now loading them, and his curiosity was peaked.

"What in the hell are you doing Wyatt?"

I held up one of the two pistols I had just capped. "Not a bad gun. I was always partial to the Colt Army Revolver."

He looked back at the Hawkins boys sitting next to the fire then back at me. "Why are you loading their pistols?"

I said, "Well I cannot give them empty guns now, can I?"

Robert took in a deep breath. I guess he was trying to decide if I was off my nut. I grinned at him and winked.

I said, "I have an idea."

Robert knew me well enough to back my play. "I am all ears, Wyatt."

I walked closer to our two guests and watched them as they cleaned their plates. I was going to go out on a limb with them, bringing Robert out with me but, what the hell. I had a good feeling about these two.

I cleared my throat and got their attention. They looked up at me with questioning if not fearful looks.

I leaned down and handed them back their pistols saying, "I cleaned and loaded them both." They took them, exchanged looks and slowly got to their feet.

Clem said, "I do not understand Marshal. What for you givin' us back our guns?"

Pete looked down at his pistol then back at me. "Yea, how come you ain't arrestin' us, Marshal?"

I stepped closer. "You boys know where Fredericksburg is?"

Clem said, "Yes sir, north about two days ride."

Robert asked, "You said you have a mule. Think he could make the trip if we gave you some feed?"

"I reckon so," Pete said. "I do not get what you is sayin' Marshal."

"Just this," I said. "We are going to cut you boys loose. We ain't gonna arrest you. We will give you some feed and grub for the trip. You get on your mule and head north to Fredericksburg. Got it?"

Clem showed confusion on his face and again looked up at the sky. "I am befuddled Marshal. What do we do when we get there?"

Robert too was confused and asked me, "Yea Wyatt. What do they do when they get there?"

I had to admit. I was enjoying myself. "When you boys get there, head to the outside of town, on the west side, and you will find some fellas building the new saloon. Look for the boss, name of Stefan Myers. Tell him that Marshals Barton and Chambers said to give you a job as workers on the new saloon. Got that?"

They both nodded their heads.

Robert said, "Now tell us what you are going to do."

Pete said, "We is to ride north to Fredericksburg and find where theys building the new saloon and find this fella Myers. Tell him Marshals Barton and Chambers said to give us a job." He smiled. "That right Marshal?"

Robert smiled back and said, "That is perfect Pete."

Clem looked uncomfortable and agitated, shuffling his feet in the dirt.

I asked, "Something wrong Clem?"

"Well sir," he began, "I do not understand why you is doin' this for us. We tried to rob you and now you feeds us, clean our pistols, load 'em and now givin' us a job. It ain't that we is ungrateful, we just do not understand you, Marshal."

I am sure it was a lot for them to wrap their heads around. To hear Clem say it he was right. It made little sense but there was just something about these two boys that compelled me to offer them a second chance. There was a lot of hope and promise for the folks in Texas so why not let these boys share in it.

Robert said, "We are giving you boys a second chance. Do not waste it."

"If I find you boys took to robbin' folks, I will hunt you down and make you pay. Understand," I said.

They both nodded.

Robert said, "Across the street is the Marshal's Office. The jailer is a big fella named Julius. Tell him what happened and what we said. He will let you sleep in the stables behind the jail, and you can keep your mule there."

I said, "If Julius is unsure tell him that Marshal Chambers sings Dixie to his horse."

Clem said, "Dixie. Yes sir."

Robert chuckled. "That should do it."

I said, "Now go and fetch your mule. We will give you boys some grub for the trail."

As they departed Robert looked at me, smiled and shook his head, then walked over to the pack horse.

I watched him as he dug through the packs and pulled out food stuffs for the boys. We were close enough to Castroville that we could part with some of our supplies. What we give up we can replenish when we get to town.

The boys came back, and we helped them load the supplies on their mule and in no time, they were ready to depart. They stood next to the mule unsure of what to do.

I walked over and offered up my hand. "Reckon you boys should get goin'."

Pete took my hand and said, "I ain't got the words to thank you Marshal. We do appreciate what you fellas done for us and we will not never forget it."

Clem shook my hand. "Thank you, sir."

Robert came over, shook their hands, and said, "Do not let us down boys."

Clem said, "We will not, sir."

They both walked off, leading the mule into the wilderness.

Robert looked at me, smiled and shook his head again then mounted his horse. He said, "C'mon Wyatt. We got places to go."

I watched the boys walking off. "Reckon so," I said as I mounted my horse.

Having already suffered through one robbery, or the attempt at robbery, we kept our guard as we neared Castroville. As we got closer to town, we came across folks along the trail going about their business. A few wagons loaded down with families and household goods heading to parts unknown. Folks looking for a better life, a new beginning and who could blame them.

As a family in a covered wagon passed us heading the other way Robert pulled up and watched them for a moment. He said, "These are brave people Wyatt."

I looked at the wagon as it slowly made its way out into the wilderness, loaded with everything they owned dragging two stringy cows behind. "They are that," I said. "To pull up stakes and start over out there, it takes a lot of guts to do that."

We continued our way into the town of Castroville Texas. It almost felt like we were returning home to the place where we began. This is where our lives had taken such a drastic turn, one for the better. I know Robert felt the same as we slowly made our way down the dust choking street. Castroville will always be special to us.

Robert looked around as we passed the many buildings. New buildings, stores, and businesses had sprung up since our absence. Even though it had not been that long ago, Castroville was growing, and the German style architecture was present everywhere.

Just before we crossed the bridge over the Medina River, we saw Helga's tent cabins on the hillside, set off the road a piece behind the small inn on the river.

I asked, "Should we check in with Helga now or go see Marshal Sweeny?"

Robert pulled back on the reins and sat his horse looking at Helga's place while massaging his right knee. I could tell the old wound still bothered him even though he tried to hide it.

"I suppose we should check in with the Marshal first. We may not even be staying when we hear what he has to say."

I said, “True enough. I had not thought about that.”

We continued through town and across the wood bridge spanning the Medina River. I looked down at the water below and saw three boys splashing in the water and thought of jumping over the side and join in with them. It was hot and dusty and sitting in the cool waters of the river seemed like a refreshing method to cool off. It was not to be as we went deeper into town to the Marshal’s office.

Robert saw the shingle hanging out over the street, ‘Town Marshal’, and we turned our mounts to the opposite side of the roadway and tied off at the hitching rail.

I dismounted and massaged my legs. I looked around and took notice that folks were looking at us as they passed. I said to Robert, “You do not suppose some of these folks remember us, do you?”

Robert too was looking around. “Nah, I do not think that is the case. They may have heard that U.S. Marshals were coming.”

I looked down at my gold badge pinned to my breast. “Yea, this thing does stand out.”

Just then we heard a deep gruff voice behind us. “Well, I will be hanged and sent right to hell! You boys look a damn sight better than last we met.”

We turned and looked up on the porch and took in Marshal James Sweeny leaning up against the roof post, just grinning from ear to ear.

He was a large man, not heavy but muscular with a thin waist and long of leg. He wore a wide brim tan hat with a high crown pushed back on his head showing his black hair. His red bib shirt, complimented with silver buttons, stood out against his deep brown pants tucked into knee high brown cavalry boots. On his chest was a five-pointed silver star large enough to be seen from a great distance. His gun belt held a Colt Army revolver on his right hip and a smaller Navy Six across his belly. With his weathered face he cut an intimidating figure.

I said, “Marshal, you sure do shine brightly in this sun. Ain’t no way a man can miss you coming.”

He laughed and stepped down off the porch while extending his hand. “Reckon you boys never seen me dressed for work. Last we saw each other I was in my nightshirt.”

Robert took his hand and said, “That was one hell of a night Marshal. Good to see you again.”

I shook his offered hand. “You are looking just fine Marshal, good to see you.”

He smiled again. "Hell boys, call me Jim. We are all in the same business, after the same thing." He looked around, glanced at our horses, and said, "Come inside boys. We got a lot to talk about."

We climbed the stairs and went into the office where we found blessed relief from the hot sun.

Jim went over to his desk and pulled a bottle and three glasses from a drawer, setting them on the desk while I looked around his place of business. I appreciated his set up. The spacious office was set in such a manner that everything had a place, and everything was in its place. A single desk on the outside wall, a round table with four chairs in the center. It was similar to our set up the exception being that his cells, three of them, were against the back wall where ours were in a separate room. All his cells were empty.

He handed us our drinks and asked, "How was the road in?"

I traded a look with Robert and said, "Un-eventful Jim."

Chapter Seven

We were sitting at the table, bottle forgotten in the center as our three glasses sat empty. The small talk finished we were waiting for the Marshal to fill us in on the crime that had brought us some seventy miles south.

He played with his empty glass and said, "Boys, I am at a loss. I cannot even tell you how many there were in the robbery."

Robert said, "I think you need to start at the beginning Jim. We have no information on the robbery."

Jim sat back and looked at us. "The Judge did not fill you in at all?"

"He did not," I said. "He only told us the bank was robbed, and you needed our help."

"Well shit fire," Jim uttered. "Reckon I should start at the beginning then. Damn strange tale."

He grabbed the bottle and filled our glasses, taking a drink before he began.

He said, "Bank manager, fella name of Cyrus Mimms comes in the jail bout eight-thirty in the morning some three days back all worked up. Yellin' the bank was robbed."

I asked, "How much did they get away with?"

Jim took in a deep breath and said, "Over ten thousand in foldin' money, nearer fourteen and another two thousand in gold coin."

"The ten thousand was the Federal Payroll," Robert asked.

"It was," Jim said. "Near another two-thousand dollars of folks money around here and the gold coin was the banks."

I asked, "Anyone get hurt in the hold up?"

Jim looked at us and said, "That is just the thing. It was not a hold up. They took it during the night."

"They blew the safe at night and no one heard it," I asked.

Jim shook his head. "They did not blow the safe Wyatt. They took the whole damn thing."

We sat there in silence for a moment thinking through what Jim had just said. That would explain why he was not out with a posse.

Robert asked, "How big was this safe?"

Jim said, "Big bastard. Cast iron safe from Italy or some damn place. Thing must have weighed in near eight or nine hundred pounds."

A multitude of questions ran through my head as I was trying to put it together. I asked, "How the hell did they get the damn thing out of the bank without being seen? Someone would have seen them coming out the door with this big, huge box."

Jim took another drink. "That is the other thing. They did not come out the front door. They came out the back."

"The back door," Robert repeated.

"No door," the Marshal said. "They went through the wall."

I sat back and took a long drink. No wonder Jim asked for our help. Sometime during the night three or four days past some unknown bandits were clever enough to not only rob the bank of its money but the very vessel where the money was secured, and all without a witness to the crime.

"Lord Almighty Damn," I uttered.

Jim took another drink. "That is just what I have been sayin' last couple of days."

Robert said, "I suppose we should go to the bank and have a look. Maybe it will give us some idea where to start."

As we stood from the table I said to Jim, "I reckon we are gonna be here for a bit. We will need to stable the animals and find a place to stay."

"Already been taken care of Wyatt. You had a choice between George's Inn or Helga's tent city." Jim said as he went to the door. "I already knew what you boys would say, so I will have one of my deputies take your animals down to Helga's. I already told her you boys were coming back to town. She was one happy lady, said her two boys come back."

I smiled. "She is one special lady."

We were standing on the porch while Jim was talking to one of his deputies on the street, giving him instructions about the care of our animals. That task completed he waved us to follow him as the three of us walked down the street, deeper into town.

Robert said, "You forgot to warn the deputy about your horse Wyatt."

I stopped and looked at him. "Oh, hell I did forget." I looked back the way we had come. The deputy was well on his way in the opposite direction. "I hope he is careful," I said.

Jim asked, "Problem Wyatt?"

"That would depend on what mood my horse is in at the moment," I said.

Jim waved away my concern. "Billy can handle horses well enough."

I hope so said to myself.

We continued our journey through town as we made our way to the bank. Memories of the last time we had walked these streets floated through my mind. Back then our concerns were so different than those we had today. Back then they were more self-serving.

We stopped in the middle of the street and Jim pointed to a single storied wood framed brick building with bars on the windows. "This is it," he said as we made our way to the door.

A hand drawn closed sign hung on the door. The Marshal ignored it and pushed it open, and we went inside.

It was a bank like any other one would find out on the frontier. Simple, basic, nothing too fancy as most of the customers were regular town folks unlike banks back east in the big cities that catered to those with an endless supply of money.

I found it dark and gloomy even for a bank. All the oil lamps were lit and the shades pulled back yet still I did not find it inviting with its wood panel walls and plank floor. It reminded me of a funeral parlor and only the presence of three caged windows along a long counter for the tellers' spoke of a bank.

A tall thin frail looking man dressed in a black frock coat, black pants, white shirt under a silver vest stepped out from behind the counter. His face, thin and bony was topped with thick grey hair combed back. On his rather long pointed nose he wore gold rimmed Pince-nez glasses causing him to tilt his head back to keep them from falling off I suppose.

Without bothering to introduce himself he addressed the Marshal directly. "Well," he began with an irate tone as he stopped abruptly in front of us. "I was beginning to wonder if you were intentionally ignoring my situation, Marshal Sweeny."

Jim took a deep breath before he spoke. "Mister Mimms, I told you I had to wait for the U.S. Marshals to arrive."

He cast a reproachful glance at us. "Are these the Marshals," he asked as he pointed at us.

Robert said, "We are Mister Mimms."

"Well," he said as he stomped his foot. "You certainly took your time getting here."

I was already disliking this man. "Mister Mimms, we came seventy miles to look into this so what say you drop the abuse and work with us."

He pulled his Pince-nez off his beak-like nose and stared at me. I stared right back.

Robert interceded before more words were thrown about. "Why not show us where the safe was Mister Mimms."

He put his glasses back on his nose, never taking his eyes off me and said, "For all the good it will do...follow me."

We followed Mimms around the counter, through a doorway into a spacious office. Here the room was bright, almost cheery, and welcoming. It could be an office anywhere. A large, polished desk, a few wingback chairs around a low table, nice rug on the floor, it was pleasant and inviting. The only detractor from the decor was the bars across the back wall. Cell like with a hinged door we saw where the safe was prior to the robbery.

I looked at the gaping hole surrounded by brick. The hole was rectangular in shape maybe five feet in height and three feet wide. I stepped closer and looked at the cage door.

"Mister Mimms," I said. "I would guess that this gate was locked when you came in that morning."

He said, "It most certainly was."

I stepped in and looked at the brick along the wall. It went from floor to ceiling and wall to wall about another six feet.

Robert said, "Mister Mimms, tell me about this safe."

Mimms groaned as if our questions were going to impose on his time. "It was an Italian Hobnail safe. It was special made and comes with two unique keys that must be worked together to open the multiple locking mechanisms."

I was looking into the void that had once contained the safe. "So, you cannot open it with just the one key," I asked.

He said, "That is correct. But even with the two keys it is sort of a puzzle to release the locks. The keys must be turned in a certain sequence at a certain time and order."

Jim said, "Sounds complicated."

Mimms smiled and said, "Not if you know how to do it Marshal. It is the latest in security. I spared no expense in getting this government contract. The safe is a fortress."

I stepped back from the hole and said, "Only if you can keep the safe from walking off Mister Mimms."

His ego, slightly deflated by my statement silenced him for the moment.

Robert turned to Mimms. "What contract are you talking about?"

Mimms pulled his Pince-nez off his nose and with a handkerchief began to polish the lenses as he spoke. "I bid on the Federal contract to house monies for the District Paymaster General. I had to meet certain requirements to win the bid, and the safe was one of them."

"What were the other requirements," the Marshal asked.

Mimms put his glasses back on and waved a hand around as he spoke. "Well, the building itself, the cage and the lock on the front door..."

I interrupted. "And the way the safe was secured on the premises, correct?"

Mimms looked at me over his glasses. "What do you mean?"

I ignored Mimms and addressed Jim and Robert. I pointed into the hole and said, "It would seem that someone has cut a few corners in building cost to meet those requirements."

Both Jim and Robert looked into the hole and saw what I was referring to.

Robert stepped back and looked at Mimms. "It seems that you either forgot to brick in the outside wall or just wanted to save some money and not do it. Which is it Mister Mimms?"

Mimms cleared his throat, and I noticed sweat started to appear on his brow.

Marshal Sweeny stepped closer to Mimms and pointed at him. "Did you do that on purpose? The entire outside wall has not been bricked in."

Mimms took his handkerchief out of his pocket and wiped his forehead before he spoke. "Now Marshal Sweeny. You must understand how difficult it was for me to obtain the brick. I did not think it was that important."

Robert looked at Mimms hard. "So, the contract called for you to brick the entire safe in, front and back, and you told them it was done." Robert pointed over his shoulder. "Yet we see here that it was not done. Is that what you are saying Mimms?"

Mimms became indignant. "Now see here Marshal. You cannot speak to me this way."

I walked away from the hole and stepped closer to the nervous banker. "Boy, you are damn lucky I do not drag your skinny ass out on the street and let the folks of this town get their hard-earned money out of you anyway they can!"

Jim looked at Mimms and shook his head. "Do you know what you have done Cyrus? I do not give a damn about the Federal money. The people of this town lost what little they had, you arrogant jackass."

Mimms retreated to his desk and sat down, put his head in his hands and wept. I reckon he had convinced himself he was blameless in the loss of the money. Now the truth hit him hard, like a ton of brick.

I said, "I am going out back and see how they got through the wall."

Robert said, "Go ahead Wyatt. I have some more questions for the banker here."

"I be comin' with you Wyatt," Jim said.

Outside we walked around the back of the bank. I immediately took notice that the rear of the building was a blind spot. Short of lighting a bonfire anything going on back here would go unnoticed.

Jim said, "There are wagon tracks going right up to the wall."

I looked down on the ground. Judging from the width of the wheels I knew it to be a heavy-duty freight wagon. We used plenty of them during the war to move the heavy loads.

"How much did the safe weigh," I asked.

"Mimms told me around eight or nine hundred pounds."

I thought for a moment while I looked at the hole and the wagon tracks. Remembering just how high a freight wagon was with the gate down I looked at the base of the hole. It was near the same height from the ground. I looked in the black void.

I said, "Once they removed the first board they cut the rest. Easy job and did not make much noise while they were doing it."

Jim pointed at the floor inside the hole. "Look at those marks Wyatt. I noticed them before. What do you reckon made them?"

I looked at what he was pointing at. The floor had been dirty and with the added saw dust from cutting a distinct outline of two parallel lines showed on the floor extending from the brick inside the building to the exit hole. The marks were about two inches wide and a bit over two feet apart.

I thought as I looked at them trying to let my imagination run wild as if I was doing the robbery. It did not take me long to come up with an idea.

I said, "It is about seven or eight feet from the outside wall to the brick on the inside. That is a hell of a distance to drag an eight-hundred-pound box out of this hole."

Jim looked in. "Yea, nearer nine. This hole is also smaller than the space where the safe was."

I nodded. "Which means the safe was on its back when it came through this hole and into the wagon."

The Marshal said, "Still. Hard to drag that much weight back to here then get it in a wagon. How many men would you need?"

I looked at Marshal Sweeny and smiled. "Two," I said.

Jim pushed his hat back on his head. "Two?"

I nodded. "They put down a narrow rail, like train tracks, rolled a wheeled flat cart along the rails into the hole then pulled the safe over onto the cart, then wheeled the entire thing into the wagon. Simple."

Jim whistled. "Well, how bout that."

Robert joined us behind the bank, and we filled him in on what we surmised had occurred.

Robert too whistled. "Clever fellas they were. Which begs the question. How did they know to go through the wall in the first place and how did they know to go in at this exact spot?"

I said, "These fellas had a lot of information before they showed up that is for certain."

Jim asked, "What else did Mimms say?"

Robert said, "According to him only he and the brick mason knew of the lack of brick and no real inspection was done by the Federal boys when it was completed. He also said that there are only two sets of keys for the box. He has one set, and the other is kept with the Paymaster in Austin."

I said, "I think we may need to send a message to Austin and make sure they still have their keys. Is that normal for them to do that?"

Robert nodded. "According to Mimms it is. It was one of the conditions to get the contract to store the money."

Jim asked, "Where was all this money going?"

"Mimms said it was for the forts the army is reoccupying in the Western District." Robert looked at me and frowned. "It was also our pay."

I took my hat off and wiped at the hat band with my handkerchief. "Well, shit."

We retreated to the comfort of Jim's office to further discuss the robbery and maybe, just maybe find out who did it.

CHAPTER EIGHT

We returned to the jail and went in to get out of the hot sun. Inside we found the Deputy that had taken care of our mounts while we were down at the bank. I noticed he had the foresight to return with our saddle bags, Robert's Spencer, and my shotgun. I also noticed he was massaging his shoulder.

I sat down at the table and looked at the young man. "Everything okay Deputy?"

He stopped massaging his shoulder and said, "Oh sure Marshal. Just fine."

I nodded, unconvinced but decided not to press it. I knew that Caliban had taken exception to him and had inflicted some sort of punishment on the Deputy for not minding himself.

Robert said, "Thanks for taking care of our horses Deputy and bringing our things back here."

He nodded and stood. "My pleasure Marshal," he said as he made his way to the door. "I will get back to work now Marshal Sweeny."

Jim said, "That is fine Billy. Thanks for your help."

Robert sat at the table and grabbed the bottle, filling the three glasses that sat empty. He said, "Wyatt, I think Caliban claimed another victim."

I took a glass and said, "I believe you are right Robert."

Jim sat and looked at us. "Something I should know? Who is Caliban?"

I took a drink and looked into the glass of whiskey grinning. "Caliban is my ill-tempered horse that has a habit of flexing his authority over folks he does not know."

Jim looked back at the door. "I reckon Billy found that out." He took a drink and looked back to me. "Good kid. He is not one to complain."

I felt compelled to apologize to the Marshal. "Sorry about that Jim. I will make it up to your Deputy somehow."

Jim waved me off. "He will be fine. Tough kid." He took another drink. "Now, how about this robbery? How you reckon we can go any further with this?"

Robert looked at me and said, "I have a couple of ideas." He turned to Jim. "Any idea how they got out of town? Did anyone say anything about a freight wagon in town?"

The Marshal sat back and looked frustrated. "No one saw nuthin'."

"Well, we did not see any wagon on the way in but that does not mean they went north," I said.

We were silent for a few moments as each of us tried to figure out the next step in this confusing series of occurrences. Both how it happened and where they went afterward and, more importantly, how we were to proceed in tracking these unknown thieves.

I stood and began pacing around the room. I was trying to burn off the energy that was building up in my body as my mind raced through what we had already learned. My Daddy always said that when faced with a problem that had no visible solution just concentrate on what you knew and break it down, think of it a piece at a time. This I decided to share with the others.

I stopped and looked at the colored map of Texas on the wall. I guess all lawmen in Texas worked off the same map as we had one at our jail.

"Damnation this is a big state," I uttered.

"What say Wyatt," Jim asked.

I turned back to the others. "We need to look at this one step at a time and figure out how they pulled this off. I think we have enough information that we can put something together here."

Robert nodded in agreement and said, "We can start with how they got the equipment they used. They did not just show up and put this together the same night."

Jim said, "The track and the cart they used. They had to have that made which means maybe a blacksmith. I do not think it was wood. That safe was too damn heavy."

I sat back down. "The freight wagon would stick out around these parts so whichever way they went, maybe they were seen passing through another town."

Now Robert was on his feet pacing about the room. "These fellas knew exactly where to cut into the wall. According to Mimms only he and the brick mason knew the particulars of the lack of brick. You have a brick mason in town?"

Jim thought for a moment then said, "We do. Fella name of Billings, Herman Billings."

The Marshal was out of his chair and went for the door. Outside we heard him calling for Billy, his Deputy.

He came back inside. "Got me an idea fellas," he said as he sat at his desk and began to scrawl on a sheet of paper.

Billy came through the door, alarmed and tense. "What is it, Marshal?"

The Marshal turned in his seat and said, "Go fetch Tommy and Jack then come back here in a hurry."

The young Deputy turned and bolted out the door.

"What do you have in mind Jim," I asked.

Still writing on the sheet of paper he said, "I am gonna send two of my Deputies out to Billing's place and another one to the telegraph office." He finished writing and turned back to us and held up the paper. "We are gonna send a message to every town and county lawman within a hundred miles and find out if they seen a freight wagon come through in the past few days."

I smiled. "If we are lucky, we can find out which direction they went when they left here."

Billy came in with two other men. One, young and tough looking like Billy, and the other older with an eye patch over his left eye. The three of them stood just inside the door and looked to Marshal Sweeny, awaiting their instructions.

Jim stood and faced his men saying, "Boys, this here is Marshals Barton and Chambers, down from Fredericksburg." He turned to us. "Wyatt, Robert, this here is Tommy Phelps and One-Eyed Jack Collins."

We all acknowledged each other with a nod of our heads.

Jim turned back to his men and began issuing instructions. "Billy, Tommy, I want you boys to ride out to the Billings cabin and grab Herman and bring him back here and be careful, he might not want to come peaceable. Jack, I want you to go to the telegraph office and send out this message to everyone I have listed here and tell that drunk Milton to stay by his apparatus till he gets an answer from all of them. I do not care if it takes all damn night."

One-Eyed Jack took the paper, read through it, and asked, "You want I should stay there for the answers? It might keep him from drinkin'."

Jim said, "Good idea. If you get one that says they seen the wagon, then come a runnin' back here. I also want you to stop at the blacksmith and tell Sim I want him here like yesterday."

The three men did not need any further instruction or motivation as they turned as one and went out the door to carry out their mission.

I went to my saddle bags and pulled out my pipe and tobacco pouch motioning to Robert to do the same.

I held up the pouch to Jim and said, "Care for some fine Virginian tobacco Marshal?"

He grinned and said, "Do not mind if I do Wyatt."

The three of us, pipes in hand decided to step out to the porch and await the arrival of the blacksmith and any news from the deputies.

I leaned against the porch railing as I smoked and looked out at the town folk going about their business. At one time I would have been envious of them thinking they had simple concerns as they ran about town tending to their needs. That was when I lived out on the range, drifting from town to town, living in the wilderness, concerned with living in an unforgiving world. But now I came to realize that they too lived in this environment, and this troubled world. Be it in town or in the wilderness, life can be all too short in both places. I admired these folks and the chances they took to make a better life for themselves.

"You okay Wyatt," Robert asked.

I turned back and said, "Oh sure. Never better."

Jim pulled on his pipe and said, "This is a fine tobacco, Wyatt. Better than those crappers Melvin pushes down at the saloon."

Robert laughed. "Speaking of Melvin. Would he object to our presence in his saloon later today? We sure could use a beer."

Jim said, "Tell you what. We talk to the blacksmith, and I will stand you fellas to a couple of rounds at the saloon. Billy and Tommy will not be back till later tonight and I do not expect anything on our message till later."

"Fine idea," I said.

Just then a short round fella wearing a black leather apron came to the bottom of the porch steps. By the size of his muscular forearms and thick hands I figured him to be the blacksmith we were waiting for.

He said, "I came a quick as I could Marshal. Jack says you want some words with me."

Jim stood and walked to the top of the stairs. "Boys," he began, "this here is Simkin Blassingame, our blacksmith. Sim, these fellas is U.S. Marshals down here about the bank."

The blacksmith nodded and said, "Pleased to know you."

"Likewise," I said.

The Marshal said, "C'mon up here out of the sun Sim. I got some questions for you."

The blacksmith hesitated for a moment then came up to the porch. "I ain't in some kinda trouble am I Marshal?"

Jim laughed. "No Sim, we need your help with something."

Blassingame seemed to relax a bit. He looked at us, visibly sniffed the air and said, "I do smell a fine Virginian shag I do," he said.

I offered up my tobacco pouch and said, "Feel free Mister Blassingame."

He took the pouch, opened it up and took out a small wad between his thumb and his index finger. Then, to my surprise he pushed it in his mouth using his tongue to work it in his cheek.

"Much obliged," he said nodding happily.

I took back the pouch, looked inside and shrugged. "Certainly," I said as I put the pouch in my pocket.

Jim said, "Want to know Sim if you had done any kinda special work the last week or so for some strangers."

Sim looked puzzled. "Whatcha mean special?"

Robert, having gotten over his shock seeing the blacksmith chew instead of smoke the tobacco said, "These fellas or fella would have wanted you to make a couple of two-inch-thick rails maybe two and a half feet wide and oh, say maybe ten or twelve feet long."

I added, "Also a wheeled flat cart to ride on the rails."

He chewed on his wad, spit off the side of the porch and said, "Like a skinny train track you mean."

Jim said, "Yes, like a skinny train track."

Sim shook his head. "Nope."

Jim looked dejected and asked, "You sure Sim?"

The little blacksmith nodded. "Sure, I am sure. Whatcha think, I would forget somethin' like that?"

Robert asked, "Would something like that be hard for you to make?"

Sim thought for a moment, even rubbing his chin as he looked up. "Nah. Not hard. Damn thing be heavy though, for sure. How much weight you put on it?"

I said, "About eight or nine hundred pounds."

"Then that cart be damn heavy too," he said.

"Would the cart be hard to make," I asked.

Again, he thought. "It would be easy if you use the wheels from one of them mining hoppers, you know, the ones they takes down the shaft. Some of them carts be about two and a half feet wide."

I looked at Jim and Robert. We had not thought of that. They could have used something already made, just change it around for the robbery. Still, they would have to have all the measurements of the safe, the wagon they were to use, right down to the floor space to set the track.

I was about to voice my thoughts when Jim said, "They used something already made. They just made it to fit the job."

Sim, confused, looked at the three of us. "Who did what Marshal?"

Jim said, "Nothing Sim. Thanks for coming down."

Sim gave a half-hearted salute, spit off the porch and bid us a farewell.

As I watched the blacksmith leave, I said, "They would still need a blacksmith to make it all fit. These boys really had a lot of information to pull this off."

Jim looked out over his town and quietly said, "That is why it is important to talk to Billings." He turned back to us. "Now, how bout that beer fellas?"

Robert happily said, "Lead the way, Jim."

We walked down the street mulling over the new information the blacksmith had imparted to us. I will admit, I was pleased with the progression of our inquiry thus far. We had a damn good idea how they pulled it off, though we wanted to know where they had obtained the information on the bank. I was hoping with that information we may be able to find out who the thieves were and where they had gone.

We soon found ourselves standing in front of the saloon.

As we walked up the steps Jim asked, "Bring back memories boys?"

I chuckled and looked at Robert. "I sure hope this visit does not end up in another gunfight."

Robert said, "Amen to that."

We went inside and stopped just inside the double doors. It had not changed one bit since last we were there. The bar on our left, still in disrepair and worn, the tables arranged around the floor, a small, elevated platform for any musician or entertainer, and a piano on the back wall.

The saloon was near empty as I suppose it was early in the day for most, so we decided to take our places at the bar. I looked at Robert and noticed that he was looking at the table where we fought it out with the gun hands. I looked too, almost expecting to see bloodstains from those we shot down.

"Afternoon Marshal Sweeny," came the voice behind the bar.

I turned and there stood Melvin, the chubby saloon keeper. I swear he was wearing the same outfit from the last time we were here. Black pants, dirty wrinkled white shirt, opened at the neck and an equally dirty white linen apron.

He looked at me then Robert and uttered as the blood drained from his face, "Oh damnation, you two."

I smiled. "Hi Melvin. How you been keeping yourself?"

He looked around his saloon then back at me. "You ain't fixin' to shoot nobody are ya?"

Robert could not help himself and said, "Now, Melvin that is no way to greet a couple of old friends."

He pointed at Robert and said, "You two. I still have nightmares cause you two fellas dun kilt five men in my saloon. It took me forever to git the blood outta the floorboards. What the hell you want?"

Robert took pity on poor Melvin and said, "My good sir. We are the law now and we just came in here for some of your refreshing beer. So, how about three beers barkeep."

He looked from Robert to me.

I said, "We will be mindful Melvin, I promise."

Jim let out a laugh. "Melvin these boys are with me. We just want some beer, nothing else."

He let out a lungful of air and said, "Okay. Reckon I can do that."

Chapter Nine

We had our beer and then some with Marshal Sweeny. It was getting late, and our stomachs began rebelling at the lack of food, the beer not being enough to stop our rumbling gut. Jim suggested we retire to Helga's, eat then get some rest.

The three of us walked back to the jail where we picked up our saddle bags and long guns.

Jim said, "You boys get some rest after you fill your bellies. Once I hear some news I will come and get you. It may be late mind you."

I grabbed up my shotgun, threw my overstuffed saddles bags over my shoulder and said, "No matter Jim. If need be, we can ride out tonight."

Robert scoffed. "Not before we get our fill of some home cooking."

Jim laughed and said, "Go on boys, git. Billy already moved your things into a cabin and bedded down your animals. Go eat and get some rest. I will come get you."

We nodded our affirmation and went out the door and proceeded down the street to Miss Helga's tent city. It was a beautiful afternoon, and the town was bustling with activity. Folks coming and going, here and there, set on their own personal missions of the day.

As we stepped on to the bridge going over the Medina River I stopped and looked down at the inviting water. The three boys were gone, off to other forms of mischief no doubt.

I asked Robert, "Ever do much fishing?"

He looked over the side and said, "Some. Not since I was back in Pennsylvania though. Trout fishing is what I like."

I looked out over the river. "Sure, would be nice to throw a line."

"That place we were at with Olen would be a good spot," Robert said referring to a picturesque place we found on the Llano River some time back.

"Yea," I said as I walked away, seeing the face of our departed friend in my mind's eye.

We crossed the river and turned up the path to Helga's. It was just as we remembered it. Even though it was not so long ago, I suppose I was expecting a change. Everything else seemed to change, to grow and expand with the influx of folks coming west.

We stepped up to the porch and went inside. The room, large and accommodating lay before us. The tables were spread out as before, each with four chairs and blue and white table clothes. The oil lamps hanging down from the ceiling cast a pleasant glow over the room. The place was packed with folks, and they all fell silent and looked at us as we came in. We ignored them for the moment and took in the smells of home cooking as it drifted through the dining area causing our stomachs to remind us of our priorities and to put an urgency in our step.

Looking to the far wall we saw the counter where the many customers checked in to receive their sleeping quarters. Just to the right of the counter was the double doors to the kitchen and at that moment they opened and a short plump woman, holding a large pot stepped out.

She looked up, saw us and uttered in German, "Ach du Lieber Himmel!"

I looked at Robert, knowing that he was well versed in Pennsylvanian Dutch, close to the German language I have been told, and asked, "You catch what she said?"

He chuckled. "Something like 'Oh my goodness,' I think."

Helga ran to one of the occupied tables, put the pot down and near broke into a run, her small legs propelling her towards us with purpose.

With her arms open wide she almost tackled the both of us yelling, "My boys, my boys are back. Oh, thank the Heavens you are back," she cried in her thick German accent.

She wrapped her arms around Robert's thin frame, then grabbed his face in both hands and pulled his head down, planting a kiss on his forehead, turned to me and did the same.

Grabbing both our arms she pulled us closer to her. "Oh my, you have come to see old Helga. Oh, how I have missed my boys."

We both put our arms over her shoulders and welcomed her affections.

She started to lead us to a table saying, "You boys must be hungry, now sit. Sit and eat some of Helga's stew. Yes, yes, that is what you will do."

As we were sitting a man, seated alone at a table called out. "Hey, old women, I am hungry. Where is my dinner?"

Helga frowned, pushed a lock of graying hair out of her eyes, and said to the irate man, "One moment, I will be coming sir." She looked at us. "One moment boys. I will return with your dinner."

As she went to tend to the loudmouthed customer I said, "I do not like rude folks Robert."

Robert looked over at the man and said, "Nor do I Wyatt, especially if it is directed to a dear friend of ours."

I watched Helga spoon out the stew to loudmouth, then she retreated to the kitchen.

"Bring me something to drink you old crow," he yelled as she disappeared into the kitchen.

I took the man in as he shoveled the stew into his mouth. Even seated I could tell he was a tall man, thick in frame, almost fat, long black hair combed back and held in place with a thick pomade or axel grease for all I knew. He wore a white frock coat trimmed in brown over white pants and brown low-quartered shoes. On the table was a brown top hat.

"Reckon we need to have some words with this fella about how he talks to our friends Robert."

Robert said, "That we do Wyatt. Fella needs to be taught some manners."

We both stood from the table and walked over to loudmouth. I came in on the man's right and Robert came in on his left. We stood there silently as he shoveled his meal in the gaping hole he called a mouth. He looked up.

"What do you two want," he asked with his mouth full.

Even with his face full of food I could clearly hear his Yankee accent. For me, that was another reason to dislike him. Not that I had any anger or disregard towards Northerners, just ill-mannered loudmouth Yankees like him.

Robert said, "We do not appreciate you speaking to our friend like that mister."

I said, "Yea, she is like a mother to us, and we get kinda riled when folks treat her badly."

He ignored Robert and focused on me. "I do not give a tinker's damn what you say, you rebel trash."

I looked at Robert grinned, looked down at loudmouth, and in one swift motion I had my Walker Colt out and jammed the barrel between his legs, and pushed down.

He let out a groan as his eyes grew wide in terror.

I said quietly through clenched teeth, "Now listen here you Yankee Carpetbaggin' son of a bitch! We asked you nicely, ain't gonna ask you again!"

Robert leaned down and said softly, "Now we are telling you. Be polite or my friend here is going to remove your privates."

I cocked the pistol and smiled.

Carpetbagger broke out into a sweat and began nodding his head so quickly I thought the man was going to have the fits. Then his eyes rolled up in his head and he fell forward with his face planting in his bowl of stew.

Robert grabbed a handful of hair and lifted his head out of the bowl, looking at his face dripping in brown gravy, beef, potatoes, and carrots. "Poor man fell asleep during his meal," he said as he dropped his head on the table.

I holstered my pistol and said, "He must have the vapors."

As we were returning to our table a well-dressed fella on the far side of the dining room stood, held up his mug of beer and said, "Bravo gentlemen. Bravo."

I nodded my head acknowledging him. As we sat down the room broke into applause.

Miss Helga came over to our table with a small pot of stew, set it in the center of the table and leaned in and kissed me on the cheek, then planted one on Robert's cheek, turned and went back into the kitchen.

I began to spoon out the stew in Robert's bowl when he said, "You are blushing Wyatt."

I handed him his bowl and said, "Oh, hush."

When my bowl was filled Helga came back and set a pitcher of beer on our table. She said, "I remember how you boys liked your beer. This is good German beer I save for special times." She leaned closer and whispered, "Just for you boys." She stood and smiled, wringing her hands through her apron.

I reached up and took her hand, giving it a squeeze. "We sure missed you, Miss Helga."

She put her other hand to her cheek, blushed and went off to tend to her other customers.

While we were eating the Carpetbagger came to, wiped his face, and stood. The room fell silent as he looked at the many faces in search of support. The looks he received told him that he stood alone, so he dropped a coin on the table, picked up his top hat and beat a retreat for the door.

“Good riddance,” I said.

The meal finished, the pitcher of beer drained we sat back, fat, happy and sassy as my Momma used to say.

Helga came over to gather up the dirty crockery. She said, “Why not go to the porch and have some of that fine tobacco of yours Wyatt, and I will bring you boys some coffee.”

Robert said, “That is a fine idea.”

As Helga was leaving, she added with a giggle, “As long as it is not those foul-smelling cigars from the saloon.”

We found a couple of rockers on the porch and set in for a pipe. As folks were leaving, either to their cabins or home after the meal, they all bid us a good evening, a few of the men even shaking our hands, thanking us for dealing with the Carpetbagger.

Helga joined us on the porch with a tray of coffee.

I asked, “Will you join us, Miss Helga?”

“Oh, no boys. I have much to do.” She looked at us, again wringing her hands in her apron. “I heard about you boys getting hurt.” A tear slid down her cheek. “I prayed so long and hard that you would get well. I pray for you every day. Such danger you boys face.”

I said, “Thank you Miss Helga. The Good Lord listened”

“Thank you, Miss Helga,” Robert said.

She asked, “How are the other two? Your handsome Indian friend and the tall man that was with you the last time?”

I said, “Long Buffalo and the Undersheriff of Karnes County, Clinton Baker.”

Robert said, “Long Buffalo is well, we were just with him a few days ago and Clinton is doing well, so we have heard.”

Helga said, “That is good. You boys need good friends with this law work you do. You look out for each other and that is good in these troubled times.” She turned to go inside and added, “I will pray for you every night. You do important work for all of us.”

We sat on the porch, drank our coffee, and smoked another pipe, our conversation lacking in anything of substance. We were talked out, tired from the trail, tired of exercising both mind and body, it had caught up with us. We decided to retire for the evening, went inside to find our sleeping arrangements.

We settled into our small but comfortable canvas draped cabin. Wood framed and half planked walls, the canvas stretched over the ‘A’ frame to keep the weather at bay. When the wind kicked up the canvas would flap in the breeze, a sound I found soothing going back to my days in the army. With our bellies full of stew and beer, the last image I had was looking at the canvas roof. We were soon fast asleep.

It seemed like minutes when I heard my name being called through the fog of my waking mind. I sat up on the bunk, looked around in the darkness and listened.

"Marshal Chambers. Marshal Barton. You fellas in there," came the unfamiliar voice.

I said, "We are. Who is out there," as I grabbed up my pistol.

The voice responded, "It is me."

I looked at Robert, who was struggling to get out of his bunk, and shrugged my shoulders.

I said, slightly irritated, "Who the hell is me?"

There was a moment of silence then he said, "Oh, me. One-Eyed Jack, Marshal."

Robert yawned and said, "Well get in here before you wake everyone up."

He came through the door and stood there, silent.

I looked at him expectantly. "Well," I said, "whatever is the matter, Jack?"

He took his hat off. "Oh, yea," he said. "Marshal Sweeny sent me to fetch you fellas. The wagon we was asking about has been seen."

All thoughts of sleep immediately drained away as I jumped to my feet. "Where?"

Jack said, "Bandera. County Sheriff saw the wagon two days past now I reckon. Said it had two fellas and an Indian ridin' with them."

Robert was grabbing his pants. "Is it still in Bandera Jack?"

"No sir," he answered. "He says it left town and went north. Said he would not have paid it no never mind cept for the Indian that was with them. Marshal Sweeny has been conversing with the Sheriff back and too. Says the Indian was decked out in war paint and had some big knife on his belt. Thought it odd. That how comes he remembered the wagon."

"What about the brick mason the boys went after," I asked.

Jack shook his head. "Could not find him. Were not at his cabin." He paused and said, "Oh yea. Austin said they have their keys. Some army major fella."

We hastily dressed, strapped on our pistols, grabbed our long guns and with hats in hand made for the door.

I asked, "The Marshal still at the telegraph office?"

Jack said, "No sir. He is at the jail. We got Billy and Tommy waitin.' Marshal is talking bout going out after them."

As we were walking down the street, I looked at my time piece. A little after two in the morning. I looked over to Jack who was walking next to me.

"How did you lose the eye Jack," I asked.

He looked at me. "Battle of Chickamauga," he answered.

"Who were you with," I asked him.

His chest puffed up a bit with pride, "General John Bell Hood." He looked at me and asked, "How bout you Marshal? Who was you with?"

I answered, "General Stuart."

Jack nodded his head, looked past me to Robert and said, "I know you is a Yankee Marshal Barton. No offense to you sir. Who was you with?"

Robert said, "None taken Jack. I was with General Buford."

Again, Jack nodded his head. "Damn shame how the man died. Ain't no way for a soldier to go out."

"You are right Jack," Robert said.

We went up the steps and into the jail. All the oil lamps were burning, and we found Jim looking at the map on the wall while Billy and Tommy were sitting at the table sharing a pot of coffee.

Jim turned around. "Sorry you boys could not get more sleep, but we might know where the wagon went."

I said, "Jack filled us in. Sounds like they went north. Reckon we should head up to Bandera."

Robert said, "I was thinking on this. How did they get to Bandera? They would have passed us on the trail when we were coming down."

I grabbed an empty cup and reached for the coffee pot. "Yea, and I would have questions about this Indian they are traveling with. Is that what the Sheriff said Jim?"

Jim picked up a small stack of paper slips. His conversation with the Sheriff of Bandera County. "I was wondering that too," he said. "Damn strange not to have seen them when you were coming down. I do not know of another way to get to Bandera cept on the North-South Trail. Do you?"

Robert said, "I rode through here in the army before the war. I know of no other way. Nothing well-traveled anyway."

Jim said, "Be hard as hell to get through that hill country. Damn near impossible I reckon with a freight wagon loaded with that safe." He put the papers on the table. "What do you boys think?"

Robert asked, “Did the Sheriff notice anything in the wagon?”

Sweeny said, “He did. Said there was a big lump under a tarpaulin. Did not see what it was.”

“Sounds like the fellas we are looking for,” Robert said. “No other reports of a freight wagon?”

Jim said, “No one else saw one. The Sheriff also said the only other wagon was a preacher man, circuit rider in a big box wagon decked out like a small church or some such. Been hangin’ round town spreadin’ the word, that was it.”

I said, “Reckon we are headin’ to Bandera. See if we can pick up the trail from there.”

Marshal Sweeny put his hands on his hips and said, “I be comin’ with you boys.”

CHAPTER TEN

Jim sprang into action, barking out orders to his three deputies while I sat and drank my coffee, and Robert studied the map on the wall. I was trying to understand how a freight wagon had gotten passed us on the journey down here. The timing of the robbery along with our departure from Fredericksburg would have put us on the trail at the same time. We would have met them at or near the turn off to Bandera, but we saw nothing.

Jim said to his deputies, "Billy, Tommy, I want you boys to go down to Helga's and get the Marshal's horses ready." He turned to One-Eyed Jack. "Jack, I want you to go wake up Slim and have him open his store. We need to pack out supplies for the trail."

I said, "We will come down with you boys to Helga's. We need to collect up our personals, we will meet you in the stables then follow you up to the store."

Jim asked us, "You boys mind if I live out of your stores. I will have Slim add to them. I am already packed out and ready to go."

Robert asked, "When did you pack out?"

Before Jim could answer One-Eyed Jack said with a smile, "He dun been packed out for three days now just waitin' on you two."

I laughed. "Feel the need for some trail time do you Jim?"

He said, "If it means catchin' these critters I would ride to China."

I looked at Robert and smiled saying, "That is a fair piece off your mark Marshal Sweeny. But I get your meaning."

With the two deputies we walked down to Helga's to hit the trail once again in pursuit of some desperados. We had a good feeling about our information and our only hope was to be able to track them beyond the small town of Bandera.

Billy, Tommy and myself turned to the stables while Robert went back to the cabin to retrieve our saddle bags. I had decided to go with the boys in the chance Caliban felt the need to express his displeasure at being handle by persons unknown to him.

Inside the stables I said, "If you boys put the panniers on the pack horse, I will handle the other two."

Billy rubbed his shoulder and said, "With pleasure Marshal."

I walked up to Caliban and rubbed his neck. "You got another victim I see," I said as I admired him. "Well, put that aside for now my friend, we have work to do."

In short order I had both Caliban and Cillian saddled and ready to go at the same time the boys were leading the pack horse out into the pen. I followed and found Robert walking towards us with Miss Helga at his side. I smiled.

Robert handed me my saddle bags and said, "She came to see us off."

I looked at the small German woman. In her hands were three wrapped bundles, much like the time before when we had abruptly departed.

She smiled and said, "I made you boys something for the journey. I know Marshal Sweeny is going so I made one for him."

I took the offered bundles and handed them to Billy to put in one of the panniers.

I said, "I wish we had more time, Miss Helga. But duty calls."

She smiled. "I do too Wyatt. Now you boys go and take care of each other. I will see you again."

I leaned down and wrapped my arms around her, then she held my face in her hands looked in my eyes and kissed my forehead. "I will be praying for you, Robert and the Marshal."

I stepped back to let Robert receive the same affectionate embrace and kiss from the women that had become like a mother to us.

As we walked away, horses in tow, I looked back to see her watching us. I said to the two Deputies, "You boys do us a favor and keep an eye on that woman for us. We would be appreciative."

Tommy answered, "We will sir. Whole town thinks the world of Miss Helga."

We walked down the darkened street, following the Deputies to the store to replenish our food stuffs. It was a good thing too as we had given up half our rations to Clem and Pete on the trail and now, we were going to have a third rider eating out of our stores.

We easily would have found the establishment without the aid of the Deputies only because of the ruckus that was coming from the lighted storefront. I reckon this Slim fella took exception to being awakened at this unreasonable hour.

We stopped at the front of the store; the front door was open, and we saw One-Eyed Jack standing with a tall very thin man towering over the smaller Deputy. He wore a nightcap on his head, spectacles on the edge of his nose and a night shirt with slippers on his oversized feet. I reckon it was Slim.

Slim said, "Why now Jack? Sakes alive why could you not wait till morning to do this?"

Jack responded, "It is mornin' Slim. Just give us what we want and charge it to the Marshal's office. Damnation man, this is law business!"

Robert looked at me and asked, "You want to get in this?"

I scoffed. "Hell no. I do not have a dog in this fight."

Billy asked, "You fellas want anything special?"

Robert, the better one at planning for the trail than I, said, "We need flour, salt, sugar, jerky, some bacon, and some horse grain if he has any."

"And coffee," I added.

Billy nodded and with Tommy in tow went inside to fulfill our needs while Jack and Slim kept arguing.

"Now see here," Slim was saying, "I am gonna get my money before the Marshal leaves. This ain't right Jack."

Jack was doing an excellent job of standing his ground. "You will get paid Slim. Jus gimme the bill."

Jim came up leading his horse and joined us. He laughed and said, "Ol' Slim is yellin' up a storm."

Robert asked, "Is this normal?"

Jim nodded. "Sure is. Cannot make that man happy for nuthin.' Always yammering on bout something or other."

While Slim and Jack were discussing payments and such the boys were coming and going from the store with arm loads of food stuffs, packing them in the panniers then returning to the store for the next load.

Billy, burdened with an arm full said, "That is the last of it Marshal."

Jim said, "Thank you Billy. Now Jack will be in charge while I am gone. You mind your mother."

Billy said, "I will sir, Be safe out there."

I exchanged a look of surprise with Robert and said as I pointed at Billy, "He is your son?"

Jim said, "Sure," as he laughed.

Slim came out and said angrily, "Now Marshal I do not know what all you fellas took. How am I to bill you when I have no idea what you took?"

Jim inhaled deeply and said, "If you had not been arguin' with Jack you might have seen what we got." He turned to his horse and said over his shoulder, "Billy will tell you. Just send the bill to my office Slim."

We all mounted up and I said as I looked at the deputies, "Appreciate all that you fellas have done. Y'all take care."

Jim said, "Jack, you are in charge. I will try and send you a message to let you know what transpires. When you boys find Billings, lock him up till I get back. I got questions that need answers." Jim paused, then said, "Send a message to Thadius and tell him we will be there tomorrow afternoon."

Robert said, "Jack if you would. Also send a message to Judge DuBose and tell him what is going on."

Jack raised his hand and said, "I will Marshal. Godspeed fellas."

The three of us turned and headed down the street, into the awaiting darkness of the wilderness.

We were soon clear of the town and got into a rhythm of sorts with our horses. The pace we set was not hectic nor was it slow and easy. We decided to take advantage of the coolness of the early hour and press on, facing a twelve-to-fourteen-hour journey. It was best to move as quickly as we could in the darkness but, without sacrificing our safety or that of our animals.

I asked Jim, "Is Thadius the Sheriff of Bandera County?"

Jim said, "He is. Thadius Dexter Polehouse."

Robert asked, "Is he a good lawman Jim?"

He said, "Yea, I suppose he is. A bit heavy handed bringing in the bad hombres. Quick to bash a fella then ask his questions after. Has a real hatred of Indians." Jim paused and thought before continuing. "I suppose that is why he took to this Indian he told us about."

"Why does he hate Indians so," I asked.

Jim looked at us. "Reckon you boys have not heard about Bandera. Real big problem with Indians going back to fifty-five when they settled the area. Indians did not like it and took to killin' the Polish settlers that came in and made the town. Killed a few of the previous sheriffs."

Robert said, "Our duties have yet to take us there. I suppose we will get educated real soon about Bandera."

"Good folks there," Jim said. "Most of the folks are Catholic. Town has not grown much since fifty-five."

I asked, "How many folks they have in town?"

Jim answered, "Oh, three maybe four hundred. The rest of the county is ranches. A lot of cattle used to move through there. Maybe when things get back to normal the cows will start moving again."

I said, "Yea, when things get back to normal."

We rode on, ever vigilant as the stars and moon lighted our way. Our conversation light, nothing to gab about as we kept our attention to our surroundings. We were on a well-traveled trail, so we felt the danger was not too great as to cause us to move at a slower pace, even though we knew the freight wagon was no longer in town. Still, we did not want to dawdle, the closer we got to them the better our chances of continuing the chase.

The sun began to show itself and we quickened our pace planning to slow as the temperature climbed later in the day. The gathering light shown on the hills to our west and I again thought of the freight wagon traveling this route and us missing it on the trail.

I voiced my thoughts to the others. "I am still puzzled as to how we missed this freight wagon."

Jim answered by saying, "I heard tell that there are some old Indian trails through these hills. I do not know of any in particular but maybe this Indian fella they have with them knows of some."

Robert said, "Possible they went that way. I cannot think of any other reason we should have missed them."

Jim said, "Speaking of Indians. How is your friend Long Buffalo?"

I could not help but grin at the mention of his name. I said, "He is well. Still doing his own thing, going his own way."

Robert said, "I am willing to bet that he would know something of a trail."

"He does know this area better than any other," I said.

"Well," Jim began, "we can speculate all the day long. First, we must find where they went after Bandera. Thad said they went north which means the town of Kerrville in Kerr County. Right in the middle of Hill Country."

I asked, "Did you hear from the Sheriff of Kerr County?"

Jim nodded. "I did. He did not see a wagon. He saw the Circuit Rider come through, that was it."

The day wore on and the temperature rose. By mid-day we decided to stop, stretch our legs, and water the animals. The Marshal found a small clear stream that suited our purpose, and we rested for a time.

I took my boots off and rested my feet in the water while I packed my pipe. I was breaking one of my standing rules knowing that smoking my pipe would add to my thirst, but I felt it was acceptable while we were sitting by the stream. Besides, we had not had coffee nor breakfast and I felt the need to indulge.

Robert came over and handed me a strip of jerky. "Breakfast Wyatt," he said with a laugh.

I held up my tobacco pouch, he shook his head and sat down next to me, rubbing his right knee.

I asked, "Leg bothering you?"

"It is," he said as he looked at me. "How about you and your wounds Wyatt?"

I pulled on the pipe, exhaled the smoke, and said, "Oh, it can be bothersome from time to time. Specially when the weather gets to changing. I have grown used to it."

"I do not see how," he said. "I was shot three times; you were shot five times."

Jim stepped over. "I heard about you boys taken on that rancher and his men. Damn fine job you did. News traveled through to us. I swear, I must have heard you fellas died three times before I found out otherwise." He laughed.

I said, "I thought we had died too. Long Buffalo found us out in the wilderness and doctored us till we got back to town."

Jim nodded. "Something to be said about a Medicine Man and his ways. I will take that before most of the Sawbones I have seen out here on the frontier."

"Hy Averbeck did a hell of a job fixing us up too," Robert added.

I put my boots back on and stood. I did not want to reminisce about that time at this moment. I wanted to get back on the trail and pursue these thieves that made off with the safe and disappeared into the wilderness. Time was wastin'.

"Reckon we should get back on the trail," I said as I tapped my pipe against my hand.

I walked over to the pack horse, grabbed the lead line, and mounted up. I looked at the others and smiled.

"Well, back to work boys. We got bad guys to chase."

Chapter Eleven

Shortly after returning to the trail, we turned west at the cutoff and headed direct to Bandera. We were now nearer than further, and we felt that we had made timely progress in our journey, despite the many issues we faced on the short ride. The heat, beginning the trail in the hours of darkness and mine and Robert's previous wounds could also add to the many aggravations.

I should have remained silent when I inquired on Robert's wound. Of course, the brief conversation would eventually have turned to mine, and I usually had the ability to ignore the pain that occasionally burdened me. True, it had only been a few short months ago when we were shot to pieces. But now that the issue had been voiced, all five of my previous wounds hurt and I cursed myself for having said anything at all. Next time I will remain silent and take it that his wound was bothering him and sympathize in silence.

I tried to distract myself from the burden of my aches and pains by taking in the countryside. The browns had given way to greens through the rolling hills around us and I found it pleasing. It certainly was not what I had envisioned Texas to be before I had arrived in the great state. I, like so many, had thought of it as a flat open expanse, dusty and dry, lacking in any kind of vegetation, with an overabundance of rocks, dirt, and cactus.

We were riding up a shallow valley with limestone and granite peeking through the vegetation at places. The grasses were greener here with scattered Live-Oak Trees and the occasional Cypress and Cedar Tree with wildflowers in abundance throughout the high meadows and rising hills. It was unique to this region of Texas as the many rivers converged through the hills to nourish the green scape. It was beautiful and pleasantly calming.

Robert said, "I had been through here only once before. Beautiful area."

Jim said, "It is that, but I hate to break up y'all's admiration of the Hill Country. This is contested territory, and we need to keep an eye out for hostiles."

I asked, "Which Indians are puttin' up the ruckus Jim?"

He said, "The Comanche and Apache. I for one would like to keep my hair as long as I can." He laughed.

I did not find humor in his statement, since scalping was a fear, I held and had done so since I arrived in the state. I began to look at the terrain as a soldier looking for an ambush, not one admiring the beauty of the countryside. I too would like to keep my hair and the scalp that grows under it. I reached down to my scabbard and slid out my shotgun, dropping it across my lap, wishing that I had my Colt Revolving Rifle.

Robert saw me do this and he withdrew his Spencer Carbine and laid it across his lap saying, "Good idea Wyatt."

Jim took this in, let out a laugh, fell silent for a moment then pulled his Henry Rifle and rested the butt on his thigh, barrel pointed skyward. He said, "Reckon it is a good idea to be ready."

The three of us allowed ourselves a brief laugh then went back to keeping guard as we made our way through the plush valley.

In a short while we came upon a rider heading towards us. We pulled up and watched. He was pulling a pack mule and made no threatening moves or motions as he plodded along. He was too far off to see his face clearly, he just rode slowly along the trail, seeming to mind his own business.

Jim said, "Hold here boys. I will have a talk with this fella."

"Okay Jim," I said as I put my hand on my Colt. "We have you covered."

Jim rode ahead and Robert cocked the hammer on his Spencer Rifle. We kept our eyes on both men as they met up.

They sat their horses and conversed, Jim occasionally pointing in our direction, their voices hushed to us as the distance was too great to hear the conversation. Jim tipped his hat turned to us and waved us forward.

As we rode up the rider passed us, pulling his mule along behind. He was an older man, white hair, and thick bushy beard. Brown derby perched on his head, brown thread bare jacket with many holes and tears as did his pants, he just smiled and nodded his head as he passed. His mule was burdened with pans, buckets, pick axe and a couple of shovels. He said nothing and continued his journey.

We pulled up next to Jim and looked at him expectantly.

Jim smiled and said, "Fella calls himself Bushy Bill Kingman. He is a miner in search of the San Saba Mine. He did not see any wagon nor Indian here abouts. He just told me of a few mines in the area"

Robert said with a laugh, "That old legend? I thought that died ages ago, and I thought that was more up around Menard County."

I looked at the other two and asked, "What legend?"

Jim said, "The lost mine of San Saba. It says that there was a Spanish Mission up that way, and they hid all their treasure in the mine. The mission burned down, and the Spaniards left without their treasure. Folks have been tryin' to find it since the seventeen hundreds or some such. Some say it is down here somewhere."

Robert added, "Even Jim Bowie went looking for it."

As much as I enjoyed a brief history of the legend, I was not seeing how this was important to us and said so. "What does this have to do with us?"

Jim pointed to the retreating figure of the old miner and said, "He told me that there are old mining digs throughout these hills. Folks looking for silver."

I suddenly understood. "That could be where they found the materials for the rail and cart."

Jim smiled. "It is possible."

We resumed our journey, pleased at what little information we had gotten from the old miner. It was possible that the equipment the bandits had used came from one of these old mining operations around us. It was not important to find which one in particular but it told us that maybe, these fellas were from the area, or at the very least familiar with the diggings.

We came out of the shallow valley and before us lay the small town of Bandera. We stopped and looked at what lay before us. After a long hot journey, it was easy to think of the few pleasures a traveler could indulge in upon arrival but for us, these would have to wait as our first mission was to seek out the County Sheriff.

We rode through the dusty streets and took in the buildings of Bandera. Most seemed to be made of granite, limestone, or rock mixed with wood planking. Shingled roofs or clay tile, the buildings were mixed and no two alike. The people were out and about, what few we saw as we made our way into the heart of town in search of the local law.

We found a small single-story building with a stone foundation, wood sides and a shingled peaked roof. Above the porch a sign, Bandera County Sheriff, told us we had arrived.

We tied off out front and stretched our legs working out the kinks, aches and pains of our bodies then walked up the steps and went inside.

I suppose each jailhouse in Texas had the same builder who worked off one single floor-plan. We stepped into a large open room occupied by a single table, a stove and desk, with the cells along the back wall laid out in a row. I looked around for anything distinct or different from what I had seen in other jails and even found the same county map of Texas hung on the wall. I reckon there was comfort in familiarity.

A large muscular middle-aged man with a clean-shaven hairless head sitting atop a thick neck stood from the desk and turned to us. His face looked as though it was chiseled out of a block of stone with a thick black mustache extending down passed his mouth and ending at his square jawline. His clothing spoke more of a farmer than a lawman. Had it not been for the star on his left breast I would have thought he was anything but the County Sheriff.

The man stepped forward and extended his hand to Marshal Sweeny. "Glad to see you made it Jim," he said.

Jim took the extended hand and said, "Good to see you, Thad. Got on the trail as quick as we could." Jim released the man's hand and turned to us. "This here is U.S. Deputy Marshals Chambers and Barton."

Sheriff Polehouse shook our hands. "Good to know you boys. I heard a lot about you and that business up north." He crossed his arms over his massive chest and looked at us. "Damn fine work you boys did. Damn fine."

I said, "Thanks Sheriff."

He waved a hand, laughed, and said, "Call me Thad boys." He looked down at my pistol belt and said, "You must be Wyatt. Heard you were the one that carries the Walker Colt. Damn fine pistol. My Daddy carried one, yes sir, he still carries it truth be told. Rode with Colonel Walker back in the day he did."

"That so," I said.

He looked at Robert. "You must be Robert, the Union Army Sergeant Major. Damn glad to know you son, yes sir."

Robert asked, "How do you know so much about us?"

Thad laughed again. "Shit son. Everyone round here heard about you two fellas. Gunnin' down those vermin in Castroville, killin' all those hired gun hands and that Yankee rancher. Hell, even burnin' down that shit-hole saloon." He laughed again. "Yes sir."

I traded looks with Robert and shrugged it off. I can just imagine how the stories were different from the truth. At least his stories got our names right.

Jim said, "Tell us about this wagon Thad."

The Sheriff turned back to his desk, opened the bottom drawer, pulled out a bottle and four glasses. He motioned to the table and said, "Have a seat boys and let us converse on this business of robbery."

We each found a chair and the Sheriff pulled his desk chair to the table and joined us. After filling our glasses he said, "Was few nights passed. I was walkin' the town down near the west end I saw this big freight wagon rollin' in. Did not think too much on it cept the hour they came in."

"What time was that," I asked.

"Oh, I reckon it was near eight that night. Just found it strange that they would travel through the valley in a freight wagon in the dark. Hard enough on horseback it is."

Robert asked, "You said they came in from the west?"

Thad nodded his big head. "That they did."

Robert looked disappointed and said, "That does not make any sense. I figured they would come in from the east. There is nothing west."

Jim said, "True enough. Then where the hell did they come from I wonder. Maybe it ain't the ones we are looking for. These fellas would be coming from the south then out of the east, like we did."

Thad threw back his drink and said, "Now hold on boys." He looked at us, laughed and said, "You boys look like someone dun slapped you sideways." He laughed again.

"What are you gettin at Thad," Jim asked.

"These fellas must have come up the forgotten trail through the valley. Old Indian trail." He laughed again.

I repeated, "Forgotten trail."

Thad said, "Yes sir. Lot of them around these parts. Old Comanche and Apache trails through the Hill Country." He waved a massive arm in the air. "Hell son, they go clear out west to the edge of Texas."

Jim asked, "Then they could have come up from the south. From Castroville?"

Thad nodded. "Yes sir. They might could do that. Be hard travelin' for some unless you knew the way."

Robert said, "Which brings us to this Indian you saw."

Thad poured another drink while ours sat untouched. He said, "Well Jim, you know what I think of Indians in general. Do not trust them, that is why I shave my head. When I go it will be with my scalp still attached to my skull bone." He laughed. "When these fellas rode through town this Indian was on a horse alongside of them. He was bedecked in warpaint and feathers comin' out of his head, big fella. He also had the biggest knife on his belt I ever did see. Damn near a sword it was."

"They did not stop," I asked.

Thad said, "No sir they did not. Took the trail north to Kerrville."

I said, "Then I reckon we are going to Kerrville."

Thad stood. "I would not recommend that journey Wyatt. Gonna be dark soon and it ain't the most hospitable trail to travel at night. Besides, they could be hold up in those hills and you could ride right past them, never see 'em in the dark."

Just then the door opened and in walked a man, small and thick dressed much the same way as the Sheriff. He too wore a star on his breast.

Thad looked at the man and asked, "What is it, Ty?"

The man handed Thad a slip of paper and said, "This just came in for Marshal Sweeny."

Jim leaned forward and took the slip. "Much obliged Deputy."

Before introductions were made the man turned and bolted out of the door.

Jim read what was handed to him aloud. "It is from Jack. He says they found Herman Billings."

Robert said, "Great. Now we can get some answers."

Marshal Sweeny dropped the note to the floor, rubbed his face, and said, "I do not believe so. They found Billings all right, but he is dead. His throat was cut, and his tongue was gone."

I grabbed the glass of whiskey in front of me and drained it. "Then I reckon he was part of it. That is where they got the layout of the bank."

Jim slammed his hand on the table. "Son of a bitch!"

I said, "Sheriff. We will need a place to rest up before we hit the trail."

Robert added, "A place to grab some grub too."

Thad's demeanor softened. He said, "Sure fellas. I will set you up at the hotel. It ain't much but the food is fairly good, and they have a bar."

Jim grabbed his whiskey and threw it back. "Thanks Thad," he said as he smacked the glass down.

Thad walked over to his desk and grabbed up his hat. "C'mon fellas. I will walk you down to the stables then get you settled in at the hotel." He put his hat on his bald head and strapped on his pistol. He too carried a Remington as did Robert. "Hell, I will join you for dinner."

We went outside, gathered our mounts, and followed Thad down the street. We were silent, each lost in the misery of our own thoughts. These desperadoes had stayed two jumps ahead of us since they pulled this off. We felt like fools, now more so since one of those we desired answers from turned up dead and the others were gone to parts unknown.

Down at the stables we unburden the animals of saddles, blankets, and the panniers. Thad joined in and we brushed and fed them then got them bedded down for the night.

Still, none of us spoke. Our misery and self-loathing were slowly replaced by anger.

Thad got us checked in at the hotel. He was correct in his evaluation of the establishment. It was not much, but it fit our needs for the moment. This was not a pleasure outing, and I personally would have been happy in the stables with the horses. We each got a separate room and Thad picked up the bill and gave us our keys.

He said, "You boys go up to your rooms, splash some water on your faces and wash the trail away. I will meet you down here in half hour for dinner." He grinned. "Mary-Ellen is makin' her chicken and dumplings tonight and it is usually pretty good fare."

"Usually," I asked.

Thad shrugged his broad shoulders. "Depends on if it has a chicken in it."

"How 'bout that," I said and walked up the stairs.

In my room I took in my surroundings. Red and gold striped wallpaper covered the walls. A bed, complete with a thick woven blanket and linen pillow looked inviting enough. A wash basin and pitcher on a chest of drawers with a broken mirror behind it. A painting of an unknown woman cradling a bunch of flowers and a window with gold drapes hanging down to the floor.

As rooms go, I reckon it was not bad. I had stayed in worse. I tossed my saddle bags, hat and shotgun on the bed and filled the wash basin with water and washed the dust off my face and out of my hair.

As I was drying myself, I had to admit, I felt better. Thad's suggestion was just the thing to wash away the anger.

I went downstairs and headed straight into the bar. Robert and Jim were already there, beer in hand.

Robert pushed a mug of beer my way as I stepped up to the bar. I said, "I thank you sir." I drained the mug and motioned the barkeep for another.

Jim said, "Before you boys say anything I am continuing on with you in the morning."

Robert raised his mug and said, "I would not have it any other way Marshal."

We were on our second round when Thad joined us at the bar. He ordered a whiskey, threw it back and said, "What say we get to the table and get first crack at dinner."

We found an empty table, sat and without a word a young lady placed a pot on the table and retreated to the kitchen.

Thad began spooning up the meal and said, "We are in luck boys. Looks to be a chicken in the pot tonight."

Chapter Twelve

The meal was as filling as it was good, and I soon found myself back in my room getting ready to turn in. The desire for sleep became overwhelming with a belly full of food and the journey up from Castroville taking its toll on both mind and body.

I soon found myself clawing my way back from a deep slumber by a slight knock at the door and Jim's voice calling to me.

"You up Wyatt," he asked.

I sat up and took stock of my condition. I was still clothed, only my boots and pistol belt had made it to the floor, the shotgun my bed mate, and the oil lamp was still burning. There was another knock.

I cleared my throat, dry and scratchy, and said, "Yea, Jim. Give me a few minutes."

He said from the other side of the door, "I have coffee downstairs."

I yawned and waved at the door thinking perhaps I should find another line of work that would allow me to get proper rest or adopt a schedule more agreeable to my present circumstances.

I stood, stretched, and said aloud, "Nah. I would become bored and restless."

I splashed some water on my face, put my boots on, strapped on my gun and with my hat on my head and shotgun in hand went out the door in search of coffee.

Downstairs I was greeted by Jim Sweeny and Sheriff Thadius D. Polehouse. They were both seated at a table, pot of coffee between them looking at me with concerned eyes.

I tried to put a smile on my face, but a rogue yawn showed itself first and I just stood there.

Thad said, "C'mon over Wyatt and get some coffee. You look like you need it."

Jim laughed and said, "Yea, you look like hell."

I nodded and said, "Good, cause that is just how I feel."

As soon as I sat and filled my cup Robert came down the stairs. I took notice that he had a slight limp in his gait as he negotiated each step and I knew that his wounded knee was bothersome. I kept my mouth shut and directed my attentions to the cup of coffee in my hand trying to will the fog of sleep out of my head.

Thad said, "You boys look plumb tired."

I said, "We will be right as rain in no time."

"Good," Thad said. "Cause I ain't ridin' out this morning with a bunch a sleepy heads."

I looked at Thad and asked, "You aim to join us?"

He put his coffee cup down. "I surely am boys. I got a bad feeling about this. If we make it to Kerrville with no trouble, I will bid you fellas a heartfelt goodbye and Godspeed."

Robert said, "Happy to have you, Thad. I hope we do not need you." He held up his hand. "No offense mind you."

"Oh, none taken Robert," he said. "I had my deputy make the animals ready to save time." He looked at me and said, "That is quite a horse you have there Wyatt."

I moaned. "What did he do to your deputy?"

Thad laughed. "Do not worry yourself about Ty. That boy knows horses and got that black demon settled down in no time."

I nodded. "Glad to hear that. Caliban can get a bit uppity."

Thad laughed heartily. "Caliban? Now there is a fitting name for that animal." He laughed again. "Never figured you for Shakespeare Wyatt."

I smiled. "Saw The Tempest some time back in Washington City before the war."

Thad smoothed down his mustache with his thumb and index finger then said, "Reckon we should be goin'. Be light soon."

The four of us went outside and found Ty, the Deputy, standing with the animals by the hitching rail.

Thad mounted up and said, "Hold things down here Ty. I reckon I should not be more than two days, three at the most. Send Sheriff Burns a message that we will be there later today and let him know the particulars."

"Will do Sheriff," he said.

I mounted up and said, "Much obliged for your help Deputy."

He said, "My pleasure Marshal. Ya'll take care out there."

Robert had been at the pack horse and came around to me and handed up one of the parcels that Miss Helga had given us. He said, "Now is a good a time as any I suppose. Enough goodies in these to make a nice breakfast for the four of us."

I took the lead line for the pack horse and the four of us turned away from the hotel and made our way down the street. It was still dark, and the sheriff moved out in front to lead the way, this being his territory and the more experienced on the route of travel.

We soon turned north and put the town of Bandera behind us as Thad navigated through the darkness at an easy pace. We put our trust in him and his knowledge of the land as he acted as our guide wandering deeper into the Hill Country. What little I could see through the darkness I understood what he meant by places unseen, places to hide and how we could easily miss a turn off or pass by a clump of trees that could hide a freight wagon or bandits lying in wait. We had thirty or so miles to travel and I looked forward to sunrise as I did not feel comfortable looking for any trouble that may be lurking in the deep shadows.

We split up the parcels that Miss Helga had prepared for us. Cooked bacon, couple of biscuits, raisins, and a small jar of apple butter, which ended up in the saddle bags for later. Again, she gave what little she had. She was always thinking of others, and we ate heartily, grateful for the offering.

The sun finally came up, the shadows of the hills around us faded and the temperature began its climb to the higher reaches. We quickened our pace.

Thad held up his hand and we stopped, not closing the gap between us as we suspected he had seen or heard something, and we instinctively rested our hands on our pistols. He was studying the sandy ground, leaning out of his saddle but remained mounted as he examined it on both sides.

He yelled back, "Wagon tracks. Deep in the sand and wide apart. I think it is our freight wagon boys."

That was promising news. We were on the track of our quarry and with luck, would soon overtake them as we could travel faster than they could. He waved us forward and we continued heading north towards Kerrville.

We were two hours out of Bandera and moving at a quickened pace when Thad held up his hand, signaling for another stop. This time he did not look for sign but cast his watchful eyes to the hills surrounding us. He showed no haste nor alarm but just looked about, searching.

He waved us forward but stayed where he was, just looking.

I pulled up next to him and asked, "What goes Thad?"

He visibly sniffed the air and said, "I smell just a hint of burnt wood. It ain't a cook fire, that I am certain."

I looked around, not seeing any sign of a cook fire and sniffed the air. Thad was correct, I smelled just a hint of burnt timber.

Thad dismounted, pulled his revolver, and said, "I believe we should look about before we move on."

We all dismounted, led our horses to the side of the trail, and tied off on a small scrub oak.

Robert took out his Spencer and said, "I will stay with the animals. Call out if you need me."

Jim looked to the west as he pulled his revolver and said, "I will look over here."

Thad said, "Wyatt," he pointed to the right. "You go off that way and I will walk a bit further along the trail then circle back to the right. Keep a watchful eye out fellas, could be sumthin', could be nuthin'."

We split up and went our chosen directions, slow and watchful as we negotiated the many obstacles along our respective paths. Thick brush, trees large and small, rocks of limestone and granite, even the wildflowers offered a hiding place. Small and large, they could hide a man or a large wagon. We pressed deeper off the trail.

I turned and looked back, no longer able to see the trail or Robert and the animals. I held my Walker at the ready, sweeping it back and forth as I searched. I sniffed the air, using my sense of smell to guide me deeper into the hills as a slight breeze brought the tell-tale odor to me. Then, behind me I heard the snap of a twig, I spun around, pistol pointed out ready to engage. I cocked the large hammer on the revolver , the cylinder rotated loudly as it turned to a loaded chamber.

"It is only me Wyatt," I heard Thad say. "I do not wish to be shot by that damn horse pistol of yours so kindly un-cock it."

I let the hammer down gently, turning the cylinder between chambers.

Thad came out of the brush and grinned. He said, "Damn near filled my breeches when I heard you cock that big 'ol pistol."

"Sorry about that Thad."

He walked up beside me and looked around. "Breeze is bringing the smell from over there," he said as he pointed to a clump of trees.

We separated and approached the suspect area from either side. He on the right and me on the left we worked our way forward in a sort of skirmish line as we made our way around the trees. It was on the other side of the brush that we found the source of the smell.

It was an unseen clearing with a narrow path coming in from the left. The path though narrow, was just wide enough to accommodate the freight wagon that we saw before us. Or more correctly, what remained of the freight wagon. It was nothing more than a pile of burnt timber and ashes.

The front was no longer distinguishable as having been a wagon. Only the metal rings of the wheels, their spokes and centers having burned away, lay atop the ashes and small pieces of blackened wood and the twisted metal fixtures. The rear of the wagon though burned, and smoldering sat on two blacked and broken wheels.

Thad walked to the remains of the wagon and looked in at what was left of the bed. He holstered his pistol and said, "No safe in here Wyatt." He looked at me and frowned.

I holstered my revolver and started to make my way through the tall grass when I stopped and looked down at the ground in front of me.

I called to Thad. "I think it best you come over here Thad."

He looked at me and made his way through the cleared ground to the higher grass where I stood. He stopped and looked down.

"Son of a bitch," he uttered.

I said, "Yea." As I looked at the bodies of two men. Bloodied laying on their backs side by side, looking up at the sky with unseeing eyes.

Thad called out, never taking his eyes off the two dead men. "Jim, Robert, come up. There is a small cut off trail a bit further up on the right. Bring the animals in that way," he said as he knelt beside the bodies.

Jim called back, "Be there directly."

I knelt, looking at the ground around the men. I saw where the bodies had been dragged into the tall grass and laid out next to each other. Then I took in the bodies, one at a time.

The man closest to me was large and muscular, well over six feet in height. The front of his shirt was covered in blood, thick with blowflies. Just below the jawline his neck had been so severely severed that his head near came off. I shooed the blowflies away and looked into the wound. I kept waving my hand over the man to keep the flies at bay and noticed that the wound had been a single cut. Whoever had done it was a powerful man. A man of great strength with a blade so large and severe he could easily cleave a man's skull with one blow.

I looked at Thad and said, "That Indian fella you saw. You said something about his knife."

Thad was looking at the neck wound of the second fella. He said, "I did. Knife was so big I thought it was one of those Roman swords you see in Bible drawings."

I pointed to both dead men and said, "I suspect that is what did these fellas in."

Thad stood and looked down at the bodies. "He was a big Indian for sure. He could have done this." He looked around. "But why Wyatt?"

I leaned in a bit to the closer of the two bodies and looked into his mouth. Then I looked at the second man and repeated the observation. I stood.

"They both had their tongues cut out too," I said in a neutral tone.

"Damnation," Thad uttered softly.

I asked, "These fellas look familiar to you?"

He looked down, shook his head.

Robert and Jim had made it to the clearing and tied the animals off then took in the remnants of the freight wagon. Both stood looking at the wreckage, hands on hips shaking their heads.

Thad turned to them and said, "You boys best come over here and have a look see."

I stepped away as they walked over. I wanted them to observe the bodies as I had with no interruptions or comments by me or Thad. I wanted them to form their own thoughts; their own opinions before we shared our observations. I waved Thad over before they arrived and the two of us traded places with Robert and Jim.

I looked at the burnt wood of the wagon. It had been one of the larger freight wagons as big wagons go. So large in fact that I found it a bit over-kill to haul a nine hundred pound safe, even through this rough countryside.

I asked Thad, "Did you see any other wagon tracks around here?"

He shook his head. "I did not."

I looked around as I thought through a few notions running around my noggin. I shook my head feeling a headache coming on. A headache born of the frustration I felt from the moment I took the telegram from Jeremiah's outstretched hand back in Fredericksburg. These fellas were well equipped, proficient at their vocation and just clever enough to remain a few jumps ahead of us. That is where the frustration boiled over, their cleverness in pulling this off. Their timetable put them ahead of us every step of the way and left us only embarrassment and humiliation, along with three mutilated bodies and the burnt remains of a wagon. I did not like being humiliated nor embarrassed by any man.

Robert and Jim joined us, and we all just stood there, staring at the wagon.

Jim said, "Lord Almighty. Why were their tongues cut out?"

It was Thad who answered. "Some Indians believe that if they cannot speak in this world neither can they speak in the spirit world."

Robert asked, "Then you think the Indian did this?"

Thad nodded his head.

I said, "I for one would like to know what happened to the safe. Thad said he did not see any wagon tracks around here, just these when they came back here."

Jim asked, "You do not suppose they buried it around here?"

I shook my head. "Nah. It went somewhere. These fellas have it planned down to the smallest detail. I reckon they will take it someplace to open it."

Jim said, "Without the keys? Some Army major said they had their set of keys in Austin and Mimms has his, and there ain't but two sets."

Robert asked, "Who is this major?"

Jim dug through his pockets and came out with the slips of paper from his conversations through the telegraph. He searched through the small stack and found the one he was looking for. He said, "Major Purdy, A.J. Purdy. Said he is the aide to the Paymaster General. You know him?"

Robert had a look as if he were searching his memory, yet remained silent.

I said, "Never thought to ask the Banker if a blacksmith could open the safe."

Jim said, "I did. He said if they tried, they would need a month of Sundays to get into it. Might end up destroying what was inside."

"What now," Thad asked.

I looked around and said, "Reckon we bury them fellas and keep going to Kerrville."

Thad said, "Since we are still in Bandera County, reckon I will be comin' along with you boys. I got a stake in this too."

I looked at Jim. "How 'bout you Marshal? You aim to come along?"

Jim looked over his shoulder at the bodies then back to the remains of the wagon. "Try and keep me from comin'," he said.

Robert retrieved a shovel from the pack horse, and we took turns digging a grave for the two dead robbers. Some would say to leave them to the buzzards but not us. We were not the ones they would answer to in the afterlife. We, or at least Robert and myself felt that they too deserved the respect of a decent burial, despite what they did. What happens to their souls was out of our hands.

When the task was complete, we gathered around our horses to plan our next leg in the journey.

I said, "Well fellas, do not know what to look for now. That big Indian I suppose."

Thad said, "Reckon we ride on to Kerrville and see if he went through there. He might have been seen. Never know."

Robert asked, "How far out are we?"

Thad said, "We have a few hours yet. We will be in there after dark. Trail gets a bit easier as we get nearer so we will not have too much trouble with that."

I had a thought and shared it with others. "I was thinking. I wonder if this Indian knows we are out here lookin' for him. I mean he seems to be killin' the men we have been after."

Robert said, "Possibly. But maybe he is killing them cause he wants all the money."

Jim asked, "What is an Indian gonna do with all that money? And how did he get the safe out of here?"

I looked at the others and said, "I do not believe the safe ever made it this far."

The others looked at me. I remained silent for the moment not wishing to share my thoughts. It was more of a feeling, maybe just speculation on my part but I believed the safe had gone off in another direction.

CHAPTER THIRTEEN

We ate a light meal and got back on the trail. Thad was out front as before while we followed in train. Robert had relieved me of dragging the pack horse and was bringing up the rear. We were not taking any chances after the discovery of both the wagon and the bodies, so we had our long guns out and at the ready.

What we surmised about the heinous death of the two wagoneers could have been wrong and that they met their end by some other means. But we felt we were on the right track in looking for the unknown Indian, so we stayed the course and made for Kerrville, staying vigilant on the trail, nevertheless.

The remainder of the day progressed as we traveled through the Hill Country and the sun fell below the horizon, once again casting us in darkness, surrounded by deep shadows as our pace slowed along the tricky terrain.

More than once, Thad had held up his hand halting us as he looked around, sniffed at the air, or just listened to the sounds of the night. Each time we stopped we instinctively looked out to the flanks, guns ready to engage an unseen enemy. Each time nothing came to pass, and Thad waved us forward.

The hours slipped by and we soon found ourselves at the outskirts of Kerrville.

Thad held us up and we gathered around him. He said as he dismounted, "We go directly to the Sheriff's Office. It might be best to walk the horses down the street. Mine is a bit tired and difficult at present."

It was an excellent idea since we had been on the trail for the better part of twelve hours and both horse and rider needed a break.

We all fell in behind Thad as we walked our mounts down the street to the County Jail. Folks were out and about even with the lateness of the hour. Coming and going to whatever night life or point of interest that brought them out they moved from place to place paying us no never mind. We passed a saloon busting with folks as music, laughter and singing could be heard from within, and judging from the number of horses tied off out front, it was a popular watering hole.

I remembered my days of drifting from town to town often ending up at a saloon either for a refreshing drink or in search of a card game as a way of providing ready funds for my meager needs.

We stopped near the center of town and tied off as we stretched the stiffness out of our joints and to get the blood circulating to our lower extremities. A lengthy time spent in the saddle often numbed parts of the body that caused discomfort when the blood flow resumed to those areas, namely one's backside.

Robert said, “Damn. I still cannot feel my ass.”

I laughed and said, “Mine has become so calloused that I may never feel it again.”

Thad laughed at our malady and said, “Surely you youngsters are tougher than this.” He laughed again as he walked up the steps shaking his head. “Tenderfoots, that what I got. Couple of tenderfoots.”

Jim stepped closer to me rubbing his backside. He said quietly, “I ain’t sayin’ a word,” and laughed.

We followed Thad into the County Jail.

Thad stepped across the threshold and said in a booming voice, “Why if it ain’t W. B. D. Burns his self! How are you pard?”

A tall lean well-dressed man with a weathered face, grey hair and a bushy mustache extended his hand to Thad and said, “Well if it ain’t Thadius Dexter Polehouse. What the hell brings you up here?”

Thad was visibly surprised at the greeting. He said, “What do you mean Bill? Did you get my wire about us comin’?”

Sheriff Burns said, “I did not Thad. The wires have been down pretty much all day. Crew is going out in the morning to find what is the cause. We cannot talk to anyone south of us.”

Thad took his hat off, tossed it on the table, and sat down. “Damnation,” he said. “What was the last message you got?”

He said, “The one from Jim Sweeny.” He looked over at us and stepped up extending his hand. “Howdy Jim. Been a long time.”

Jim took his hand and replied, “How you been keeping yourself Bill?”

“Oh, fair to midland,” he said.

Jim turned and waved a hand at us. “These here are the Deputy U. S. Marshals that I asked in on the bank robbery.” He pointed to me, “This is Wyatt Chambers,” then he pointed to Robert saying, “And this is Robert Barton.”

The Sheriff shook our hands and said, "You fellas out of Fredericksburg. Glad to make your acquaintance. Heard much about you two."

He motioned to the table. "Grab a seat boys. Ya'll can fill me in on this bank robbery and why it brings you up here?"

Jim took the lead and began to explain to Sheriff Burns everything we knew thus far about the crime, the missing safe, the wagon and the two dead wagoneers, finishing his narrative with our pursuit of the mysterious Indian.

Sheriff Burns put a bottle of whiskey at the center of the table and produced five glasses. He said, "That was one hell of a tale. Damnation if they ain't clever doin' this."

Thad asked, "You see any Indian the last day or two come through Bill?"

"No sir, I have not. No strangers have come through here," he answered.

I said, "Damn odd occurrence you cannot talk to anyone south of here."

Bill asked, "You thinkin' it has something to do with your bank robbery young fella?"

"I do," I said.

He looked at me for a moment and said, "So do I."

Robert asked, "What the hell do we do now?"

Thad took a drink and set the glass down hard. "Well, if you boys do not look like you been whipped." He refilled his glass. "If it was me, I would head north back to Fredericksburg."

"Back to Fredericksburg," I asked. "Why?"

He took another drink. "There ain't nuthin' west of here worth goin' to cept those old army forts on the plains."

Jim said, "Most of them are being reoccupied by the army. The whole area is crawling with Blue Coats."

Robert said, "He could have doubled back on us and went back to Bandera or Castroville."

Thad shook his head. "I do not think so. That safe went north, and so did that redskin."

"How you figure," I asked.

Thad stood and paced around the room while he reasoned it out to us, and maybe to himself as well. "We followed the wagon. Maybe these boys wanted us to do that or figured it would happen. Somewhere before or just after Bandera the safe went on another wagon, that much we figured. They stayed ahead of us all the while and now the wires have been cut between here and there. They put us on that trail knowin' we were gonna come up here."

Robert said, "Then killing the two men was always part of the plan as was killing the brick mason down in Castroville. Someone is silencing those that took part in the robbery."

Jim said, "They damn sure would not be dumb enough to go back to Castroville. They been too smart through all of this."

I smacked my hand down on the table. "They been making fools of us from the beginning!"

Bill said, "Easy there young fella. From all you boys told me, you been doin' damn good at figurin' this through. Seems to me you have been keeping them on the move." He leaned in closer. "You best not stop now Wyatt."

I looked at his weathered face, his piercing blue eyes and knew that he was right. I merely nodded my head.

He sat back, smiled, and said, "Good."

I said looking at Robert, "Sergeant Major, we best be headin' back to Fredericksburg tonight."

Robert stood and said, "We have about twenty-five miles to go, time is wasting Captain."

I stood and extended my hand to Sheriff Burns. "Much obliged Bill."

Thad walked over and shook my hand. "The trail north ain't too bad. Do not venture too far off it if you are fixin' to rest."

I said, "Thanks for all your help, Thad."

He nodded and shook Robert's hand saying, "Been a pleasure ridin' with you boys. Send word if you need any help. I will be there."

I walked over to Jim and said, "Jim, it has been...," he cut me off.

"You ain't leavin' me here Wyatt, no sir. I be comin' with you boys. I still have a stake in this."

Robert grinned and said, "I would not have it any other way Marshal Sweeny."

We went outside and grabbed up our horses, mounted up and looked at Thad and Bill standing on the porch.

I said, "We are indebted to you fellas. We truly are."

Bill smiled and said, "If you boys need a gun-hand just send word to 'Ol William Bill Dalton Burns, Sheriff of Kerr County and I will come a runnin'."

“We will,” Robert said.

We turned our horses and retraced our steps on the way out of town, again passing the busy saloon. It was now busting over with folks gathered on the porch. I nodded my head as we passed acknowledging, if not envying the fellas as they stood with mugs of beer in hand watching us.

Jim said, “Wish we had Thad and Bill along with us.”

I turned to Jim. “Why is that,” I asked.

He repositioned himself in his saddle then said, “Oh, just a feelin’ I reckon. They sure are two damn good gun hands. A lot of history between the two of them.”

Robert asked, “Oh, how so?”

Jim again shifted in his saddle trying to get comfortable. “Ol’ W.B.D. was a Texas Ranger before the war then went off to fight under the same flag during the struggle. Thadius himself has a reputation of a tough lawman and Indian fighter before the war. Cannot make it this long in this life without being able to handle yourself.”

I said, “I kinda felt that about them, tough lawmen.”

Robert asked as he pulled his Spencer out of the scabbard, laying it across his lap. “Still, you think we are in for some trouble Jim?”

He slowly shook his head and said, “Like I said boys, just a feeling.”

Kerrville fell behind us with the lights and noise fading away as we turned north and headed back to Fredericksburg.

The moon was full as it rose in the sky lighting up stars from one end of the horizon to the other, easily showing the way as we navigated the wide well used trail. Our pace was steady as we clearly saw any obstruction or danger area along our route of march. We figured that we should make town sometime in the morning.

Jim was still shifting in his saddle and more than once I saw him looking over his shoulder. His anxiety was contagious as both Robert and myself were getting a bit antsy, constantly looking out to our flanks and at our rear. It is difficult to explain to those that never lived on the edge of life and death as we had for so long. One develops a sense about such things and learns to trust in those feelings for it is safer to pay heed and be wrong than to ignore it and be dead.

Jim said, “Fellas, I got the feelin’ that we are being dogged.”

I looked over my shoulder. The moon and stars provided enough light that I could see a considerable distance behind and off to our sides.

Robert said, “Maybe one of us should hang back and check it out.”

Again, Jim looked over his shoulder and said, "Nah. If we are being dogged no tellin' how many there are and separating will not do us any good if they come at us."

Robert nodded, "I suppose we should push on. Be foolish to come at us at night."

Jim laughed, "Have you ever met a desperado that was not foolish?"

Again, I looked behind us. I said, "Reckon we should keep going till daylight and see what they do, if there is anyone there."

Jim said, "Oh, they are there boys, that they are. You can count on it."

Now it became a game of staying one step, if not two, ahead of the unseen parties on our tail. Though we had not seen them, heard them, or even knew for certain they were there we trusted Jim's instincts. To ignore it would have been foolish as our lives could very well hang in the balance.

Everywhere we looked, left, right, ahead and behind we assessed the threats, real and imagined. Our minds worked at potential defensive positions we may occupy should the desperados come at us. Every rock formation, every tree could help or hinder our defense, so we would have to choose wisely when the moment came upon us. We would rely on experience of battles past, experience in marksmanship and experience in keeping our wits about us when the lead started to fly. Once you lost your head in a fight, you were as good as dead.

Time ceased as we continued in our nocturnal journey through the wilderness. We remained vigilant, guns at the ready, eyes and ears seeking out movement, the slightest of oddities that would cause us concern. The closer we got to Fredericksburg, the better off we would be.

Jim said, "Reckon we are nearer to town than further. I fear if they are gonna hit us it will be soon."

I pulled my Walker and worked the action ensuring that it was free of dirt or obstructions. "If they are comin', I hope they do it sooner than later. I for one am growing tired of waitin'. Was never that good at sittin' on my hands," I said as I holstered the pistol.

Jim smiled and looked at me saying, "I thought you soldiers were good at waitin'."

Before I could answer Robert said, "We will not have to wait much longer." He pointed out to our right flank. "Take a look fellas."

We looked to where he was pointing and saw the distinct outline of four riders in the distance. They were trying to hide among the brush but made the simple mistake of allowing themselves to be shadowed by the horizon behind them.

I said, "Damn fools puttin' the horizon behind them like that. Do you reckon that is all there is?"

Robert said, "Doubt it. These fellas look like they are trying to get ahead of us. There is probably more coming up the rear. Probably going to hit us at the front and rear at the same time."

We looked to our front for a possible defensive position. We were still too far out of town to make a run for it.

Jim said, "Well, let us see just how bad they want to tangle with us." He looked at us and grinned. "What say we make a run for it till we find a good place to set up a defense."

Robert said, "Marshal Sweeny. We would not have it any other way."

With that the three of us yelled out, kicked our horses, and took off at a hard gallop. We were going to see just how bad they wanted to take us on.

CHAPTER FOURTEEN

We rode hard and fast. Robert held the lead line to the pack horse tight in his grip hoping that he would keep up. Should he fail to do so, I knew Robert would cast the animal off hoping to retrieve it later.

I looked to the rear and sure enough here they came. I did a quick count of the riders coming up at us. Ten to the rear about one hundred yards out and four on our right flank that were trying to get ahead of us.

I yelled to the others, "Here they come boys!"

Robert looked over his shoulder and released to lead line to the pack horse. He yelled, "Hope you fellas are not hungry. There go our supplies."

Jim answered back saying, "I was gettin' tired of hardtack anyway."

Humor and danger sometimes go hand in hand. Our dark humor was as much a part of the battle as fear, grief, sorrow, and bravery. It was just one way to handle the desperate situation we were faced with.

Jim yelled out, "Up ahead! On the left, off the trail is a rock formation!"

I yelled back, "You boys get set up while I will try and scatter them!"

Before they could respond I turned Caliban around, pulled my Walker Colt and rode straight at them. I got low in the saddle and aimed my massive pistol at the center of the mass of men and horseflesh and squeezed off a shot, knocking one rider out of the saddle.

I pushed Caliban harder as we closed the distance, he responded well to my command as I felt his powerful muscles, felt his hot breath blow back in my face as he did not faulter nor deviate from our path. I took in a lung full of air and introduced these boys to the infamous Rebel Yell.

"Woh-who-ey! Woh-who-ey! Woh-who-ey," I screamed.

Frazzled by my aggressive attack, the bewildered riders had yet to fire off a shot though I saw a few had filled their hands so I kept at them, squeezing off a second shot sending another rider to the ground as I rode right into the mass of men and horse.

The reduced group scattered as I mixed in with them, I fired off another round at a desperado who lost control of his mount sending his body into a second rider that was trying to pull his pistol and they both fell to the ground under the panicked horse's hooves. Others in the group rode after Robert and Jim as I turned Caliban in a tight circle in search of another target. One rider, having a change of heart, decided to hightail it out of the area and took off out into the open expanses of the wilderness.

Another man got off a shot and missed because his frightened horse was not conditioned to the sounds and pungent odors of battle. I put a ball into the man's chest flipping him ass over head out of the saddle.

With one bullet left in my pistol I holstered it and pulled my shotgun free of the scabbard, cocked both rabbit ear hammers and rode after those that chased after Robert and Jim.

As I neared, I saw my friends at the base of the large rock formation with their backs to the natural fortress, rifles in hand standing their ground. Even in the light of the moon I could see the desperados clearly as they tried to gain the advantage on Robert and Jim. Both men picked their targets, Jim working his Henry Rifle and Robert his Spencer. I saw Robert drop two men and Jim nailed another. The four riders from the flank had joined the fight and were trying to come at Robert and Jim from the blind side on their left. I rode at them.

Before I neared a strange occurrence happened as a shot rang out and one of the men fell off his horse and hit the ground, dead. I could not see where the shot had come from as I pulled up searching for the unseen shooter.

Just then two riders came from behind the rock fortress and rode right into the fight, pistols in hand yellin' with excitement they engaged the outlaws bringing down the other two.

It was Thadius Polehouse and W.B.D. Burns.

One man had fallen from his horse and tried to run away on foot when Thad kicked his mount and, catching up to the man, trampled him into the ground, turning back to the fight just as Jim dropped the last rider.

I kept Caliban in motion, turning in tight circles as I searched for a target, another desperado meaning to do us harm. Even in the darkness I could see the smoke from the spent powder hovering in the air. It reflected off the moonlight and cast the area with an eerie blanket over the bodies and riderless horses. Nothing moved, silence had taken over from the recent sounds of the fight.

Thad broke the silence. “Is anyone of you boys hurt,” he called out.

Silence.

I dismounted and walked Caliban over to the rock formation just as Thad and Bill joined up. We all just stood there looking at each other, breathing heavily, trying to slow our bodies down from the excitement of battle.

I asked, “Thad, Bill, how is it that you are here?”

Thad and Bill exchanged looks. It was Bill who answered.

“Right after you boys left, we took notice of some cowboys at the saloon watching you leave town. I knew of some of these fellas from a ranch outfit before the war. They was always troublemakers, bad hombres.”

Thad said, “Bout an hour after you boys were gone, they all mounted up and lit out after you. Figured they were up to no good.”

Robert said, “Well, we are in your debt.”

I asked, “You say you know these fellas?”

Bill said, “That I do. Most of ‘em worked a ranch west of here as cattle drovers. It went belly up during the war. Thought it odd when they all showed up in town yesterday before you boys did.”

Before another question could be thrown at the two lawmen, we all heard a cry out in the darkness.

“Oh, I have been shot. Someone help me, I am bleeding,” moaned the unseen voice.

We all pulled our pistols and spread out to begin a search of the area for the desperate voice. It was Jim who found him.

“On your feet youngster,” Jim said.

We saw Jim in the low light holding up a small looking man with one hand while sticking his pistol to the fella's neck, barking orders at him.

“C’mon, move yer ass son for I finish the job,” he yelled.

The man moaned and said, “Oh Lord do not shoot me again. I am shot bad mister.”

Jim pushed the man towards us saying, “Git over there with the others, damn you!”

The man stumbled up to us holding his right shoulder, blood seeping through his gloved hand as he fought to stay on his feet. He looked at us with wide eyes of fear mixed with the pain of his shoulder wound.

He was a ragged looking character. Short and slight, unshaven with unruly hair coming out from under his hat. His jacket, torn and dirty matching his brown pants and boots. Around his waist was a simple belt that held a worn holster, empty of revolver, and a bone handle knife.

I looked at his face, thin, exaggerating his cheek bones making his fear filled eyes seem bigger.

"How old are you son," I asked.

To answer he pushed his wounded shoulder closer to me saying, "Ain't you gonna help me mister? I am shot."

Thad smacked him on the back of the head, knocking his hat to the ground. "The Marshal asked you a question youngster."

The man looked surprised. He looked at me and asked, "You a Marshal?"

I reached over and removed his knife from his belt and tossed it aside. "We are all lawmen you damn fool. Why you think we wear this tin on our shirts?"

He looked at each of us in turn. Shaking his head, the shoulder wound now forgotten he said, "Oh Lordy, Lord. He did not say you was lawmen. Oh, Lordy, Lord." He hung his head.

Bill grabbed the boy by his jacket and asked, "Who are you talking about? Who did not tell you we were lawmen?"

The boy looked up. "What will become of me now?"

Bill yanked him off his feet. "Son, I can tell you this! You do not start tellin' us what we want to know I will make damn sure you will be hurtin' more than you are now! Who told you about us?"

Fear overcame the boy as he cried out, "It were a big Indian! He paid us in gold to kill you fellas!"

Bill let go of the boy, who fell to the ground and began to weep.

I looked down at the boy and said, "I for one am getting damn tired of hearin' about this big Indian."

The boy looked up and said, "I am gonna bleed out Marshal. Ain't you gonna help me?"

Robert said, "You better keep quiet son. The way we feel right now may bring a bullet to your head."

He hung his head down and uttered, "Oh Lordy, Lord. I am done for."

Jim said, "Reckon we need to get moving. No tellin' what else this Indian has in store for us."

Robert said, "I will go off and find the pack horse. He could not have traveled too far."

"I will go with you Robert," I said.

We retrieved our horses, mounted up and went out in search of the pack horse. As we moved to the trail we navigated around the bodies of the fallen cowboys turned outlaw, viewing each as we passed. They were all dead, the boy being the only survivor of the battle. Him and the fella that had run off.

We rode in silence side by side, happy to have survived yet another skirmish, another battle, another day behind the pistol. They had brought the fight to us, and we met it with equal force dispatching them to the next world, wherever that may be. Heaven or hell, each man will be judged, each man will answer for his wrongdoings.

Before long we spotted the pack horse on the trail. Without direction he had continued his journey along the trail, seeking us out while dragging his tether on the ground behind him. As soon as we neared, he stopped, looked at us and waited as we pulled up next to him.

Robert picked up the lead line and said, "I guess we will have dinner tonight."

I smiled. "Oh, wonderful. Salt pork and hardtack. My favorite."

Robert turned around and we headed back. "Do not forget the beans Wyatt," he said as he laughed. "We must have the beans."

We rejoined the others at the rock formation where we found Jim doctoring the shoulder of the young cowhand.

Jim looked up and said, "Went clean through. He will be fine."

I said, "Too bad."

We took a moment to reload and check our pistols and rifles to have them shoot ready should the fight not be over. This Indian had set a trap for us to which we were fortunate to have come through unscathed. The next time may prove to be more difficult a task to overcome.

Thad said, "I suggest we set up camp here fellas. Two men on guard then we all go into Fredericksburg together."

"You fellas gonna come in with us," I asked.

Bill said, "We ain't goin' to turn you lose out here a second time. That redskin may have another surprise waitn' for you."

The cowhand looked up. "What you goin' to do with me Marshal?"

I looked at the others before I answered. "Reckon you are comin' with us. You have a name?"

He nodded. "Yes sir. My name is Johnny Thorton."

Bill walked over and grabbed a handful of the boy's hair, pulled back, and looked at his face. "You one of the Thorton boys?"

Johnny nodded his head, staying quiet.

Bill said angrily, "Where are your two no account brothers?"

Johnny pointed out towards the trail and said, "Out there. You dun shot them too. Theys dead fer sure."

Bill released the boy, looked at us realizing an explanation was in order. "The Thorton family come out of San Marcos," he began. "The Pappy was the worst. He has been dead long time now." He looked down at the boy. "Left behind three no account boys, him being one of them."

Jim said, "I heard of his Pappy. Meaner than a snake that one. Got gunned down for cheatin' at cards."

Johnny looked up and said, "He were not cheatin'! He was a good Pap!"

I shook my head and said, "Boy, you ain't got the sense God give a dog."

Robert looked out over the mass of dead bad guys and said, "We gotta do something with these fellas."

I said, "Ain't right leavin' them out here."

Sheriff Burns put his hands on hip hips, looked out over the area as if he was making up his mind then said, "Reckon you are right. Might as well lay them over the saddle and bring them in."

I said, "Robert, if you will get a fire going, we will tend to this."

"You sure Wyatt," Robert asked.

I patted him on the shoulder and said, "I sure could use a cup of coffee."

We set about the grim task of policing up the bodies, guns, and whatever items we came across that had belonged to the outlaw cowhands. Be it hats, jackets, gloves, and boots we collected it all and placed them in a small pile while we took each body, draped it over a horse, and tied them off.

A few of the mounts had taken off during the scrap and we had to burden the stronger of the animals with two bodies. As we tied each one off, we led the animal and passenger to the backside of the rock formation and tied them to a line we had strung. It was time consuming but a task that needed to be done.

We saved one of the horses for our wounded prisoner and tied him off with our mounts.

The boy watched us and said, "That ain't my horse."

Bill walked over to him and looked down. "Boy, you are damn lucky we do not make you walk to Fredericksburg. Now shut your mouth!"

By the time we had finished the task of gathering the dead, Robert had our grub prepared and we greedily attacked the simple meal as we stood around the small cook fire, keeping watch over the wilderness before us.

Bill said, “I will ride around the perimeter if one of you fellas keeps watch at the top of the rock.”

I said, “I will take the first watch.”

I grabbed my shotgun, filled my pipe, and handed Robert my tobacco pouch saying, “Good a time as any for a pipe my friend.”

He took the pouch. “Thanks, Wyatt. I sure could use a good pipe about now.”

I filled my cup with coffee, and with pipe and shotgun I climbed to the top of the rock formation without spilling a drop and settled into my watch.

I looked out through the dim light of the moon and saw the vastness of the Texas wilderness. I felt small in comparison and said a quiet prayer of thanks for coming through yet another battle. Then I added a quiet prayer for the protection of the Almighty that we should make it home. We were going to need it.

CHAPTER FIFTEEN

One by one we brought the animals that were given the task of carrying the dead to the front of the rock formation. We had nine horses, three being burdened with carrying two bodies instead of one, our five mounts, the pack horse, and the horse for our wounded prisoner. Fifteen animals carrying six live souls, twelve dead bandits and our supply of food stuffs. It was going to be slow trek back to town.

We figured we would have made Fredericksburg sometime late morning but now, with our additional burden of animals and bodies we figured we would arrive late in the afternoon if not early evening.

Also adding in the task of combating any enemy that may be before us, our journey would be arduous at best. We would have to remain vigilant on the trail seeking out threats of ambush, bushwhackers in hiding or an enemy trying to cut us off from reaching our destination. We had to be ready for anything.

Thad and W.B.D. Burns rode out front, often changing positions, scouting the flanks, the front. One would ride off, seeking out danger while the other remained up front, moving us forward. Any area that presented an opportunity for the bad guys to get the jump on us was searched and searched aggressively. Both men kept their rifles at the ready, always moving, searching, hunting for an unseen enemy.

I had five of the horses carrying the dead following me in train. Jim had the other four while Robert had the pack horse and our prisoner, who was in chains, also in train. I was on the left and behind Robert, my shotgun resting across my lap while Jim was on the right, his Henry rifle on his leg, barrel pointed skyward while still holding the reins of his animal.

Our plan was simple. If we were jumped anytime during our journey we would let go of the lead lines of the dead and the pack horse, kill Thorton and hightail it to Fredericksburg. Each step of the horse, every mile we traveled brought us closer to safety.

Every footfall gave us a sense of accomplishment, if not relief. That was one more step down, an unknown number yet to travel, but we were moving forward. We felt strong in our numbers, confident in our fighting posture, ready to take on whatever was thrown at us. Fourteen desperados came at us the day before hell bent on dispatching us only to meet their end by our hand. Ours was an experienced force, a force to be reckoned with. Still, we did not want to become overconfident in our abilities.

Be it the big Indian we kept hearing about, or an unseen person not yet known to us, they were recruiting gun hands that, for the most part, lacked experience or even the know-how in making war. Those that went up against us were lacking in this ability which gave us an edge. Slight as it may have been, we were able to exploit it and turn the tables on our enemy.

It is easy for one to strap on a pistol, perhaps practice with it and become proficient at shooting but it was another to maintain that proficiency while your target, the other guy, was also shooting at you. There was a marked difference when shooting at a tin can and shooting at a man. The tin can could not kill you.

We rode in silence for the most part, keeping our senses focused on what could be waiting for us in the wilderness. Occasionally our prisoner would let out a moan, mumble something incoherent or just hang his head and cry.

Jim leaned over and prodded Thorton with his rifle saying, "Boy, you best keep it to yourself. Your whining is getting on my nerves."

Thorton lifted his head and said, "But I am shot. It pains me something terrible."

Robert looked over his shoulder and said, "You should have thought about that before you threw in with this rabble."

Thorton replied, "Theys ain't rabble Marshal." He hung his head. "We just tryin' to earn us a living."

I shook my head. "Boy, you should have taken to the plow. You ain't any good with the iron."

He said, "I ain't got nuthin' more to say to you fellas. You do not care if'n I live or die."

I laughed, "You are not as dumb as I thought."

Robert and Jim laughed then we fell into silence as we went back to the task of seeking out danger while trying to get home.

The temperature climbed as the sun made its way high in the sky and the hard packed earth gave way to a fine powdery dust that seemed to surround us, engulf us as our strange train of man and animal plodded along. It was choking, miserable and irritating. Often fighting the desire to reach for my canteen I found myself hoping for a respite. Though we were nearing the town we still maintained our water rationing, fighting yet another enemy on our journey.

It was late in the afternoon when Thad rode back to us. We held up, instinctively reaching for our guns.

He said, "Found a stream just around the bend. We can water the animals and wash some of this dust out of our mouths."

Robert said, "Lead the way, Thad. We could use a break."

We followed Thad for near a quarter mile then turned off the trail and went out into the wilderness. The dust was not as bad as we navigated our way through the brush and up a small rise. At the top we saw the stream to which he spoke. I would have enjoyed casting off the lead line and make a dash for the cool inviting water but I, and the others, maintained self-control and led our train to the water's edge.

It was wide enough for me to bring all the animals into the stream where I then tied off the lead line to a mesquite tree. For some strange reason I did not want Caliban to join with the horses, those carrying the dead, while partaking of the refreshing water, so I walked him further upstream and dismounted.

Leaving Caliban, I walked through the water as the others made their way into the stream. Oddly enough I noticed that Jim had led his string of horses to the same spot I had deposited my train of animals. Then he brought his horse alongside Caliban and dismounted, joining me up stream.

He stood next to me and said, "I did not feel right letting my horse drink with the dead."

I chuckled. "I felt the same way."

I knelt in the stream, splashed some of the water on my face and over my hair and immediately felt refreshed. As I stood, I saw that the others had the same idea as we all gathered in the stream, except W.B.D Burns who remained mounted, keeping watch over us.

I walked back to Caliban, mounted up and moved next to Bill saying, "I have the watch."

He looked at me, smiled and said, "Much obliged Wyatt. I feel like I swallowed half of Texas these last few miles."

I sat my horse in the middle of the stream and looked out over the landscape. I said, "How much further Bill," I asked.

Bill was kneeling in the stream, splashing water on his face. He took his hat off, submerged it filling it with water and promptly dumped it over his head as he stood.

He looked about and said, “Couple of hours at least. We should make it well before nightfall if we do not run into trouble.”

“Yea, if,” I said.

We had gathered in the stream and Robert handed out strips of jerky as we let the animals drink and cool off as best they could under the hot Texas sun.

Our prisoner was sitting in the water looking at us and mumbling to himself. I was not the only one that took notice of this, as Thad went over and gave him a once over, then walked over to us.

He said, “I fear the boy may be suffering from the heat.”

Robert asked, “Think he is trying to fool us into thinking he is out of his head?”

Thad looked back at the Thorton boy. “I cannot be sure, truth be told. Could just be foolin’.” He looked back at us. “The sooner we get him out of the heat the better. He ain’t gonna last much longer out here if he is out of his head.”

Robert looked at Thorton and said, “Still, he could be faking it.”

Bill said, “He is one of the Thorton boys, he ain’t that smart.”

I said, “We will let Doc Averbeck look him over when we get to town.”

Thad said, “Reckon we should get back on the trail boys. We ain’t home yet.”

So, once again we gathered up our string of animals, pushed Johnny Thorton back on his horse and followed our two scouts, Thad and W.B.D. Burns back to the trail to resume what we hoped was the last leg in our journey.

We resumed our defensive posture as before as we rode through the choking dust. Thad and Bill rode scout, running through the brush trying to flush out any hidden adversary, almost daring them to fight it out with us. Thankfully, there was no enemy lying in wait as we continued along the trail.

Theirs was the tougher job, as it is with any scout charged with protecting the main force. Always moving, working their mounts, searching, seeking out those bent on bringing harm to the rest of us. Much like hunting where you drive the prey to the awaiting guns, we were not going to allow them to bring the fight to us. We would drive it to them.

This went on for the remainder of the trip. We remained vigilant throughout the day and were soon rewarded with the sight of Fredericksburg on the horizon.

We stopped and took it in.

Thad yelled back to us, "We ain't there yet boys. I will not rest till we are safe at the jail!"

With a renewed charge we resumed our quest to be rid of the dead and dying and find relief from the oppressive heat.

At the very edge of Fredericksburg, we all sat a bit taller in the saddle knowing that all eyes of the folks out and about with their daily routines would see us come into town. Though we were filthy, disheveled and covered in dust from head to toe we still represented the law of the land, and as such, we would ride proudly down the street knowing, if only to ourselves, that we had overcome the odds and conducted ourselves as true Texas lawmen.

Our formation grew tight as Thad and Bill led the way into town, rifles pointed skyward looking straight ahead followed by Robert in the center with the pack horse and our chained prisoner in tow. I was on the left dragging my string of dead and Jim was on the right pulling the ugly reminder of our work behind him.

We rode in silence, slowly moving down the center of the street. People stopped; riders and wagons pulled to the side to give us the way. I heard women gasp in horror as we led our procession along, past the stores and shops. Six dirty tired souls bringing with them twelve bodies draped and tied over nine horses. There was a noticeable silence as no one spoke nor welcomed us home. The shock of our work following along behind us, reminding those that stared in disbelief that ours was a deadly business.

They pointed, averted their eyes, or put their hands to their mouths suppressing a scream or anguished cry. It was not our intent to show this macabre display with pride or pronouncement of our abilities as shootist but to, perhaps, serve as a warning to those that teetered between lawlessness and a peaceable life that we as lawmen will carry out our duties and restore order to a turbulent time and place, no matter the cost.

It was the ugly side of our life; our jobs and we accepted it.

We passed Mark and Chelsea's shop on my side of the formation. I saw Chelsea standing on the porch looking in disbelief as we plodded by. She brought a hand to her mouth, turned and went inside calling out to her husband.

We soon came to the jail, our journey at an end.

As I was dismounting, the door to the jailhouse opened and Julius, shotgun in hand stepped out and stood stock still as he took in our miserable collection of animals and men.

"Oh Lord Jesus," he uttered

I coughed, spit out a mouthful of trail dust and said, "How goes it my friend?"

He stepped off the porch and came over, wrapped his powerful arms around me and hugged, then turned and grabbed hold of Robert, hugging him as well.

Embarrassed and somewhat confused as to this welcoming show of affection I said, "Lord have mercy Julius. You look as if you have seen a ghost. We have not been gone that long my friend."

Julius recovered and said, "We feared the worst Cap'n. Last we heard you and the Sergeant Major left Castroville headin' to Bandera. That was the last anyone heard of you. Then we got telegrams asking if we seen the town Marshal and two sheriffs. Theys also missing."

Jim, Thad, and Bill gathered around listening to the story as told by our jailer.

Jim said. "We are all here." He offered his hand to Julius and said, "Marshal Jim Sweeney of Castroville. You must be Julius, the Jailer. Heard much about you."

Julius took the offered hand and said, "Yes sir, I am Julius. I got a telegram from your deputy sayin' how you is missing."

Just then Chelsea pushed her way through the gathering crowd and wrapped her arms around me and held on. She said, "Thank God you and Robert are okay." She turned and grabbed hold of Robert repeating, "Thank God."

Mark Lauderback worked his way to my side and took my hand in both of his. "We feared the worst Wyatt. We heard all sorts of things when the telegraph started up again." He looked over our collection, shook his head and said, "I can see that most of what we heard was true."

Robert asked, "What have you heard? We have only been gone five days."

Chelsea said, "Six days, nearer to seven. When we heard that the Marshal left with you and the Sheriffs of Bandera and Kerr Counties were also gone, we did not know what to think."

Julius added, "Those two boys you sent up told us what brought them here and the preacher man coming to town said he never seen any of you on the trail. We were figurin' the worst Cap'n."

"Preacher man," I asked.

Mark said as he pointed across the street, "There he is, next to Pepper's Place Wyatt. Came in the other day."

I looked across the street and saw the oddity of this wagon I had only heard about. It was huge. It was shaped like a small church complete with a bell steeple on a pitched roof. It was as wide as it was long and high with steps going into a back door. Stained glass windows, three on each side depicting scenes from the Bible with colorful angels', trumpets in hand playing from the heavens stood out against the darkened paint.

Something else caught my eye. On the top step, standing in the open door a slim figure of a man, his hair black and straight, parted in the center fell to his shoulders and matched his thick black eyebrows and thin black beard. He was dressed in a long ankle length black cassock with a sash tied around his thin waist with the ends hanging down his side ending in fringes. He just stood there watching, unmoving. I found his image disturbing as I turned away.

I asked Thad and Bill, "Is that the wagon and the preacher fella you saw?"

Bill answered. "Sure is. Looks bigger in the daylight. Lord Almighty that thing is big."

Thad said, "Looks like the preacher I saw. Does not look too heavenly you ask me."

I ignored the wagon and preacher for the moment as introductions were made all around and we then addressed the need to clear the street of our cargo and get the horses tended to. Without wanting, we were drawing a crowd of townsfolk taking in our macabre collection of dead men and horses.

Everyone pitched in and we walked the animals around the back where we found our two would-be robbers, Clem and Pete washing up at the pump.

"Hello boys," I said as I saw them.

They both stood, nervous at seeing us. Pete said, "Marshal. You made it back. Glad to see you." He turned to his brother and lightly smacked him on the chest saying, "Ain't we glad to see him Clem?"

Clem looked down at the ground and said, "Howdy Marshal."

Robert asked, "Why are you boys so nervous?"

They traded looks and Pete said, "We figured once you came back, you'd be lockin' us up for what we done."

I laughed. "Have you boys been working on the new saloon like I said?"

"Yes sir," Clem answered. "Every day since we got here. We just finished up for the day and was fixin' to get somethin' to eat, we was."

Julius said, "Cap'n, they been helping around here too. I been feedin' them for their trouble."

Robert said, "Well good. You boys can pitch in here and help us get settled."

I turned to Julius and said, "I need you to fetch Doc Averbeck, our undertaker and see if Jeremiah can come here, we have some messages to send out." As an afterthought I said, "Carry your shotgun, Julius."

Julius nodded and said firmly, without question, "Will do Cap'n."

Robert directed Pete and Clem to move the animals that carried the dead to a place away from the stables while everyone tended to our mounts then Robert took our prisoner inside to await the arrival of the Doc.

I took a moment for myself and went to the pump. I was about to put my head under and begin pumping when Chelsea came over and offered her assistance.

She said smiling, "Get your head under there Wyatt, I will work the pump."

As she pumped the cold clear water poured out and spilled over my head. It was refreshing and invigorating as I let it flow over me, washing away the trail dust.

I stepped back, ran my fingers through my long hair pushing it back when Chelsea offered up a hand towel.

As I took it, I said, "Thank you my dear. I feel like a new man already."

CHAPTER SIXTEEN

All the tasks complete save for the collection of the dead; we went inside leaving Clem and Pete with the animals to await the arrival of the undertaker. I promised them it would not be too long of a wait, and they could assist Mister Kramer when he came to collect.

Robert had our prisoner seated, still in chains, off to the side. Thorton was quietly mumbling incoherently to himself and did not pose a danger to us, so we let him be. Perhaps he was off his nut. When the Doc arrived, we would let him make that call.

We gathered around the table as I produced my tobacco and pipe, offering it up to those that wished it.

There was a knock at the door as we all fell silent. Mark walked over, pulled a revolver from the small of his back and looked out the window before stepping to the door.

He said, "Well I will be damned," as he opened the door.

In stepped a thin redheaded girl, pale in complexion and covered with freckles, carrying two buckets of beer, smiling from ear to ear as she set them down, squealed with delight and ran right at me.

I barely had time to stand when she wrapped her arms around me, kissed me on both cheeks, pushed me aside and grabbed at Robert, holding tight.

Pepper squealed with delight again and said, "Lordy I thought you boys was dun in for sure and for certain! You ain't dead!" She clapped her hands, jumped once more, and wrapped her arms around my neck.

Thad cleared his throat and said, "You fellas want to introduce us to this young lady bearing gifts of beer and hugs?"

Everyone laughed as I tried to peel Pepper off my neck. I said, "Now hold on Pepper. I want you to meet a couple three fellas."

She stopped bouncing and wrapped one arm around my waist and the other around Robert. "Why sure, Wyatt honey," she said as she looked at the unfamiliar faces.

I said as I pointed to Thad, "This is Thadius Dexter Polehouse, Sheriff of Bandera County." I pointed to Jim and said, "This is Jim Sweeney, Town Marshal of Castroville and this," I said as I turned, "is Sheriff William Bill Dalton Burns of Kerr County."

Pepper whistled and said, "Lord Almighty sure is a lot of names to remember. I am Pepper Leeds and that is my place across the street." She paused, pursed her lips then said, "The saloon. Not that church house on wheels. Wish that fella would park that thing elsewheres."

I said, "I will be happy to chase him off for you Darlin'."

Pepper turned to me and said, "Would you Wyatt? That fella makes me nervous. Has a name I cannot rightly pronounce. Call himself Brother sometin' or the other."

I said, "Be glad to."

Robert asked, "How is the place coming along Pepper?"

She said, "Oh fine. Gonna start lookin' for someone to play the piano and maybe a fiddle player or two. The card room is nearly done too."

Mark said as he put the two buckets of beer on the table, "Hear that, Wyatt, a card room. Now you can play poker with other folks and stop taking our money."

Pepper said, "Well, I got to go y'all. Got me a fella who is gonna run the bar for me. Come by and meet him."

"We will," I said.

Pepper planted another kiss on my cheek and one on Robert's, turned and went out the door.

Thad asked, "Was she the girl that worked at the old place? That shit hole, Heart of Dixie?"

"She was," I said. "Fella that ran the place beat her senseless for helping us."

Thad nodded knowingly and said, "Then it was you that beat that jackass near dead."

I remained silent and answered with a smile.

Thad said, "You should have shot the bastard."

Chelsea had produced beer mugs from our collection that we had liberated from The Heart of Dixie, before I burned it to the ground, and Mark took on the job of tending bar, filling each mug and passing them around until everyone, save our prisoner, had a beer.

Mark raised his mug and said, "Welcome home fellas and welcome to our three new friends."

As we drank a voice called out to us from the street. “Hello in the jail, it is me, Julius.”

Mark went to the window then to the door granting Julius, with the Doc in tow, entrance to the jail.

“Hello Doc,” I said as he came in.

He stepped over, extended his hand, and smiled. “Glad you boys are safe.”

Robert took his hand and said, “You are looking well Doc.”

He waved his hand at Robert. “Oh, horseshit!”

I smiled at his comment but took notice that he did look tired. In fact, he always looked tired. His hair had turned prematurely grey, the growth on his face was three or four days old but it was his gaunt features that gave me pause. When we first met soon after we had arrived in town, he was a bad-tempered country doctor that drank a bit too much. Always one to show genuine concern for his patients he was a good sawbones. We quickly learned that he, like Robert and me, was a soldier and a doctor in the war. We may have made the casualties, but it was Doctor Hiram Averbeck that had the thankless task of putting them back together, and not always whole. I knew that he too was haunted by his past.

I pointed to the prisoner seated behind him and said, “This young fella has been shot. We doctored him best we could, but I fear the sun may have done him in.”

Doc sighed heavily and said, “I will take care of him.” He looked again at his patient. “Why are they so damn young Wyatt?”

I shook my head and said softly, “I do not know Hy. I wish it were not so.”

Julius said, “While you are here Doc would you check on our other prisoner?”

I looked at Julius and asked, “You mean Mack the Knife is still here? The Marshal did not send anyone to get him?”

Robert stepped over. “Did I hear that Mack is still here?”

Julius said, “Yes sir Sergeant Major Robert. Still causin’ a fuss and keeps sayin’ Mack the Knife is his given name.”

I returned to the table sat down facing the doc and picked up my beer. It was then that I noticed a pair of brown eyes surrounded by a furry face looking at me. I closed my eyes for a moment and opened them willing the apparition to go away. It had not. Instead, it cocked its head at an odd angle as if it were studying me, sizing me up. It was then I noticed the room had gone quiet.

I cleared my throat, took a drink, and looked at Julius standing off to the side of this apparition. "Julius," I asked, "am I seeing a dog?"

Julius looked down, nodded, and said, "Yes Cap'n."

I said, "Good, good," nodding my head. I then asked, "Julius. Why am I seeing a dog?"

Julius said, "Well, Cap'n. He showed up the day you and the Sergeant Major left, and he has been hanging around. Kinda made this his home I reckon."

I nodded again. "He kinda made this his home because maybe you have been feeding him?"

Robert said, "C'mon Wyatt. He is friendly enough."

I turned to Robert and asked, "You knew about this animal?"

Thad answered, "We all seen him Wyatt since we first came in. I thought he was your dog for pity's sake."

I looked at the dog. He was not a large dog, bigger than most I suppose. Brown and black, a Shepherd of some sort I believe. He was still studying me, his head cocked, pointed ears up, sitting in front of me just looking.

Doc interrupted and said, "Okay Julius, I will see the other prisoner now."

"Right away Doc," Julius said as he turned to retrieve the prisoner from the cell.

I continued to study the dog as he studied me. When Julius came out of the cell only then did the dog turn his attention to something other than me.

Julius led our prisoner over to the Doc who was seated in front of the Thorton boy. Then in a quick motion, Mack the Knife shoved Julius into Doc, sending both men crashing to the floor in a heap. I dropped my mug, sprang to my feet, and reached for my pistol only to stop in my tracks, my Walker halfway out of the holster.

The dog, either sensing something was amiss or reacting with lightning reflexes as it happened lunged at Mack the Knife. With open mouth the dog clamped down on the prisoner's crotch bit down and forced the now screaming man against the wall. From deep down inside the animal there came a guttural growl that raised the hair on the back of my neck. The dog forced his weight against the man keeping him against the wall.

Mack the Knife, ever defiant and uncooperative screamed in agony or fear, I am uncertain as to which, pleading for help while the dog remained steadfast, his powerful jaws clamped onto the man's privates.

Mack the Knife screamed out, "Git this animal off me! He will rip out my pecker!"

I slid my pistol back in the holster while Robert helped Julius and Hy to their feet. Everyone was standing now watching as the dog continued to hold the prisoner against the wall.

Mack pleaded with us as sweat poured down his face. "Oh Lord, help me! Do not stand there gawkin', git this animal off me!"

I picked up my mug and asked Doc and Julius, "You boys, okay?"

They both nodded, transfixed by the unfolding spectacle as I walked over to the beer bucket and refilled my mug. I took a long drink and slowly walked over to our near catatonic prisoner who began to shake uncontrollably.

I stood next to the dog, took a drink, and calmly said, "You seem to have gotten yourself into a bit of trouble here boy." I took another drink, savoring the sweetness of the beer. "What do you think we should do to resolve this?"

The man barely turned his head, only glancing at me briefly while he returned his frightened eyes back to the dog. "Oh Marshal," he cried out. "Do not let this dog castrate me, please. I beg of you Marshal."

Robert joined me while the others gathered around behind us. Robert said, "You have been less than helpful when we asked questions of you." Robert crossed his arms over his chest. "In fact, I believe at one time you told Marshal Chambers to go to hell." Robert looked at me. "Is that not right Marshal Chambers?"

I nodded. "It is Marshal Barton. That he did."

"I hate rude people," Robert said. "Is that not so Marshal Chambers?"

I nodded. "Oh, absolutely Marshal Barton."

Mack the Knife's face dripped in sweat, eyes wide with fear while the dog's growl grew deeper, fiercer. "I am sorry," he said. "I am sorry...I am sorry...I am so sorry I said that, Marshal."

I grinned. "Let us start with something simple. Like your name," I said.

The man nodded and said, "I could do that Marshal. Yes, I could do that."

Yet he remained silent. I shook my head. "Boy if you was any dumber you would have to be watered twice a day. Now, what is your name?"

The sweat was dripping into his eyes causing him to blink repeatedly to clear his vision. "Oh, you want I should tell you." He looked down at the dog who held fast to his privates and offered up another deep growl. The frightened man said with a quaking voice, "Horace is my name. Horace."

Robert asked, "Horace what?"

Horace swallowed hard and said, "Horace Bartholomew Oakley."

"Lord Almighty," I said as I looked at Robert. "I like Mack the Knife better."

Robert said, "No wonder he changed it. Do we have any papers on a Horace Oakley, Marshal Chambers?"

I said, "I believe we do Marshal Barton."

Just then the dog growled, shifted his weight, and pushed Horace harder against the wall. Horace, fearing the worst moaned and I noticed his eyes come up on him. I called the dog off by gently resting my hand on his head. The dog let go and Horace now free of his bonds promptly fainted and fell to the floor.

I looked down at the unconscious heap on the floor and said, "Doc, you got another patient to tend to."

Doc nodded and said, "So it would seem Wyatt."

"I believe this one has the vapors," I said looking back to Doc.

Robert looked down and added, "A lot of that going around."

I turned back and found my chair. As I sat, the dog came up to me and laid his head on my lap. I rubbed him behind the ears, lifted his head, and looked into his brown eyes. I said softly, "I reckon you can stay. You will make a fine Assistant Jailer."

The dog licked my hand, turned and sat next to me, keeping a watchful eye on our two prisoners.

Again, there was a knock at the door. Mark looked out and said, "It is the undertaker and Jeremiah."

I took another drink. "Damnation, we should just leave the door open."

Mister Kramer, tall and gangly stepped across the threshold, dressed in his usual attire of black. Black on black over black. The only garment he wore that was not black was his white collarless shirt, barely visible under his black waist coat and jacket. He removed his top hat, again black and bowed slightly at the waist.

Standing next to him was the small frame of our telegraph operator, Jeremiah, oval glasses perched on his nose, black and gold conductor's hat squarely on his head.

I stood and said, "Mister Kramer, it is good to see you sir. Jeremiah, you as well."

Again, Kramer bowed. “The pleasure is mine Marshal Chambers.” He acknowledged Chelsea and the others with a nod of his head.

I said, “Robert, if you will help Jeremiah with the notices we must send out, I will take Mister Kramer out back and deal with the other issue.”

Robert agreed and led Jeremiah to the table as I escorted Mister Kramer through the back door.

I said to the undertaker, “We had a run it with some desperados on our return trip Cyrus and require your services.”

He said, “Of course Marshal. Am I to assume that it is the same price as before.”

I rested my hand on the middle of his back, smiled, and said, “You have correctly assumed sir. Five dollars apiece.”

He sighed. “Ah hell Wyatt. How many this time? Five, six men?”

I stopped and pointed to the string of horses tended to by Clem and Pete. “No Cyrus. We have twelve this time out.”

Cyrus Kramer’s jaw fell open as his gaze followed the direction I was pointing. “Twelve? Oh, good heavens Wyatt.” He turned back to me and said, “Have you ever thought of arresting these people?”

“Sure,” I said. “I always give them a choice. Only one fella took me up on it though.”

He shook he head and looked at the ground. “Do you know who they might be?”

I said, “No idea whatsoever. If you find any papers on them telling you who they might be just inform the sheriff and he can post their names, and you can have the Sheriff of Kerr County help you out. He is inside. I will send two fellas with you to help unload them. They can bring the horses back.”

Cyrus nodded and sighed. “Of course, Wyatt.”

I waved Clem and Pete over and gave them instructions. “Boys, I want you to go with Mister Kramer here and help him unburden these animals. Keep all the guns and belts, saddles and such and bring them back here with the horses. Can you manage that?”

Pete and Clem exchanged looks and Pete said, “Yes sir. We can do that.”

I smiled, reached into my pocket, and pulled out two one-dollar coins and handed them to Pete. “When you boys get back, come inside for some dinner and beer.”

They both smiled and followed Kramer to the string of horses.

CHAPTER SEVENTEEN

I returned inside and took notice that our mixed posse of lawmen were gathering up personal possessions of clothing, shaving gear and such.

Robert said, "Gather up a change of duds there Wyatt. We are all off to the bath house."

I would admit that the prospect of a hot bath and a shave was welcoming but so was a restful sleep and a decent meal . I said, "Well I was figuring..." I was interrupted.

Chelsea said in a commanding tone, "Orders Marshal Chambers. While you boys get cleaned up, I am going to cook you a nice meal. Ya'll could use both." She put her hands on her hips and said, "Now, git."

I smiled and said meekly, "Yes ma'am."

Doc said as we were leaving, "Wyatt, I am going to take this fella down to my surgery and keep an eye on him for a couple of days. He may be out of his head from the heat."

I nodded and said, "When he can talk Doc, if you will let us know. We have some questions that need answers.'

"I will," Doc said as he guided the near catatonic youngster to the door.

The five of us, clothing and shaving gear in hand, walked down the street in search of soap and hot water. It had been a long trail, difficult to say the least, and the prospect of a hot bath renewed our spirits.

The town folks had gotten over the shock of our grisly parade through the center of town earlier in the day and came up to us offering congratulations, hardy handshakes, a few pats on the back and general well wishes. Some implored us to recap our adventures in the wilds of Texas, some offered prayers of protection knowing that ours was a terrible and deadly vocation. Others just expressed their gratitude and thanks offering words of inspiration and one gentleman even handed out cigars.

At the bath house we settled into the routine of cleaning our bodies. The hot soapy, perfumed water was welcomed as I submerged my filthy frame down into the brass tub. I applied match to cigar, laid my head back and closed my eyes feeling the tension slip away.

The others must have had the same experience as none of us said anything. Not a word was spoken during our collective soaking. Each alone in his own tub of steaming hot water, smoking the gifted cigars, heads tilted back looking up with unseeing eyes.

It was not long before the pangs of hunger forced their way through our relaxed state, and we began to work our way out of the rejuvenating bath and made our way to a shaving mirror to complete our ablutions.

One by one we paid and made our way to the exit door, refreshed and invigorated.

As I was standing on the porch, savoring clean clothes and the fresh scent of the perfumed soap I heard my name being called.

Jeremiah, with papers in hand called out, "Marshal Chambers." He waved the papers over his head. "I have a message for you sir."

I took in a deep breath and forced a smile. Whatever news the little telegraph operator had for us, good or bad, I had come to expect the worst. He was merely the messenger, and such was our fate that he seemed to be the bearer of unwelcome news, and usually when we were about to partake in a home cooked meal.

He climbed the stairs and stood next to me. He said, "They told me at the jail that I could find you men down here." He held up a small stack of papers. "I have answers to some of the messages I sent out for you, Sheriff Burns, Sheriff Polehouse and Marshal Sweeny. I also have a letter for you and one for Marshal Barton."

I looked at the little man and asked, "Are we going to like it?"

He dropped his hands to his sides. "I do not know Marshal. Ain't really my business to say."

I rested my hand on his shoulder and said, "I know Jeremiah. You sir are the messenger. No need for disappointment or concerns."

I took the messages, thanked Jeremiah, read through them, passing them off to each recipient before I read my own, holding the sealed letters for later.

Robert sided up to me and asked, "Are we to eat hardtack and salt pork or Chelsea's lamb stew tonight?"

I read through the lengthy message and said, "It is from the Judge. He congratulates us thus far and offers caution. Seems we have stirred up some army folks in Austin, and they want to know if we have recovered the money. They are sending some army major out here and sent more money under armed escort to pay the soldiers."

Robert asked, "Is this army major from the Paymaster General's office?"

I looked back at the message. "Says his name is A.J. Purdy."

Jim said, "I asked you if you had known him and you never did say."

Robert shrugged his shoulders and said, "I knew of a Purdy on General Buford's staff during the war. Cannot be the same fella, I know that man to be dead."

I said, "Well, he is coming here. The payroll was dispatched three days ago headed out to the frontier." I turned to the others and asked, "What about you fellas? Gonna head on back home?"

Jim said, "I am staying on to the end. This started in my jurisdiction and the folks back home deserve some answers."

W.B.D. Burns said, "Me and Thad will be pushing on tomorrow. As much as I would like to see this to the end, I got my own county to protect."

Thad said, "Same here. You boys got a hotel we can room at?"

Robert said, "Nonsense, you can stay with us."

Sheriff Burns said, "Do not want to put you boys out but an invite given is an invite taken."

Cleaned and refreshed we started to make our way back to the jail anticipating a decent meal. Hardtack, salt pork, beans and pickles will be forgotten for a time to be replaced by a more nourishing, fulfilling meal. We quickened our pace as our stomachs, seeing the images we held in our brains, began rebelling at the lack of food.

As we neared the jail, a lone figure of a man, thin, dressed in a black cossack stood in the center of the street watching our approach. It would seem he had been waiting for our return. He neither walked towards us nor acknowledged us. He just stood there clutching a large leather-bound Bible to his breast, watching us.

I nudged Robert and motioned with my head. "Seems his Eminence would like an audience with us."

Robert chuckled and said, "It was bound to happen sooner or later."

As much as I would have liked to ignore the preacher, I thought it best to get the visit out of the way as I had promised Pepper, I would chase him off, or at the very least have him relocate his church wagon.

I said, "You boys go ahead to the jail. I will see what the preacher wants."

Robert again chuckled, "Oh no. I do not want to miss this meeting. I will be joining you."

The others separated from us and made their way to the jail and the welcoming meal that Chelsea was preparing for us.

We stopped in front of the preacher and took him in.

He was tall and thin. A sort of pale if not pasty complexion that highlighted his long black hair, bushy black eyebrows, and black close-cut beard. His skin was pulled tight on his face giving him a fierce condemning look and his eyes were dark, penetrating and accusing. His features were such that should one feel the need to confess to this holy representative of the church, the journey to guilt would be short and harsh. His eyes alone would inflict shame upon the sinner.

I said, "Afternoon preacher."

At first, he said nothing, just clutched his Bible to his chest with long thin fingers. He just looked at me then Robert before he spoke. "Good afternoon, sir. I take it I am addressing the Deputy Marshals for this area?"

Robert said, "I am Deputy Marshal Barton, and this is Deputy Marshal Chambers of the Western District."

He nodded his head and said, "I am Brother Adrian Tremellius of The Church of Our Savior. I am pleased to meet you."

I found his voice, if not his tone condescending. I said, "What can we do for you preacher?"

He held up a finger and cast a reproachful look at me. "It is Brother Tremellius, Marshal." He paused, his tone softening. "Or, if you feel more comfortable, Brother Adrian will do."

Robert said, "What can we do for you Brother Adrian?"

He turned to Robert and said, "I only want to discuss what I saw earlier today when you and your posse arrived." He turned and pointed to his wagon and continued, "It will only take a moment of your time, but may I suggest that we go into my church out of this oppressive sun."

I looked at Robert than back to Brother Adrian. "Sure thing."

He nodded, turned about without a further word, and walked to his wagon. We fell in behind him and traded looks.

Brother Adrian stopped at the base of the stairs and waved us into the open door saying, "After you gentlemen, please."

As I started up the short staircase I looked over to the jail across the street. Jim, Bill, and Thad were standing on the porch, watching us closely.

I took off my hat; a habit developed from attending church as a youngster and walked into the wagon. It was impressive the way he had utilized the space. A craftsmen would have appreciated the workmanship of the little church. It was larger than I had expected. A double row of chairs was on the left, six deep, and a single row of chairs was on the right leaving a narrow walkway down the center. The interior, unlike the exterior was painted white which reflected the varied colors of the stained-glass windows down both sides. At the front was a small, raised platform, carpeted with a lectern draped in a purple velvet cloth that extended down to the floor with a large gold embroidered cross on the front.

I, being a tall man at over six feet, took notice that the ceiling replicated the pitched roof and extended beyond my reach.

I walked to the lectern and laid my hat on top of it as Robert too joined me at the front. I rested an arm on the slanted top surface and waited for Brother Adrian to address us.

He stood in the center of his church, or wagon, set his Bible on one of the chairs and opened his arms saying, "I witnessed the demonstration earlier today when you gentlemen arrived. It was most disturbing, to say the least."

I began to respond when he held up a hand stopping me.

He said, "I understand the dangers of what you men do. I merely want to offer my services as a Man of God to those families that may be affected by this terrible set of circumstances."

Robert said, "We thought you were going to condemn us in some manner Brother Adrian."

Brother Adrian said, "I may be a Man of God brothers, but I also understand the ways of the world." He put his hands together looked up and said, "A time to kill, and a time to heal; a time to break down, and a time to build up." He grinned. "Ecclesiastes three, three."

I said, "Well, Brother Adrian. We appreciate your services, and I think it best that you get with Mister Kramer at the funeral parlor. He would have all the particulars you may need."

Brother Adrian smiled again, showing off his white teeth. I found his smile, well, menacing.

He said, "Alas, I must push on in the morning brothers. I am heading into the frontier to seek out the settlers that may need to hear the word of God. So, I will go down to this Mister Kramer this evening and do whatever it is I can." He smiled again.

I was pleased to hear that he was leaving, thus saving me the conversation of asking him to relocate. I reached into my vest pocket and fished out a five-dollar gold piece, handing it to him.

"Here," I said, "take this as an offering of thanks for your services Brother Adrian."

He took it and said, "Bless you Brother Chambers. Mine is a poor existence and every little bit helps. Bless you."

I looked at Robert and said, "You ready to go Brother Robert. Dinner awaits."

Robert suppressed a laugh and said, "Lead the way Brother Wyatt."

I turned back to retrieve my hat from atop the lectern and as I did, I whacked my knee on the corner, sending a lightning bolt of pain down my leg. I bit my tongue to prevent the string of cuss words that wanted to escape my lips, and I immediately grabbed my knee and rubbed.

Brother Adrian came forward. "Are you all right Brother? My goodness that must have hurt."

I exercised my leg, back and too, making certain that it was still functional. Embarrassed, I grabbed my hat and straightened up.

"I am fine, just fine," I said. "Thank you again Brother Adrian."

We made our way to the exit, my knee throbbing a bit, and I hobbled down the stairs.

Brother Adrian joined us, put on a large black floppy hat against the sun. He bowed slightly and said, "Again, brothers. I thank you. I shall now make my way to the undertaker." He turned, walked away, and held up a hand saying loud enough for us to hear, "Go with God brothers."

As I watched him go, I felt relief that our meeting, short as it was, had come to an end.

Robert said with a laugh, "You see. God punished you be being a wise ass in his church."

I rubbed my knee again and said, "Oh, is that what he did?"

Robert laughed again. "I am sure that your offering has put you back in good graces with our Lord."

I shook my head and said, "Just put that five-dollar offering on the expense report for our little accountant friend in Austin." I looked at Robert and smiled. "C'mon. I want to tell Pepper that the preacher is leaving in the morning."

As we walked to Pepper's Place, we heard music coming from inside. As we neared, the distant sound of music became clearer to our hearing, and it became more of a noise than music with someone trying to sing along with a scratching fiddle and an off-key piano player.

We went through the saloon's louvered doors and took in the grandeur of the new watering hole for the town.

It was large and spacious. In front of us near two dozen round tables were placed on either side leaving a pathway down the center to the back of the saloon where an ornate sign hung above an arch announcing the entrance to the Poker Room. On the left side, extending under the second-floor wrap around balcony was a small restaurant with square tables covered with red and white checkered clothes.

The bar was on the right side, also under the second-floor wrap around balcony. It was long ornate polished woodwork accented with a brass foot rail running the length of the bar, and a beautiful silver trimmed mirror behind it reflecting the many bottles of liquor on multiple glass shelves.

We looked around as workers went from place to place, each with a job or tasking, each working towards the completion of the saloon while the musicians scratched out another tune, competing with the sounds of hammer and saw as the craftsmen continued to work despite the noise produced by the inept musicians.

We could not see Pepper among the many faces, but we saw a man behind the bar, and he seemed like a suitable candidate to inquire as to her whereabouts.

We stepped up to the bar and he came over and smiled, taking notice of our badges shining brightly on our clean clothes.

He stood just shy of our height, yet he was small of frame and features. Long brown sideburns coming down to his jaw, mustache, and goatee. He wore a black derby with a small red and white feather in the band; a flashy black vest trimmed in silver stitching over a white shirt and black string tie.

He took the stub of a cigar out of his mouth and said over the noise, "You fellas is the U.S. Marshals I expect."

I said, "That we are. I am Wyatt Chambers, and this here is Robert Barton."

He put the cigar back in his mouth and extended his hand to us. "Pleased to meet you fellas. Heard much about you and I saw you ride in earlier today. My name is Michael Andrew Piercefield. Folks just call me Drew."

We shook hands and I asked, "I hear a southern accent there my friend. Where do you hail from?"

He smiled and said, “Bryan County Georgia.”

I shook his hand again and said, “Son, I am from Coffee County Georgia.”

Drew smacked his open hand on the bar and said, “Well how ‘bout that! That calls for a drink!”

He turned around, grabbed a bottle from the shelf, and produced three glasses. As he was filling them, he asked, “Where you hail from Robert?”

Robert said, “Lancaster County Pennsylvania.”

Drew held up a glass in toast and said, “Well, we will not hold that against you Robert. You are a Texan now.” Drew held his glass up higher and said, “To Texas!”

We held our glasses up and repeated the toast as the musicians switched to another torturous tune.

“I surely hope Pepper is not thinking of hiring these hog-callers for entertainment,” I said.

Drew laughed and said, “Not if I have any say in the matter. These boys is givin’ me a powerful headache. Miss Pepper ain’t around at the moment.”

I raised my voice over the shrill singing, “No matter. Just tell her the preacher is leavin’ town in the morning.”

Robert added, “I think if this keeps up my ears will start bleeding.”

It was then a large, dirt covered cowboy stumbled through the swinging doors and made his way to the bar. He smacked his hand down, steadied himself against the bar and yelled, “Whiskey barkeep! Make it fast, I have a powerful thirst on.”

Drew looked at the drunk cowboy, took the cigar out of his mouth and said, “Sorry pard. We ain’t open yet. Not for a week or so. You can go down the street a way and get plenty to drink.”

He looked at Drew with anger and yelled, “Horseshit! I want a whiskey right now damn you!”

Drew put the cigar back in his mouth and said, “Look friend, we ain’t open for business. So, hit the trail.”

The drunk cowboy straightened up and announced, “Then I be comin’ back there and serve myself.”

I looked over and said, “I would not do that friend.”

The drunk said, “Who aims to keep me from doin’ what I want?”

Before I could answer Drew walked to the end of the bar and came out onto the floor. To my surprise I saw as he came around the bar that he was only four feet in height. I quickly looked over the bar and saw that he had been standing on a raised platform that went the length of the bar.

He stopped in front of the drunk.

The cowboy, towering over Drew looked down on him, laughed and said, "Go home little boy. You ain't supposed to be in here." He laughed even louder.

Robert stepped a bit closer, and I put my hand on his arm. I noticed that while the cowboy was looking down, Drew had slipped his right hand into his back pocket. I shook my head at Robert, waited, and watched.

Drew said with the cigar clenched in his teeth, "You gonna leave boy?"

The drunk cowboy looked surprised raised his arm up to strike and yelled out, "Why you little..."

Before the man could finish, Drew pulled his hand from his pocket and threw a perfect jab right into the crotch of the drunk cowhand, sending him crashing to the floor, clutching his bruised privates, moaning in agony.

Drew looked down on the man, removed the brass knuckles from his hand, returned them to his pocket, and walked back around the bar.

Standing in front of us he asked, "You fellas fancy a beer?"

CHAPTER EIGHTEEN

We had a beer and talked more with the new barkeep, learning about his past and what had brought him, like so many others west. His reasons were the same as the immigrants that came before him, the immigrants that came with him and the ones that had yet to arrive. He was in search of opportunity, adventure, a chance to carve out a new life from the ashes of a war-torn south. Cities, towns, and communities had been left in ruin from a vengeful army that had been set on bringing the war to the people in the hopes of inflicting enough suffering and force the conflict to a swift conclusion. It had worked.

The war had ended, the people had suffered but the misery went on, so they came west, bringing with them a renewed hope of a fresh start away from the devastation left behind. That is what brought Drew here. He left what little he had in Georgia and came west.

I sipped my beer and asked, "When did you make the journey out here Drew?"

He lit a fresh cigar and said through the rising smoke, "Right after Sherman brought his Yankees into Savannah." He puffed on his cigar, "Most folks had already left the area thinkin' he was gonna burn the town and everything around it like he did Atlanta. I had no family to speak of, so I left."

I shook my head and pulled on the cigar that Drew had given me. "Damn shame what happened to Atlanta. Damn shame."

Drew looked at Robert and said, "Do not mean to speak evil of you folks Robert. But Sherman raped Georgia when he marched through."

Robert said, "Not all of us agreed with the way he conducted his campaign."

I nodded in agreement with his statement. Had we this conversation a year ago, I might have taken issue with any man from the north when it came to the campaign through the south and Georgia in particular. Since that time, I had met many a man, Robert especially, from the north and heard that they too took issue with the conduct of Sherman's Army and his so-called March to the Sea. I also met those that not only agreed with the General's conduct but wished more harm on any Southerner regardless of whether he had taken up arms during the struggle or not.

My stomach soon reminded me that it was time to go. I said, "Drew, we must be going. If you could let Pepper know that the preacher will be gone in the morning and I asked not to hire these hog-callers on for entertainment." I extended my hand. "We appreciate the beer my friend and look forward to the Grand Opening."

Drew took my hand and said, "It has been a pleasure, Wyatt. No worries about these fellas, I am fixin' to show them the door." He turned to Robert. "It has been a pleasure to meet you, Robert. No offense given from our conversation."

Robert took his offered hand. "None taken Drew. I understand how you feel."

"Before you leave," Drew said stepping off his platform, "take a couple of pails of beer with you for all them folks you have over there."

We watched Drew as he muscled the pails under the tap, filled them and walked around to the opening in the bar, setting them on the floor.

I reached into my vest pocket and asked, "What do we owe you Drew?"

He pulled the cigar out of his mouth smiled and said, "Not a thing fellas. Least I could do for the men that burned The Heart of Dixie to the ground."

I exchanged a look with Robert, then picked up the two pails of beer.

Robert said as he pointed at me, "It was his pleasure."

Drew then handed Robert a fist full of cigars saying, "This is for later tonight for all you fellas. My way of sayin' thanks for what you done."

"We are grateful to you Drew," I said.

We departed, working our way past the many craftsmen, and made our way outside. Across the street we saw our three lawmen friends had been joined by Mark and Julius, awaiting our return.

Thad stepped to the top of the stairs as we approached and said, "We was concerned for you fellas, but I see what you have been up to."

I said, "Just wanted to tell Pepper that the preacher man will be leaving in the morning. Got to jawin' with the new barkeep."

Robert added, "He is also from Georgia so you can imagine that conversation."

They all laughed and followed us inside where I stopped and looked for a place to put the pails of beer. The table had been set in such a way as to accommodate all of us to a sit-down meal, leaving no room for the buckets.

Mark had grabbed the small secretary's desk by the door and cleared off the wanted bills. "Here Wyatt," he said as he slid it up near our banquet table.

Chelsea came in and with two hands set a large stew pot on the one free spot in the center of the table.

I inhaled the aroma of the contents and immediately set off a rebellious growl from my empty stomach. I asked, "How is it that you made this on such short notice?"

She wiped at her forehead and said, "Truth be told I was making this yesterday for your return and made too much." She looked around the room. "Which seems to be a good thing seeing how many hungry mouths we have here."

Everyone stood around, unmoving, as if we were waiting for the command to commence.

Chelsea put her hands on her hips and said, "Well boys, what the hell are you waiting for? Get started."

That was all it took as we raced for a seat at the table and what was sure to be a delicious and filling meal.

The meal was, in fact, delicious. In addition to the lamb stew, Chelsea, with help from Julius, a good cook in his own right, had made biscuits and cornbread. It gave us a choice to which we all took both.

The conversation at first was light as we devoured all that was in front of us, not wanting to waste the energy on anything but consuming the meal. Then, as seconds were passed around the conversations varied as each of us found a partner to talk to. We spoke of the robbery that currently had our attention. The journey home and the shootout with those that tried to ambush us. Each retelling their portion of events, injecting a bit of drama into the stories as if they were for entertainment, offering up humorous anecdotes though there was little humor in the facts of what had happened.

That was just the way it was. Ours was a dreadful task and in retelling the many tales' humor was a release from the stresses of living on the trail in pursuit of desperados. I had often wondered as a boy, when hearing such tales from those that had lived these events how they were able to laugh, joke and poke fun at fellow participants when it all sounded so desperate and dangerous to me. Now, sitting here among friends and fellow combatants, it was easy to understand the motivation to seek out a laugh, a smile or even just a look of awe.

During this time Clem and Pete had returned and announced that their task was complete, the horses had been returned and bedded down. We invited them to join us, and the boys dug into the meal with gusto.

The meal finished, the dirty crockery removed from the table we set about in the task of cleaning up after ourselves with the end goal to retire to the porch, enjoy a good smoke, beer, and fellowship.

Julius took Clem and Pete out back to collect up the guns, saddles and odds and ends we had obtained from our journey. The guns would be given to Mark and Chelsea as they can find either new owners, or spare parts for those in need. The horses, saddles, and such we will sell to the many ranchers in the area. When word got out about our booty, they would stand in line for the chance to make an inexpensive buy on the mounts.

We all retired to the porch, the day coming to an end as the sun made its way below the western horizon. Robert handed out the cigars to those that wished one and we all continued our conversations with beer in hand and cigar clenched in our teeth, sending a grey cloud of tobacco smoke surrounding us as we enjoyed the moment.

Across the street we saw the preacher, Brother Adrian Tremellius, walking back to his wagon church. He turned to our gathering and bowed slightly at the waist, acknowledging our presence.

Bill looked at the black clad man and asked me, "What did you think of the preacher Wyatt?"

I pulled the cigar from my mouth, studied the man as he retired to his church and said, "Odd sort of fella to be sure."

Robert said, "Not a man that exudes the presence of God you ask me."

Julius stepped to the edge of the porch. "When he first came to town he came over here and asked about you Cap'n. You and Sergeant Major Robert."

"Oh," I asked. "He ask for us by name?"

"No sir," Julius said. "Just asked if you was around. I tol him you and the Sergeant Major will be back directly." Julius paused. "I did not feel good talkin' to him. Made me feel cold, he did."

Chelsea looked concerned and asked, "How do you mean Julius?"

He looked at her and said, "He ain't no preacher man for sure. Not in his heart he ain't. That fella is full of hatred."

I put the cigar in my mouth and thought that Julius had an interesting observation. I too felt as he did. I did not feel the presence of any Holy

Spirit or otherwise goodness when I spoke with the man. Those that felt the calling to serve usually projected if you will, their love of the Lord and shared that with others. Quoting scripture did not make you a Holy Man any more than putting doctor tools in my hands, make me a surgeon.

"No matter," I said. "He is lightin' out in the morning, and we will be rid of him."

"Amen Brother Wyatt," Robert said laughing.

Before I could respond Robert told the tale of our meeting with Brother Adrian, of me having whacked my knee on the lectern as a form of punishment thrust upon me and of my donation to the preacher man's cause of spreading the word. It brought on laughs, good natured ridicule, and jokes from all.

Still, I thought. There was something about the fella that I found disheartening.

The hour grew late, and our gathering broke up. Mark and Chelsea returned to their shop as we settled on sleeping arrangements in the jail. It was not long before we all fell into a well-earned slumber.

Sometime during the night, while in a deep sleep he came to me. His face was how I remembered it. His smile, reflecting a mischievous intent, his unruly blonde hair under his grey kepi, his short cavalry jacket with two gold stripes on his sleeves, he came to me. Unlike before when he led us through the desert that night, silent at the head of my horse as he took us to safety, this time he spoke.

He spoke of our friendship, our time in the saddle together, the good times we had and the bad. He spoke of our last moments together, the last battle that took him from this world and left me questioning the merits of our cause, mourning his loss.

His tone was reassuring; his message was one of admiration, love and understanding. He then apologized to me. He apologized for disobeying my final order. He told me that he heard my command but felt compelled to carry forward, feeling indestructible, immune from danger as he sought out the enemy. He said he was sorry for having disregarded my order to stand fast.

He also said goodbye.

I woke with a start, catching my breath as I looked around the darkened room. I listened to the sounds of the others as they snored, they breathed in and out, lost in their own dreams.

I quietly put my pants on, my boots and made my way out of the room, out the back door and out into the darkened night. I slowly walked trying to clear my head, shake the visions away from my waking mind wondering if it had been real.

I found myself alone, away from the jail. I looked up at the star filled sky and felt a tear roll down my cheek. I said softly, "Goodbye Cleet. I shall always miss you, my friend."

I walked back to the jail and went inside. Looking at my time piece under the low light I saw that it was close to the waking hour and decided to start the day. I felt refreshed and unburdened. Unburdened of my troubled memories. It had happened just as Long Buffalo had said. It came upon me when I least expected it and in the form of my friend reassuring me that there was no blame in what happened. It was war, it was what we did, and it was over.

I sat in the darkened room at my desk and reached for my tobacco and pipe, filling it to the top and striking a match to the dried leaves bringing on the desired smooth taste of the fine Virginian shag.

As I was smoking in the darkness, I heard light footfalls coming around the corner from the back. Robert, pistol at his side came into view, looked at me and breathed a sigh of relief.

He asked, "What goes Wyatt?"

I exhaled the smoke and said, "Nothing Robert. All is well."

He laid his revolver down on the desktop, and even in the darkness, I could see concern on his face. He remained silent and sat on the corner of the desk.

"I swear to you my friend, all is right with the world," I said.

Robert nodded his head, understanding my meaning. He said, "That is good to know Wyatt."

Just then Julius came around the corner, shotgun in hand. He said, "Lord Almighty I thought I heard somethin'."

I chuckled and said, "There is no sneaking around with you fellas on the job." I stood and asked Julius, "How about some coffee. The others will be awake soon."

Julius went off to the kitchen, Robert returned to the living quarters, and I continued smoking my pipe in the darkness, enjoying the solitude for the time being. The dog, having bedded down with Julius, came in and sat next to me searching for attention.

I reached down and scratched behind his ear. "A good morning to you, my friend. Had a restful sleep, did you?"

Julius came into the room. "Coffee be ready directly Cap'n."

“That is fine Julius,” I answered as I continued to stroke the dog’s ear. “Have you named this fine critter yet?”

Julius said, “I have not. I cannot think of a name for him.”

I looked at the dog and recalled his swift action in taking down Horace the day before. I said, “How about Argos?”

Julius was thoughtful for a moment then asked, “What does it mean Cap’n?”

I said, “In Hebrew it means swift or quick. In Greek mythology it means shinning and a city that was known for strength.”

Julius smiled, showing his white teeth. “I like that just fine Cap’n. I surely do. It fits him well.”

I looked down at the dog and asked, “How does that suit you, my friend? Do you like the name Argos?”

The dog stood looked at me, then Julius, wagged his tail and began barking.

I laughed and said, “It is settled then. Argos it is.”

“Reckon so Cap’n,” Julius agreed.

As Argos went around the room happily announcing to all he had been given a name I heard the stirrings of the others in the back. Moans and groans came from the room as they were jolted out of their slumber. It would seem that they were none too pleased to have their sleep interrupted by the energetic and loud pronouncements of our canine companion.

The day now began for us all. W.B.D. Burns and Thadius Polehouse would be hitting the trail to return to their own jurisdictions while the rest of us would decide on how we can further pursue the robbers, the big Indian that has eluded us thus far and hopefully, the recovery of the stolen money.

Julius made breakfast for us while we made ourselves ready for the day. While performing my morning necessaries I recalled that Jeremiah had passed on two correspondents to me the afternoon before. One for Robert and one for myself. I retrieved them and handed Robert his, knowing it was a letter from Gwendoline in San Antonio, while mine was from my lovely Arabella all the way in Kentucky.

I found a quiet place on the porch to read the letter while thinking of her angelic face, soft voice, and the feel of her hand in mine. As I sat in the chair, I noticed that Brother Tremellius had departed for places unknown. Good riddance I thought.

Her letter was full of love and hope. She spoke of our future together, the prospect of a family, a home of our own and a lifetime together. I too wanted these things and often thought about them, having stated the same in my return correspondents to her. We both decided that though it was going to be so, the time at present was not such that we could commit to such a venture with the assurances that our future would be secure enough to raise a family. Too many factors dictated otherwise for us. From the current state of the security of Texas to the rampant crime forcing us to be on the trail more than being at home.

There was even talk by some of taking up arms once more against the Federal Government in the hopes of restoring the Confederacy. These are the things we thought about when we planned for our future. Until then, we reaffirmed our love for each other and our commitment to make it happen.

I returned inside and found the others at the table drinking coffee and patiently awaiting the morning meal.

Thad asked as I sat at the table, "What the hell was that dog yapping about this morning Wyatt?"

I poured my coffee, smiled, and answered, "He was happy to finally get a name befitting his personality."

Jim said, "Julius told me you named him Argos. Fitting name for him Wyatt."

Bill looked around the table and finally asked, "Okay. One of you fellas' care to tell me if it means anything?"

Robert said, "In Hebrew it means swift or fast. Greek mythology it means strength or something like that."

Bill shook his head. "You boys with your educated ways." He laughed. "I would have named him Dog."

Julius brought in two plates, one of fried eggs and one of bacon. Once he sat at the table, we all attacked the food forgetting our manners for this meal as there were no women present, and we surrendered to our morning hunger.

After we finished the meal, I looked through the destruction we left behind on the table, the floor and even our clothes. Six hungry men had willingly cast all manners aside in an attempt to satisfy our hunger in the shortest time available to us. I for one, guilty of such an egregious infraction of table manners felt a bit embarrassed but did so with a full belly. Even Argos had been satisfied with our simple meal as everyone offered him samples of the fare.

I said, “I need to walk this off. I believe I will take my clothes down to the Chinese laundry.” I stood from the table. “Robert, Jim. You boys have anything you want cleaned?”

Robert said, “I do. I will go and get them.”

Jim said, “I have a couple of things to go.”

Thad looked at Bill and said, “Reckon we can go down to the store and get some grub for the return trip.”

Robert said, “I will go see Jeremiah and get another message off to the Judge then check in with Doc about our prisoner.”

We collected up our plates and soon set about our tasks.

CHAPTER NINETEEN

I folded and rolled my clothes tightly and repeated the same for both Jim and Robert's clothes making them easier to carry under one arm, leaving my right hand, my shooting hand, free. It was an old habit, one that I would not soon abandon.

We all left the jail about the same time. Robert striking out for the telegraph office, Bill and Thad for the general store, Jim elected to remain behind and tend to the animals while I set off for the laundry.

It was a beautiful day, one that promised to be hot again, but, at the moment, it was tolerable, and I walked down the street greeting passersby with a nod of my head, a simple greeting of the day or a wave of the hand. Folks were out and about beginning their day, each with a destination in mind or a task that required their attention. It was a day like any other.

As I walked down the street, an uneasy feeling came over me. As on the trail when I felt as though we were being dogged, I thought I was being watched. Not by the curious towns people, wanting to know of our exploits, but by someone with other intentions.

As I walked, slowing my pace a bit, I casually looked about trying to see what was out of place. A person or a thing perhaps. Something that caused this uneasy feeling I had. I searched faces, followed movements and actions of those nearby. My eyes searched store fronts, boardwalks, and alleys, even the space between horses tied off at the many hitching posts thinking that someone may be lying in wait to ambush me, assassinate me.

I stopped at a store front, one with general merchandise, and looked in the window. I used the glass like a mirror, searching the crowd of folks moving around behind me through the uneven panes of glass. It was then I found them.

Across the street there were two men. There was nothing distinctive in their appearance other than they were covered in trail dust, it was more what they were doing, or more precisely not doing. They were just standing near a hitching rail, with no horses tied off, just watching. They seemed to be making a point of not watching me while they stole extended glances in my direction. They were both heeled and wore leather chaps like cowhands.

I slowly moved away from the window and back out to the street, continuing my walk to the laundry. My mind raced as to what could or would happen when and if they made their move. The many scenarios I thought through all amounted to one thing. It was me against them and I needed an edge. Something to make them overconfident, secure in the knowledge that it was two against one and it was they that had the upper hand.

I soon found myself in front of Mark and Chelsea's shop and a plan came together. I went inside.

Mark was at the counter and looked up. "Well, good morning, Wyatt. How are you this beautiful morning?"

I put the bundles of clothes on the glass countertop and said, "I need you to look over my shoulder out on the street and tell me what you see."

He sensed the urgency in my voice and without question, knowing what it was he was to be looking for he glanced over my shoulder, not making a show of it.

He said, "I see two men covered in trail dust. Leather chaps, pistols. One has a green vest the other a brown one. They both have beards, dark hair."

"What are they doing right now," I asked without looking.

He looked again and said, "They seem to be making a show of not doing anything. Not very convincing though." Mark looked at me. "Do you know them, Wyatt?"

I shook my head. "I do not. I had a feeling of being dogged when I left the jail and spotted these two." I thought for a minute then said, "I need a weapon that I can hide in these clothes. If I come out without my Walker, it may bring suspicion."

Mark looked at the three bundles of clothes and said, "I have just the thing." He went to the back of his shop and when he returned, Chelsea was with him.

I said, "Chelsea, I need you to stay in the back for a time. I think I have two fellas out there that will try to assassinate me before I make it to the laundry."

Chelsea looked at me with alarm and Mark put his hand on her forearm. "Do not react dear. They are watching us now. Just go to the back and bring me the box of Snider shells."

She inhaled deeply and said, “Right away.”

When she left Mark put a large wood box on the counter directly in front of me, denying the two on the street a view of what he had. He lifted the hinged lid back, removed a gun from inside and in a quick motion pushed the box to the floor behind him.

I looked at the gun, whistled and asked, “What the hell is that thing?”

Without holding it up in his typical showmen style of selling his wares, he said as he slid it closer to me, “It is a Howdah Pistol. English, and shoots a five hundred seventy-seven caliber metal cartridge,”

I looked at the twin barrels, side by side with two separate hammers and two triggers, much like the shotguns we carried only this was a pistol. It was massive, as large if not just a bit larger than my Walker Colt. I reached down and lifted it, turned it over in my hands admiring the woodwork and metal fixtures, the curved wood grip. Heavy but not so as to require both hands to use.

Chelsea came in, trying to hide her anxiety and placed a large paper carton on the counter and stood next to Mark looking over my shoulder at the two men on the street. She too was able to spot them by their lack of activity while trying to act as though they were engaged.

She said, “Not very good at hiding themselves, are they?”

I gave her a reassuring smile. “No, they are not.”

Mark opened the carton and pulled two massive metallic cartridges out of the box. They had to have been more than a half inch in diameter and close to three inches in length. Again, I whistled.

Mark broke open the breech of the pistol, again, much like a shotgun, inserted the two cartridges and handed it back to me.

He said, “Now that thing will kick like a mule when you fire it. Damn thing was made to bring down a charging Rhino or Tiger.”

I took one of the bundles of clothes and unrolled them putting the pistol on the end, cocked both hammers and rolled the pistol up in the dirty laundry. “Well,” I began, “I just need it to bring down two assassins.” I smiled again trying to put them at ease, though my heart was racing. As an afterthought I grabbed four more shells and put them in my pocket.

Mark asked, “What do you plan on doing Wyatt?”

I said, “Gonna take my laundry down to get it cleaned.” I picked up the bundle, leaving the other two behind and turned to leave.

Mark called after me, “I will be ready to back you up Wyatt, count on it.”

I looked over my shoulder and said, "I know Mark. Just be ready for anything."

I went to the door, looked through the glass at the two cowhands, opened it, and stepped outside.

I walked to the edge of the porch and paused before stepping down. My concern was not so much for myself but the people of the town. The last thing I wanted was for them to be caught up in a street fight. I had to keep the assassins close when the fight began.

I stepped off the last step and turned to resume my trek to the Chinese laundry, though I was shy two bundles of clothes, I still had to act as if I was ignorant of their presence.

I had not gone far when I heard a woman's high pierced scream, and a man call out to me. I turned around.

"Marshal! We is callin' you out," yelled the man in the green vest.

He stood in the center of the street next to the man with the brown vest who held a woman by the back of her hair, with his gun pointed at her head. The two of them were grinning.

I yelled, "Let the woman go! She has no part in this!"

Green Vest shook his head and the two of them stepped closer, Brown Vest pushing the women in front of him. Brown Vest said, "No sir! We will let the woman go when you drop your gun belt Marshal!"

Folks out on the street scattered and sought cover. A few of the brave ones, brave or just plain stupid, crouched low along the boardwalks hoping to witness a shootout. The woman screamed again and began to cry.

Brown Vest shook her by the hair and yelled, "You shut your mouth woman!"

Green Vest laughed and again, the two of them came closer.

I said again, "Let her go, this is between us!"

The two of them took another step closer. The woman was sobbing uncontrollably now as she held onto the hand that held onto her.

Green Vest was getting impatient and yelled, "Drop your gun, Marshal! I ain't gonna tell you again, or the woman dies!"

I gritted my teeth hoping, almost willing them to come closer. Just two more feet and I have them.

"Okay," I said still holding the bundle of laundry under my left arm. "I will drop my gun belt."

I slowly reached down with my right hand and unfastened my belt at the buckle. For some odd reason, the memory of the day Chelsea had given me the belt and holster flashed through my mind. I continued to unfasten it.

The belt came free, unwrapped from around my waist and I held it up and in front of me showing the two gunmen that I was unarmed.

"Now, let the women go," I said.

Green Vest laughed and with a motion of his head signaled to his partner to release the woman, which he did.

The woman, still sobbing stumbled for cover while I stood there holding my rig above the ground, waiting for the woman to get clear and hoping the assassins stepped just a bit closer.

Brown Vest holstered his iron, much to my surprise, and the two of them stood there looking at me.

Green Vest said, "Now drop that belt boy."

As he said this the two of them took three steps closer to me. That was all I needed, and I dropped the belt. When it hit the ground, I quickly moved the bundle of clothes with the Howdah Pistol concealed within in front of me, put my right hand on the pistol grip and my finger on the first of the two triggers.

Sensing something was amiss, Green Vest went for his pistol, but he was too late as I pulled the first trigger.

A large flame erupted from the end of the bundle of clothes as the gun roared like thunder and sent the large caliber bullet right into the chest of Green Vest, lifting him off his feet. The force of the impact threw him back a good five feet where he landed in a cloud of dust, rolled ass overhead twice before coming to a stop, face down.

His partner watched in shock, reached for his pistol and as soon as he turned to me, I let loose with the second barrel, sending him airborne where he landed flat on his back with an audible thud, kicking up a cloud of street dust.

The bundle of clothes, on fire now, I cast aside bringing the pistol out, broke it open and reloaded both barrels. I cocked back both hammers and held the pistol at the ready, searching for another target.

Mark joined me, pistol in hand and covered my back while Chelsea stood on the porch, holding a shotgun, searching for a target.

I reached down and picked up my Walker and handed the Howdah Pistol to Mark while I strapped on my gun belt. Once done I took the Howdah back and looked at the two dead assassins.

I was about to thank Mark for backing me up when shots rang out further down the street.

I said, "Robert is in trouble."

I began to run down the street with Mark at my side, searching for yet another ambush along the way.

Folks were running about. All were seeking cover, running from the danger as more shots rang out. Screams of panic, doors being slammed shut, people running and yelling as mayhem erupted in the once quiet town. Everyone was running away from the gunfire while we ran towards it.

As we neared the scene, we saw clouds of dust and spent powder hanging in the air. I saw Robert standing in the center of the street crouched low turning in a tight circle. To the right I saw Thad standing over what looked to be Sheriff W.B.D. Burns laying on his side propped up on his elbow with his pistol pointed out. Thad too was searching for a target.

I called out, "Robert, Thad it is me and Mark comin' in."

Robert responded, "Come ahead but keep a look out for more assassins."

As we neared Robert, we noticed the bodies strewn about the street. I did a quick count as I ran past. Six lay in various positions of death. Face up, face down, on their sides with guns in hand, blood on their clothes, eyes open, unseeing the world they left behind.

Mark went to Thad and Bill while I stood with Robert. I asked as I joined him in his search, "How many?"

He looked around and said, "Six. We got them all but one of them shot Bill in the leg before he fell."

I looked over at Bill, he waved that he was okay as Mark tended to his leg, Thad guarding his two friends at his feet.

Just then a short round man, gun belt with a holstered pistol around his thick belly and a five-point star on his shirt waddled up to us. His pudgy face, drenched in sweat and bulbous nose showed his love for alcohol. He was our newly elected county Sheriff, Wilhelm Strasburger.

He stopped, winded from his long walk a few doors down, hiked up his pants and said in a thick German accent, "What is it that you men are doing?" He pointed around the street at the bodies. "You men have killed these other men!"

I looked at him, trying hard to contain the anger that welled up in me. I said through clenched teeth, "Where in the hell have you been Sheriff?"

He looked around as if he were searching for an answer or an excuse. "I have been working at the jail, I have been."

I shook my head and remained silent.

Robert said, "Well Sheriff. You and your deputy have a mess to clean up, so get to it."

Sheriff Strasburger huffed and puffed, waving his arms around and said, "But I have nuthing to do with this shooting. You is the Marshals and it is you who must clean this up."

Thad stepped over, holstered his pistol, and said, "Not so, Sheriff. This falls to you my friend so hop to it!"

Strasburger huffed and puffed a bit more and asked, "Who is you?"

Thad pointed to his own star and said, "I am the Sheriff of Bandera County. I know what is and what ain't the job of sheriff." He snapped his fingers in the smaller man's face and said again, "Now get to it boy!"

Strasburger turned and walked away mumbling in German as he went.

Thad asked to no one in particular, "How did that fella get elected?"

I said, "Damn if I know." I looked at Bill as Mark was helping him to his feet. "How is Bill?"

Thad looked back at his friend and said, "Went clean through. Still, we need the Doc."

Robert said, "We will grab him on the way back to the jail."

I looked up the street. "Reckon we need to check on Julius and Jim."

Robert asked, "Thad, can you and Mark see to Bill while we go to the jail?"

Thad said, "Go on boys, git."

We took off at a run, uncertain as to what we would find but we felt that they were safe as we did not hear any gun shots from that side of town. But still, we had to be sure, so we wasted no time.

As we passed Mark and Chelsea's shop I stopped while Robert went ahead. Chelsea was still on the porch with the shotgun. I said, "Mark is fine. Bill took one in the leg, we need to fetch the Doc, we are going to bring everyone down to the jail for a spell."

She forced a smile and said, "Okay Wyatt."

We went a few doors down and went into Doc's office. As we did, I was surprised that he had not been out on the street, ready to tend to those that were wounded. When we walked in, we found the Doc, sitting in a chair his face white staring at the floor with a blank look.

I approached him slowly recognizing shock when I saw it. I said softly, "Doc, what is the matter?"

He looked up, inhaled sharply, and said, "I went to check on the prisoner this morning and when I went upstairs," he sighed heavily. "He is dead."

Chelsea put a hand to her mouth.

"What happened Doc," I asked.

He lowered his head and said quietly, "Someone cut his throat during the night."

CHAPTER TWENTY

I looked at Doc, turned and ran up the stairs to his makeshift hospital. I took the steps two at a time and burst through the door and stopped dead in my tracks as the sight unfolded before me, my mind trying to absorb the image my eyes held.

On the far side of the room the white walls, white sheets and what had been a remarkably clean floor was mixed with a dark crimson. It was almost brown as the blood had dried. The bed was covered in dried blood as was the walls and floor.

As I neared, I had to look twice for what I was sure was the body of the Thorton boy. His right arm hung limply over the edge of the bed; the linen sheet was still pulled up to his chest. His head was tilted back exposing the awful wound. The attack had been quick as it was terrible.

I hesitated for a moment before I continued deeper into the room. There was one thing I had to check before I returned downstairs. I knew the man was dead, that was a certainty, but what else had been done to him is what I needed to ascertain. I had to will my legs forward.

I approached the body and looked down. His mouth was open, and I knew without a closer examination that his tongue was gone.

The Indian had been here.

I looked up at the ceiling and inhaled deeply then took one more look, turned and walked over to the other bed on the opposite side, removed the bedsheet and brought it back, covering the body.

"Sorry kid," I said as I walked out of the room.

Downstairs I instructed Hy to gather his doctor tools and with he and Chelsea left his office and headed for the jail.

Thad and Robert were on the porch as we approached. Both armed with long guns standing guard in case there were more assassins about, just waiting for an opportunity.

Doc and Chelsea went in without a word while I stood at the top of the steps looking out over the deserted town. Everyone remained indoors, safe, and secure behind their walls as we stood out in the open, ready to meet the danger.

Robert had seen Doc and Chelsea go inside. He asked, "Doc does not look too well." He looked at me. "Something happen Wyatt?"

The images of the Thorton kid were still fresh in my mind. I said, "The prisoner is dead." I paused and looked at Robert and Thad. "Same as the others."

Thad stepped closer. "You mean that Indian got to him?"

I merely nodded my head and remained silent.

Robert and Thad said nothing. They, like me, were getting tired of living in the destructive wake of this murderous villain. All those we sought out, chased, tracked across three counties were being brutally murdered by someone we had only heard about. Someone we had never seen, an evil apparition that moved silently about leaving dead men behind as his calling card. His way of telling us he was here among us yet unseen by the living except at brief moments. He was almost teasing us, telling us he was real by leaving yet another poor discarded soul, only to disappear into the wilderness along a forgotten trail.

I asked, "Who do we have at the back?"

"Julius and Jim," Robert answered.

Thad said, "With Bill gettin' shot and these bastards tryin' to kill us we are gonna stay on for a few more days Wyatt. You boys need help and you damn sure ain't gettin' none from that Sheriff."

I nodded, suddenly exhausted, turned and went inside.

Doc was working on Bill's leg. He had it elevated on a chair, pant leg cut away while Chelsea, easily returning to her previous vocation, assisted Doc in his procedure. Mark was sitting on one of our two desks, silently watching.

Bill looked as I came in and said, "You look like hell Wyatt." He pointed to the table, a bottle of whiskey sitting all alone in the center. "Take a couple of drinks my friend. You will feel right as rain in no time."

I suddenly realized I still had the Howdah Pistol in my hand. I took off my hat, set the pistol down on the table and sat looking at Bill with admiration and respect. Here was a man with a bullet hole in his leg telling me I looked like hell. I had met some real tough fellas in my time, but W.B.D. Burns was one of the toughest.

I poured a drink, threw it back and said, "Thad tells me you are stayin' on a couple more days."

Bill laughed and replied, "Well we ain't gonna leave you fellas now. No sir. You can use the extra gun hands."

I smiled. "We are obliged to you and Thad."

Robert came into the room, leaving the front door open, and sat at the table across from me. He grabbed the bottle of whiskey, filled a glass for himself and refilled mine. He said, "Here is to surviving another one." He threw the drink back.

I raised my glass and said, "Amen to that."

The room fell into an odd silence as each of us went through the day's events. It had started as any normal day and ended in a tragic gun battle in the center of our town.

I suddenly remembered the task that had sent me down the street. I uttered, "Ah, hell. I left a couple of bundles of clothes in your shop Mark."

Before Mark could answer Robert interrupted and said, "You left with three bundles Wyatt."

I cleared my throat and said, "Yes, I did Robert." I picked up the Howdah Pistol. "I wrapped this gun in one of the bundles and hid it from those two fellas that wanted to shoot me down. I had no idea the power of this fine pistol." I set the gun down. "It lit the bundle of clothes on fire. I reckon they are smoldering in the street, nothin' but ashes now."

Robert smiled. "That is one powerful gun. Shame about your clothes Wyatt. But I suppose it was for a good reason when you give it a think."

I nodded and replied, "Glad you feel that way Robert." I turned and looked at him with a smile. "Cause they were your clothes."

Robert just stared at me with gaping mouth.

Doc, Mark, Chelsea, and Bill tried to suppress their laughter. They all turned away from Robert in a pitiful attempt to be polite but failed. The humor of the incident was there for all to behold, and the room soon erupted in laughter. Even Robert joined in.

That was all it took to get our spirits back up, our minds back on track as the weight of the morning's activity was lifted from our collective shoulders. Now was the time for planning. Now was the time for action. True, we had our backs to the wall, but we were far from beaten.

I held the big pistol up and looked at Mark. "Mark, I would like to add this to my arsenal. Name your price and I will gladly pay cash on the barrel."

"Only if you let Chelsea make you a holster for it," Mark said.

"Done," I answered. "But make it for my saddle. If I carry two pistols of this weight I will not be able to walk straight nor keep my pants up."

Again laughter.

Thad stuck his head in and asked, "What is so funny?"

Chelsea, still chuckling answered, "Oh, twas nothing. Wyatt just burned Robert's clothes when he fired off that big gun."

Thad said, "That was what that explosion was? Damnation, I thought it was cannon fire." He laughed and went back to the porch.

Doc stood, stretched out his back and pointed at Bill saying, "Mind that leg for a couple of days. I will be around to change the bandage tomorrow." He turned to me, a serious look on his face. "I am going to grab the undertaker and take care of that kid in my surgery."

I stood and reached into my pocket. I pulled out ten dollars in coin and handed it to Hy. "Give this to Mister Kramer and tell him to give the kid a decent send off."

Hy took the money, pocketed it. "I will Wyatt. Thanks."

Bill said, "Even though the boy was a no account, he did not deserve to go out that way." He looked at the Doc. "You be mindful out there Doc. That Indian is still runnin' about."

Doc said, "Ah hell Sheriff. If he were gonna kill me, he would have done it last night."

We all watched Doc Averbeck pick up his bag and leave. The weight of the world seemed to be on his shoulders.

I looked about the room, my thoughts moving towards our next step in our strange pursuit of those that have been bringing death upon us. All of us wanted to bring this to its conclusion. I felt that it was now more than recovering the money lost in the robbery, though that was the initial objective of our cause, we had to remain alive to complete our quest. We had been thrust into a world where life did not matter to those that had perpetrated this crime.

I said, "I reckon we should figure out what we do next."

Robert stood and said, "I will get Jim in here, he may have some ideas."

We all gathered around the table while Julius remained out back with Argos and Thad stationed himself in the open door, still maintaining his vigil of guarding the front.

I began the informal gathering by stating the obvious. "I, for one, am at a loss as to where we go from here."

Jim said, "You ain't the only one. Seems every time we figure out something these fellas go off in another direction."

Thad added, "They are keepin' us guessing for certain."

Bill shook his head and said, "I do not believe that is the case. Whatever we do makes these boys answer back. They know we are hot on their heels, and they are sure tryin' to stop us." He waved a hand in the air. "Hell, they tried to kill us, twice."

"Reckon we are makin' them a bit nervous," I said.

Robert said, "We only know that some big Indian is killing anyone involved in this and they got their information from someone in the know. The bank layout, our pursuit of the wagon, the switching of the safe."

Chelsea sat forward in her chair and asked of no one in particular, "Have you been sending wires since the beginning of this adventure?"

I said, "We have. Except when the wires were cut and we came back here."

The room fell silent.

Jim said, "Someone is reading our messages."

"Well, shit," uttered Bill.

Jim said, "Hell, that could be anyone. We have been sending out wires from the first day. Half of Austin knows what happened."

"Reckon we will just have to stop sending out messages for a while," I said.

Robert asked, "Then where do we go from here?"

Before anyone could answer, Thad spun around and walked outside. We heard him say, "That be far enough soldier. State your business!"

I grabbed the Howdah Pistol and went to the door, looked out only to have my view blocked by Thad's large frame. I stepped out onto the porch, Robert right behind me.

Standing at the foot of the steps were two Federal Soldiers. A major and a sergeant. I found the scene a bit humorous as the sergeant towered over the major. He had to have been a foot and a half taller, thick in chest with a shockingly large mustache joining his low sideburns across his cheeks. His blonde hair stood out against the blue kepi on his head. Thick gauntlets on his hands, his left resting on his saber, his right on top of his flap holster, he stood erect and tall that spoke of a disciplined trooper.

The major, thin, and short, not so as our new friend at Pepper's Place, but small none the less, stood next to him. His cavalry hat, folded up on the right side, sat squarely on his head. He too sported a mustache. Whereas the sergeant's blonde hair stood out against the blue uniform, the major's hair was black, matching the deep dark blue of his jacket. His mustache was thick across his upper lip and curled upwards at the ends. On his chin was a small square patch of black hair, or dirt for all I could tell.

Though his posture was not as disciplined as the sergeant, he grasped the handle of his saber with his left hand, his right hung down by his side, he tried to look the part of a serious man.

The major spoke to Thad, "Now just hold on there, sir. I have business with the Deputy Marshals of this district." He tilted his head slightly, cocked an eyebrow in an almost arrogant gesture, and grinned. "Would you be one of the two gentlemen to which I am inquiring about?"

Thad kept his rifle at the ready and said, "Who might you be?"

The major cleared his throat, stood a bit taller and said, "I sir, am Major A.J. Purdy from Austin." He turned and gestured with his hand, "This is Sergeant Archibald O'Hanlon, my aide to camp."

Thad said, "That a fact?"

Major Purdy was growing impatient. "It is so, sir. To whom am I addressing?"

Thad cradled his rifle across his chest and said, "You are addressing Thadius Dexter Polehouse, Sheriff of Bandera County."

I was about to step forward when Robert put his hand on my arm. I turned and looked at him, he shook his head, staying silent. I nodded slightly and stepped next to Thad.

Looking down at the stuffy little major I said, "I am Deputy Marshal Chambers. What can I do for you?"

He stepped closer. "Ah, at last we meet sir. I have come about the missing payroll and to hear a first-hand account as to why it has not yet been recovered."

Try as I might, I could not find anything about this arrogant fella that did not bring my temper to rise. While the sergeant stood silent, keeping his disciplined posture, the major began to shift his weight from foot to foot, giving us the evil eye as my mother would say. He was obviously impatient at this perceived delay at gaining entrance to parlay with us, and I am sure the hot sun did not make his disposition any better. I was beginning to enjoy myself at causing this Yankee annoyance.

I decided that I needed to hear the man out and give Robert the opportunity to express his concerns, in his own manner.

I said, "You best come inside then major."

The major turned to his aide to camp and said, "Sergeant, considering all this brouhaha of this morning, I believe it best if you remain out here on guard."

The sergeant clicked his heels together, looked down at the smaller man and said, "Yes sir!"

I turned and went inside, Robert right on my heels.

Robert whispered to me, "I do not believe this is the Purdy I once knew Wyatt."

I nodded and whispered back, "I will let you feel him out. I will stick with the business at hand."

The major came in, crossed the threshold, and surveyed the environment before him. He looked around, saying nothing and clicked his tongue while shaking his head. Try as I might, I could not find a redeeming quality in the man.

Playing the part until I could get more out of him, I made introductions around the room. He was gracious when introduced to Chelsea but not so much with the rest of our group.

Chelsea excused herself, claiming that she was going to prepare the evening meal and Mark went outside to join Julius in the rear guard.

As we seated ourselves around the table Robert introduced himself to the major, only getting a neutral response which I found curious. Thad stood at the doorway, listening intently to our conversation.

I began. "So, what is it that you wish to know Major Purdy?"

The major twisted the ends of his black mustache with his fingertips and said, "I am here on behalf of the general and he, as well as myself, would like to know why you have not recovered the payroll."

I said, "We are working on it. We have been sidetracked with other issues of late."

He looked at me, wide eyed for a moment and said, "Sidetracked." He paused. "Oh, yes. You are referring to this morning. I am sorry, I fail to see what a street fight has to do with the missing safe."

Bill leaned closer and, not bothering to hide his anger said, "This morning had everything to do with the missing safe Major. We are getting close to finding these desperados and they tried to assassinate us."

Purdy said, "Really? How dramatic."

Jim added, "Did you come down here just to insult us Major, or is there a point to this visit?"

"Oh yes, gentlemen," he began, "there is a point to all of this. I will return to Austin and make a recommendation to the general that if I find you are incompetent in your duties, I will have you removed and as such have this investigated by the army." He paused. "Frankly, I was against having your involvement from the very start. I do not trust the loyalties of the parties conducting this inquiry."

I sat back and took in a deep breath.

CHAPTER TWENTY-ONE

Robert leaned forward in his chair and looked right at the offending man across from him and said, "Just what loyalties are you referring to Major Purdy?"

Purdy returned the stare without flinching and grinned ever so slightly. He said, "Well sir, I can see you are a man of the North and as such your allegiance is not in question." He looked at the rest of us before he continued. "The rest of you gentlemen have Southern roots, and I suspect fought for the rebel army. So, I doubt you are all that anxious to work towards a successful conclusion in this matter, seeing that the money belongs to the federal government."

We remained silent.

He added, "I also suspect that none of you has been granted a pardon for your actions during the war, so I feel you cannot be trusted with such a major undertaking."

My anger was fixin' to boil over, however, I felt he would derive some satisfaction at seeing me lose my temper. I said softly yet firmly with all due conviction, "No man in this room needs a pardon."

Purdy took a snuff box from inside his jacket, took a delicate snort, and said, "That remains to be seen Deputy Chambers."

Bill said through clenched teeth, "You little bastard! You best watch what you say boy for I come over there and beat you senseless!"

"Oh, come now gentlemen," Purdy said abruptly. "Violence is not the answer. I am merely stating facts as I see them. I do not wish to offend."

Bill said, "Well, you are offending a bunch."

Robert interrupted the exchange, "Understand Major, we all fought in the war. Did you fight in the war Major Purdy?"

He looked at Robert and answered, "I did sir. I fought alongside General John Buford. Who did you fight with Deputy?"

I saw a look of surprise swiftly pass over Robert's face. As quick as it was there, it disappeared. Robert answered, "I was with the 1st Pennsylvania Regiment of Volunteers at Gettysburg."

Purdy nodded and said, "Ah, yes, Gettysburg. I believe we may have crossed paths. I recall some of you men from the 1st at the start of the battle."

Robert sat back and crossed his arms over his chest. "Perhaps we did. What sir is your given name, it may bring something to mind, though I did not associate much with West Point officers. I, myself, was a lowly Corporal of Infantry."

Purdy said, "My given name is Arius James Purdy. I too was an enlisted soldier at the beginning of the war. I received a field commission later."

Robert again nodded and fell silent as we watched this exchange between the two men. I, knowing of Robert's background during the struggle, knew that he had gotten what he sought during the somewhat friendly conversation. Now to be rid of the major as we could discuss this newfound information.

I stood from the table and said, "Well, Major Purdy. If you will excuse us as we would like to discuss our next steps in this matter."

Purdy seemed taken aback to be excluded from this pending conversation. He said, "If that is your decision then I have no other course but to recommend to the general that the army should relieve you of this matter and take over the inquiry from here."

He stood from the table and turned towards the door, paused and looked back. "I suggest you stand down gentlemen. The army will handle this matter." He put his hat on his neatly parted black hair and said, "I will ride back to Austin at once and inform the general of my decision. Good day."

Before he crossed the threshold I said, "You tell the general whatever you like Major Purdy. We work for Judge Dubose and the Federal Marshal and as such we take our orders from them, not you. We will continue our inquiry, and you sir, can go to hell."

He turned back, looked at me then left without a word.

We remained silent as we watched his retreat, grateful that cooler heads had prevailed though he did deserve a severe ass whoopin' for his insults and general demeanor.

I went to the door and watched as he and the sergeant walked down the street, side by side, the sergeant standing tall over the little man. I shook my head and went back inside.

Thad remained at the door. He said, "That was certainly a difficult conversation. More than once, I wanted to pistol whip that arrogant little bastard." He looked at Robert and asked, "What was that nonsense about being a corporal in the 1st Regiment?"

I sat back at the table and said to everyone, "I believe Robert has something he would like to share with us."

All eyes turned to Robert as he sat, arms across his chest, lost in thought.

I said, "Robert."

He looked at me, then the others and stood from his chair and went to the coffee pot on the stove. We all watched him, anxious yet patient for whatever Robert had to share with us. He returned to the table and sat down.

He said, "That is not the Purdy I knew during the war."

Jim said, "You rode with Buford." He pointed to the open door. "He said he too rode with Buford, yet he did not recognize you, nor you him. What the hell is going on here?"

Robert took in a deep breath. "Let me start by saying that I saw Major Arius James Purdy during the war and that man was not him. The Purdy that was with General Buford was killed at Gettysburg."

Bill asked, "Could you be mistaken Robert?"

Robert shook his head. "I am not. I was at Major Purdy's burial. I saw the man going into the ground while standing next to General Buford."

I said, "What else did you learn Robert?"

He sat forward. "I told this man here that I was with the 1st Pennsylvania Regiment of Volunteers at the Battle of Gettysburg." He paused and looked at each of us before continuing. "The 1st Regiment never fought at Gettysburg. They had been disbanded three months into the war back in sixty-one."

Thad whistled softly and said, "He said he knew of you fellas."

Robert replied, "He did. He also said he received a field commission. The Major Purdy I knew graduated from West Point. I heard General Buford mention it when he learned of the man's death, something about him being in the class behind the general at the Academy."

"Then we need to know just what the hell he is up to," I said.

Bill asked, "Do we arrest him?"

Robert shook his head and said, "I do not believe we should. He is up to something, and Wyatt is right, we need to know what that is."

Just then Chelsea came into the room and said, "I do not mean to intrude. But I for one believe he is involved in this matter of the money and the safe."

We all looked at her expectantly, waiting for her to explain.

She blushed a bit but continued. "He wants you boys out of the way. He made that decision long before he came here. I also believe you just met one of the men behind all these occurrences." She smiled, "I do not trust that little shit as far as I can spit, boys."

We laughed at this last remark having forgotten that Chelsea was as tough as the rest of us as she occasionally would cast off that persona of a gentile creature and Southern Belle.

Bill said, "I say we arrest him and beat the truth outta the mangy dog."

Robert suddenly stood from his chair and made for his desk, grabbing an envelope and sheet of paper. "We need to get a message to the Judge," he said as he began to write.

I reminded him, "We cannot use the wire, Robert. If he is part of this then he will know we are on to him."

Robert looked up and said, "We will not use the wire. We will use a messenger."

I knew exactly what he was thinking, and I grabbed my hat, the Howdah Pistol , stuck it in my belt, and raced out the door making my way across the street.

I ran into Pepper's Place and looked around. The workers were fewer than before as I guessed the construction was near complete. I searched the faces and saw him.

I called out, "Pete, come over here."

Pete, carrying a hammer and saw, quickly came over to me. "Yes sir, Marshal. Whatcha need?"

I said, "Grab your brother and come to the jail. I have an important job for y'all."

Without question he dropped the tools and said as he went in search of his brother, "Right away Marshal. We be right there."

I returned to the jail.

I said, "Clem and Pete will be here directly."

Robert looked up then returned to his scribbling saying, "Good. I will tell the Judge all that we know and let him corner the major when he returns to Austin."

Clem and Pete came in, removed their hats and stood by silently as all eyes were on Robert as one sheet of paper turned into two as he wrote out our suspicions and actions thus far. This being a hand delivered message the need for brevity was of no consequence and all details could be written out in plain English.

Robert folded the pages and put them in the envelope. Then, striking a match to a small candle on his desk he began melting the sealing wax onto the back of the envelope. Once enough of the red wax had formed into a small puddle, he used our official stamp and sealed the letter.

He called the boys over and issued instructions for their journey. "Boys, I have an important letter that must get to Austin as quickly as possible." He held up the sealed document. "It must be hand delivered to Judge Dubose and only to the judge, no one else. Do you understand?"

They both nodded but it was Pete who answered. "We do Marshal. Judge Dubose in Austin and no one else."

Clem asked, "Awful big town Marshal. How do we find him?"

I said, "Seek out the Federal Marshal's office and have him take you to the judge. But the letter goes from your hand to Judge Dubose's hand and not another soul."

"Yes sir," Pete said.

Robert handed the letter to Pete. "Go and saddle a couple of horses, grab up your gear and come back here. We will have Julius fix you boys some grub for the trip."

I went out the back and called Julius inside.

Julius, with Argos at his side asked, "Yes sir Cap'n. What do you need?"

I said as the two boys made their way past us, "We are sending these boys to Austin on an important matter. If you could help them, make ready with their gear, food, and water. Enough for three days at least."

"Right away Cap'n," he said as he went outside.

Jim came over and asked, "You sure you do not want to arrest Purdy here?"

Robert answered, "I thought that through and believe we should let him stay ignorant that we may be on to his activities."

"Besides," I said, "he may have already done whatever he needed to get done when he got here. No, I reckon we should let Judge Dubose, and the Marshal handle him. I suspect we are gonna have our hands full here directly."

Thad, still at the front asked, "What makes you say that, Wyatt?"

I grinned, "Oh, the look on Purdy's face when I told him we were not gonna stop."

Bill said with a laugh, "I thought that look was for you tellin' him to go to hell."

Jim added, "Just like Miss Chelsea said, that is why he came here, to try and have us back down. They ain't had much luck in tryin' to kill us."

Chelsea and Julius soon had the boys packed out with supplies for the eighty-mile journey. Food, water, bedrolls, rain slickers, long guns and pistols, ball, and powder, they were ready, waiting with their mounts behind the jail.

As we came outside, they both mounted, ready to set off, the eagerness on their faces as they understood the importance of their task.

I handed Clem a small leather pouch. "There is some money in there should you boys need anything. The judge will tell you to come back or hang around for a bit. Buy what you need."

Clem said, "Thank you Marshal."

Robert added a word of caution. "Do not stop and do not converse with anyone on the trail. No one is to know what it is you are up to. Should you come across a big soldier riding along with a smaller one, stay clear." He paused then said, "In fact stay clear of anyone you see. That letter must get to the judge."

Pete said, "You can count on us Marshal."

The brothers looked at each other and took off, never looking back. I know, cause I watched them. Without seeing the content of the message nor knowing all that was happening around them they took their task without question, set on completing that which was given to them, never protesting nor complaining. They were good boys and again I was glad we had given them a chance.

We all resumed our postings in and around the jail. Chelsea remained in the kitchen preparing a meal for us, Thad on the porch, Julius, Mark, and Argos guarding the back while Bill sat in a chair and elevated his wounded leg on a stool.

I went to the coffee pot and went around the room topping off everyone's cup that so desired a taste.

Before I could sit and enjoy the coffee Thad called out from the porch.

"Rider comin' in," he said. "Lord Almighty he is a mountain of a man all decked out in buckskin."

I looked at Robert and smiled. "Sounds to be Skinner," I said.

We went to the door and sure enough, there he was, Skinner Stevens. Tall in the saddle, dressed head to toe in buckskin, thick head of black hair and an even thicker beard blowing in the wind, he rode with the confidence of a man without fear. His eyes scanning all around, taking in all that he saw, dismissing the irrelevant and assessing the dangers knowing that there was nothing that will keep him from his appointed task. His long heavy caliber rifle, his weapon of choice, lay across his lap.

As the Buffalo Hunter neared, I said, “Do not shoot him Thad. He is with us.”

Thad said, “Lord Almighty Damn, but that fella is huge.”

Robert chuckled and said, “Just do not get on his bad side. We have seen that fella run through a locked door.”

“I will make it a point not to,” he said as he looked at Robert. “A locked door you say?”

I said, “It was. Fella on the other side took a shot at him, made him mad.”

Skinner pulled up at the hitchin’ rail and sat his horse. “Afternoon gents.” He looked around. “What goes? Ain’t no folks out and about.”

I said, “Get off your horse Skinner and we will tell you all about it.”

He said, “Spect I will Wyatt. I came in to tell you fellas of somethin’ I come across in the wilderness couple days back. Sort of distressing it was.”

Robert looked at me then said, “Oh? Trouble Skinner?”

He dismounted and tied off his horse. “Spect so Robert. It ain’t good for certain.”

Skinner came in and we made introductions all around. Before he got down to his tale he went out back insisting to greet Julius and Mark, stopping to give a hug to Chelsea.

He came back in, sat at the table, and asked, “Got some of that tabakie Wyatt?”

“I do,” I said as I handed him my tobacco pouch. “Help yourself.”

He stuffed his pipe, struck a match to it, and got it going. Exhaling a cloud of smoke he said, “Bad business boys. Bad business indeed.”

“What goes Skinner,” I asked.

He puffed on his pipe and looked at us, shaking his head. “Couple days back, out passed Fort Mason I come across some dead soldiers. They’d all been shot and left for the coyotes.”

Robert asked, “Could it have been Indians?”

He shook his head. “No, it was not. Cause one of the fellas was still alive when I found them. Fella tol me everything for he too died.”

“How many soldiers, “I asked.

He took another puff off his pipe and answered, “It were six soldiers.”

Bill asked, “What did this soldier tell you?”

Skinner set his pipe on the table and reached for his cup of coffee, stopping before he drank. “He tol me they was ambushed by other soldiers who made off with the cash box. Fella said there a lot of money in that box.”

CHAPTER TWENTY-TWO

We sat there quietly for a moment mulling over what Skinner had just told us. The situation was obviously the work of our unseen nemeses. Or, at the very least, they had guided the hands that killed the soldiers when they took the money. Many questions flooded our thoughts as the moment of silence continued.

It was Robert who spoke first. "I suppose you should start at the very beginning Skinner."

Skinner put his cup on the table, took a hard pull on his pipe, and said through the cloud of exhaled smoke, "Reckon I should. Make more sense to do that fer you fellas. Might get you fellas to make more sense for me to understand why the hell Blue-Bellies be killin' Blue-Bellies."

I said, "I expect the answers to be comin' for you Skinner." I looked at the others. "Not so much for us I fear."

Skinner set his pipe down and began. "I was ridin' about fixin' to come to town to see Momma, havin' just finished sellin' my skins when I seen vultures off in the distance. Normally I would pay it no mind but theys a bunch of them, so I figured to have a look see." He picked up his coffee cup, took a sip and set it down, looking at it with a grim, sadness on his face. He continued. "When I got there the soldiers was all on the ground, shot to pieces, dead they was."

I asked, "Any horses?"

Skinner shook his head and said, "Not a one. I got down and checked on each soldier, make for certain theys dead when the last one opened his eyes and grabbed hold of me. He near scared me to death he did. He started babblin' on and on 'bout how they got the money, took the wagon and horses and left him for dead." He paused and looked at his coffee cup again.

I watched him for a moment. Often, when revisiting a traumatic experience one can step back in time and relive the emotions that accompanied the drama. I knew Skinner, as tough and seasoned as any man, was having such a moment. I stood and retrieved the bottle of whiskey and filled his cup.

He looked up and grinned. "Much obliged Wyatt." He took a drink. "I admit them fellas spooked me some. Some of them was shot six and seven times."

Jim, sympathetic to Skinner's plight said softly, "Go ahead with your tale Skinner, we got time yet."

"Yes sir," he said. "I found this fella alive, tol me his name, Sullivan it was. Said they was carrying payroll to all of them forts the Blue-Bellies be movin' back to. They was headed to Fort Mason to deliver the box of money then go back to Austin. He said near fifteen soldiers rode up sayin' they come outta Fort Mason and was there to escort them."

I asked, "He said fifteen?" I whistled and looked at the others saying, "They seem to have themselves an army stashed off someplace fellas."

Thad, still in the doorway said, "Ain't hard to do comin' out of a war. No work, no land to be had cept out west and no money. It would be easy to recruit an army of no accounts."

Skinner added, "I seened plenty of no accounts out on the range here of late. More than I ever seened before truth be told."

I asked Skinner, "Do you reckon they are hold up at one of the empty forts?"

Skinner asked, "You mean like before?" He shook his head. "I been near Fort Terret and some of the others and ain't no one livin' there I could see. Not like we found the last time Wyatt," he said referring to our last trip out to Fort Terret.

"Did Sullivan say how much was in the cash box," Robert asked.

"He did," Skinner said. "Told me it was near twenty thousand dollars paper money and gold coin. Some was payroll and some was for buildin' the forts back, supplies and such."

Jim asked, "Then what happened Skinner?"

"Well, he said theys all ridin' together all pleasant like then these fifteen soldier boys is all pointin' their guns and the shootin' starts. Sullivan says these fellas is laughin' and havin' a grand time killin' and shootin.' Yellin' and carryin' on about still fightin' fer the cause or some such." Skinner stopped and shook his head as if to clear the bad images that came to mind. "Then he got all upset and says he was shot off his horse and played dead hopin' he would be left alone. He tol me one of them fellas rode from soldier to soldier shootin' holes in them laughin' all the while and another collected up all the horses and guns. This fella had only one bullet left when he shot Sullivan again, at least that is what he told me, then he up and died on me."

The room fell silent once again then I said quietly, almost to myself, "The Cause."

All eyes were on me. It was nothing new, to have folks stare at me when 'The Cause' was mentioned in conversation. I reckon it was a natural or even an unwilling reaction knowing that I had once pledged allegiance to 'The Cause', as did so many of us, not so many years ago, and they felt compelled to view my reaction or response. I cannot say theirs was a reaction of sympathy, anger, blame or even, in some instances, one of mistrust.

For me it was just a word, a phrase that brought about something from folks knowing of my past, perhaps feeling that offense was given when the phrase was uttered or spoken, especially in a derogatory manner, though it was never taken. At least not by me. I also cannot say that I was as true to 'The Cause' as others who wore the grey, contrary to some beliefs. I had my reasons for choosing the side to which I fought as I have my reasons to stand proud of that decision to this day.

The shame that I brought out of the war was not because of the allegiance I took nor the uniform I wore, or even for the fact we had lost. It was for the lives that were lost. Some boys wore grey, others wore blue.

I ignored the looks for the moment and said, "I have heard that there are some who wish to continue fighting for 'The Cause'. Hell, we have all heard of such notions." I looked around the room before I continued. I intentionally made eye contact with every person so as to be certain that my words were heard by all. "I have been hearing of bands of Confederate soldiers joining up in the wilderness and forming holdout camps wishing to continue the fight against the Union." I stood, straightened my gun belt and vest. "I for one wish it to stop. So, what are we to do about it?"

Robert asked, "Do you think this is part of it? We are dealing with some holdouts from the war?"

Bill said, "You know boys. That is the best idea I have heard about this occurrence yet."

Thad said, "Bill is correct. It makes sense when you give it some thought. If you want to continue the war you must have money. The only way for them to get it is to..."

"Steal it," I said. "We have been looking at this in the wrong light boys."

Jim asked, "Then why are they killin' their own?"

I answered, "Reckon they were only hired hands to do one part of the job. Once that was complete, they killed them." I looked at Thad and Bill. "You fellas said you recognized some of them as boys from a ranch that went belly up during the war. They hire local ruffians knowing that they will get killed, and if they do not, that big Indian finishes it."

Robert asked no one in particular, "So, how do we find them, or their camp?"

Chelsea came into the room and said, "I expect some of you boys will need to ride out to Fort Mason and ask the troopers if they have had any trouble, or strange occurrences here about." She turned to go and added, "I will tell Mark and Julius to make everything ready while I get more grub together."

We all looked at her in silence as she walked back into the kitchen, the expression on our faces said it all. It was like my Momma used to say when the obvious just slapped you in the face and you could not think of any response or acknowledgment. You was slack-jawed and silly-eyed, she would say. That is just what we were too.

Bill, finally brining us around said, "Reckon me and Thad will stay here and help Julius."

"Mark and Chelsea too. They are in this now," Thad added.

From the kitchen Chelsea said, "We have been in this, as you say, since we moved to this town. This is our home too."

I said, "That you have Darlin' and that it is." I turned to Skinner. "Feel up to another ride my friend?"

Skinner was quick to answer. He said, "Reckon so Wyatt. Cannot let you fellas go it alone and I would like to get my hands on them that dun this. Gonna have to live out of your stores for the journey as I am cleaned out. Sides, I am a special deputy for you fellas, and I can take you to where I buried them poor souls."

Robert asked, "Do you think we should catch this Purdy fella before he leaves and tell him about the cash box?"

Jim said, "Hell no! He already knows you ask me. Sumbitch knew about it when he came in here, twas his doin'."

Robert said, "Wish we had something on him so we could lock him up."

"Hell, wish we could just shoot him," Bill said.

I said, "Bill, if he shows up after we are gone, feel free to shoot him and be done with it."

He laughed, "Do not think I will not do it Wyatt."

We then imparted our tale to Skinner Stevens. From the first telegram, the missing safe, the dead wagoneers, the ambush and the journey back to our town. We told him of our meeting with Major Purdy, or whoever he was, and of the street fight with the assassins then sending the two boys off to message the judge in Austin. When we finished, Skinner just sat there.

Finally, he said, "Reckon we best be on our way for somethin' else goes bad."

Everything had been set in motion. We were a well-disciplined and functional unit, each knowing his job as we set about carrying out the many smaller tasks that would eventually put us in the saddle for our journey into the wilderness. Food, water, ball and powder, essentials for the trail were all laid out and packed. Panniers for the trip, well stocked, were strapped onto Buster the pack mule as we would be going over some rough country.

Julius and Mark packed us out to accommodate four riders. Jim, again insistent, was to be part of the expedition, wanting to see this to the end, no matter the cost. It had started in his jurisdiction, his town, hurting his people, his friends and he was determined to bring those responsible to justice or to see them dead. By his hand or ours, his desire was to be part of bringing it to a successful conclusion and perhaps, return the lost money to the people of his town.

I decided that I would bring my Colt Revolving Rifle in addition to the shotgun, my Walker and the Howdah Pistol. All circumstances were to be planned for, and I packed accordingly, even secreting my Remington derringer on my person. My rationale was simple, straightforward in my choice of weapons. If I were to be killed, it was not going to be for a lack of shooting back. My possibles bag was stuffed with shells, powder, ball, and cap.

Robert had taken notice of this and said, "The only thing we lack is a cannon."

I looked at Robert, grinned and said, "I know where we can get one."

Robert laughed. "I am sure you do Wyatt." He turned to walk away, stopped and looked back. "You are joking, are you not?"

I shrugged my shoulders and went back to the task at hand, that of loading my arsenal.

A brief discussion was had by all as to when we should depart for Fort Mason. There was merit in the argument to leave fresh in the early morning hours, but a sense of urgency consumed us as we were now days into the events that led us here, and waiting was not a desirable notion we took to. We had a few hours of daylight left to us and we decided it best we get on the trail right away.

Julius and Mark had brought all the animals to the front of the jail while the rest of us remained inside, saying our goodbyes, passing on last minute advice and whispering those words of caution to take care, be aware and be ready for anything.

I stood at the threshold next to Chelsea and said, "It would seem that this is getting to be a habit, you seeing us off like this."

She offered a reassuring smile. "It is the times we find ourselves in Wyatt."

I looked outside as Mark stood with Julius. "Mark is a lucky man Darlin'."

Her smile grew and she said, "I know he is." She laughed quietly, hugged me, and said, "Be safe Wyatt. This whole thing scares me."

"As it does me," I said as I walked out the door.

Julius handed me the reins to Caliban and asked, "How long you reckon, Cap'n?"

I mounted up. "Cannot rightly say Julius. We are not certain what we are lookin' for, so I reckon a day out there, a day back unless we find somethin' of interest. Figure on four or five days."

He nodded, offered up his hand. "I got everything here Cap'n. You and Sergeant Major Robert be mindful of these men. They is evil fellas for certain."

I took his hand and said, "They are my friend." I looked at the top of the stairs to the porch. Argos sat there watching us. "You keep Argos with you wherever you go Julius. He is a good hand and be mindful of 'Ol Horace. Hopefully, the Marshal will send someone to pick him up."

Julius laughed and said, "Between his missing teeth, broke nose and bruised privates I do not expect too much trouble outta him Cap'n. He ain't got much left to give."

Mark came over and handed me a holster, minus a belt and said, "Here you go Wyatt. This will do for the Howdah Pistol till Chelsea makes one for you. It loops over your saddle horn."

I took the holster. It was brown in color, worn, well broken in and larger than the one I wore for my Walker Colt. I took the flap, with a hole cut in the center, and put the saddle horn through it. Taking the Howdah from my saddle bag, I slipped it in the holster, hanging off the left side, so allowing me to draw with my right. I tried it a couple of times, pleased that it came out with ease. Using the leather strip at the top of the holster, I lashed the pistol down to keep it from coming out during a hard ride.

I shook Mark's hand saying, "I thank you sir. This will do me well. Let me know what I owe you, my friend."

"Just come back Wyatt," he said in return. "Just come back."

Jim sided up to me. "Lord Almighty Damn," he began, "you think you have enough arms there Wyatt. The only thing you lack is a cannon."

Robert said, "Do not encourage him, Jim. He may just get us one."

"I will not complain if he does," Jim answered back.

Skinner, his buffalo-gun across his lap was already on the street.

I looked to the big man as I grabbed up the lead line to Buster and said, "Ready when you are Skinner."

He called back, "Reckon I will be lead scout Wyatt. Do not want these vermin tryin' anything on us."

"Fine by us Skinner," I said as we turned as one to the street and rode off, out of town and into the wilderness of West Texas.

None of us looked back. There was no need as we had been doing this far too many times of late and the scene that was behind us was the same as it was since we began our inquiries into this matter. Be it here, Castroville, Bandera, or any other town we stayed in, we were saying our goodbyes more often while in pursuit of desperados. We were men of responsibility and as such accepted our fate in coming and going, only staying long enough to replenish our bodies, our supplies and rest our animals. Julius had been correct in his observations of these men. They were evil and we had taken on the unenviable task of stopping them. The price was high. It was us or them, and we were going to use everything we had to stop them. So, for now, the goodbyes were accepted, the scenes we left behind were repeated and the journey was welcomed as it brought us closer to the end.

Chapter Twenty-Three

It was not long before Fredericksburg fell behind and the unspoiled lands opened before us. Our pace was quick and steady, our desire to get as much distance into the wilderness as possible before the darkness overtook us. The heat, oppressive as usual, was not too much of a concern as we would only have to hold this pace for a brief time before the sun went down and darkness took its place.

Skinner was out front, moving us along, his head moving from side to side taking it all in. He had the eyes of a hawk as he sought out danger. His hearing and sense of smell was uncanny as he worked these three senses together as one without a conscious thought in doing so. His years as a buffalo hunter had made this man one of the best trackers and scouts, I had ever seen.

He was a powerful man, fearless in the face of danger and hard to anger thus keeping his wits about him in tough situations. Many a man had found that to anger him will bring the wrath of his might down on top of you and it would be as swift as it was terrible. But there was never a better man to have as a friend and comrade in arms.

We rode on through the remainder of the day as darkness soon enveloped us and the temperature fell bringing relief from the brutal Texas sun. It also slowed our pace as we had left the beaten trail, turned northwest, and struck out through unchartered terrain, taking what we believed to be the most direct route to our destination.

Jim, never had ridin with Skinner before asked, "This fella know where he is goin?"

Robert said, "That he does. Never was there a better tracker than Skinner. Wish I had him with us during the war."

I laughed. "I do not believe Skinner would allow himself to don a blue coat."

"I believe you are right Wyatt," Robert said with a laugh.

We rode on through the night, a slow steady pace. Sometimes we dismounted and walked our animals, a benefit to both them and us, as we did not want to suffer from the cramps of being in the saddle too long. Sometimes we stopped if we came across water allowing the horses to drink and rest as we too partook in nourishment and relief.

Such was our life on the trail, dangerous as it was difficult, not that we were fussing about it, mind you, it had to be done. Our duty as lawmen brought us out in search of the outlaw who often hid from the town or community he terrorized, thus causing us to seek him out in the wilds. We were not the type of men who would be content with another vocation, be it a banker, shop keep or even a farmer, we were not cut from that cloth for such a life. Ours was one that kept us in the saddle, searching for the lawbreaker set on taking it away from the banker, shop keep or farmer. We knew our place, accepted it, and continued to strive at being the best at what we knew.

Some were born into it, like Jim Sweeny. Having found his skills behind a gun he chose to put it to good use and pinned on a star, serving the people of his town. Though being a good gun hand did not make you a proficient lawman he also had the strength of character, high moral values and knew right from wrong. Always willing to put himself in harm's way to bring the law breakers to justice, straight up or over the saddle, it shall be done. His was a dedication to be admired, and that is what made him an exceptional lawman.

I looked over at him in the dim light of the early morning hours. I was glad he chose to stay in the fight. Both Robert and myself, though not born into the profession of lawman, learned much from men like Jim Sweeny.

I brought myself back to the present and asked Robert, "What do you know about Fort Mason?"

Robert thought for a moment before he answered. "I had never made it that far out when I was here before the war. I understand it to have two dozen or so buildings, the smaller ones being for the troopers."

"Any walls, or parapets around it," Jim asked.

"Not that I know of," Robert said, "It was one of the forts that was set out in the wilderness to provide protection to settlers traveling west, so the troopers were always in the saddle." He looked at me and grinned saying, "I understand Robert E. Lee was posted there."

"That a fact," I said, surprised by this knowledge. "I will admit that it is hard for me to see the Great General in a life before the war, let alone in a blue coat." I laughed.

Jim looked around in the darkness. "Lonely place to find yourself in for extended periods you ask me."

Robert said, "It is. Back then it was hard to keep troopers at these outlying posts for any length of time. Real problem with desertions."

I looked around, knowing that what I could see of the landscape was the same as what I could not see out in the darkness. It was a lonely land, void of the comforts of living, harsh and unforgiving. But still, I found it comforting, knowing that even in this unspoiled harsh land, there was life to be found.

The hours passed as we continued our trek deeper into the wilderness. The sounds of the night came to us out of the darkness. Those animals that lived in the blackened desert-like land would speak as we rode by, alarmed by our intrusion, never to approach but to keep a watchful eye as we passed. The coyote or the desert fox, yipping a warning to others that interlopers were about, crossing their territory, interrupting their nocturnal activities or the evening hunt.

The sun rose over our shoulders, casting the landscape in a reddish-brown illumination that showed the beauty of the harsh environment. Shadows cast by the hills, rocks and mesquite trees provided the last shades of respite for the animals that lived in the night. It was time for them to retire, seek shelter from the coming sun. They, unlike us, would bed down to escape the brutality of the heightened temperatures and the merciless sun.

We pressed on, ever forward.

Near mid-day Skinner stopped, turned in his saddle and yelled back, "We be at the place I buried them fellas."

We joined Skinner, dismounted and looked about.

Skinner ground tied his mount, rested his rifle over his shoulder, and pointed. "Just over that small rise. Figured it be as good a place as any."

We followed the Buffalo Hunter over a small hill and stopped at the crest, looking at the small mound of dirt with a crude cross at the center. We all removed our hats as it seemed the proper thing to do. This was sacred ground. Men had fallen here, had died here. This was the final ground they stood before they were taken away and, rightly so, they rested in it.

Skinner said quietly, "I dun the best I could."

I put my hat on and said in return, "You did just fine Skinner. They were soldiers together in life and now they rest together in death. It was real respectful of you."

He exhaled loudly. "I could not leave them for the coyotes nor vultures."

Jim asked, "Where was it you found them?"

Skinner said nothing as he walked down the slight hill, passed the grave, and stopped. We followed.

He said, "They was layin' all about here. The fella I found alive was over there," he pointed to his left, "the others were here, kinda in a circle."

We immediately spread out and began a search of the ground. We did not expect to find anything of importance, but we did not want to overlook something that could provide us with answers to the many questions. Where did they go after they massacred the troopers and who were they?

Robert was some distance off when he called out. "I have wagon tracks over here."

We joined Robert and began following the tracks. The bandits made no effort to hide their exit from the killing ground as we followed the tracks in the sand and dirt. In addition to the wagon tracks there were multiple horse tracks. Near as we could figure there were at least fifteen outriders along with the team of two horses pulling the wagon and a further four horses in tow.

We had walked a few hundred yards out when we stopped.

Jim said, "They headed directly south. What the hell is south of here?"

I said, "They did not go to Fredericksburg, that is for certain. We would have seen them. The only other town to the south would be Kerrville and Bandera."

Robert took off his hat and wiped at his forehead with his arm. "It seems that we are tracking in a circle."

Jim asked, "What do you mean Robert?"

"Well," Robert began, "it all started in Castroville. It took us to Bandera, Kerrville and back to Fredericksburg now the trail leads us back south to Kerrville."

"You reckon they might be hidin' in the mountains," I asked.

Robert put his hat back on. "I believe so."

I turned to Skinner. "How much further we got to go to Fort Mason?"

Skinner looked back to the north as he stroked his thick beard. It was his tell, when he thought something through, stroking his beard helped in his thought process. He said, "Reckon a couple more hours we should be there."

"Then we best be on our way," I said as I walked back to the animals. "We still have to let the garrison know what happened out here."

We retrieved our mounts and continued our journey to Fort Mason. As much as we would have liked to continue our pursuit of the bandits, we thought it best to inform the army of their loss of both troopers and cash box. The villains had gone south to seek refuge in the mountains around Kerrville, that we felt certain, and we would pick up the trail on our return trip.

We again fell in behind Skinner as he blazed the trail to our destination. We were more alert, ready for a fight. Seeing the grave of the fallen soldiers left us with an overwhelming desire to settle the score. To make those responsible for these occurrences, these tragedies, pay, either at the end of a rope or the end of our pistols.

Our conversation light, lacking in any substance we pretty much kept to ourselves letting the anger simmer as we plodded along.

The time passed quickly, and before long Skinner stopped and looked over his shoulder. He yelled back, "We are here gents."

We joined Skinner and looked in the distance. There it was, Fort Mason. It was a small garrison, much like Robert spoke of. Two dozen or so buildings set in a square formation. Four large buildings on the northern perimeter made of stone and brick, and eight or so smaller adobe structures on the southern perimeter with a few more on the east and west sides leaving the center as a parade ground.

I took my spy glass out of my saddle bag and surveyed the fort for activity.

"Does not look to be anyone at home," I said.

Jim asked, "Reckon they all deserted?"

I looked closer and took notice that many of the buildings were in some manner or form of disrepair. I lowered the glass. "I would not blame them seeing the condition of the place."

Robert said, "No better way to find out then pay them a visit."

So as not to cause undue alarm, should they be observing us, we took our time riding through the open space between us and the fort. If anyone was present, we did not want to pose a threat nor spook them.

The closer we got, the more the condition of the fort was revealed. It had been neglected for some time. I reckon some of the monies taken were to be used to resurrect this and other forts like it.

Slowly, cautiously we entered the confines of the garrison and pulled up in the center of the parade ground, looking about. It was then, from the door of one of the larger stone buildings, two soldiers stepped out on the porch and looked at us.

I called over, "Afternoon soldier. We are deputy marshals come about some business with the commander of this post."

One of the soldiers stepped off the porch and down the steps, stopping at the foot of the stairs. He was young, almost child-like in his appearance. Narrow face, short hair under his cavalry hat. He wore his long blue uniform jacket buttoned up to the neck, hardly appropriate for the saddle. His saber hung by his side almost dragging the ground. He seemed unfamiliar, almost out of sorts in his uniform. It was then I noticed the shoulder boards on his jacket. Gold rectangle braiding on a yellow field. The absence of a rank insignia told me he was a brand-new second lieutenant of cavalry.

His voice was that of a boy, lacking in confidence or force as he stated, "I am Lieutenant Wilbur Monroe. I am the Second in Command of Fort Mason. Who are you sir and state your business?"

I looked at Robert and said, "So, it is going to be like that." I looked back to the small officer. "I am Deputy United States Marshal Chambers."

Lieutenant Monroe pointed to us and asked, "Who are the others? Are they your prisoners?"

Jim, not bothering to hide his anger yelled, "Prisoners? Why you little shit! We are all lawmen come to convey some news to the commander of this here fort." He took in a deep breath. "Are you him or ain't you?"

Monroe took a step back at the tone to which he was addressed. I took this as a man who did not do well with confrontation. I decided to take a different approach with the young officer.

I dismounted and slowly walked towards him. "Lieutenant Monroe, no need to get riled up. We only came to tell you that we have news of six soldiers that have been killed and a cash box stolen."

His face whitened as he reached up and tugged at his collar. "Killed you say? My God man, where?"

Skinner said "Bout two hours south of here. I buried them."

More soldiers started to appear on the parade ground. We were a curiosity as they gathered around looking us over.

Monroe cleared his throat, regained his composure, and asked, "How were they killed? Was it Indians?

I said, "It was not. That is one reason why we came here. We are going to have to let the commander know about this. Is he here?"

The young officer said, "No he is not Deputy Chambers. He is leading a patrol up north in search of renegade Indians. I expect him back today or tomorrow."

I looked around at the gathered soldiers. I counted only eight, which I found distressing. Less than a handful of soldiers led by an inexperienced officer to defend a garrison in the wilderness of West Texas. I shook my head and wondered how it was we lost the war with dunderheaded decisions like this.

"You do not have much of a troop to defend this place Lieutenant Monroe," I said.

Lieutenant Monroe quickly snapped back, "We have a sufficient force here Deputy. We only have one prisoner to guard, a renegade Indian."

Robert, forever an experienced Cavalry Sergeant Major, pointed out, "Yet you leave the fort unguarded as we just came in without challenge or confrontation."

Monroe said angrily, "That is no business of yours sir. We have plenty of hardened defenses to ward off any attack. I assure you I know what I am doing as I am a graduate of West Point."

I stepped a bit closer to Monroe and said, "You best be mindful of who you speak tactics to Lieutenant. That there happens to be a former Sergeant Major of Cavalry under General John Buford."

He looked from Robert back to me. "You sir have delivered your message. I will convey it to the captain on his return."

Again, I shook my head. "Boy, you got a lot to learn. Reckon we will be on our way then."

As I turned to rejoin the others another soldier came out of a building that was situated behind us. He was a tall corporal with hair down to his collar, short waist coat uniform jacket and a black top hat bedecked in colorful feathers on his head. On the bridge of his nose, he wore a pair of blue spectacles.

I turned back to the Lieutenant and said forcefully, "I want to see this prisoner right now!"

Lieutenant Monroe was caught off guard by my abrupt change in demeanor and he began to stutter his way through a response, "Well...you cannot, now see here Marshal. You...I cannot allow this."

Robert took notice of my change in attitude as did Skinner and Jim. The three of them dismounted knowing that something was amiss.

Robert asked, "What goes Wyatt?"

I turned back and pointed at the corporal behind them, who was now smoking a cigar on the porch.

I turned back to Monroe. "Boy, you best take me to your prisoner, or I will put my boot up your ass!"

Lieutenant Monroe quickly realized that he stood no chance if he refused my demand, as I would surely put my boot up his ass. I had guessed correctly when I thought he was a man that did not do well with confrontation. How he got his commission in the cavalry was beyond my understanding.

He inhaled and said, "Very well Deputy Chambers. Follow me."

As we walked past the others I said to them, "Be ready for anything boys. This could go easy or hard."

I followed the Lieutenant as Robert, Jim and Skinner spread out on the parade ground, hands on their pistols hoping for the best but preparing for the worst. They had seen the corporal on the porch and knew what we were going to do.

We went up the steps, ignoring the corporal for the moment and went inside. It took a moment for my eyes to adjust to the dim light as I took in my surroundings. It was a simple space occupied by only a single desk in the center of the room. Even though the windows were open it was hot and stuffy. In the back of the room was a large square cage of thick metal bars on all four sides and over the top. It had been built inside the room as it was a stand-alone cell with a single door held closed by a thick chain and a massive padlock. A man of my height could not stand erect while inside.

Inside the cell, lacking in any furniture or bunk, was a slop pail in one corner and a sitting figure of a man in the opposite corner. His legs were drawn up, head down between his knees, his long black hair falling to the sides hiding his face. From his dress there was no mistaking who it was.

Long Buffalo looked up with tired eyes, bruised face, and said, "Hello my friend. How is it that you are here?"

CHAPTER TWENTY-FOUR

Stunned I turned back to the Lieutenant and said through clenched teeth, "Turn him loose right now, damn you!"

Monroe said defiantly, "I will not. He is a renegade, and we have been tasked with rounding up those that cause trouble."

Just then the corporal stepped in and asked, "Problem Lieutenant?"

Monroe looked over his shoulder and said, "No, all is well Corporal Meecham. The Deputy Marshal here wants me to release the prisoner, and I just informed him he cannot have this," he pointed to the cage with a look of disgust, "this Redskin."

The corporal, cocky and self-assured, sauntered further into the room. "That a fact. Well, I expect this here Johnny Reb thinks he can just walk in here and do want he wants cause of that tin badge on his shirt." He took the spectacles off and smiled, still wearing the top hat. "That what you think Johnny Reb?"

I quickly took the man in. He was a bit bigger than me by at least thirty pounds, muscular and well-toned. He was obviously a man that took care of himself, and my guess was probably good in a fist fight.

I took two quick steps towards him as I drew back my right fist and let him have it right on the nose and followed that with a left to the side of his face that sent him back out the door where he landed on his back, rolled over and down the stairs landing in a heap, unconscious and bleeding. The top hat sitting upright at the top of the stairs.

I turned back as the Lieutenant made for his revolver. With my left hand I grabbed his wrist before he withdrew the pistol and backhanded him with my right sending him to the floor. Before he recovered, I took his gun and saber, tossing them into the far corner.

I took in a deep breath. "Now Lieutenant. Shall we try this again? Release the prisoner or I will beat on you some more."

Robert called from outside, "You okay in there Wyatt?"

I yelled out as I looked at the young officer as he rubbed his face where I struck him. I said, "We were just discussing letting Long Buffalo out of the cell and had a bit of a disagreement. We are fine now."

I knelt next to Monroe, "Is that not correct boy?"

He nodded his head. "Yes, I will let him go."

I patted him on the leg, stood, and said, "Good thing son. You are going to give my friend all his belongings back, his pony as well."

Lieutenant Monroe picked himself up off the floor, brushed off his uniform and nodded again as he made his way to the desk. "The keys are in the desk," he said as he made his way to the other side.

I watched him closely as he reached down for the top drawer and began to pull it open. I knew what he had in mind by the look on his face, as I could read people making me a good card player, and this man just showed his hand. I took the three steps separating us, reached over the desk with my left and pulled the drawer closed, pinning his hand inside. He let out a scream of pain and I hit him in the mouth with my right. Down he went, unconscious.

I stepped around the desk and opened the drawer. Sure enough there it was, a pistol. In fact, it was Long Buffalo's pistol along with the keys to the cell.

I took the keys and unlocked the cell door as Long Buffalo stepped out on weakened legs. We embraced and I looked at him.

"You look like shit my friend," I said.

He nodded and said, "Good. That is how I feel."

I looked at his bruised face and said, "Looks as though they beat you some. Maybe took the boot to you as well."

"They did," he said weakly.

"Can you ride," I asked.

"I can."

I put my arm around his waist as he put his arm over my shoulder and we made our way to the door. I asked, "What in the hell happened? How long have you been here?"

He said, "Four days. I was just riding past the fort when they came out and took me. Called me renegade Indian and locked me in cage." He stopped and looked back. "My things, in the desk."

"We will retrieve them my friend. Right now, we need to get you the hell out of here."

I stopped and picked up his top hat, put it on his head as we made our way down the steps. At the bottom of the stairs the corporal was stirring. I stopped and looked down at him as he tried to pick himself up off the ground.

"This the fella that beat on you?"

Long Buffalo said, "He did, and he liked to kick too."

I addressed the prone figure at my feet, "Put the boot to my friend, did you? Well...," I brought the heel of my right boot down hard and fast against the side of his bloodied head. "...how does it feel son?" Down he went, again.

We made our way to the others. While I had been dealing with the Lieutenant and Corporal, Robert and the others had gathered up the soldiers, stripped them of their sidearms and had them standing tall as if in a formation. The Sergeant Major in Robert took charge of the disorderly undisciplined mob of troopers and reminded them of what it meant to be in the army.

Robert came over to us. "Lord Almighty what did they do to you, my friend?"

Long Buffalo said, "I do not remember much of it. It was the corporal that did most of it."

I said, "Robert, Long Buffalo's belongings are in the desk inside. I will have one of these soldiers get his pony saddled up."

Skinner and Jim came over and relieved me of Long Buffalo and I addressed the gathered soldiers. "I want two troopers to get this man's pony saddled up and brought out here right now!"

The soldiers just stood and looked at one another, unmoving.

I stepped closer and pulled my Walker. "I ain't gonna say it again boys." I cocked the big pistol. Two troopers' broke formation and ran for the pole barn used to house the mounts and quickly set about saddling Long Buffalo's pony.

In short order they returned with the pony, and we got Long Buffalo mounted just as Robert came down the steps with his belongings. When he reached the bottom of the stairs the corporal again stirred and tried to push himself to his feet. Robert, with his free hand laid his fist into the side of the man's jaw, he moaned once and collapsed back in the dirt.

I said to no one in particular, shaking my head, "That boy ain't gonna learn."

Jim said, "One more thing yet fellas." He mounted up and pulled his horse to the gate of the pole barn, leaned out of the saddle, and opened it. He navigated to the backside of the corral, pulled his pistol, fired once in the air, and yelled, "Go on now, git!"

With that, all the horses made for the open gate, into the parade ground and ran off in different directions as Jim chased them off, leaving the soldiers without a way to pursue us.

As we turned our horses to leave, I looked back at the soldiers. "You boys have a nice day now."

We rode south out of the fort with the intention of putting as much distance between us and Fort Mason. There was still a patrol that was out and about with their commander, and we had no intention of meeting up with them.

We rode for a couple of hours more before we considered stopping for a rest. Skinner found a place that provided suitable cover and concealment on high ground among a rock formation.

We helped Long Buffalo off his horse and Robert dipped into our stores and prepared some food for our wounded friend.

I asked, "How long since you ate something?"

He took the plate from Robert. "Four days. Since they took me."

Robert said, "I am sorry it is cold rations Long Buffalo. We better not start a fire just yet."

Long Buffalo managed a smile as he bit into a strip of jerky. "Do not worry my friend. Bark of tree never bitter to hungry squirrel."

We all exchanged a brief look and broke out in laughter.

Long Buffalo ate slowly, knowing that his stomach had not had food in four days and eating too quickly would make him sick. While he ate Skinner took up a position to observe all around us and Robert tended to Long Buffalo's injuries between bites of food.

I was tending the horses when Jim came up to me and asked, "What now Wyatt?"

I looked back at Long Buffalo. "Reckon we head back to town and get Long Buffalo checked out by the Doc."

Long Buffalo heard me and said, "I need no doctor. I think you are looking for someone and I can help."

"Oh," I said. "Who might that be?"

Long Buffalo put his plate, now empty, on the ground and pushed himself up. "You look for the spirit that moves about, unseen and brings death."

We fell silent and just looked at our friend.

Long Buffalo said, "I have heard of this one as well my friends. He is silent, unseen yet he kills with brutality of one who enjoys it. He calls himself Achak."

Jim asked, "How is it that you know of him?"

Long Buffalo stepped among us. "This one is evil. He fought with the Greys out here during the war. He favors the long blade. He is a bad one my friends, yes, very bad."

"Do you know where we can find him," I asked.

Long Buffalo thought for a moment, walked around exercising his stiff legs and said, "I need some whiskey and tobacco."

Robert handed Long Buffalo his possibles bag while I dug out my tobacco pouch and the bottle of whiskey I had in my saddle bag.

Long Buffalo, as was his manner, stuffed his pipe, took a drink from the bottle, then struck a match pulling hard on the pipe, all before he spoke. He exhaled the smoke looking up at the sky and closed his eyes, while we waited.

He said, "This is fine tobacco Wyatt. Good Virginian shag." He smiled.

Jim, not used to the ways of Long Buffalo impatiently said, "Oh for pity's sake Long Buffalo, tell us."

Long Buffalo surrendered to our will and spoke as if he was telling us a story, a tale of times past. He said, "Many years ago there was a warrior among the Navajo people that was banished from his tribe. He fought hard as a warrior, but not for his people but for himself. He liked to kill; he became dangerous to his people and was sent away." He took another pull on his pipe. "He came out here during your war and joined with the Greys because they wanted him to kill the Blue Coats. Now the war is gone for but a few who still fight."

I interrupted Long Buffalo and asked, "For a few, you mean the holdouts?"

Long Buffalo nodded. "I have heard of some that want the war to go on. They live along the forgotten trail to the south. They are growing in numbers and planning to fight the Blue Coats once more."

Robert asked, "How long have you known about this?"

He shook his head. "Not long. I heard whispers of these men but only now have I heard of this Achak. I was coming to tell you of what I learned when the Blue Coats grabbed me and put me in the cell."

"Do you know of this forgotten trail," I asked.

"I can find it. But I do not know where they hide. It is many trails, not one. Much to search, hard country," he said.

Jim said, "Still, it is more than we have known so far."

"What does Achak mean," Robert asked.

Long Buffalo said, "It means spirit. But he is not so. He is evil and must be stopped."

I looked at Robert. "Do we have enough supplies to continue the search?"

Robert thought for a moment. I knew that he was going through our stores in his head, always the better one at logistics and planning for such an expedition. "I believe we can stay out for another three days, four if we stretch it."

Jim added, "If need be, we can resupply in Kerrville or Bandera."

Skinner, who stood atop the rock formation called down, "Hell, I can shoot me a big Shaggy and keep us in meat for a month."

I looked at Long Buffalo and asked, "Care to join us my friend."

He smiled, took another drag off his colorful pipe and said through the smoke, "It is I who will lead us to the forgotten trail."

I looked at the others and spoke. "I reckon we should get back on the trail and put more distance between us and Fort Mason. If that army patrol comes back anytime soon, they will be a bit upset with what we done."

Robert added, "I think we need to pick up the trail where Skinner buried the soldiers and follow it from there. We need to find this hold out camp and see what it is we are truly up against."

So, we decided to return to the task at hand, and find this guerrilla army.

Long Buffalo felt refreshed after his meager meal of hardtack, jerky, pickles and raisins and we quickly mounted and returned to the trail. Skinner took his position as scout and tracker while Long Buffalo rode with us giving him more time to heal before he would take over the tracking duties.

Our direction was direct, cross country to the gravesite of the fallen troopers. Taking the well used trail would have been easier on us and the mounts, but it would cost us precious time. A sense of urgency began to settle over us as we understood that events had been set in motion for a reason. A reason, unknown to us at present.

We had no idea of their timetable or their plans. The truth was, we knew nothing about these men, only that they were out and about. Not their location, their strength, or their make-up. Were these rogues a mounted cavalry unit? Perhaps they were artillery or dismounted infantry? What sort of support did they have in the field, weapons, and such.

These were the same questions I had asked myself many times during the war when I led scouting patrols in search of the Federals opposing us on the field of battle. The information I gathered was used before we engaged the enemy. Its value was as great as ammunition for the soldiers. To attack the enemy blindly was as though you went into battle with one boot, a lame horse, or an empty pistol. Information was an asset to a successful campaign.

We soon found ourselves back at the gravesite. Though we felt regret for the fallen soldiers we spent no time mourning over their loss, instead picked up the exit trail of the wagon that they took from the troopers. They had not made any attempt to hide when they fled the killing field, instead chose a quick retreat over the caution of hiding their numbers or direction of travel.

As we followed Skinner I said, "These boys are a certain kinda dumb not to hide their tracks."

"I was thinking the same thing, "Robert said. "Perhaps they did not figure on anyone following them."

I took in the landscape as the terrain began to change. The hills and mountains could be seen off in the distance reflecting the setting sun. The vegetation was getting thicker; more colors began to appear all around us as we moved further south. The browns gave way to greens giving what I thought was a deceptive sense of safety for the traveler, for it was still blazing hot and available watering holes were few and far between. At least at present, and beneath this expanding vegetation was still the dirt and sands of an unforgiving land.

We pressed on following the tracks left by the desperados in their escape. That is, until the sun slowly dipped below the horizon, casting the area around us in shadows and darkness. It was then we decided to stop for the night.

We found a suitable spot and set up camp, each with his own duties, again, born out of necessity and experience. We were a cohesive fighting unit, and I pity the hombre that takes our force for granted.

Long Buffalo, feeling better and stronger, still moved about with the aches and pains of one who had been put through a terrible physical ordeal. I looked at him and saw the many bruises and cuts on his face and neck and wondered what was beneath his shirt. The anger at his maltreatment grew in me as I watched him. I wanted to get my hands on the corporal that was the responsible party for inflicting such misery on my friend.

I knew that, though it would make me feel better to beat on this fella some, it would not change the sadistic nature of the man. His was the sort that viewed Long Buffalo as an inferior, a lesser man in his world. There was also those that encouraged this sort of behavior, enabling him to carry out his aggressions on others with impunity, free of judgement. That is, until he came upon us.

I stepped over to Long Buffalo and said, "How are you feeling my friend?"

"I am doing well. I do not hurt as much since I can move around," he responded.

I put my hand on his shoulder. "Good. We will get a cook fire goin' and have a decent meal then get some rest as I feel tomorrow will be a busy day and we need your help."

He smiled and nodded.

Robert got the fire going and we soon sat down to a decent meal of salt pork, biscuits, and beans. Some foods, though simple, were comforting in the wilderness. Those that travel along the trail can find relief in the simple pleasures of a filling meal cooked by the fire in the darkened hours of the night. It was something that a hungry man can count on after a long day under the hot sun.

After the meal, a guard schedule was established with me taking the first shift while the others laid out their bedrolls and hoped for a restful night's sleep.

Armed with a cup of coffee, pipe, my pistol, and Colt Revolving Rifle I set out away from the camp to keep watch.

CHAPTER TWENTY-FIVE

I found a large rock and sat with my rifle across my lap. I listened to the sounds of the night as those creatures that thrived in the darkness came out to start what was their new day. Searching for food, water or seeking out a mate, night after night they came. Theirs too was a harsh world. Predator and prey, they set out into the darkness. The only difference between them and us, I suppose, was the reasons to kill. Whereas theirs was a necessity for survival or food, ours had become routed in greed, anger, and a perceived injustice.

I struck a match to my pipe, suddenly angry at myself for the direction my thoughts had taken me yet again.

"Wyatt," came the unseen voice behind me. "It is me, Robert. Care for some company?"

I glanced over my shoulder and said, "Come ahead."

He joined me with a cup of coffee and pipe. "Do you have some more of that fine shag my friend?"

I handed him my pouch saying, "Of course I do, help yourself."

As he was stuffing his pipe he said, "You know, all this time I have known you I have never asked this." He paused as he laid a match to the bowel. "Where do you get this tobacco Wyatt? You never seem to run dry."

I took the pouch back and said, "That my friend is a secret. Should I tell you, then you will no longer be in my debt for every pipe of this fine Virginian tobacco you smoke." I laughed.

Robert laughed and pulled on his pipe, silent for the moment, yet I sensed something was on his mind.

I asked, "What troubles you, my friend?"

His exhale of smoke was more of a sigh as he looked at me, "You ever get tired Wyatt? Tired of what it is we do, day after day. The killing, the gun play I mean."

I too was feeling the melancholy from the responsibilities that came with our vocation. Our task was such as to keep the peace while protecting the citizenry, but at what cost?

Just then Jim came behind us and said, "Gun play? I never heard it put that way before Robert. That sounds to be somethin' of a child's game my friends."

We turned and there he stood, one hand resting on his pistol, the other holding a coffee cup.

I said, "This rock seems to be large enough to accommodate three, care to join us, Jim?"

"Do not mind if I do," he said as he sat next to Robert.

I said, "Robert was just asking about our job of late."

Jim pulled out a cigar, struck a match and got it going. He took it out of his mouth, looked at the burning end then said, "I did not mean to stick my nose into your conversation boys, but I think I can provide you with some helpful knowledge." He put the cigar in his mouth and said as he bit down, "You see, I have been at this for more than twenty years come next month."

Robert said, "You have our attention, Jim."

He pulled on the cigar, exhaled around it. "Well, let me start off and ask if you fellas is feelin' the melancholia sneakin' up on you?"

I looked at Robert then back to Jim and said, "At times we do, yes."

He nodded in understanding. He pulled the cigar out of his mouth, spit on the ground and said, "I tell ya boys. I been livin' behind the gun for a long time. Over twenty as a lawman, a few before that as, well, somethin' else. I know what it is you feel, I have been down that dark trail myself."

"Yet, you stay with it," Robert pointed out.

He nodded. "I do. I have stayed with it because I am good at it and there are folks out there that ain't. It is for those that cannot protect themselves that I stay behind the gun, and I ain't never killed them that did not have it comin'." He turned to both of us and continued. "Boys, there is evil in this world, tis a fact. There will always be evil in this world intent on takin' what they want from folks that cannot fight back. That is why we are here." He stood and looked out into the night. "Like it or not, you boys are good with the iron. You can use it for evil, or you can fight the evil that is set upon us. What you boys did in the war is beyond my thinkin', but knowin' you two as I do, it was not evil that you did, no sir, twas not, it was soldiering!"

I looked down at the ground, pulled absentmindedly on my pipe and remained silent, as did Robert.

Jim turned back to us. "I think of when I first met you boys that night in the saloon. You took on some evil sons a bitches that ever walked the ground, and you sent them to hell cause you seen what evil men can do." He started to walk away, stopped and turned back adding, "You just remember those fellas that had their throats cut, that boy in the hospital bed. These sons a bitches chose to come at us, and I will be damned if I let them get any further past me. You boys remember that."

We both watched him walk into the darkness toward the camp.

Robert said, "I think he has a point, Wyatt."

"I believe he does, Robert."

"I suppose it is a matter of one's perspective," Robert observed. "I have never taken a life of a man in cold blood or a man who did leave me any other choice."

I thought before I spoke. So many years of living with a gun strapped to my hip, in the saddle scabbard, in my pocket. It was difficult to see myself without one. I said, "What troubled times we live in my friend. Reckon we will go on as we are as long as this evil is beset upon us."

Robert asked, "What was it that George Washington said about being President?"

I smiled and answered, "The office chooses the man."

"I suppose that can apply to our job Wyatt."

"Reckon so," I said.

Robert bid me a good night and returned to the camp while I maintained the guard, smoked my pipe, and expressed my thanks to The Almighty for having come through yet another day.

Morning came, and we, having passed an unmolested evening, stirred from beneath our bedrolls. No critters, soldiers nor gunmen sought us out during the night, so we went about the task of breaking camp, having breakfast, and caring for the animals.

Once back on the trail, Long Buffalo feeling much like his 'ol self, joined Skinner as we navigated our way further south, still able to follow the tracks left by the desperados. The wagon and horse tracks were visible to all which spoke of stupidity on the part of the bandits or over-confidence as we had no difficulty in pursuing them.

The hours in the saddle crept by as the flats gave way to hills, trees and thick green brush causing us to move in single file as we entered the Hill Country.

It was mid-day, and Long Buffalo was the lead rider. The trail was not so present as before and our pace slowed, but we continued, moving deeper into the hills putting our trust in Long Buffalo and his abilities to read sign left by the fleeing bandits.

It was soon after this that Long Buffalo stopped, held up his hand and looked around at the ground under him. Our column stopped and we sat our horses as Long Buffalo dismounted and walked around his pony in an ever-widening circle.

Robert turned in his saddle and said to me, "Should we dismount Wyatt?"

I watched Long Buffalo from my position at the end of the column as he continued his circular trek around his pony, stepping a bit further out with each rotation. I shook my head and said, "Not yet Robert. He is on to something, and we best let him go about it."

No sooner had I said this when Long Buffalo stopped and looked off to the east, never uttering a word nor making a motion to us. He just stood there looking for a moment, nodded his head, then made his way to the rest of us.

I dismounted, tied Buster off on my saddle horn and made my way forward as did the rest of our party, meeting Long Buffalo at the head of the column.

"What goes," I asked.

Long Buffalo pointed to the east and said, "They took the wagon that way and returned without it, then continued southeast. They all gathered around the wagon before they did this, I do not know why. The wagon went in the brush but did not come back. Only two riders came back."

Jim said, "Reckon they dumped the wagon in the brush."

Robert asked, "Why dump the wagon after coming this far?"

Skinner stepped away from us and visibly sniffed the air. He turned to Long Buffalo and asked, "Smell that?"

Long Buffalo nodded and said, "I do. It is burnt wood and something else I do not know."

Jim said angrily, "Sons a bitches did it again! They burnt the wagon, damnation!"

I smelled nothing. "We best go and look," I said. "No sense gettin' worked up just yet till we see it."

"Well, you know they did it, damnation," Jim uttered.

Robert said, "I will stay with the animals."

I looked at him. "You might want to get your rifle. Do not know yet how close we may be to them."

I followed Jim, Long Buffalo, and Skinner into the brush. It was thick but not so as we could not get through it. As we walked deeper into the foliage I could see where they had brought the wagon back through the area. Limbs from small shrubs, broken and bent, tall grass trampled down, and bushes torn up by the roots. They brought the wagon back here sure enough and it was not long that I too smelled burnt wood with something my sense of smell could not identify yet smelled vaguely familiar.

In short order we came to a small clearing and everything revealed itself for all the senses to behold. It was the wagon, burnt to blackened chunks of wood and warped steel from the heat of the flames. It had been a hot fire, enough to burn the surrounding ground and grass.

I bent down and picked up a small piece of burnt wood, it was cold to the touch, the fire long since burned itself out. I smelled it, recognizing the stench of lamp oil. They used lamp oil to start the fire, a lot of it by the looks of the remnants.

Long Buffalo had something in his hand. It was loose, not hard like wood, and he brought it to his nose. He said, "This is the smell I did not know. It is clothing."

I stepped over to him, found a thick, long branch and stirred the area where he had found the article. As I stirred, embers and smoke were released to the air as they were still hot and smoldering beneath. I pulled a small scrap from the pile and looked it over carefully.

I held it up for the others and said, "It is a uniform. A Federal Army uniform."

Jim stepped over, took the charred piece of clothing, and examined it. "Damnation if it ain't. You can still see the color of the dark blue." He kicked at the smoldering pile, bent down, and pulled a small piece from smoking mass of burnt cloth and held it up. "It is a brass button," he said. "They burnt the Yankee uniforms."

I said, "I thought the smell was familiar."

Jim cast me a puzzled look and asked, "How is it familiar to you?"

I cocked my head, raised my eyebrows, and just looked back at Jim.

He took my meaning and said, "Oh, yea. Sorry."

We stood around the remains of the wagon and just stared. There was no sense in digging through the burnt wood to find the cash box. The money and gold were gone and the box ended up as fuel to an angry fire that took everything. There was no need to discuss what was obvious.

Jim shook his head and said, "Shit."

I said, "Best get back to Robert and figure out where the trail goes from here friends."

Jim asked, "Why they always burnin' up good wagons?"

I chuckled and said, "Reckon they have no use for them, like the uniforms."

We gathered at the animals and told Robert of our discovery and began to discuss our continuing on, deeper into the Hill Country in search of these killers. It was not so much as to traveling and our supplies holding out, but could we follow this forgotten trail that was known to them, not so to us. True, we had two of the best trackers to be had, but this was rough country we had entered, and it was their ground.

I asked, "So how about it Long Buffalo? Think you can pick up the trail and follow it?"

He looked around, his mouth and jaw set as he gave it some thought. He said, "I think with Skinner up front with me we can do this. We can find these men."

Skinner added, "We surely can Long Buffalo. We can track 'em to hell if need be."

I said, "Then we best get at it. Be dark in a few hours and I hope to find them before the sun goes down."

We mounted up with Skinner and Long Buffalo in the lead while I brought up the rear dragging Buster through the brush. At Long Buffalo's suggestion we spaced our column out beyond the normal distance between mounts and added extra space between our two scouts and us. The tactic we employed was one of safety should we be discovered. The enemy may discover the lead scouts, Long Buffalo and Skinner, but may not see us following at a greater distance behind, thus giving us the opportunity to seek cover or provide a distraction. From my position at the rear of the column I could not see our two lead scouts.

It was a typical sweltering day as we cut through the thick vegetation. The foliage grew tight and thick along the trail pressing in from both sides. More than once, I caught myself questioning our route of march as I could not see how Long Buffalo or Skinner followed any trail, read any sign, or observed any tracks. We remained silent as we slowly made our way deeper into the Hill Country, each left to his own thoughts.

I looked at the back of Caliban's head as he pushed along the trail. He too felt the heat and discomfort of the expedition but continued giving his all. Branches and vines reached out to us along the trail scratching his flanks, his head, and neck. I leaned forward and patted his thick muscular neck as a way of telling him I was aware of his sacrifices made on this journey, and that I was appreciative of his efforts.

On and on we traveled. The hours passed un-noticed as our silent train of men and animals moved through this unknown wilderness. We had no idea as to what we would find, when we would find it, or if we would find what we sought. Much like the patrols I led in search of the Yankee army during the war, each step either brought us closer to our prize, or further into the unknown, only to find...nothing.

Though it was an arduous task to navigate through unfamiliar ground it was more trying on a man to remain vigilant to the unseen dangers. To be aware that around every bend in the trail, over a slight rise in the ground, there the enemy waited. The silence of the ride caused one to retreat to his own thoughts, his own concerns, thus becoming ignorant of what lay ahead, behind or to the flanks. One must force himself to concentrate, work the senses beyond what could be seen. Sounds, smells, and the general feeling of the situation was a never-ending task, daunting at times but necessary none the less. To lapse into complacency was inviting death.

It was late in the hour, and I took my time piece from my pocket and looked at the watch for the first time that day. It was after six o'clock and still, we were in the saddle. I returned the gold watch to my pocket, shook my head as I felt anger creeping into my thoughts. Not an anger at our party but an anger at my lack of participation. Much like the early days of the war where I was anxious to go into battle, I felt that now, I needed to do something, anything other than ride along, dragging the pack mule in tow.

I pushed these thoughts from my mind, remembering that in the early days of the struggle we held an unrealistic notion of war, a sort of romantic idea filled with drama and heroic deeds. Riding off into battle to fight for our cause only to learn that in the end, the cause meant nothing and had been replaced with the death and misery that accompanies war and conflict, and yet we fought on. Only later, we would be fighting for each other.

These memories, these thoughts pushed the anger from my mind as we rode on. My time to contribute would come soon enough and as was my way, I would give it my all for my comrades, for the folks I had sworn to protect, for the justice of a deserving people.

I remained steadfast in my observations of the situation around me, contrary to my drifting thoughts, yet I cursed myself for the brief breech in discipline. It was then that I saw Robert hold up his hand, signaling a halt.

We had arrived.

CHAPTER TWENTY-SIX

I sat my horse and waited. It was not long before Skinner, on foot, sided up to Robert. I saw him speaking softly to him as Robert leaned out of the saddle to hear what it was, he was being told. Robert nodded and dismounted while Skinner made his way to me.

Skinner was tall, almost a giant of a man some would say, as he stood next to me. I did not need to lean too far out of the saddle as his head came just below my chest.

Softly he said, "We got us a whiff of smoke up ahead. I reckon we found them. You and Marshal Robert is to go up front with Long Buffalo, and me an' Jim will tend the mounts."

I said nothing, merely nodded my head and dismounted. Almost as an afterthought, I grabbed the shotgun and put a few extra shells in my pocket. I had seen Robert grab his Spencer which would give us the long-range protection whereas the shotgun was more suited for close actions in the thick foliage.

Silently I made my way forward, closing the space between Robert and myself, joining him as we came upon Jim. He was dismounted and held the reins of both Skinner's horse and Long Buffalo's pony.

I stepped close to him and quietly asked, "What goes Jim?"

He said, "Long Buffalo says there is a camp up ahead. I am going to take the horses back to the rear while you boys do your cavalry stuff and scout it out."

I smiled and whispered, "I knew we came along for a reason."

Jim grinned and whispered back, "Oh horseshit. You boys be careful."

We made our way forward, bent slightly at the waist searching the immediate area for danger. We did not move swiftly as it would seem we were on the enemy's ground now and the discovery of our party would mean death.

I led the way, pushing through the thick foliage in search of our friend. I dare not call out as it would give our position away and alert this hide-out camp to our presence. Even though we had not seen nor heard anything to tell us where it was, the fact that Long Buffalo wanted us up front was enough to tell us we were close and knowing him as I did, he would suddenly appear to us as he was a master of concealment, in spite of his colorful dress.

I stopped, knelt on one knee, and scanned the area in front of me. It was a small rise, and the trail was now evident as the foliage seemed to widen making it more a trail than the goat path we had been following.

Off to my left I heard a whisper, "I am here Wyatt."

I turned, startled, and there he was, squatting in the scrub brush grinning. We moved closer.

I whispered as I came alongside him. "I do not know how I missed you."

Robert said softly, "Scared me out of ten years of my life."

Long Buffalo suppressed a laugh. He whispered, "You look but fail to see. One day I will teach you."

I ignored his comment and said, "What have you to tell us my friend?"

He pointed to our front and quietly said, "The camp of which we are looking for is up ahead a short way. I have seen it. I will let you go on the scout to get what it is you require while I remain here until you return."

"It may be dark when we return," I said.

He nodded his understanding and said, "I will remain here and keep a watchful eye and guide you back. When the darkness comes, it is a blackness in this wild place so, be careful my friends."

I grinned and turned to Robert. "You ready?"

He said, "I am, lead the way, Wyatt."

We turned, keeping low we made our way along the edge of the path should someone come along, forcing us to seek cover in the brush. We moved slowly, cautiously with our guns at the ready just creeping along looking and listening to our surroundings.

I stopped and turned to Robert. "I smell smoke."

He said, "They are probably making dinner." Then he asked, "Think they have any pickets out?"

I had thought of that. "Be foolish if they did not have a few posted."

"Foolish or complacent," Robert pointed out.

We continued our trek to put eyes on the camp.

As we neared, we heard voices in the distance. At first it sounded like someone was calling out to another. Then there came more voices. I found the sounds familiar, even though I could not make out the words.

Many a time I had gone out to scout Federal positions and listened to the sounds of camp-life coming from the other side. The routine business of living by the open cook-fires, sleeping in the heavy canvas tents, soldiers playing cards, laughing, and carrying on was oddly comforting to me. The sounds and the activity were the same in our camps throughout the war, mostly it was an attempt to quell the boredom, relax after battle or be alone and reflect. I surmised that the life of a soldier in the field was the same in every army.

We slowed our advance, moving closer to the ground as we noticed the brush was thinning out. I turned to Robert and held up my hand signaling to stop. Using rudimentary hand gestures, I instructed Robert to stand fast as I would go forward to put eyes on the camp, then return.

I took off my hat and laid it aside. Then I took my Walker revolver from the holster and slipped it into my gun belt at the small of my back. Lowering my body flat on the ground I slowly dragged myself up the small rise, not ten or so feet in front of me while Robert faced to the rear of our position, rifle at the ready.

Ever so slowly I eased my head over the crest of the rise and looked out in front of me, and there it was. Laid out in a large clearing was a military camp in all its disciplined order. Tents, large and small, separated and arranged at right angles by size spread through the edges of the camp forming a box with open ground in the center. The open ground, though small, served as a parade field or formation area for the troops with a flagpole inside a rocked rectangular box, and atop the flagpole, flapping in the breeze was the Stars and Bars, the Confederate Battle Flag.

I quickly looked over the camp then focused my attention to the wood line that defined the shape of the camp. We needed to establish an observation post where we might watch the comings and goings of the soldiers and get a better idea as to their strength, equipment, and what type of unit they had formed. I saw a useable spot off to the right about fifty or so yards that looked down on the camp.

I slid back away from the rise and joined up with Robert. He continued to watch our rear as I put my mouth close to his ear. I whispered, "It is them for sure. It is a holdout camp all right. We need to move off to the right to get a better look and put the glass on them."

Robert only nodded his head as I crouched low and moved slowly to the right, pushing through the brush, Robert directly behind me.

We found our position overlooking the camp not seventy-five yards from the perimeter's edge. From our observation nest we saw the entire camp and immediately set to work establishing strength, type of unit and weapons. Robert lay next to me with his spyglass at the ready.

Robert whispered, "Odd that they do not have pickets posted."

"Overconfident would be my guess," I said.

We divided the normal observation duties between us. I would establish the unit by the number of men and what they were currently doing, while Robert would observe and record the types of weapons and equipment, they had to include the horses.

I brought the spyglass to my eye and began a count. Working from right to left I scanned over the camp keeping the number in my head as I panned the glass slowly over the men. I saw the faces of the grey clad soldiers as they went about their activities in the compound. I felt oddly detached from my duty as observer as I watched and remembered. Here I was, spyglass in hand, watching an active Confederate Army camp, and me, a former Confederate Cavalry officer. The oddity if not the absurdity of the situation suddenly struck me. Not so long ago I could remember doing this identical type of mission, but against the Yankees.

I lowered the glass before I finished my count trying to accept or understand this odd feeling that came over me. I mentally ran through a gamut of emotions as I tried to figure my sudden concerns and issues. Was this betrayal? Were my actions as such that I was going against my own kind, the very notion that had brought me into the Confederacy at the start? Were these men, these soldiers whom I had stood side by side through those four long years my comrades? The more I thought through my internal conflict the more confused I became.

Robert must have taken notice of my lack of activity and gave me a slight nudge with his elbow. I looked at him and said nothing.

He looked down at the camp then back to me. He leaned closer and whispered, "What troubles you, my friend?"

I shook my head, suddenly ashamed of myself for feeling the way I did. I returned to the task at hand and began my count, again, moving from right to left.

As I neared the center of the camp, I took notice of a lone soldier, bugle in hand stop and stand at attention in the center of the parade field. He brought the bugle to his lips and blew out a familiar set of notes.

I said quietly, "Assembly."

Soldiers came from all corners of the camp and gathered in a tight well-disciplined formation in front of the flagpole. I did a quick count of the four rows of men standing at attention. Ten in each row, four rows yielded forty men. Then off to the side of the formation another group of soldiers, wearing the uniform of officers, formed into another four rows. This had four men per row, another sixteen soldiers.

I lowered my spyglass and shook my head. I whispered to Robert, "Lord Almighty Damn son. That is fifty-six soldiers down there."

Robert, still looking through his glass whispered back, "If you like that take a gander at the large tent, far side of the camp at eleven o'clock. Soldier came out of there and left the flap open."

I brought the glass to my eye, scanned over, and stopped on the open tent. I could not believe what it was that I saw. "Son of a bitch," I uttered quietly. "They got them a twelve-pound Napoleon Cannon."

Robert answered, "It would appear so my friend."

I looked over the artillery piece under cover of the tent. Its brass reflected what light remained of the day, the wheels and carriage clean with a fresh coat of black paint telling me that it had been well taken care of which also meant that it was serviceable.

I said, "Well if that does not make my ass want a soda cracker!"

I noticed out of the corner of my eye Robert had lowered his spyglass and cast a bewildered look at me. I was unsure if he heard me, or he was trying to suppress a laugh or, more than likely, did not understand.

He leaned over and asked, "What the hell does that mean, Wyatt?"

I looked over at him while keeping my spyglass up. "I am not rightly for certain Robert. My Daddy always said it when he was mad."

At this Robert put his hand over his mouth as he tried to choke back a laugh.

I lowered my glass and rested my chin on my hands. "We got a whole heap of trouble Robert."

"That we do," he answered. "I also saw a rope corral up that small rise to the rear of the camp. I guess each man has a mount and a team to pull the cannon."

"We can assume that they have a caisson slap full of ammunition for the cannon," I added while my mind was working out the details of a coordinated attack on the compound. "Still," I continued, "we could come in from the left and right at the same time."

Robert said, "I admire your sand Wyatt, but I do not think the five of us can take on fifty plus men with a cannon."

I grinned at him and said, "You may have a point my friend."

From the camp below the command of 'Attention' was barked out and the gathered Confederate soldiers stood ramrod straight and still. From inside the largest of tents, directly in front of the flagpole a small officer, in full parade dress bearing the insignia of a major stepped out and stood before the gathered men.

Again, I raised the glass to my eye and rested it upon what I presumed to be their commanding officer. Rotating the shaft of the spy glass to bring the figure in focus I rested it on the man's face and froze.

My heart immediately began to beat faster, harder, almost threatening to explode from my chest as I took in the black mustache, thick and curled upwards at the ends, the almost boyish face and black hair of Major Arius James Purdy.

I reached out to my left and grabbed Robert, shaking him as I was unable to speak. He looked at me then back at the camp and raised his glass to his eye.

He said quietly, "What was that about a soda cracker?" He lowered the spyglass and looked at me. "That little bastard has been playing us from the start."

I said, "Well, we knew that but not like this."

"What do you think we should do," Robert asked me.

I looked down at the despicable man as he addressed his soldiers. We could not hear the words, but we knew what he was saying. I said, "I believe you should take your Spencer and put one right between his eyes."

Robert said, "I would be more than happy to fulfill that request my friend, but I fear we would not make it out of here alive."

"I know, Robert. It was just a thought." I looked up at the sky through the thick leaves overhead. "Be dark soon, we best be gettin' back."

We backed out of our position ever mindful of making any noise and decided on a direct line to rendezvous with Long Buffalo. As we were leaving, I took one last look over my shoulder, thinking to myself that my feelings of earlier, my strange feelings of betrayal, were no longer of any consequence. These men were murderers and thieves, nothing more.

Their allegiance to the Confederacy and their desires to keep the conflict going was of no importance to me. These men had crossed the line between right and wrong. The war is long over and we in the Southern States had lost. Our armies and our cause ceased to exist when General Robert E. Lee put pen to paper and surrendered at Appomattox on the 9th day of April, eighteen hundred and sixty-five.

Though many units chose to fight on in isolated parts of the country and the CSS Shenandoah did not surrender until November of the same year, the war was over. Yet these men chose to cause more suffering on a people that had suffered enough, and our aim was to stop them from doing so. Personally, my aim was to bring the wrath of hell down on Arius James Purdy.

By the time we had returned to the general location where we parted with Long Buffalo the darkness was near complete. We slowly made our way around the general area, not daring to call out, just hoping that we stumbled across our friend or he found us.

We stopped, sat on the ground, and looked through the darkness, hoping for a sign when we heard a whisper, "You almost tripped over me twice my friends."

I exhaled loudly then whispered, "Why did you not say something then?"

I thought I heard him chuckle when he said, "You were moving in circles and would not stop long enough for me to speak."

"Oh, just get us out of here," I answered.

We followed Long Buffalo out of the area, a bit quicker than our arrival due to the darkness, and soon rejoined Jim and Skinner with the animals.

Jim asked softly, "What did you find boys?"

I said, "You ain't gonna like it fellas."

I looked at Jim through the shadows and spoke. "We found the camp. They have roughly fifty-six soldiers and officers with mounts." I paused. "They also have a twelve-pound cannon."

Jim said, "You were right. I ain't gonna like it."

Robert said, "That is not all. We saw their commander."

I interrupted Robert and said, "You really ain't gonna like this."

Robert finished. "We found out what Major Purdy is up to. He is the commanding officer of these holdouts."

Jim's anger was clear even through the darkness. His jaw tightened as he mashed his teeth together and said a bit too loudly, "I am gonna kill that miserable little bastard!"

CHAPTER TWENTY-SEVEN

Jim gathered his emotions, and we decided it best if we retreat. We thought by getting away from the camp we could talk more freely and formulate a plan. From the information we gathered so far, the unit size, weapons and even their commander, it needed to be one hell of a plan, and my mind raced as we walked the animals away from the camp in the darkness.

Long Buffalo led the way through the dense foliage as we pulled our mounts along. No talking, moving slowly to keep the noise to a minimum we stayed on the move with no set location to stop, to rest or even set up camp. We had an overwhelming desire to put as much distance between us and the holdout camp as we could.

The hours passed as we trudged through the Hill Country along the goat path. I can speak only to myself when I say I was not tired, nor did I have the need to stop for a rest. My mind had taken over and became the sole driver, the single motivator as we pushed on, ignoring all else. I kept seeing Purdy's face in the lens of my spyglass as he addressed his troops, standing there speaking to his men as I had done so many times during the war.

How had he accomplished such a ploy, such a scheme in adopting a dead Union Army Officer's identity, obtain a position on the Paymaster General's staff, and facilitate multiple robberies of Federal monies throughout Texas?

The more I dwelled on the particulars the more it made sense to me. I am certain the others have been exercising their brains while on this arduous trek out of the wilderness and had come to their own conclusions, developed their own theories as to how this could be. The more I thought on it the more the desire to stop and discuss it with the others came upon me. We needed a plan to stop this and the trek along the goat path was becoming frustrating.

My anger and frustration stewed within, and it was not until midnight that we stopped. We had walked from the camp to the small clearing where they had burned the army wagon and their Federal Army uniforms.

We gathered near the remains of the wagon and stood in a loose circle.

I said, "Reckon we can camp here tonight. One man on guard while the others rest up."

Jim said, "Rest up? Hell, that ain't gonna happen. I am too riled up!"

Robert chuckled, knowing the frustration Jim felt and tried to make light of it. He said, "Seeing how you are not tired, you can have the first guard shift Jim."

Jim fell silent and looked at us. It did not take long before he smiled and said, "Ah hell boys. I been thinkin' on that Purdy fella since we left the camp. Kinda worked myself up I did. I did not mean nuthin' by it."

"What say we bed down the horses and come up with a plan," I suggested to the others.

We unsaddled the mounts, unburdened Buster of the panniers and tied them off on a rope line strung out between two trees as Robert put together a cold dinner for us.

I sat back against my saddle and crossed my arms over my chest. I said, "I have been giving this some thought," I looked at the others and saw that they were nodding. "Figured you boys been doin' the same so I will just say that we found out what Purdy is doing and now we just have to figure on what we can do to stop him."

Long Buffalo asked, "Who is this Purdy to which has you so angry?"

I had forgotten that Long Buffalo had not been privy to the happenings of Major Purdy since he was imprisoned by the army at Fort Mason. I began by telling him of our first and only meeting with the man, our suspicions from the very onset to this latest revelation as to his identity and motives.

He nodded his head and said, "I too would be angry. This man has fooled so many people, so easily."

Jim asked, "So what are we to do about him?" He stood and paced in a tight circle. "I say we just kill the man."

Robert said, "Not so easy getting to him. Remember, he has over fifty men with him and a cannon."

Skinner cleared his throat and said, "You give me a clear line I can take his head off at over hundred yards."

"Fellas," I began, "we are forgetting that killing him is just part of the solution. Robert is right. He has near sixty men, and they have been robbing payrolls throughout Texas for the last few months."

“And killing people as well, “Robert added.

I said, “Right. We must deal with them as well and there ain’t but five of us.”

Jim stopped pacing and said, “Okay, so we need a bit of help.”

Robert asked, “You have a plan, Wyatt?”

I looked at my friend and said, “I am at a loss Robert. At this moment, I cannot think of a damn thing to give us the edge.”

Jim was going to say something but stopped before he uttered a word.

I took notice of this and said, “Go ahead with what you were going to say Jim.”

He took in a breath and said, “As soon as I thought of it, I know it ain’t goin’ to work. I was gonna say we could go to the army and ask for help.”

I chuckled, cleared my throat to suppress further laughter, and said, “I do not believe they would be too willing to help us after what we did at Fort Mason.”

Long Buffalo smiled then said, “Do you think they will still be angry at us Wyatt?”

Robert said with a snicker, “I am willing to bet angry does not describe what they feel right now.”

I sighed heavily, frustrated again but this time because we could not come up with a plan. I said, “Reckon we should get some rest and think on it some more.”

Jim said, “I will take first shift on guard. Doubt I can sleep now anyway.”

Surprisingly, I was able to catch a few hours of rest. I did not think it possible, but I opened my eyes to the morning sun and looked around at the others as they were stirring under their blankets.

I saw Long Buffalo near the trail standing guard, rifle cradled in his arms looking off in the distance. I looked over at Jim and asked, “I was never roused from sleep to stand guard Jim.”

Jim scratched his head and looked at Long Buffalo. “Long Buffalo relieved me. I reckon he stood watch all night, Wyatt.”

“Yea,” I said as I looked at my Indian friend. “He has something on his mind.”

I stood, stretched my legs, and made my way to him, not wishing to intrude on his thoughts, yet concerned that there was something that troubled him and I may be able to help.

I came alongside him and asked, “How are you this morning my friend?”

He turned, looked at me, then looked back at the trail. He said, "I will not rest until we have returned to town." He looked back at me, smiled slightly then said, "You have come here to ask what troubles me. Is that not so?"

I shook my head and grinned. Cryptic, even mysterious at times, nothing escaped Long Buffalo's attention. I said, "No gettin' anything past you, my friend. What is it that troubles you since you brought it up?"

"It is this evil one, Achak," he said. "He is out there waiting, watching for the next moment to strike. He is the one that must be stopped. He will go on killing until he himself is dead. He enjoys it."

A chill ran down my spine as I listened to Long Buffalo. It was not so much what he said as how he said it. I will admit that I had been so consumed by my anger over Major Purdy that I forgot about this murderous Indian that had been killing all those we sought. I said nothing.

Long Buffalo looked out towards the trail. "I must kill him," he said softly.

I put my hand on his shoulder, gave it a slight squeeze, and turned back to the camp. I understood my friend's desire, his need to rid the world of this evil. It was not that Long Buffalo was akin to this man, this Achak, because they were both Indians, but I felt that Long Buffalo believed and understood the blackness that resided in Achak's heart. An evil spirit possessed this villainous Indian, and the medicine man felt compelled to send this demon back from whence he came.

We began to break camp, eating light as we accomplished the few tasks required to get us back on the trail. We spoke little, agreeing that a more formative plan can be made when we return to town drawing on the assets and experience of Thadius Polehouse and W.B.D. Burns. Still, it did not sit well with me as I felt we were leaving the field to the enemy.

I was leading Caliban into the camp when I took notice that Long Buffalo was not standing by the trail, he was nowhere to be seen. Fearing something was amiss I drew my Walker and said quietly to the others, "Where is Long Buffalo?"

The others, sensing my alarm drew their pistols and looked about.

Robert said, "Better get the horses under cover."

We pushed, pulled, and prodded the animals back to the rope line and returned to the burnt remnants of the wagon, spreading out in a circle to cover all directions.

As we were searching for our friend, we heard a ruckus back by the trail. There was a loud thud followed by an unfamiliar voice crying out, in fear or anger it was not known to us as the words were unintelligible. There followed another cry of a man, a high-pitched neigh of a horse, then silence.

I cocked my revolver and pointed it at the direction of the trail, waiting.

Long Buffalo called out, "I am coming into the camp my friends."

I answered, "Come ahead Long Buffalo."

Through the tall grass and shrubs, I spied Long Buffalo's colorful garb. He came through the foliage pulling a horse with his left hand and what appeared to be the foot and leg of a man through the grass with his right.

He stopped, breathing heavily, looked at us and said, "I can pull the horse or the man into the camp, not both together."

I stood, holstered my pistol, and ran forward with Robert right behind me.

As I stopped next to Long Buffalo, I saw that he did have a man in tow. He was holding him around his leg, dragging him through the brush. The man, dressed in the full Confederate Uniform of an Artillery Corporal, was unconscious, bleeding from a wound on the side of his head.

I said, "What the hell! Where did this fella come from?"

Long Buffalo dropped the leg and said, "I heard him coming down the trail. I knocked him off his horse then hit him on the head with my pistol."

Robert bent before the unconscious form. He said, "He is still alive." He looked up at Long Buffalo. "You whacked him pretty good."

Long Buffalo shrugged his shoulders and said, "Of course. My gun is heavy, that is why I used it."

I laughed. "He the only one?"

"I saw no more behind him," Long Buffalo said. "I think we should go because there may be more coming."

I grabbed one leg, Robert the other and we pulled the soldier into our camp. Dropping his legs we set about reviving the man in the hopes he could answer some questions. Once awake we were taking him with us.

Robert poured water over his face and lightly slapped his cheek. "Wake-up soldier," he said.

The man moaned but remained unresponsive.

I knelt beside the man, looked into his face, and peeled open an eyelid. I said, "I reckon we need to persuade this fella to wake up." I slapped him hard across the face and said, "Stop faking it boy and wake up!"

He cried out, reached up and rubbed his reddening cheek. "Damnation Marshal. You do not need to beat me so!"

His statement struck me odd at his specific mention of me being a Marshal. I had removed my badge the night before as I did not want it to reflect off the sun and moon and maybe give our position away. "How did you know I was a Marshal?"

He looked back at me, closed his mouth, and shook his head.

I briefly studied the man. He was tall and thin; his uniform was loose fitting. It was either someone else's clothes or the man had lost some weight recently. His face was weathered, his hair, though light, showed signs of greying at the temples. I put the man in his early thirties maybe a bit older. It was hard to tell as those of us in the war aged well beyond our years, and this man had been to war. It was easy to tell as I looked into his eyes. There was the sadness that we all carried long after the guns fell silent.

I pulled him to his feet and said, "You may want to reconsider your position son. In the meantime, you are comin' with us."

Robert came forward with manacles and put them around both his wrists. The corporal showed no resistance and submitted peacefully, almost dejectedly.

I said, "I suggest we gag him too. Do not need him callin' out should we come upon some of his friends."

Robert fashioned a gag from a rag used to wrap the jerky. Before he put it in the man's mouth he said, "Last chance soldier. You want to tell us your name."

The man again closed his mouth as if he feared the words would come out on their own, shook his head and submitted to the gag.

I said to all, "I think it prudent that we skedaddle from the field as quickly as we can manage. We can make our plans when we get back to town."

Robert said, "As much as I find the idea of retreating hard to swallow, I believe you have a point, Wyatt."

Jim asked, "You boys were actually thinkin' of attacking?"

I laughed and confidently announced, "I spent four years fighting against the odds Jim. The thought had crossed my mind."

"Why do you think the war lasted four years," Robert said. "Fellas like Wyatt never worried about the odds."

We gathered up the animals, pushed the corporal onto his mount and formed up for our return trip to Fredericksburg. Be it a retreat, an escape or perhaps a redeployment to the rear we departed the field with due haste as we understood how badly we were outnumbered. To fight now when so greatly out manned and out gunned would have been a foolish gesture on our part.

Long Buffalo took the lead followed by Skinner, Robert pulling our prisoner in tow, Jim, with rifle at the ready behind the corporal then me bringing up the rear dragging Buster on the lead line.

Our pace was quick and steady as we knew that we would not be safe until we reached Fredericksburg. Our stops would be few and short as the hot summer's day will wear both man and animal down and we did not want to suffer casualties from the oppressive heat of the day.

Morning hours gave way to mid-day as we continued our march to the north. The ground was becoming familiar to us as we were back on the well-traveled trail and the thought of reaching town motivated us to push on. Thoughts of rest, cool water, decent food were pushed aside as we thought of only the safety of our jail, our town, and our friends. Those desires of food and water meant nothing if we were to die in the unforgiving land. Be it by the hand of our enemy or by the harsh environment we traveled through, our priorities were to get home, regroup, and find a way to combat the forces of Major Arius James Purdy.

I thought on this man while we rode. His true name was of no interest to me, only his intentions. He had brought his army to this place for a reason. That reason, I surmised, was to continue fighting the Federal Forces and perhaps incite others to join him. Perhaps there were other units scattered about Texas and the south with the same intentions as his. Regardless of his intentions he and his men had committed crimes against folks that just wanted to put their lives back together and carve out a piece of a prosperous future.

Purdy and his men, refusing to accept defeat, had robbed and killed to finance their selfish desires. I thought of my hesitance when I first glassed over the camp, seeing the uniforms of grey, thinking of my years in the struggle, fighting alongside these men. My initial feelings of betrayal had confused me at first only because I had forgotten what brought me there, to the edge of that camp. It was only the memories, the feelings, the camaraderie of my fellow soldiers that had grabbed hold of me at that moment.

These men, like the corporal in chains riding silently in front of me, were no longer my comrades, not my men. Though it tore at my heart to watch General Lee commit pen to paper and surrender, it, much like our retreat of this day, was necessary.

Sometimes it is best to walk away.

CHAPTER TWENTY-EIGHT

We soon found ourselves looking at Fredericksburg on the distant horizon, relief was in sight, and we pushed hard through the final few miles anxious to dismount and retreat to the comfort and safety of our jail.

As we arrived Mark, Julius and Thad greeted us while we were tying off, obviously pleased we had returned safely and surprised that we had two additional members in our party.

Thad said as he pointed to the corporal with his rifle, "Got you a prisoner I see. He must not have had anything worth listenin' too for that gag in his mouth."

Robert said, "He has not uttered a word since his capture. We just did not want him calling out to his friends when we made our escape."

Thad cast a glance at Long Buffalo, puzzlement clearly on his face as he asked, "Who might this fella be?"

I looked over at Long Buffalo then back to Thad. "He is a friend of ours. We sprung him from Fort Mason."

Mark said, "That would explain the angry message we got from the Captain of Fort Mason."

I looked at Mark, then Robert trying to suppress a laugh. I said, "Well that did not take long."

Julius stepped down off the porch, shook my hand then Robert's. "Glad you back Cap'n. The boys made it back from Austin with a letter from Judge DuBose for you and Sergeant Major Robert." He took the reins from me and said, "Go inside, I will take care of the animals Cap'n."

"Thank you, Julius," I said, then addressed the rest of our group, "Come gentlemen, let us retire to the comfort of the jail and get caught up on the latest news."

Mark stood at the top of the stairs and greeted us, mirroring the good-natured humor of my statement. He bowed at the waist and said, "Welcome gentlemen, your lovely accommodations await."

I grinned and winked at him as I walked past. It was good to be home.

Inside Chelsea came and hugged each of us as we crossed the threshold, overjoyed that we had returned safely. This expedition had left her fearful for our well-being, understandably so. Since the beginning of this matter the violence directed against us had only escalated, causing each one of us to cast an extra look over our shoulders, be wary of blind corners and potential hiding places. It also caused me to carry extra firearms.

I sat at the table and was soon greeted by our ever-faithful companion, Argos. He too was grateful for our return.

Robert brought the prisoner in and sat him in a chair on the far side of the room and removed his gag. "You hungry soldier," he asked the corporal.

Again, the corporal closed his mouth, said nothing, and looked at the floor.

I exhaled loudly in frustration. "Son, you best understand your position. The war is long past, and you are a criminal, not a soldier." I stood and walked over to him, Argos by my side. "We are not goin' to treat you like a prisoner of war but like a criminal. It can go bad for you, or it can go easy."

He looked up at me then at the dog. For a moment I thought he was going to speak, only to drop his head and stare at the floor.

Argos growled and showed his teeth. He would be the hard way if the corporal so chose.

Just then W.B.D. Burns came limping in from the back. He said, "Welcome back boys." He stopped and looked at the prisoner. "Well Wyatt, I see you brought one of them in. That is just fine since your jail is empty, he can have the cell to himself." Bill laughed.

Robert asked, "The Marshal sent someone to pick up Mack the Knife?"

Bill answered as he grabbed a chair and sat. "He did. Two fellas in the jail wagon come through and took the boy away." He turned his attention to Long Buffalo. "Well, I will be hanged. Long Buffalo, it has been a while, how have you been keeping yourself?"

Long Buffalo smiled and said, "I am well my friend. You seem to be injured."

Bill said with a wave of his hand, "Ain't nuthin'. Fella plugged me in the leg. Last thing he ever did by God." He laughed. "Just tryin' to get around, damn uncomfortable sittin' on my ass."

I returned to my seat and sat heavily in the chair. "I am not surprised you two know each other." Then I asked, "We got anything to drink around here? Fella will die of thirst before he is offered a drink."

Mark produced a bottle of whiskey and a handful of glasses, to which I filled and motioned for all to help themselves. Once I had mine down, I felt renewed, refreshed, and ready to carry forward with the inquiry.

I looked around and asked, "Where are the boys, Clem and Pete?"

Bill looked over his shoulder and said, "Out back helping Julius and Skinner with the animals." He repositioned himself in the chair trying to get comfortable. "I tell you Wyatt. Them fellas would not give us that sealed letter from the judge. Said it was for you and Robert only."

"Reckon Judge DuBose told them as such," I said. "They are good boys."

Thad, standing just inside the door said, "In the meantime, how 'bout you fellas fill us in on all that has happened."

I grinned at the big lawman and said, "Reckon we could do that." I pointed to our prisoner. "I suggest we get this fella settled in his new home before we begin."

Robert stood, grabbed the keys off the desk, and escorted the corporal into the back, pushing him into the first cell.

As Robert came back, he said, "One of these days we will get that new cell put in."

I ignored his comment, understanding how he felt and began to tell everyone of the expedition from the moment we departed to our return. With help from Robert, Jim, and Long Buffalo, who filled in the forgotten or missed details, we spoke of our adventure from Fort Mason to the Texas Hill Country, and the discovery of the Confederate camp hidden away in the wilderness. We spoke of the dangers, the sorrow of seeing the grave of the fallen soldiers, the anger at discovering Long Buffalo's unwarranted imprisonment and our forceful extraction from the confines of his cell. We told them of our trek south, finding the forgotten trail, the burnt wagon, and the hidden camp. We covered all the details of the expedition, save one.

Everyone was quiet, captivated if you will by our tale. Julius, Skinner, and the boys had joined us, watching our faces, hanging on our words.

I said, "The only detail that I have not spoken of is the discovery of the commander of these ex-soldiers."

Bill leaned forward in his chair and asked, "You found out who is leading these villains?"

Robert looked at me and said, "We did."

I crossed my arms over my chest, sat back in the chair, and said, "You ain't gonna like it."

Thad said impatiently, "Well damnation, tell us."

Robert said, "It is Major A.J. Purdy."

The room was silent as looks were exchanged between everyone, disbelief hanging in the air like a dark cloud. I will admit, even as Robert had uttered the man's name, I still found it difficult to believe, even though I had seen him with my own eyes.

Thad began to speak while suppressing his rising anger. "You mean...why he was sittin'...that son of a bitch...we should have..."

Bill said, "You are right. I ain't gonna like it."

I turned my attention to Clem and Pete. "You have a letter for us boys?"

Pete stepped forward and removed a folded envelop from his pocket. He handed it to me saying, "Judge tol me not to let no one touch this cept you and Marshal Robert." He dropped his hands to his sides and rubbed them on his pant leg. "Truth be told Marshal, it felt like that there letter was burnin' a hole in my pocket waitin' fer you to return."

I looked at the letter, the wax seal still intact. I smiled and said, "You boys did good. We are proud of what you done."

Clem stepped closer and held out the leather pouch of money I had given the boys. "Here you go Marshal. We did not spend any since the judge tol us to high tail it back here with this letter."

My smile spread across my face. "You keep it boys. Consider it fair pay for a fine job."

The boys exchanged looks and grinned.

I broke the seal on the letter, removed the folded correspondence, and read through it before I read it aloud so that all may hear.

I said, "It is addressed to Robert and myself. The judge says he appreciates the information and that he has passed on our suspicions of Major Purdy to the General. He also says the General is so old he remains in a befuddled state of mind and will not be of any help, so we are to do what is necessary to bring this to an end." I paused thinking of an old General, one past the age of sound reason, handling all the funds for the State of Texas. I shook my head and continued my reading, asking myself once again, how did we lose the war.

"The judge says we are to continue our correspondence through messenger to him and him alone. He fears we will have to handle this ourselves, but he is sending help."

Robert asked, "What help is he sending?" He looked at Clem and Pete. "Did the judge say anything to you boys about help?"

Pete answered. "No Marshal, he did not say nuthin' bout no help."

Thad stepped across the threshold into the room. "Does the judge say anything else in the letter, Wyatt?"

I turned the page over and said, "That is it. He signed it but says nothin' more about who he is sending to help."

Everyone just stared at me, waiting, wanting an answer.

Just then a deep gravelly voice said, "He sent me."

Thad spun around and leveled his rifle at the large figure standing in the doorway. He asked, "Who might you be mister?"

The large man slowly raised his hands and said, "Do not shoot me, Sheriff. Judge Dubose sent me; thought I could help."

I stood, let the letter fall from my hands, and stepped around the table while taking the man in.

He stood well over six feet tall, broad of shoulder and a muscular chest. His face was hard, deeply lined with a thick brown mustache across his wide upper lip. He was dressed in a charcoal-colored sack coat over a light grey vest, white collarless shirt, and matching pants draped over his boots. Atop his head he wore a bowler tilted at a cocky angle to the right.

He dropped his hands to the front of his waist, hooked his thumbs into his gun belt, two nickel plated Colt Army Revolvers with black ivory grips hung on each hip.

I stopped a few feet from the man and said, "The question still stands mister. Who might you be?"

He grinned and said, "Easy does it Marshal. I have a letter of introduction from Judge Dubose."

Slowly he reached into his jacket and pulled out a sealed envelope, passing it to me. I took the envelope and looked at the wax seal. It was that of the judge, so I ripped it open, and read through the short correspondence.

I said, "Mister Ezra Theodore Walker the Third of The Pinkerton National Detective Agency." I looked up from the letter as the Detective opened his jacket and showed a large silver Pinkerton shield pinned to his left breast. I folded the letter and handed it back to the man. "What do folks call you?"

He took the letter, returned it to his jacket pocket, and said, "Folks call me Ted. Only my mother calls me Ezra, and she passed on."

Bill said scornfully, "A Pinkerton Man, well how 'bout that."

The Detective looked at Bill. He said, "You would be W.B.D. Burns, Sheriff of Kerr County."

Bill looked at the Pinkerton Detective with suspicion. "Now how might you know that mister?"

Detective Walker looked around the room. "I know most of the lawmen here I believe." He looked at me and said, "You are Wyatt Chambers, former Captain of the Confederate Cavalry Corps," he turned to Robert. "You are Robert Barton, a former Sergeant Major under Buford, and you," he said as he turned to Thad, "are Thadius Polehouse, Sheriff of Bandera County." He then turned to Jim. "You sir must be Jim Sweeny, Marshall of Castroville."

Jim said, "That I am."

Thad said, "You seem to know most everybody. How 'bout you tell us how you came by this knowledge."

He took off his bowler, brushed the dust off the crown with his hand and said, "I do my research whenever I take on a new case. Judge Dubose filled me in with most of it, the rest." He put his hat back on, covering his thick wavy brown hair. "Hell, who does not know of you fellas."

"Flattering," I pointed out. "How is it that you can help us, Ted?"

He inhaled deeply before answering and hooked his thumbs in his pistol belt. "For a start I can tell you about this Major Purdy."

Robert said, "We only just now discovered that he is not who he claims to be. How is it that you know about him?"

Ted looked around the room and said, "I have been on his trail for the last six months."

I smiled and said, "Would you like a drink, Ted?"

At this he took off his hat, returned my smile and said, "Thought you would never ask, Wyatt."

Introductions were made around the room as we all gathered around the table. Glasses were refilled, drinks thrown back and everyone found a seat as we waited for what Ted had to impart to us.

Like an accountant preparing to balance the books Ted pulled a small notepad from inside his jacket, a set of oval reading spectacles and a pencil, opened the book, flattened the pages down with his hand, then put his spectacles on, seating them low on his nose.

Bill was looking on in bewilderment and asked, "You sure you are a lawman? Just where are you from boy?"

Ted looked up over his glasses and said, "Chicago, Sheriff, and yes I am a lawman."

"Chicago," Bill repeated with a slight note of contempt.

Ted looked down and referred to his notes as he spoke. "First off, Purdy is not his real name. His true name is Percy Rawlings, from Richmond Virginia. Before the war he was an actor, not a good one I am told."

"Hell," I interrupted, "good enough to fool us into thinking he was a Yankee army major."

Ted continued. "When the war broke out, he got a commission from a state senator with the Army of Northern Virginia. By the end of the war, he rose to the rank of major. Somehow, he and some of his officers deserted before General Lee surrendered and he made his way to Texas, picking up stragglers along the way."

Jim said, "Yea, we saw some of those stragglers. Fifty-six of them."

Ted looked up from his notes, obviously surprised. He asked, "Oh, you have seen them?"

I held up my hand and said, "Keep on Ted. We will tell you what we discovered when you are finished."

He nodded. "Fair enough, Wyatt." He went back to his notes. "Now, the rest is speculation, but well-founded mind you. These holdouts robbed a paymaster when they arrived in Texas some seven months ago. One of these soldiers they killed was the new aide on his way to assume the duties as assistant to the General in Austin. Rawlings adopted the identity of A.J. Purdy, knowing that no one would recognize him, and stepped into the role working with the Paymaster General using a phony letter of introduction."

Thad asked, "How did he know about the real Major Purdy?"

It was Robert who answered. "Simple. Major Purdy was killed the first day of the Gettysburg Battle. We lost the ground the next day to the Army of Northern Virginia where we buried the major. Rawlings must have come across the grave marker and remembered the name and his particulars, then invented the rest."

Ted made a note in his book. "Well," he said, "that explains that mystery. Anyway, after that he stepped into the role as aide to a senile general which gave him all the routes and timing of all Federal monies coming into Texas. He and his men just had to pick and choose what they wanted." He looked at Jim Sweeny. "I surmise that they could not turn away from the safe in Castroville. At the time that was the largest shipment of money to be brought into Texas." He closed his book and looked at us.

Jim sighed and said, "Still have not found that damn safe yet."

I asked, "Anything else on this fella?"

The Pinkerton Detective opened his book again and paged through his notes. He said, "Once I figured he was tied into this I did some background on him. He is not married, both folks are dead. He has a brother, name of Clifford Rawlings, somewhere, I have not been able to find him."

Thad said, "He is probably ridin' with his no-account brother."

Again, Ted closed his book. "Possible, but I doubt it. Fella was some sort of minister in Virginia. Union troops put his church to the torch, and he disappeared after that. Oh, and that sergeant that you may have seen with Rawlings, Sergeant Archibald O'Hanlon was found dead on the road to Austin. Shot through the side of the head."

At first, I did not hear what Ted had said. I thought I heard him correctly, but it was not something I was paying close attention to. I asked him, "Wait, you said his brother was a what?"

Ted looked at me and said, "He was a minister."

I jumped out of my chair sending it crashing over, the excitement getting the best of me. I looked at Robert and said, "I do not believe it."

Robert too came to his feet. "Could it be," he asked of no one in particular.

Julius stepped closer and asked, "Cap'n, could it be the preacher man that was here?"

Now Ted was on his feet. "What preacher man?"

I could hardly contain my excitement. I looked at everyone and said, "By God, I know where the safe is!"

Chapter Twenty-Nine

I walked around the table to the center of the room, ignoring the stares of everyone and looked down at the floor as my mind raced, reviewed, and otherwise went over the brief meeting I had with Brother Adrian Tremellius. It played back in my mind as I saw his face, his eyes, his very mannerisms as I recalled the slightest detail of the man.

The color of his hair, his wide stare, his thin face. It was then that I realized there was a resemblance between our A.J. Purdy and Brother Adrian, a resemblance that I had failed to see because I was too consumed, distracted by the very rudeness, the arrogance of Purdy.

I looked at Robert and said, "Do you remember that I hit my knee on the lectern when I reached for my hat?"

"I do," Robert answered. "What of it?"

I said, "I did not think of it then but now..." I paused as I recalled the feeling as my knee struck the side of the lectern. "It was hard, but not hard like wood. It was metal."

Thad stood and asked, "You mean he had the safe in his church wagon?"

"Yes. It was covered by that purple altar frontal," I said. "The one with the cross on it."

Ted removed his spectacles and asked, "Would someone care to enlighten me? What is it you are talking about?"

It was Robert who offered up the explanation. He said, "When we came back to town a few days ago there was a church wagon parked next to the new saloon across the street. We met the preacher and went into his church to talk."

Ted asked, "How big was this wagon?"

Bill said, "Damn thing was big. Looked like a small church on wheels and this preacher man was, well, he did not look to be no man of God let me tell you."

Julius added, "He looked evil Mister Ted."

Ted had his notepad open, spectacles perched on his nose, scribbling furiously as everyone gave their impressions of the preacher and his church. He looked up from his writings and asked, "So you think the safe from Castroville was in this church wagon, Wyatt?"

I said, "I do not think, I know." I kicked off my boot and rolled my pant leg above the knee and showed everyone the bruise that, though smaller and subsiding, was still yellowed and blackened. "A wood lectern would not have caused this."

Chelsea said, "That was near a week ago Wyatt. That was one hell of a contusion."

I dropped my pant leg, smiled, and said, "I thought I broke my knee."

"I believe we found the brother," Robert announced.

Ted stood from the table. "So, where is this preacher and his church wagon now?"

Long Buffalo, who had remained silent throughout the excited conversation, cleared his throat before he spoke. "I saw this wagon the day the soldiers took me. It was near Fort Mason, heading southwest, moving very slowly."

Ted asked, "But why ride around with the safe? Why not open it and dump it in a river somewhere?"

"Because they cannot open it," Robert said. "It is some sort of custom Italian safe that requires two special keys, which they do not have."

I shook my head and said, "They do now." I sat down and thought through the last few days. It may have been speculation, but it was simple to put the pieces together now that they had been presented to us. I continued, "That was the true reason Purdy came here. He did not come to warn us off but to bring the keys to his brother. I suspect they were to meet here and open the box, take the money to finance their private war."

Thad asked, "What about that cash box with the twenty thousand dollars they took from the soldiers?"

I said, "I believe that was an opportunity that Purdy created. He must have convinced the General to send more money, knowing he would come here then disappear for good. He got what he wanted, and I reckon that he might just start makin' a move with his army."

Robert looked at the Pinkerton Detective and asked, "Ted, in your inquiries did anyone ever mention a Circuit Rider, a preacher, around the time the other robberies happened?"

Ted lowered his head and rubbed the back of his neck as he thought. He was silent, eyes closed, rubbing his neck as we all watched.

He looked up and uttered, “Son of a bitch!” He looked around the room. “It was outside of Hillsborough, near Old Fort Graham. That was one of the first robberies. Old man that witnessed the robbery had mentioned the church wagon in passing. I thought nothing of it.”

“Well,” I said, “it would seem that Brother Adrian has been in on this from the very beginning. They would pass off the money, the cashboxes to him and he would hang about waiting, above suspicion while the others made a getaway, clean. If they got stopped, they would not have the money on them.”

Robert said, “I believe it is time to speak with our prisoner. He may be able to fill in the gaps and tell us when they plan to make that move against us.”

A clear look of surprise showed on the Pinkerton's face. “You have a prisoner that knows something about this?”

I said, “I told you we would tell what we know after you told us what you know, Ted.” I laughed. “Now it is our turn.”

Julius went into the cells and brought our captive soldier out and sat him in a chair in the center of the room. The corporal, obviously frighten by the size of his audience, looked around the room then lowered his head, staring at the floor.

I looked at the man more closely. His emaciated frame, thin facial features spoke of a limited diet, one of near starvation. He was either sick or had not had a decent meal in sometime. It gave me and idea.

I went over to Chelsea and spoke quietly. “Do we have anything to eat in the kitchen?”

She looked at me, curious at first but trusting my intentions. She glanced at the corporal then said, “I could put something together right quick.”

She went back into the kitchen while I herded everyone back to the table. They all looked at me with questioning eyes, confusion on their faces, but I gave them a reassuring look, a nod of my head, and a smile on my face. I pulled Robert aside.

“Back my play on this,” I said quietly.

He nodded. “Of course, Wyatt.”

Chelsea came out carrying a plate of stew, biscuits, and a few pieces of goat cheese. She handed it to me and retreated with the others.

I grabbed a chair and set it in front of the prisoner, sat and held the plate close to me as I got comfortable. I said, “Now, I have some questions for you son.” I paused took up a spoonful of stew and ate it in front of the man. "You do not mind if I eat while we talk, do you? My stomach thinks my throat has been cut for sure."

He closed his mouth and shook his head.

"Well, that is fine then," I said as I took another mouthful. "I can do the talking and you can just sit back and listen." I took another mouthful, and a bite of the biscuit. "Damnation Chelsea, but this is good lamb stew.'

She said, "Thank you Wyatt. Plenty more where that came from."

The corporal, silent, eyed me with contempt all the while, involuntarily, licking his lips.

I called the dog over. "Come here Argos." He came and sat next to me, eyeing the prisoner. I took a piece of lamb and fed it to the dog. I said, "Good stuff, ain't it boy?"

The dog's tongue made several rounds about his mouth, never taking his eyes off the prisoner.

I turned my attention back to the prisoner. "You know son, we kinda figured everything out about you fellas and the camp you have set up in the Hill Country." I paused and took a bite of the goat cheese. "You know that the war is over," I continued, "and we lost my friend. Like it or not, we got soundly whooped in the field by the Yankees." I took another spoonful of stew.

The corporal looked at me and mumbled something incoherently, then dropped his head.

"You say somethin' son?"

He lifted his head and asked, "You fought for The Cause?"

I took another bite of cheese and said between working my jaw and chewing, "I surely did. I rode with General Stuart during the struggle. Who were you with?"

He said softly, "I were with Colonel Alexander's Artillery."

I nodded my head, took another spoonful, and said with a full mouth, "That a fact? I reckon we stood side by side more than a few times my friend." I shook my head. "Yes sir, they were good times, they were." I turned to the others and said, "I could sure use a cup of your coffee Robert."

Robert stood from the table and said, "You got it my friend."

He came over and handed me a cup. I said as I offered up my plate, "Care for a piece of this cheese? It is damn good Robert."

He reached for a piece. "Do not mind if I do." He tossed it in his mouth and said, "You are right, that is good cheese."

I grabbed another chunk of lamb and fed it to the dog, while looking at the prisoner. His eyes were focused on the plate of food; his tongue was actively licking at his lips. The man was starving.

"Yes sir," I said. "Those were the days. We sure did give them Yankees a troublesome time." I reached over and playfully swatted the corporal's knee. "Did we not?"

He nodded his head, still eyeing the food.

I looked at the man's face and noticed a tear slide down his cheek. "So, tell me friend, what do they call you?"

He mumbled something and tried to blink away the tears welling up in his eyes.

I saw my moment and leaned in closer, handed the plate to Robert and said softly, comfortingly, "The war is over my friend, and it is time to come home." I softly laid my hand on his knee. "There ain't no shame in what we did soldier, no shame at all, so, let it go."

He looked at me, the tears flowing freely now, tried to speak and only wept openly. He brought his hands to his face and lowered his head. I reached out and put a reassuring hand on his shoulder and squeezed. I whispered, "It is okay soldier, let it go."

I turned to the others. "Chelsea, would you get this man some food. Fella has not eaten a decent meal in days." I looked back at the corporal and said softly, "Eat now friend, we will talk in a bit."

I stood, turned, and walked out to the porch, suddenly ashamed of myself.

I leaned against the roof pillar looking across the street at Pepper's Place, hoping for a distraction. I took notice of the colorful banners that had been hung in preparation of the Grand Opening. It was going to be an affair like no other. The entire town was planning to attend and celebrate in true Texas fashion. It was more than just the opening of a new business, another saloon for the townspeople, it was like a rebirth. It was a sign that through the degradation, the deceit of Reconstruction, growth and promise was possible in this new frontier.

Robert came out to the porch and handed me my pipe and tobacco pouch. "Thought you could use this," he said.

I took the pipe and tobacco and nodded my thanks.

Robert sat at the top step and looked across the street. "Pepper's Place will be open in a couple of days. Good thing too as I am growing weary of drinking whiskey all the time. I do miss a mug of beer."

I packed my pipe and said, "Reckon if we go across the street Drew may accommodate us with a mug or two. Besides, I reckon we should let him know that trouble is brewing."

Robert stood, brushed off the seat of his britches and said, "What the hell are we doing over here then?"

I smiled as I looked at my friend and called out to those inside, "We will be back directly."

We walked across the street, up the short staircase and went into the welcoming environment of the saloon, taking notice of the lack of workmen about. Those present seemed to be occupied with setting the place right for the opening, moving from table to table arranging chairs, putting tablecloths and place settings on the tables at the restaurant side, putting the final touches on what certainly will be a grand affair.

We saw our friendly barkeep behind the long, highly polished bar arranging bottles on the glass shelves in front of the large mirror.

I called out to my fellow Georgia native. "I say there barkeep. Can you possibly pull a couple of mugs of beer for two weary lawmen?"

He turned, cigar in his mouth and smiled. "I might could do that Marshal. But first you must prove that you are weary."

Robert said, "Would a yawn suffice for proof?"

Drew took the cigar out of his mouth and said, "Ah hell, git your tired tails up to the bar my friends. Two beers comin' up."

We stepped up to the bar and offered up our hands, pleased to see our friend.

Drew produced two mugs of beer, placed them in front of us and said, "I see you fellas made it back okay. How was the expedition?"

I took a long drink then said, "Reckon there ain't much kept quiet in this town, that is for certain." I looked at him, smiled and said, "It went well. Learned a bunch of what has been goin' on of late."

Drew pulled on his cigar and exhaled the smoke over our heads. "I suspect none of it good."

"That is a true fact Drew," Robert said. "Things could get worse before they get better, I am afraid."

I said, "I do not mean to alarm you my friend, but I hope you have something other than those brass knuckles of yours."

Drew smiled while biting down on his stogie. He reached to the small of his back and produced a small frame Colt '49' Wells Fargo revolver in thirty-one caliber. "Got another one hid under the bar, and I can shoot with either hand," he said.

Robert said, "That will do it."

Drew put the pistol back in his belt. "How bad is it goin' to get Wyatt?"

I took another drink. "I do not know Drew. We discovered a holdout camp down in the Hill Country. Near sixty men and a damn cannon. Reckon they are gonna start something before too long and thought it best we gave you some notice cause it could be us they are comin' after. We also might ought to stash some guns and powder over here if the fight comes to this side of the street."

Drew nodded. "Just let me know how I can help my friends. I have a place to keep the guns." He put both hands down on the bar and said, "Now, you fellas could use a few pails of beer to take back to that army of lawmen you have stashed in the jail."

I looked at Robert. "You see, I told you. Cannot keep anything quiet in this town."

We finished our beer while Drew filled three pails of the brew for us to take back to the jail for the others. As an added gift, he handed me a fist full of cigars.

Though he declined I threw a couple of dollar coins on the bar. "No arguments my friend. If this keeps up, we will drain you dry of beer and cigars with nothing to show for it."

He bid us goodbye as we returned to the jail with our bounty, just in time for the evening's meal.

Thad, standing in the doorway, rifle at the ready greeted us as we came up the steps. "You boys must have your beer."

Robert walked past and said, "You complaining Thad, cause we can drink your share."

He laughed and said, "Hell no. Ain't nobody drinkin' my share."

We put the pails on the table and once again Mark began to fill the many mugs we had collected, and I handed out the cigars. As I was doing so, I took notice of our prisoner, still seated in the chair, an empty plate on his lap. I filled a mug and carried it over to him.

I handed him the beer and said, "What is your name friend?"

He took the beer and offered me a slight smile. He said, "Milton. Milton Habernacke. Folks just calls me Milt."

I sat across from him. "Where you hail from Milt?"

He took a sip, holding the mug with both hands. "Place called Hickory Tavern in North Carolina."

"I admit Milt, I ain't never heard of it."

He took another sip of beer, his hands shaking. "It be near sixty miles northwest of Charlotte in Catawba County."

I nodded and said, "Not too far from Georgia, Milt."

He looked at me. "That right? That where you from Marshal?"

Again, I nodded. "It is. I am further south, closer to Florida in Coffee County."

He said, "I thank you Marshal, and not just for the food and the beer. I thank you for them kind words, it sure struck a chord with me."

His sincerity struck me as I gazed into his eyes. I said, "Just relax Milt. We will talk later."

Chapter Thirty

The table set, pots of steaming stew, biscuits, beans, and corn were spread out for all to partake. I had already eaten my share as did our prisoner, Milton, so I elected to sit with him on the opposite side of the room while the others enjoyed their meal. Even Ted enjoyed the hospitality extended to him as a newcomer to our table.

I looked on at what Drew called our army of lawmen. The years of experience, the firepower we carried and the resolve we held, reassured me that we could prevail. Though a few of our group were not lawmen they brought experience to the fight that we could use.

I turned my attention to Milton Habernacke formerly of Hickory Tavern North Carolina and more recently, a soldier in the army of one A.J. Purdy also known as Percy Rawlings.

"So, Milton," I began, "tell me about Major Rawlings and this army of his in the Hill Country."

He said, "Sure Marshal. What is it you want to know?"

I sat back in the chair and said, "Why not start at the beginning, when you joined up with them."

He took in a deep breath and said, "Okay Marshal. Reckon it was after the surrender, and I was makin' my way home. I was on my horse when Major Rawlings and a bunch of his officers come up on me. They said they ain't surrenderin' none to the Yankees and theys headed to Texas cause theys still fightin' down there." He paused, took in another breath before he continued. "I do not rightly know why I joined up with them Marshal. Cept, I do not have no family to speak of. Maybe that was the reason."

I asked, "How big was this group of soldiers when you joined them?"

He looked up at the ceiling as he thought. "Oh, I reckon near twenty men. Mostly from his company, some from different regiments."

"Go ahead Milt," I encouraged.

"Well," he continued, "we camped at different places on the journey, got food best we could. The Major stayed with his officers most times, they would go off at times tellin' us to stay put. When they came back sometimes, they had food, more men, or guns."

I asked, "How long was the journey?"

He said, "Near two months it was, maybe longer. Some days we went without food, but the Major kept us goin' and one day was much the same as the other. Kinda lost track of time those days. Hungry all the time, tired."

"Why did you not pack it in Milt? Just leave?"

"I thought on it Marshal, honest to God I did. I had no other place to go, and it was kinda like bein' in the army, which I always liked. In the beginning it was anyway."

"What changed," I asked him.

He said, "It was after we built the camp in them hills. By the time we got there we had wagons, a cannon, lots and lots of guns, more men, and horses. We built the camp and the Major, and his officers changed. Said they would shoot anyone who deserted. Beat some of the fellas too."

"What about the robberies Milt? Did you or the other men do any of the robberies, the killins'?"

He shook his head vigorously as he spoke. "No sir! We did not! It was him and his officers that done it. They is bloodthirsty sons a bitches they are. Most of the men fears them. They hung one fella from South Carolina for stealin' food."

I looked over at the table. The room fell silent as all eyes were on us as we conversed.

I asked, "Do you know what his plans may be?"

"Well sir. I do not know much cept to say that he hates you fellas and said somethin' 'bout attacking the town to bring the Yankee soldiers in so theys can fight them."

Robert came over and asked, "Did he say when this was going to happen Milt?"

"He did not Marshal. I know it must be near the time cause he tol me to make the cannon ready and then sent me here to scout a place to set it up. I am to report back to him in two days' time."

Jim joined us and asked, "What can you tell us about this Indian that has been doin' these killins'?"

Milt's face drained of blood, turned white with fear. His voice cracked as he spoke. "That there is the Devil, he is. He likes the killin', he laughs and shows us the knife he uses on them that the Major hires to help in the stealin'. He tells us he will find us and cut out our tongues, slit our throats if'n we desert."

"Does he stay at the camp," Jim asked.

"He does not. He just shows up now and again. We all stays clear of that one."

I asked, "I will ask you one time Milt." I leaned forward and looked into his face. "Did you have anything to do with the killings or the robberies?"

Milt sat straighter in his chair, held up his right hand and said, "I swear to you Marshal. Me and the other boys had nuthin' to do with that. He hires ruffians, dregs and saddle tramps for most that work."

I patted his leg and stood. "That is fine Milt. I thank you for bein' honest with me."

Ted came over, hooked his thumbs in his gun belt, and asked, "Anything else you can tell us Milt?"

Milton thought for a second then said, "The boys is very unhappy and there was talk about desertin' and headin' off to Old Mexico." He looked down at the floor and added, "Sure wish they would have gone for I got caught. I would sure like to leave this place."

I went out to the porch, lost in thought as the others cleared the table. I lit a cigar, rolled it through the flame to burn it evenly and tossed the match aside. I pulled hard and exhaled the smoke closing my eyes, trying to understand all that we had learned today.

The information that Milt had imparted to us, though beneficial in knowing what we faced, did not offer up a plan to keep us alive. What we learned from The Pinkerton Detective, Ted, also beneficial, showed us we were up against an experienced force of ex-soldiers, if not killers. We needed a plan, and a damn good one if we were going to live.

Robert joined me on the porch. He lit his cigar and looked at me. "I suppose you are thinking of a plan, Wyatt."

I pulled on the cigar. "I am tryin' to my friend. It ain't gonna be easy."

Clem and Pete stepped out and looked at us.

Pete said, "Marshals, we gonna go help out in the saloon right now but we want you to know that we are with you, all of you."

Clem said, "That is right Marshal. We might not shoot straight but we can make them duck for cover to be sure."

I traded looks with Robert then said, "That is fine boys. Since you feel that way you best keep your pistols strapped wherever you go from now on."

Without a further word they returned inside to pick up their guns.

I turned to Robert. "Good boys."

Robert said, "That they are. I am glad you did not shoot them."

I laughed, "Not as glad as they are."

We smoked in silence as we watched the comings and goings of the folks through town. The sun was going down, relieving us of the late afternoon heat and we saw lightning off in the distance. Perhaps we would get some much-needed rain through the night, though it will only add a high level of humidity to the morning. It did not seem to be a fair trade off to me. Blessed relief from the strangling summer heat with a cool evening shower in exchange for a humid day as the moisture returned to the air above. It reminded me of the rainy season in Southern Georgia.

Skinner came out to the porch, lit a cigar, and said, "Me and Long Buffalo got us an idea."

"Oh," I said. "I would like to hear it since I ain't comin' up with anything worth a damn."

Skinner called back into the jail. "Long Buffalo, c'mon pard and tell 'em what we talked about."

Long Buffalo came out of the jail with an unlit cigar in his mouth. He looked around, patting his vest with both hands and said, "Who has match?"

I stepped over, struck a match, and held it on the end while Long Buffalo rolled it through the flame. When he got it going, he blew the match out, nodded his head in thanks and said, "I like the cigars from the Castroville saloon better."

Robert laughed and said, "You better not let Miss Helga hear you say that."

"What is your plan Long Buffalo," I asked.

He stepped over to the top step and looked across the street. He said, "Skinner and me, we will go out and stay on the trail and keep watch for the soldiers then ride back to warn everyone."

Skinner asked, "Whatcha think Marshal?"

I puffed on my cigar, nodded my head, and said, "It has merit. You two will be our forward pickets." I turned back to Robert. "What do you think?"

He took the cigar out of his mouth and said, "Yes, that will help. How far out do you think they should go?"

I looked at Skinner. "How far you reckon?"

He stroked his beard and spoke aloud through his thought process. "Well, we travel light and live out the saddlebags for a time. We will need to ride fast to get back to warn you and I was figurin' they would come up the trail."

Long Buffalo interrupted. "We can return directly, away from the trail to save us time."

Skinner nodded. "Reckon that would be a help in gettin' back." He dropped his hand and looked at us. "I reckon no more than ten miles."

I said, "We need to have a look at the map."

We all went inside, and Thad took up his post at the open front door. Skinner and Long Buffalo had started us to thinking of a plan. Like a snowball rollin' down a steep hill, it grew and grew as it gathered speed. Their idea of setting a picket out along the incoming trail had given us the right push to put together our war plans.

I opened the map and spread it out over the now cleared off table.

Ted looked down at the map, whistled and said, "Wish we had maps like this in the war. We might not have lost."

All eyes turned to Ted.

Bill asked, "Well, ain't you just slap full of surprises. You fought for the Confederacy?"

He looked around the room, surprised that his comment had been received so. He said, "You thought I was a Yankee?" He quickly cast a glance at Robert. "No offense given sir."

Robert grinned and said, "None taken."

I said, "Well, you said you were from Chicago."

"That is where I live at present," Ted said. "I was born and raised in Knoxville, Tennessee. My father passed when I was a teenager and left my mother enough money to send me East to school."

Chelsea asked, "Where did you go to school, Ted?"

He said, "Harvard Law School, class of eighteen hundred fifty-nine."

Bill was even more bewildered. "You are a lawyer too?" He shook his head in disbelief. "Well, I will be hanged."

Ted grinned and said, "I am sorry Sheriff. You seem to be running low on reasons to dislike me."

Bill laughed. "Oh, I like you just fine son. Do not mind me, reckon I am a distrustful sort. Been at this job too damn long."

I said, "Now, back to the business at hand." I pointed to the map. "Skinner and Long Buffalo are going to scout out the trail south of us as pickets. As soon as they see the Major and his army heading this way they will hightail it back here."

Robert leaned over the map and traced the trail with his finger. "We figured maybe ten miles south." His finger stopped and he leaned in a bit closer. "Right here the trail splits. This side comes up to the far side of town while the other brings them right up here, to us."

Skinner leaned down and said, "That be a good place to set up. I know just where we can watch without us bein' seen."

I asked Robert, "You figure the Major will split his forces there and send half to the far side of town?"

Robert stood back and looked at the map, giving him a larger picture of the battlefield. "I think he will. He wants to kill all of us and take over the town to draw the army in."

Jim pointed at Fort Mason on the map. "Think the Federal boys will engage the Major?"

I said, "They will not have a choice. It is why they are here."

Ted said, "He may have another plan in mind gentlemen. Just a notion I had."

I looked at Ted. "Please share it with us Ted. We are all friends here."

He leaned his large frame closer to the map and pointed to the split in the trail. "You studied tactics at VMI Wyatt, think on this a moment. What if he splits his forces but not until he gets closer to town. He sends a portion in to kill us while the main body moves on Fort Mason." He looked up at me.

I said, "Go on."

"It will be easier for him to take and defend Fort Mason, should he capture it, then it would be to defend this town," he said as his finger rested on Fort Mason. "A defensive campaign will keep his army alive longer than one that is on an offensive campaign." He stood. "We learned that fighting in Tennessee towards the end of the war."

I looked hard at Ted. I knew his assessment of the situation was sound, as it had been proven in the closing months of the war, especially for those armies in the western theater of operations. A defensive campaign kept the army intact, forcing the enemy to commit more men to overcome fixed defenses and troops that were dug in.

I suddenly came to a realization and said, "You were at Chattanooga."

His face softened. He nodded and said softly, "I was with General Braxton Bragg during the war and the defense of Chattanooga in the end."

Jim asked, "What did you do Ted?"

He reached into his vest and took out a pouch and rolled a cigarette as he spoke. "I was a captain on General Bragg's staff. I was in charge of intelligence."

I nodded knowingly. The structure was the same in our theater of operations. The intelligence officer used the cavalry as his eyes and ears taking the information we gathered and put it into a comprehensive and detailed report for the planning of battles, the maneuvering of armies in the field.

Often the intelligence officers themselves would venture out, alone at times, and gather this much-needed information and often during the heat of battle. Theirs was a dangerous job, sometimes requiring them to infiltrate the enemy positions to obtain a clear picture of the ever-changing battle. Most never returned.

The more we learned of our Pinkerton Detective, the more he garnered our respect.

I looked from Ted to Robert. "What do you think Sergeant Major?"

Robert said, "It make sense Wyatt. If the Major does not split his forces before the town, we will know that he is going to move on Fort Mason." He looked at the map. "That will help us as we will not have so large a force to fight, and it will keep the fighting on this side of the town."

Thad said from across the room. "If he does that we can ride out and attack them before they get here. It will keep the fight out of the town all together."

I looked across the room at our prisoner, who sat silently by. I said, "Milt, come over here."

He was startled to hear his name, looked around and rose from his chair. He stepped over and stood by my side. "Yes Captain, what can I do you for, sir."

I asked, "Did the Major mention anything about Fort Mason?"

He thought for a moment, then said, "He did sir. Some of his officers wanted to attack the fort instead of the town. The Major said he would think on it but was set about killin' you and the rest of these folks."

I sighed heavily. "Reckon we will find out soon enough." I looked at the faces of our small army. The time had come to put a plan together. I said, "Skinner, Long Buffalo grab what you will need for three days and get ready to head out first light. Mark, Chelsea, we will need more guns here and across the street at Pepper's place. I already spoke to Drew, and he has a place to stash them."

Robert said, "We can keep Clem and Pete over there for the duration."

"Good idea," I said. "Julius, I want you to stash some long guns and pistols outside in case we need to get to them on the run. Load them up and keep 'em dry, I think it is fixin' to rain."

Julius said, "We still have a bunch of guns from them fellas you brung in Cap'n."

"How are we fixed for food," I asked.

Chelsea said, "We have enough for a couple of days at the most."

"Well," I began, "there is eleven of us here and three across the street, that is fourteen with Skinner and Long Buffalo headin' out for a spell but coming back. We are gonna need more grub for sure."

Mark said, "We will see to it. I will grab a buckboard and get the General Store open then grab our guns and powder from the shop."

Thad asked, "What about the sheriff? Reckon we should tell him for what it is worth."

Ted said, "I will see to it."

Thad told him, "I will come with you. Do not expect any help from that fella though."

Robert said, "Everyone goes in pairs and armed."

"I reckon it is a start," I said. "I pity the sons a bitches that come at us."

Still, I thought, if I had a choice I would like to keep the fighting out of the town altogether.

CHAPTER THIRTY-ONE

Our plans, though not set in stone, had been laid out with enough detail but not so to commit us to one plan of action. Battles were fluid, ever changing from the moment the first shot was fired to the last. Field commanders had to adapt as the fight raged on. What worked before may not work a second time, forcing leaders to change their plans of attack, move troops to areas thought safe when the enemy exploited a weakness or changed their plans to overcome a difficulty, an impasse.

As the night wore on, we gathered our food, guns, and ammunition. Weapons were emptied and reloaded fresh to insure reliability in their use. Some of those taken off the desperados from our earlier fight were discarded or repaired, having been neglected by the previous owners.

Slowly it all came together. Even our prisoner threw in and helped. His reasons were such that he felt he had made a terrible mistake and attempted to atone for his misdeeds.

Milt said to me, "I will help where I can Captain. I can cook good too, but I will not take up the pistol nor rifle against these fellas. I still feels a kinship to some of these men."

"That is fine Milt," I said. "I would not have you do that."

He grew quiet and stepped closer to me, lowering his voice. "Can I ask you a question Captain?"

I was slightly puzzled at his formality but accepted it none the less. "You may," I said.

He cleared his throat and asked, "Not meanin' to be personal Captain but how is it that you can fight against those that fought with you in the war? I am puzzled by this."

I could not be angry at his ignorance of such matters. For me, though I still carried the memories and scars of battle, the war was long over. For him, the understanding of the wars end was more recent, and it was all that he knew and understood.

I put my hand on his shoulder and softened my tone when I addressed him. "You see Milt, for me and the others the war is long past. We have a new job now, that being the helping of others to live peacefully and without fear that someone it going to take that away."

He nodded, thinking on this.

I continued by saying, "Those like the Major refused to accept the loss and want the war to go on even if it means to fight those that had nothing to do with it. He and his officers have been killin' and robbing from folks that just want to live." I recalled what Jim had said that night I was sitting on the rock with Robert, manning the nighttime guard watch. "You see Milt, we aim to protect those that cannot protect themselves and these are the folks that the Major and his men are hurting. I cannot allow that." I looked at him closely. "Do you understand?"

He looked back at me. "I do Captain. I understands and thank you for tellin' me that. I am appreciative."

I patted his shoulder as he went to the kitchen to offer up his culinary skills to Chelsea and Julius.

Ted came over. "That was nice what you said Wyatt." He looked at me. "Sorry, did not mean to eavesdrop."

"No matter," I said. "What about you Ted? Why do you do it?"

He said, "Reckon it is the same reason as yours."

"You reckon," I said as I laughed. "You stay here much longer, and we will have you back to your Southern roots in short order my friend."

He shook his head and chuckled. "Oh. My poor mother must be turning over in her grave."

It was past midnight when our tasks were complete. We spoke to Drew and the boys telling them what to expect and Drew in turn spoke with Pepper and set the boys up at the saloon. Thad and Ted returned from the sheriff's office without any promises of help from him or his deputies telling us it was federal business. They parted company with Thad calling the sheriff a horses-ass and Ted promising to run against him in the next election.

I tried to give up our sleeping quarters to Mark and Chelsea, but they would not have it, instead elected to throw bedrolls down with the rest and Thad and Bill set up in the cells along with our prisoner. Julius remained out back saying he was comfortable and felt better about being outside, closer to the start of the action if it came.

A guard rotation was made with one man out front on the darkened porch and the other out back walking through the shadows, keeping an eye on the animals. It was our blind spot and any soldier with an ounce of sense knew that and would make an early move to exploit it.

As an afterthought I had Julius and Milt saddle all the animals thinking that, should we lose the jail, we would continue the fight on horseback. We were not going to make it easy on the enemy, by no means. If the Major wished to carry the day he would do so with the lives of his men.

It was near five in the morning, I was manning the front, Robert at the rear when Long Buffalo and Skinner came out to the porch. They both wore their pistols, saddlebags filled with foodstuffs, possibles bags loaded with powder and ball. They were ready to depart.

Skinner offered his hand and said, "We be off Wyatt. We should be at the spot at dawn."

I shook his hand and that of Long Buffalo's. I said, "Good luck fellas. Do not try and hold them up, just come back here and we will fight them on our ground."

"We will," Long Buffalo said.

Skinner added as he turned to go back inside, "We will walk the animals the back way out of town, case someone be watchin' us."

I nodded and watched them go.

I had the watch until sunrise and used the time to review our plans. Never let it be said that I devised a plan and let it go without suffering over the minor details. My Daddy always said that I would make a fine officer in the army because I was such a stickler for the details in all that I did. Again, battles were fluid, and change must be implemented in a timely manner or all could be lost. This also included its preparation. One minor detail overlooked, ignored, or forgotten could change the outcome before it even began.

So, I suffered through the details of the plan, trying not to second guess our decisions and choices.

The darkness of the night gave way to the rising sun soon enough. The rains never came so we would have the normal dry heat of the summer without the humidity of the rains. Some blessings, though small, were still well received.

Chelsea and Milt manned the kitchen and prepared our morning meal. Milt, it turns out, was more than a good cook. He informed us that he had the additional duty as cook in his artillery unit under Alexander during the war. He said he specialized in preparing wild game for the dinner table and gave us a notion to go on the hunt and put his skills to the test, until Bill reminded us of our current situation.

I was sitting at the table thinking through that very situation when I said, "We need to contact Fort Mason and let them know what may come to be."

Robert said, "I have been thinking about that as well." He sat at the table with me. "We cannot take a chance and send them a message in case the major has a way to listen in."

"We cannot send one of the boys as a messenger as it would mean giving up a gun," I added.

Bill hobbled over and sat. "What about Milt? Think he would, do it?"

I said, "Let me think on that for a bit."

Time dragged on through the morning as we tried to occupy ourselves with games of poker, checking and re-checking the guns and our fortifications, drinking coffee, smoking, and telling tales of exploits past.

I asked Ted, "So why have you not put your education to work and hung out a shingle for your own law practice?"

He said, "Well, I like the outdoors more than the confines of a nice office."

Bill pointed out, "But you live in Chicago. How is that brick city with its stone streets the outdoors?"

Ted laughed and said, "I only have a Chicago post address at the Pinkerton Office. I have not lived anywhere permanent since before the war. I am always on the move."

"No wife or family to speak of," Jim asked.

"No sir. I am free to come and go as I please," he said. "My only tether is my job with The Pinkertons."

Chelsea came in and stood at the table. She asked, "Do you miss a home life at all?"

"Not really Miss Chelsea. The only home I knew was growing up. Always knew I would go out on my own soon enough then the war came soon after I graduated. Well, I just like to stay on the move I reckon."

I laughed. "There you go again Ted. You can take the boy out the country, but you cannot take the country out the boy."

He laughed, hung his head, and said, "Oh, Lord have mercy."

Chelsea turned to go back to the kitchen, giggling and said, "Bless his heart."

The room broke out into laughter.

I went out to the porch armed with a cup of coffee and a cigar with the intention of taking a moment free from the concerns of the day. I lit the cigar and savored its sweet taste, took a sip of coffee, and looked out at the land beyond the town. It was then that I saw them.

Two riders were coming in hard and fast. There was no mistaking them as they rode low in the saddle, hunched over the horse's head pushing the animals as hard as they could.

Skinner, for his size, handled his mount with expert skill as he and Long Buffalo, equally skilled as a rider, made a direct line for the jail.

I tossed the coffee aside and yelled with alarm inside the jail. "Long Buffalo and Skinner comin' in!"

The jail emptied out onto the porch, watching as the two riders came in fast, only pulling back a few feet from the hitching rail. Long Buffalo was off his pony before he came to a complete stop and was propelled up the stairs to the porch.

Out of breath he grabbed hold of the railing, steadied himself and said, "They come. Many of them."

Skinner tied both animals off, also out of breath as he made his way to the bottom of the stairs. "They headed this way. Near thirty or more of them."

"How far behind," I asked.

Skinner looked over his shoulder then back at us. "One hour, maybe less."

Bill limped over to a chair and sat. "Son of a bitch! They comin' sooner than we feared!"

I looked at Robert and asked, "Think we are ready?"

He said, "Ready as we are going to be." He looked out at the land beyond the town. "Do you want to ride out before they get here, slow them down?"

"We stand a better chance holdin' them off here," I said as my mind began to work through the problem. "Thad, I need you to go across the street and tell Drew and the boys to get ready." I turned around and addressed everyone. "Julius, Jim, and Mark go around back and keep an eye out if they come in that way. Robert, me, and Ted stay here, and Bill and Chelsea stand by the windows with long guns. Keep the front door open till the shooting starts. Last man in close and lock it."

Skinner asked, "Where you want me and Long Buffalo. Wyatt?"

I said as I pointed down the street. "Run those folks off the street, then you boys take your mounts around back, stay in the saddle and fight from there."

I took a deep breath. "Once the fight starts keep your heads about you. Do not take time to reload, just drop your piece and pick up a fresh one. Those that are outside when the fight begins try to keep moving forward. If you mix in with them that makes it harder for them to shoot you down." I suddenly ran out of words of encouragement, so I just nodded and smiled.

Before Skinner and Long Buffalo mounted their animals I asked, "Did they have the cannon with them?"

Long Buffalo said, "They did not."

Skinner said, "It were the damnedest thing, Wyatt. We no sooner set up our watch when they came ridin' down the trail, raisin' up all sort of dirt and dust. They came on ridin' two by two with one fella in the front."

Robert said, "Standard cavalry formation."

"Great," I said. "Cavalry troopers. Well, at least we will know how to fight them."

"That we do, "said Ted.

Everyone had taken up their post, and I stood on the porch with Robert and Ted. I produced three cigars and handed them over. A match was struck, and we got our cigars lit as we moved to the porch rail. I leaned out, watching the landscape to the west while Robert sat on the rail facing the open door and Ted leaned against the post looking across the street.

Ted raised a hand and waved to Thad who was standing on the porch of Pepper's Place with the boys, all armed with long guns and pistols. Drew came out, gun belt around his waist, a short barrel Navy thirty-six in a holster, his two thirty-one Wells-Fargo pistols in his belt and a double barrel shotgun over his shoulder.

Ted said, "That little fella plans on a fight."

I laughed as I glanced across the street. "Us Georgia boys are known to be scrappers."

Ted smiled. "I figured that when I saw you stick the Howdah Pistol in your belt next to that Colt Walker. I pity the men you go up against."

Robert said, "You are not too badly armed yourself Ted." He pointed at his rig. "Two Army forty-fours."

Ted pulled both guns from the holster at the same time. Spun them forward on his index fingers and dropped them back in each holster in the blink of an eye.

I nodded approvingly and looked out on the horizon. Off in the distance I saw a cloud of dust making its way up to the sky. It took many a horse to raise the dust so and I knew it was the Major's army heading our way.

"Here they come fellas," I said.

I pointed at Thad then pointed at the western horizon, letting him know that they would soon arrive. He waved back and signaled the boys to retreat inside for the time being. I gathered that his plan being to surprise them as they came at the front of the jail. Hitting them at the rear at the beginning of the fight was a sound plan.

The dust cloud grew as they neared. What little wind there was, merely spread it out across the sky as they crept forward.

I went back inside to my possibles bag and grabbed my spyglass. Once they were within sight of the magnified eyepiece, I wanted to observe how they deployed their numbers and what sort of formation they would take. It would help in our defense.

I stood at the porch rail watching, never moving my eyes off the target area where I was sure the lead rider would be visible. I was soon rewarded with the sight of a lone horsemen riding tall in the saddle. I brought the glass to my eye.

I said, "There they are boys. I got the lead rider in the glass."

Robert said, "Wyatt, I just realized something."

I lowered the spyglass and asked, "What would that be my friend?"

Robert pointed in front of the building and said, "Look at the shadow of the building. We got the sun to our back."

I looked down and sure enough he was correct. "Well, I will be damned. That may give us an edge."

I brought the glass back to my eye and scanned the incoming formation of riders as a brief wind pushed the dust away and their true numbers were revealed. There was many a man atop a mount. Each soldier bedecked in the uniform of the Confederacy, each with a pistol, some with two, they rode in a tight two-man formation.

I glassed over to the lead rider, and it was then I took notice that he held a staff that extended up past his head and out to the side. Its base was hooked into a loop hanging down from his saddle. It was a staff for a banner, a guidon, but no flag flew from it. I found this odd at first but thought how much more of an oddity was it to have a troop of Confederate cavalry riding at me with intent on killing us.

I lowered the scope and listen for a moment. The wind brought the sounds of the horses as they rode over the hard packed ground.

Behind me Bill asked, "How many Wyatt?"

I sighed. "Near forty I would guess. They have not set to the attack formation yet."

Robert pointed out, "They should have done that by now, Wyatt."

I just nodded.

The sound grew louder as they neared. They were close enough to be seen without the spyglass and yet, they had not changed the formation. They continued to ride right at us, two abreast.

The lead rider held up his hand, and the troopers slowed their pace, yet they still came forward. It was then I saw the lead horse soldier unfurl his hidden banner. It was a white flag. A flag of truce.

"Lord Almighty Damn," I uttered.

Ted looked at me and said, "What the hell are they doin'?"

Robert pulled his Remington as they came across the town limits, slowing to a quick walk. The sergeant out front, clearly showing the white flag.

Again, Bill sounded off, "Do not trust them, Wyatt. They could be settin' a trap."

I said, "Everyone hold their fire." I signaled Thad across the street to stand fast. "Keep your guns at the ready."

The sergeant pulled up to the front of the jail and sat his horse as his troopers fell into formation behind him, spreading out in a parallel line in front of us. He said nothing. He just sat his horse, holding the staff to the flag of truce and looked at me.

I looked down the street and noticed that the townsfolk had all retreated to safety.

CHAPTER THIRTY-TWO

I slowly pulled the Howdah pistol free of my gun belt and stepped over to the top of the stairs. I stood there looking at the sergeant some twenty feet in front of me. He was blinking his eyes as the sun hit him directly in the face.

The sergeant sat a bit taller in his saddle, cleared his throat, and said, "I am looking for Captain Wyatt Chambers."

His voice struck me hard. I looked closer at the man's face now, whereas I had been looking at man and horse as a whole, now I looked at the figure in the saddle. By God I knew this man!

I said, "Would that be Sergeant Blackjack Hightower?"

He grinned, and settled back in his saddle. "It is Captain, it is me."

I stepped down one step and stopped. No need getting excited just yet at this odd reunion of sorts. I said, "Sergeant, you best have a damn good explanation for all of this, and I mean a damn good one!"

"I do sir," he answered. "May I get down off my horse?"

I thought for a moment. I turned to Robert and said, "You boys cover the flanks of the formation. Get the fellas from the back to come up and keep their guns on these men." I turned back to the formation and called out. "Thad, come out and keep them covered from the rear."

I stood and waited while everyone got into position, in case the flag of truce was nothing but a trick to get us to lower our guard, and knowing this man as I did, time and circumstances can do some peculiar things to redefine people and their former relationships. Meanwhile, the sergeant sat atop his mount, waiting.

Satisfied that everyone was in place I signaled the sergeant to dismount, and I stepped off the porch.

The sergeant handed the white flag off to one of his troopers and stepped up to me, stopped and came to the position of attention.

I shoved the Howdah Pistol back in my gun belt and looked at my former comrade, then promptly brought my fist back and punched him in the jaw, sending him to the ground.

He looked up at me through a cloud of dust, rubbed his jaw with his gloved hand and said, "Shit Cap'n. What for you dun that?"

I yelled as I pointed at him, "What the hell you think that was for you dumb bastard? Were you expecting a hug and a kiss? You best start talking Sergeant and it better be good!"

"Yes sir," he said as he rose to his feet, brushing the dust off his uniform. "Before we get into it, I am going to say that not a man here means to bring harm upon you or your people nor anyone in this town, Captain."

"That is good to know," I said angrily. "You will forgive me if I do not order my people to lower their guns. Circumstances being what they are and all we have been through so far, you can understand where I am coming from."

Sergeant Hightower said, "I understand sir." He paused before continuing, lowering his voice. "I gotta tell you Captain Chambers, I about fell out when I heard you was the Federal Marshal here."

I exhaled loudly and said, "Jack, I wish you would get to the point. You came here to kill us, that I know. What is different now, and do not tell me because you found out I was Marshaling here."

He looked around nervously and said, "You are right sir. Truth of it is we all agreed that we made a mistake joinin' up with Major Rawlings. We all agree we should have just gone home and forgot 'bout the war."

I eyed him suspiciously. "What happened Jack?"

"Well sir," he began, "it was right after Lee surrendered and I was ridin' home when Major Rawlings and his officers offered to keep me on. I was mad as hell after the surrender Captain, and Major Rawlings made it sound like it were a mistake." He turned and pointed to the formation of soldiers behind him. "He told all of us the same. So, we joined up thinkin we was gonna fight the Yankees down here in Texas."

I nodded. "I heard it before Jack. We have one of your soldiers inside."

He looked over my shoulder at the jail and asked, "You have Corporal Habernacke?"

"We do. Captured him two days past when we found your camp."

He said obviously relieved, "That is good cause the Major sent his Indian out to find him and cut his throat." He looked around nervously. "Hell, that sumbitch, he is probably watchin' us right now."

"What are you boys going to do now," I asked.

Again, he looked over his shoulder. "Some of us with families is goin' home and others is goin' to Old Mexico. The only reason we came here first was cause of you. Figured you was owed a explanation."

I cast a firm look at my old comrade and said, "Sergeant Hightower, I will ask you one time, and I want the truth."

He stood at attention when he answered. "Yes sir."

"Did you or any of your men have anything to do with the robberies or murders of them that are part of this?"

"We did not sir, I swear to you."

"Did you or your men have any part in the hurting of innocent folks since this nonsense began?"

He stood stock still. "We did not Captain. We are nothing but cannon fodder to the Major and his officers. He was hoping that most of us got killed when we came here."

I nodded in understanding. "What is he doing with the money?"

Sergeant Hightower shrugged and said, "Damn if I know Captain. He fed us little; did not pay us like he promised. Hell, he even hung one of the boys for stealin' food."

"What are his plans now Jack?"

"Well sir. Near as we know he plans on attacking Fort Mason tomorrow night with a force of near twenty-five, thirty men and a cannon. I also heard him say sometin' about meeting a wagon to pick up the money then moving in for the attack. I have no idea what that means Captain."

"I do," I said.

Sergeant Hightower shifted uneasily on his feet and looked down at the ground. "What happens now Captain?"

I turned to Julius who was standing on the porch and said to him, "Would you tell Milt to come out here please?"

"Yes sir, Cap'n."

Milt soon appeared at the door and Julius motioned him to join me on the street. As the man stepped closer, unsteady, and nervous he stepped up next to me, acknowledged his friend with a simple nod, and turned to me.

He asked, "You want to see me, Captain?"

I said, "Go get your horse and come back here."

Milt just stared at me, unmoving.

I repeated my order, a bit more firmly, "Go and get your horse Milt, then come back here. Now git."

He turned and went back inside while I turned back to the sergeant. I told him, "I ain't gonna arrest you fellas. What is going to happen is you boys get the hell out of Texas. Go back to your homes, go to Old

Mexico or even California but you will all leave Texas." I held up a warning finger to the sergeant's face. "If I find one of you boys on the wrong side of the law, I am just gonna shoot 'em down and be done with it. Do you understand me, Sergeant Hightower?"

Hightower stood straight, grinned and responded with a commanding voice, "Yes sir!"

I allowed myself a slight grin, waved him away and said in a softer tone, "Get the hell out of here."

I turned and started back for the porch when Milt came from the back of the jail on his horse. He pulled up next to me and leaned down then extended his hand.

He said, "Thank you for your kindness, Captain. I will never forget you sir."

I smiled as I shook his hand. "Stay out of trouble Milt. I wish you the best."

Hightower mounted his horse as Milt joined the formation. The sergeant turned his mount to face the men and yelled out, "Column of twos, by the left turn...march!"

As the troopers turned their mounts Sergeant Hightower turned back around and rendered a crisp salute. I came to attention and, as a soldier at heart, I respectfully retuned his salute.

He said before he departed with his men. "You best get ready for Major Rawlings, Captain Chambers. Knowin' that damn Indian is out and about he will get word to the Major that we did not fight it out, and the Major has a real hatred for you. I will not put it past him to attack you here and forget Fort Mason."

I said, "We will be ready Sergeant Hightower."

His troop turned as one and went off into the wilderness the way they came in, heading west to parts unknown and an uncertain future. It was just as well. We did not have the space to house all of them should we have placed them under arrest, and if what the sergeant said to me was true, the only crime they were guilty of was that of making an unsound decision in joining the ranks of Rawlings' rogue army. Last I checked, stupidity was not a crime.

I followed everyone back inside.

I said as I crossed the threshold, "Reckon you want to know about me and the sergeant."

Bill propped his leg up on chair. "I understand not arresting them, Wyatt. But how is it that you know this fella?"

I took a deep breath and found a seat. "He was one of my soldiers in the war." I looked out the open door thinking that perhaps I would see Hightower standing there. "He was a good soldier and a true believer in 'The Cause', good fighter to have on your side."

Jim said, "It sounds like Rawlings found him a bunch of true believers."

Robert sat next to me and addressed everyone in the room, "It was right to let them leave, they did not break any laws that we know of. But that leaves us with the Major and his loyal corps of officers. They are surely going to attack us now."

Thad had walked inside, and asked, "How you figure that?"

"Well," I began, "you all heard the sergeant tell me about the Indian. You can bet that he just witnessed this entire affair, and he is makin' tracks back to Rawlings right now as quick as he can with the news."

"What does that mean for us," Thad asked.

Robert answered. "It means we attack first."

I smiled as I looked at my friend. Always aggressive in his tactics, Robert was not one to sit and wait.

His was sound logic born of four years of fighting for the North. It was the philosophy of the Federal Army during the war to always drive the fight whereas ours was mostly a defensive campaign in the hopes of preserving the army in the field. Both tactics had merit, not that one was more sound than the other, each was used with equal success by both sides. We just had the smaller force, and as such, fought a more conservative campaign often forcing the Yankee armies to chase us across the country until we found ground suitable to defend.

This time, however, though we had the smaller force the enemy would not be expecting us to attack. Especially on his ground.

I stood and said excitedly, "Let us have another look at that map."

The table cleared, the map was rolled out and we all gathered around.

Robert pointed to the general location where we came upon the camp. He said for the benefit of those that did know, "This is where we found Major Rawlings and his camp." He turned to Skinner and Long Buffalo and asked, "Do you know of any other way into the camp, other than the trail we took in last time?"

Skinner leaned forward and traced his large index finger along the route we had traveled. He said, "I thought I seen a trailhead near the spot where we found the burnt wagon." He looked at Long Buffalo. "Reckon there be another trail to the camp?"

Long Buffalo looked at the map, thought for a few moments before he answered. "I know of a trail behind the spot with the wagon. It goes east and joins another trail that goes north and south. This trail will lead to the camp."

I began to voice my thoughts for the others, "We could divide our forces into two groups, move on the camp and hit them from two sides."

Robert joined me in voicing his thoughts. "We can count on the Indian getting to the Major near dusk. That means he will move on us first light. If we move in tonight, we can trap them at the camp."

Long Buffalo said, "This we can do. It will be full moon tonight and we can move through the wilderness."

"How many of us is there," I asked as I looked around the room.

Robert looked at the faces of our group as he spoke. "Well, who wants to go?"

The room was quiet for a moment, not because we were debating about going or staying behind, but who was going to speak first. When it came, everyone in the room said at the same moment that they were going, including Chelsea.

I said, "I kinda figured on that." I looked at Chelsea and said, "Darlin'..."

She interrupted me, held up her hands in mock surrender and said, "I know, I know Wyatt. I will stay."

"Julius, "I said. "We need you here. We still do not know where the preacher is."

He looked at me, trying to hide his disappointment and said, "I know Cap'n. I will watch out for him."

I turned my attention to Bill, who was leaning hard on the table.

He looked up at me with a grim determination and said firmly, "Do not even think about it Wyatt. That fella is in my county, and I will be damned if I let this happen without me. Do not worry about me, I can ride."

"What about the boys," Robert asked.

I said, "I reckon it is time to send them out with a message."

"You figurin' on lettin' the judge know about this, "Thad asked.

I shook my head. "No sir. I believe it is time to let the army know what is going on."

Thad said, "I will go and fetch 'em."

"Ask Drew if he can spare us a few minutes too Thad," I said as he went out the door.

"Well," Jim said. "You boys have the experience at fightin' and planning. How do we go about this?"

I looked at Robert. "There is nine of us, how do you want to do this?"

Robert studied the map, traced his finger around the areas of the Hill Country we would be traveling through and stopped on the spot where the camp was located. He began to tell us the plan, "Long Buffalo takes the east trail from the burnt wagon with me, Mark, Thad and Bill while Skinner takes you, Ted and Jim along the other trail." He looked at Long Buffalo and asked, "How long to travel this trail to the camp."

Long Buffalo thought, glanced down at the map and said, "The same on both trails."

"Good," Robert said. "We split up where the wagon was burned then move to the camp. The best time to hit them will be at first light."

I said, "Skinner. I know a spot you can set up and pick these boys off while we move into the camp when the fightin' starts." I looked at Robert and asked, "Do we go in mounted or dismounted?"

"Mounted at first. We can get down into the camp and mix in with them," Robert said.

Just then Clem and Pete came in followed by Thad and Drew.

I said, "Sit tight boys, while Robert drafts another message for you."

Pete asked, "We goin' to see the judge again?"

Robert stepped away from the table and walked over to his desk. "No, you boys are going to get the army at Fort Mason."

"You fellas know where that is," I asked.

Clem said, "You point Marshal, and we will find it."

I stepped over to Drew and offered my hand. "I want to thank you for backing us up on the street."

He took my hand and said around his ever-present cigar, "You know us Georgia boys are always willin' to join in a good fight."

I pulled him aside and explained to him what it was we were going to do and of the concerns that the preacher man would show in our absence.

He listened then said, "You sure you do not need another gun hand on this expedition?"

"We could but if any of them get away or this preacher man shows up it could spell trouble for the town. Besides, we think the preacher still has the safe they stole from the bank in Castroville."

Drew chewed on his cigar. "If he does, do I get to shoot him?"

Ted came over and said, "You Georgia boys do love a scrap."

He took the cigar out of his mouth and said, "I just do not like a theivin' Circuit Rider. Seen enough of them of late and got no trust of any of them."

I waved Julius over. "Here is your backup, Drew."

Drew put the cigar back in his mouth and looked up as Julius stood before him. He said, "You is a big fella to be sure Julius." He smiled. "I think between the two of us we will take care of things around here."

Chelsea came over and said, "You mean the three of us."

Drew looked at me, concern on his face.

I said, "Do not have any worries about her Drew. She shoots better than all of us."

CHAPTER THIRTY-THREE

The preparations for the journey were quick as we had everything on hand from our previous battle plans. The animals had already been saddled as was Buster set with the panniers. It was just a matter of moving our stores to the animals, gathering up ammunition and spare guns not knowing how long we would be committed to this endeavor. A day, a week, who knew.

What we did know was that we were now the aggressors. We had decided to take the fight to them.

We had gotten lucky when Hightower and his men road into town, giving up the fight before it began, especially considering the size of the force he commanded. We never wanted the fight to come anywhere near our townsfolk, but we did not have a force large enough to stop them let alone slow them down.

This time we had such a force. Even though we were outnumbered more than two to one, we had the element of surprise, the ability to create fear and confusion with our aggressive tactics. The Major, we were hoping, would be preoccupied in planning for an attack on the town, not preparing for an attack on his own position. This was how battles were planned and executed. You find the weakness, exploit it, commit your troops, and drive the fight. You had to rob the enemy of the initiative, hold it and keep moving forward, putting the enemy on their heels.

This we planned as we made ready to depart.

An odd, if not eerie silence hung over us as we made our preparations for the coming battle. Robert composed his letter to the commander of Fort Mason, sending the boys out into the wilderness without ceremony, only brief well wishes, handshakes and words of caution. We all gathered up supplies, guns, water, and the like running from the jail to the stables and back again, often bumping into each other without so much as an acknowledgment or apology. We were focused on the task at hand, determined and committed to get it done.

In short order we were ready and gathered at the table one last time.

I looked at the map, committing its detail to my memory, then said softly, "We have all been in a fight, so we know what to expect. These fellas we are going up against are seasoned fighters coming out of a war with four years of hard experience. Once we are in the camp just keep moving forward. Mix in with them, make it hard for them."

Jim asked, "What about that damn cannon?"

Robert answered. "It will be hard for them to use it inside the camp if we mix it up with them, just like Wyatt said."

I added, "Try and stay on your horse as long as you can. If you find yourself on the ground, pick your fight." I paused. "First chance I get, I will take care of the cannon."

Thad looked surprised and asked, "Just how are you gonna go about that?"

"Yea, Wyatt. How you gonna do that," Bill added.

I grinned and said, "A little trick I learned in the war, so, if you see me runnin' away...just try and keep up with me."

Ted chuckled. "Oh, I cannot wait for this."

Robert looked around the room, settled on me and nodded.

I said, "Okay, time to go."

I pulled Julius aside and spoke in a low tone. "I wish you could come along my friend, but I need you here."

He nodded and extended his hand to me. "Do not worry Cap'n. I will take care of Miss Chelsea. I know what to do."

I took his massive paw-like hand and smiled. "Keep an eye on Pepper's Place too. If a big Indian with a long knife shows up, well, you know what to do."

Again, he nodded. "I do Cap'n. That goes for the preacher man too."

I said, "In my desk is two letters. One to my father and one to Arabella."

Julius looked sad as I said this and responded, "Sergeant Major Robert has 'em as well in his desk. I will take care of everything Cap'n."

Chelsea followed us out the back door as we mounted up. Her goodbyes to her husband had been done earlier, words exchanged, their devotions for each other revisited, it reminded me of the days when we went off to war. The goodbyes exchanged, the worries ignored, and the love expressed as we departed from home.

Chelsea looked at us and said, "I expect you boys' home in a couple of days. I will have a feast ready for you so do not be late."

I said, "Count on it Darlin'. We will be here."

Robert said, "Long Buffalo, Skinner, if you would lead us out."

Our two scouts turned their mounts and led us out front, all of us behind in train as we came around the front of the jail. Drew was standing on the porch of Pepper's Place, smoking his cigar, shotgun over his shoulder, pistol hanging from his hip. He raised a hand and held it up as we rode past, out into the wilderness.

Skinner and Long Buffalo were out front. Skinner kept us on the trail while Long Buffalo rode scout, seeking out unseen dangers, riding off to either flank, riding ahead in search of a possible enemy in hiding. Ours was speculation that the Major would attack us the following day, but a good field commander would have sent out his own scouts. That is what Long Buffalo sought out.

Ted rode alongside me as I pulled Buster behind. I took notice that he was at ease in the saddle, and I could tell that he was an accomplished rider, an expert horseman. There were those that, though they could ride, exuded an awkwardness atop the animal, never gaining confidence in riding. Not so with Ted. He was comfortable in the saddle, that I could tell, and I still found it hard to grasp or see him as a big city lawyer type.

I looked over his horse, admiring the spotted coat, the black and white mix, unusual for this region of the country. I knew it to be an Appaloosa, having seen them before, and knowing where they came from, I found it curious and knowing what little I knew of Ted, I could surmise that there was a story behind its origins.

Ted said, "You want to ask, Wyatt." He looked at me and smiled. "So, ask."

I laughed, shook my head, and said, "So you can read minds as well. You sir, need to set yourself up in a tent at the circus with a crystal ball."

He laughed. "What makes you think I have not done so."

"It would not surprise me to learn that my friend." I looked at his animal and asked, "So, how did you come by this Appaloosa Stud?"

"Well, I will tell you," He began, "my first assignment with the Pinkertons was in the Pacific Northwest. Bunch of miners started invading Indian land out there and the agency sent me to quiet things down. The Chief of the Nez Perce Tribe gave me this fine animal as thanks for what I did. Fella by the name Joseph the Elder."

"I knew there was a story," I said. "Impressive."

Ted said, "Yea, for all the good it did. I suspect those fine peoples will not keep that land much longer. Too many folks moving west. It is just a matter of time." He looked at my animal, pointed and said, "You have a fine mount yourself."

I leaned forward and patted Caliban's neck. "It was not always so." I pointed to the front of our column and said, "Long Buffalo sold me Caliban shortly after we met some time back. This beast did not take too kindly to me a first. He is still the meanest animal this side of hell."

"Hence the name I gather," he said. "I saw 'The Tempest' in Washington City before the war. Did not care for it all that much to tell you the truth."

"Well, we may have been at the same event. I went to see it before the war, after I graduated from VMI."

He looked surprised and said, "So, you wore a blue coat before the grey."

"I did," I said.

He looked at me, grinned and said, "I will not hold that against you, Wyatt."

We both laughed.

The day progressed as we rode on, and the temperature rose with each mile we put behind us. It was the time of year when the sun brutalized the land sending man and beast to seek out cooler climes, often without success.

The clouds were few and the threat of rain gone. It would be a full moon come dark, giving us the needed light to move about through the thick vegetation of the Hill Country. Still, rain would have masked our movements enabling us to penetrate the edges of the camp unseen, an added edge. We would just have to be diligent in our approach to the camp, mindful of every step, hopeful that a restless horse, the snap of a tree branch, or a watchful sentry did not expose our position.

We entered the Hill Country just as the sun fell to the western horizon, casting shadows all around us. We fell into a line formation as the trail crept in from both sides. As before, we put our trust in Long Buffalo and Skinner as they led us deeper into the hills, each step bringing us closer to our objective. Each step bringing anxious anticipation to our desire to begin the fight in earnest.

One does not wish for a fight, but will accept what will be and prepare, each in his own way, to carry through to the end. There were some, I suppose, that longed for a fight. They sought it out, influenced matters in such a way to bring the fight on. Those we were going up against were such men, this we knew and accepted. When posed with the threat of a fight, men like those I found myself with, we stepped up and faced it. Ready to take on the challenge, ready to stand against those that brought it to us, ready to dispatch those guilty of such a desire.

We rode on.

We soon came to the clearing near the burnt wagon, our separation point, and gathered at the charred remains of wood and steel and dismounted. Our tones became hushed, our movements silent knowing that we were now in the enemy's backyard.

Robert addressed us as we stood in a circle. He said, "This is where we divide into our groups. We have a few hours yet to get in position, so we need not rush." He looked at me and asked, "How do we kick this thing off Wyatt?"

I had been thinking on this during the last hours of our ride. "First light Skinner will touch off the fight by taking out whatever man shows himself in the compound."

Bill said, "Hopefully it will be that little shit, Major Rawlings."

Thad said, "We should be so lucky."

I said, "As soon as that man falls to the ground we ride in fast and begin taking those out that choose to fight." I looked at Robert. "You boys will be closer to their corral, so one of you scatter the horses."

Mark said, "I will do it."

"Skinner," I continued, "pick your targets. Hopefully, they will try and seek cover enough for us to move around during the fight."

Jim asked, "What about prisoners?"

I had also given this some thought. I said, "I will leave that to each of you. But know this. These boys made a choice to rob and kill for whatever reasons. I would not trust a one of these villains to do anything honorable or decent. They would have done that long ago."

Thad said, "Time to start the show boys, c'mon."

We separated into our groups, and I looked at Robert. I said, "See you in the camp my friend."

He smiled. "See you in the camp."

I sided up to Skinner and asked, "You have enough cartridges for that gun of yours?"

He held up his Springfield trapdoor .50-70 Government rifle. He looked at it admiringly and spoke as if it was a person. "We be ready Wyatt. No worries with us. We will keep them duckin' fer cover."

"Good. Then lead the way my friend."

Skinner turned his mount and headed back to the trail followed by Jim, Ted then me pulling Buster along. We moved slowly through the brush as I recalled our previous trek through this area. I reviewed all that I knew of the terrain, the trail and the surrounding area.

I did some figuring in my head as to the time we would be on the camp; the remaining hours left until the sun rose, and where we would position ourselves prior to the attack. I did not want us mounted for the few remaining hours we had until Skinner fired that first shot. Skinner had to be in position ahead of us while we remained in the brush with the animals.

I saw the camp in my mind and recalled the spot where we met Long Buffalo and thought it perfect to hold the animals there. The trail from that position led straight into the camp giving us our entry point when the fight kicked off. Skinner can set up where we had established our observation nest in the tree line, giving him a clear field of fire on both sides of the camp. It was all coming together as I thought it through. All except the fight itself and its outcome.

After a time, living behind a gun you accept what could be your end. Going into a fight, alone or with others, your mind is occupied by planning and preparation, not so much your own mortality. You develop a skill of ignoring what could be your demise, your life ending in such a violent manner. Some say they ain't afraid of dying, to which I must say is an untruth. Hell, it is horseshit. You just learn to ignore or even suppress that feeling, that desire to the point that it becomes a habit. I have seen many a man utter their fearlessness, exclaim their bravado in the face of death only to recant such notions in the end.

Perhaps I accept what could be or I ignore it with such skill and practice that, should I give it some thought, I might pursue another, safer, vocation. What I do know and readily accept is that the Good Lord has not, as of yet, felt the need to call me to the hereafter. Even though I accept it, does not mean that I do not fear it, for it is unknown to us.

I cleared my mind and stayed focused on the task at hand. Before facing death, we had to be in the fight, and before we got into the fight, we had to be in position. This is where my mind turned.

Skinner stopped and sat his horse. I dismounted, tied Buster off on my saddle horn and made my way forward.

I looked up at Skinner as he towered over me on his horse. He leaned in as I whispered in his ear.

I said, "How close you reckon?"

He remained silent and pointed to his front. I nodded and slowly moved forward as my eyes searched the darkness, and my ears listened to the wilderness around me.

I came to the small clearing I remembered from our last visit and did a quick search of the ground for anything that may trip up man or beast. I found it sufficient to tie the animals off for the duration while we waited for daylight.

I moved forward, up a small rise and lowered myself to the ground as I recalled this to be the spot we had first laid eyes on the camp of the rogue army. As soon as I cleared the small mound I was greeted with a well-lighted camp at rest.

Before I took in the camp I reviewed my position, satisfied that we would be hidden in darkness of the vegetation, I felt confident that we could sit out the remaining hours undetected.

I turned my attention back to the camp, surprised that it was so well illuminated with many oil lamps hung about in front of tents, from poles and stakes throughout the camp. I looked for activity, for guards and only noticed two, on opposite sides of the compound. I surmised that they were confident in their hidden location within the Hill Country that pickets outside the confines of the camp were not of a concern.

I shook my head and retreated to the others.

When I returned Jim and Ted stood with Skinner, who was still mounted, and I came along side. I motioned Skinner to dismount, and I gathered them all together and spoke in a whisper.

I said, "The camp is just up ahead. Thirty feet straight up the trail is a small clearing of sorts we can tie the animals off and wait for daylight." I turned to Skinner. "Once we tie the animals off you come with me to a spot, I picked out to watch the camp, and you can shoot from there. We walk the animals in from here."

Ted said, "I will grab your horse so you can lead us in."

I waited a few minutes for Jim and Ted to retrieve the horses then I led everyone into the clearing. I noticed as Ted walked by; he was massaging his shoulder while he got the animals settled. I stepped over to him.

I asked in a whisper, "Something amiss?"

He massaged his shoulder once again and said, "Your animal bit me."

I said quietly, "Yep, meanest animal this side of hell."

CHAPTER THIRTY-FIVE

I brought the three of them up to the rise and we spread out abreast of each other, low to the ground and observed the activity in the camp.

I looked down at the parade ground and noticed that they had moved the cannon from its tent and married it to the caisson. They intended to take it along, that being the town or Fort Mason. Either way I needed to render it useless as quickly as possible when the fight started.

Ted leaned over and whispered, "Shameful behavior of these fellas. No pickets, enough light coming from the camp I could almost read a newspaper up here."

"A mistake they will soon come to regret," I whispered back.

Jim leaned over Ted and whispered to me, "Where will Long Buffalo and the others come in?"

"They will come in from the opposite side. That is where they keep their horses."

I looked at my pocket watch and noted the time. We had two hours yet before the sun came up.

I turned to Skinner and whispered, "Come with me and I will set you up." I turned back to Ted. "You and Jim stay with the horses and keep them settled. I will be back directly."

I led Skinner through the foliage to the observation spot we had occupied earlier. It gave him a commanding view of the compound, allowing him to target both sides and center. Those that took refuge behind a tent, obscuring Skinner's view, would have to deal with us as we rode through the camp.

We lay down on the ground and I whispered, "What do you think?"

He brought his long rifle to his shoulder and looked through the sights, moved it left, then right stopping in the center of the compound. He said, "Tis good Wyatt. I can play hell on these boys from here."

I said, "The cannon on the far left. When you see me move on it, try and keep them off me as I will be occupied."

He nodded. “What are you goin’ to do that you be occupied?”

I smiled at him. “I am going to spike it.”

Even in the low light I saw a bewildered look on his face. He asked, “What does that mean, spike it?”

“Just watch the show and when I run, you might ought to duck.”

“Ah hell,” he said.

I said, “I will be back over there with Jim and Ted. Come first light you will be able to see me, and I will signal you to start the show. As soon as the first fella goes down, we will ride into the camp and finish them off.”

“We will be ready Wyatt,” he said referring to himself and his rifle.

I patted him on the back and moved back to our original position, meeting up with Jim and Ted.

We knelt in front of the horses, who thankfully remained quiet and content for the moment, and I finalized our plans for the coming assault.

I said in a low voice, “I will signal Skinner, and he will touch off the fight. We will be mounted when he shoots so ride hell bent for leather down to the camp. Try and push the fight away from the cannon and send them into Robert and the others.”

Ted asked, “How many you figure?”

“Well, Sergeant Hightower said there was near twenty-five men,” I answered. “I am hoping that we surprise them well enough we can cut that number in half in the first volley.”

Jim said, “We will give it one hell of a try.”

I returned to the small rise, took off my hat and watched the camp. I did not need to look at my time piece, but the urge to do so came upon me as it often did during moments such as this. I forced my attention to the camp, looking, searching for something that may cause alarm, cause me to rethink our plan of attack.

There was nothing. It was just a camp, sleeping in comfort and ignorance of what was about to befall them come first light.

I lay on my belly watching the camp, shifting my gaze from one spot to another at random. How many times had I been in this position doing this exact same thing through the years? One hundred, two hundred times, more? If I gave it any serious thought, I was certain that I would be able to recall each time I had snuck in to observe a Yankee camp. Often entering the camp during the hours of darkness to gather more precise information or just to satisfy my ego and steal a memento of my visit. A hat, a pair of boots, a jacket, or gloves, it did not matter. Every time I returned to our lines, I would give the trophy to one of my deserving troopers who was in need of a pair of boots or gloves, even a hat.

Admittedly, I enjoyed it. It was something that got my heart racing as I found myself alone, stealthily moving through their camps, as if it was a game. Confidence in my abilities was such that I knew I would never get caught or killed. Confidence or arrogance, it was a dangerous game to be sure, one that I excelled at.

But this time, this moment felt different to me.

I could not discern what it was exactly. Was it just the uneasiness I often felt before the start of a battle? Or perhaps the anxiety I felt had attached itself to my feelings of exhaustion which worsened this concern. Had I forgotten something, overlooked an important detail? I forced these rising issues out of my mind and back to the here and now.

It was time to go to work.

I grabbed up my hat and slid away from the rise, moving back with the others. Without speaking I motioned Ted and Jim to mount up as it was near time for the assault on the camp.

We slowly moved our animals up to the small rise, leaving Buster tied off, and sat our horses watching the camp come to life while we checked our firearms.

Grey clad soldiers of the rogue army came out of their tents, gathered up gear, congregated around the flagpole and prepared to begin their day as we stood three abreast in plain view watching them move about.

I looked over to Skinner as he lay prone with his buffalo gun resting across a fallen tree. He was watching me over the top of his rifle as I removed my hat, held it in the air, and looked at the camp below one last time.

A lone soldier, standing in the center of the compound turned and looked in our direction. His mouth fell open as he raised his hand and pointed at us. I dropped my arm, signaling Skinner to fire.

The sound of the heavy caliber rifle resounded through the trees and brush as the bullet traveled the one hundred yards and struck the soldier just as he raised the alarm.

I spurred Caliban into action, and we took off down the trail into the camp. Closing the distance quickly as we came down the rise, I pulled the Howdah Pistol from the saddle holster and cocked both hammers. Behind me I heard Jim and Ted as we crossed the boundary to the compound.

The camp was in a complete state of chaos as we rode in among the soldiers, hitting one here, knocking one down there as they fell under our horses. We moved deeper into the camp at a full gallop as the confusion we created grabbed hold of the rogue troops sending them in all directions, without guidance, without leadership.

I knew this state of disarray would not last long as the shock would be replaced with a soldiers resolve to stand their ground and fight.

I looked to the opposite side of the compound and saw Robert leading his force into the camp and I turned Caliban around and rode at a group of soldiers coming out of a tent as they grabbed at their weapons. I did not give them a chance as I raised the double-barreled pistol high and took a bead on a tall soldier as he pointed two pistols at me. He cocked his revolvers as I let go with the first shot. The pistol roared, bucked high in my hand as I watched the bullet strike the man in the chest, sending him back into another. The others scattered and ran for cover as I rode into them.

Gunfire erupted all over the camp as shots were traded, the initial shock and confusion had been replaced with the need to fight for survival as we rode through the camp, often sending an unsuspecting adversary under our horse's hooves. The fighting grew close, the smoke of spent powder hung over the battlefield like a low hanging cloud as the horses from the corral, frightened, ran through the camp seeking the protection of the forest.

Movement being the key to survival. I watched as Ted, a pistol in each hand, kept his mount moving through the enemy, picking his targets, and making each shot count. He never faltered; his animal responded well under fire as soldiers tried in vain to remove him from the fight.

I spurred Caliban deeper into the camp when I noticed an officer on the far side raise his saber and attempt to rally a small group of men to charge at Jim, who was now on his second revolver, firing as he moved. I rode straight at the soldier and leveled the Howdah Pistol as I neared. He was wearing the long grey coat of a captain, his glimmering saber held high as he yelled instructions for a charge. He looked at me as I came right at him, suddenly aware of the mistake he made, that of standing still in the middle of a fight.

I fired, again the pistol bucked high and threatened to come free of my hand as I watched the bullet strike the captain high in the chest, sending him backwards to the ground. As I rode past, I looked down, holstering my pistol. He still held onto the saber, a look of surprise on his face as his lifeless eyes looked skyward, his light blonde hair, neatly combed and parted.

I turned Caliban yet again and pulled my shotgun free of the scabbard just as a man grabbed at my leg. I brought the barrel of the shotgun down on his head and he let go, stumbled back then reached for his pistol. As it came free of the holster I let loose with one barrel, the buckshot throwing him through the air. I moved on to the next fight.

Thad and Bill were on the far side of the camp raising hell as they rode through the gunman trying to unhorse them. Those that tried quickly felt the strike of a bullet, the steel shoe of a horse's hoof and once, the swift kick of a boot to the face as one grabbed onto Thad's leg. They fell, one after another as the fight raged on.

Those that sought the protection of the woods were met with the bullets from Long Buffalo's pistol as he chased them about. There was not a safe place to be had.

I turned and saw Robert at the flagpole as two men grabbed hold of him and pulled both he and his horse over. I urged Caliban forward and jumped off him before he stopped, propelling me into the fight as Robert took on both men. I brought the barrel of my shotgun down on the back of the neck of the closest man and he went down just as Robert pushed the second man away, pulled his pistol and put a bullet into his head. I spun around just as the man I clubbed rose, pulled his pistol, and leveled it at Robert. I stepped between them and fired the shotgun sending the full force of the buckshot into the man's face.

Robert, out of breath grinned and said, "Thanks Wyatt."

I took a quick look around. The fighting, still going on was not as fierce and I thought it was a good time to fallback and regroup.

I said, "Get the others up to the corral while I take care of the cannon."

Robert mounted his horse and moved through the camp, still engaging the enemy all the while trying to get our men to safety.

I saw Mark and waved him over as I ran to the cannon. I called out, "Mark, give me a hand at the cannon."

He waved and turned his horse to the cannon as I mounted Caliban and made my way to the artillery piece.

We met at the caisson and dismounted. I put two fresh shells in the shotgun and handed the weapon to Mark saying, "Skinner will back you up but if any get close use this."

He asked, "What are we doing?"

I threw the lid back on the magazine box and began searching through the contents of shell, cannon balls, powder bags and tools. "We are spiking the gun so they cannot use it on us."

I continued my search through the box, getting frustrated at not finding what I sought as the battle continued around us, then finally I found what I needed.

During normal use, the artillerymen ignited the charge in the cannon with a primer set above the flash hole on the backside of the piece. We needed more time to escape as I had no intention of launching a projectile from the gun, so I pulled an old style of fuse that was used as a backup source of ignition from the box. It was rolled around a spool, more than enough for my needs.

As I put this under my arm Mark called out.

"Behind you Wyatt!"

As I turned, I saw a man run at me with a saber raised high, screaming at the top of his lungs. Mark raised the shotgun just as a shot rang out from afar and the man fell forward at my feet, dead.

I turned back to Mark and said, "That would be Skinner. Now, I need you to start feeding me powder bags."

I moved to the muzzle of the Napoleon Gun and removed the ramrod from the gun carriage. Mark began walking from the magazine to the muzzle handing me pre-measured bags of powder. With each trip I stuffed the bag into the barrel, repeating this each time Mark brought one over. After a few trips I took the ramrod and stuffed it down the barrel, pushing the powder deeper into the gun.

I asked, "How many was that?"

Mark was standing next to me holding another bag. "Was I supposed to be counting?"

I shrugged my shoulders. "Hell, I do not know." I grabbed the bag in his hands. "Bring two more and see if they fit."

Mark shrugged and turned back to the caisson while I stuffed another bag of powder into the barrel.

I added two more bags, satisfied the gun had been filled and went to the magazine box, dug through the bottom, and came up with a long thin steel spike.

Mark asked, "What is that?"

I held it up and said, "It will pierce the first bag of powder. Then I slip in the fuse, light it and we run like hell."

We looked around and saw that the fighting had become sporadic and only on the far side of the camp. Those of the rogue army that were still able to fight had set up a small defensive position and tried to engage our force that held the higher ground of the corral.

Bodies lay everywhere, both wounded and dead, both men and horses as the battle was coming to an end.

I returned to the cannon, took the small spike, and thrust it down the flash-hole above the breech. I felt the spike meet a slight resistance, giving way as it entered the bag exposing the powder to the fuse. I then grabbed the roll of fuse cord and inserted one end into the hole pushing it down until it too met resistance. Rolling out the fuse a couple of feet I took my knife, cut it, and tossed the roll aside.

Mark asked, "Will that be enough of a fuse for us to get away?"

Again, I shrugged my shoulders in doubt. "Damn if I know. Reckon it might be. This bein' the second time I did this."

Mark looked incredulous. "Oh, shit."

"No need for concern," I said. "Now, go get me a couple of rocks to jam in the end of the barrel."

Mark grabbed the shotgun. "Rocks," he uttered as he walked away.

He returned with the rocks which I stuffed in the barrel with the ramrod, leaving the ramrod sticking out of the cannon.

I said, "Bring the horses over here will you."

Once he led the animals over, he mounted up and I took one last look around the camp. Our exit will take us over to the defensive position the desperados had set up, which meant we would have to fight our way out.

I said, "You ready?"

He nodded as I struck the match and held it to the fuse. The ignition of the powder fuse took a moment but lit off with a bright flash and a puff of white smoke as it hissed along its journey to the powder bag.

I quickly mounted up and announced, "Get the hell out of here pard!"

I pulled my Walker and spurred Caliban back into the fight as we made our escape to the corral through the unsuspecting men that still held out. We rode right into them scattering their numbers as both of us fired into the fleeing rogues. I counted two more down as we went up the rise and took shelter in the wooded area.

As we dismounted, I turned and saw a handful of the ruffians running back to the cannon. I figured that they were hoping to roust us from the woods with the artillery piece. The gun, pointed in our direction, would have been an excellent option for the few survivors of the battle, had I not set rigged it to explode.

I yelled to the others, "Take cover boys, she is about to blow!"

I pulled Caliban behind a thick tree and leaned against the side, waiting for the blast. Time seemed to cease as I mentally counted the seconds, thinking that I had used too long a fuse, giving the bad guys the opportunity to put the gun back in service.

I waited and wondered if I had failed. I pushed away from the tree and turned to look around the trunk.

The fuse had reached its end and lit off the first bag of powder, creating a chain reaction up the barrel igniting each bag in succession all within the span of half a second. It built up such a force of pressure in the steel and brass barrel of the 12-pound Napoleon gun it exceeded its design strength and blew apart with such power that a visible pressure wave went out in every direction, leveling everything it its path.

The flash of fire and light was so bright that shadows were cast all around us as the eruption of the explosion threatened to break our ear drums.

I held onto the reins of my horse, trying to keep him close, throwing my hat over his eyes as dust and debris flew past us in a gale force wind.

As quickly as it was upon us, it was gone.

I worked my mouth trying to get the ringing in my ears to cease and shook my head, taking stock of both me and Caliban.

I yelled to the others, "Is everyone okay?"

Silence.

I called out again. "Is everyone okay?"

W.B.D. Burns answered back. "Think you used enough powder there Wyatt?"

Chapter Thirty-Six

I came out from behind the tree and looked over the devastation. It was complete. The tents, where they once stood in neat rows, at right angles in military precision were gone. The flagpole, once flying the Stars and Bars of the Rebel camp was also gone. Trees, brush and the ground itself was scorched, burnt and smoldering. A massive hole was all that remained of the cannon, its destruction complete. As if it was never there. Small fires burned as the last bits and pieces of the Rebel camp were consumed, completing the destruction.

Then there were the bodies. Laid throughout the camp, twisted, burnt and broken, they too had been consumed by the explosion.

We just stood there looking, taking it all in, unsure of what we were to do next as a slight breeze blew through, cool and pleasant, pushing the smoke clear of the battlefield, revealing the scorched ground and debris in its entirety.

I called out, "Skinner, are you okay?"

He answered from his observation nest, "I am Wyatt. Once this dammed miserable ringin' in my ears stops, I will be down directly."

Robert said, "We should look for wounded."

"We should look for the Major is what we should do," said Thad.

Sheriff Burns asked, "Did anyone see that bastard during the fight?"

No one answered.

He then asked, "How about that Indian? Anyone see him?"

Again, silence.

I sighed heavily and said, "I reckon we should go and look."

We tied our animals off and walked down into what was left of the camp. Our pace was slow, hesitant as we were not looking forward to the task at hand. It had to be done, as it had been so in many battles past. Move through the devastation and carnage, seek out the wounded, assess the damage, verify the dead. Dreadful though it was, it had to be done.

One by one we moved into the camp, spreading out, taking it slow, mindful of our steps, weapons still in hand.

I looked to the ground, moving among the debris and the dead. I looked at the men as I slowly walked past. Some I did not need to check as they were obviously gone, while others I knelt for a closer examination. I came across the captain that had tried to rally his troops for a charge. He was untouched by the explosion, the massive fireball that I had created. He lay on his back, saber in hand, the look of shock still on his face, his hair neatly combed and parted.

I looked down at his face and silently cursed him for compelling us, for compelling me to take such a drastic step in stopping them from their reign of terror. I cursed all these men for forcing us into this terrible ordeal, for taking up arms on such a grand scale, for bringing harm on the folks we were sworn to protect. For believing in a cause that continued to destroy families across a nation.

Perhaps, at one time, it was a noble cause that brought us to war. Now it was a sad memory as those of us who had taken up arms, chose a side and fought, now desired peace.

I looked across the battlefield and cursed these men for what happened.

Jim called out, "Hey, I got a live one over here!"

I looked at the far side of the camp, to the right of the corral and saw Jim, pointing at the ground by his feet. We all made our way to him as I shook off my anger and walked away from the dead captain.

The survivor was a young man, near my age, sitting up against a tree. His face was dirty and bloodied, smeared with the remnants of burnt powder and debris from the explosion making his blond hair a mix of black and brown. His uniform was equally dirty and disheveled from battle. He was a lieutenant, his insignia and gold braided sleeves still shone through the dirt. His breathing was shallow, quick and I realized that this man had not long to live as a small line of blood appeared at the corner of his mouth.

I knelt in front of him and looked into his eyes as he looked at me. His green eyes, perhaps once filled with compassion, were now filled with hate.

He asked, "Would you be the Marshal that was a Union Sergeant Major or the Confederate Captain?"

I said, "I was a Confederate Cavalry Captain. My name is Chambers. By what name are you known?"

He grinned, showing his bloodied teeth, then he spit on the ground. "My name is of no consequence. You be the traitor the Major always talks about. Turn your back on your kind you did," he said then spit again.

I took a deep breath fighting the urge to grab hold of this man and shake some sense into him. "I betrayed no one Lieutenant, you and yours are not my kind."

Bill leaned in and said, "Boy, you are nuthin but a murderin' thievin bastard that got what he deserved."

Again, the Lieutenant grinned and said, "It does not make no never mind if I killed then or now. Yes, I have killed as I have been corrupted by war and killin comes easy, and I suppose I will answer for it."

He began to cough. It was deep and guttural as he tried to catch his breath. He was dying.

Robert looked at our group as we looked at the wounded man and asked, "Has anyone found the Indian or the Major?"

It was the dying Lieutenant who answered. "You will not find them here. The Major and the Indian took six men to Fredericksburg to kill all of you traitors to The Cause." He looked at me, the anger clearly on his face. "He has a hatred of you Captain the likes I ain't never seen before. He has special plans for you."

Ted knelt before the dying man and asked, "When did they leave?"

The Lieutenant coughed again and spit. "I reckon it don matter none to tell you. They left yesterday and ordered us to attack Fort Mason. He was to meet us there when we had taken the fort and y'all was dead."

Ted said, "Sorry to spoil you plans Lieutenant."

"Makes no never mind to me," he said. "I am dying. Reckon I will see you all in hell."

I stood and looked down on the man, shaking my head. "We all must answer for our deeds in this life son. Reckon you go first."

I turned my back on him and walked away trying to collect my thoughts, absorb the information the dying man had imparted to us. The accusations leveled at me and the notion that I had betrayed my kind.

I walked through the debris, ignoring the dead at my feet, as my mind picked apart the statements made, the accusations thrown and the information about the Indian and the Major.

Knowing that I had never betrayed any person, persons or cause, I quickly dismissed what the wounded Lieutenant had said and concentrated my efforts on the news that the Major was not here. Our mission to stop both he and his men had only partially succeeded. The Major and the murderous Indian had departed with a handful of devout followers, leaving his soldiers to face the wrath we had brought down. Those six men, probably chosen for their loyalty and skill with a firearm, were set on killing us and were now roaming free to continue to terrorize the populous.

Ted and Robert stepped over to me.

Ted said, "He died. Never expressed any remorse for what he done."

"Well," I began, "we all knew of such men. They liked the killing, and it got the best of them. Traded their souls for a pistol and the chance to kill."

Robert said, "I guess we need to get back to town."

I looked around and saw Skinner coming into the camp, leading both his horse and Buster. I said, "That we do. We need to be quick about it."

Ted said, "I do not believe the Major will be stupid enough to lay siege to the jailhouse. Once he figures out we are not there he will wait and watch." He shrugged his shoulders and added, "Perhaps."

I looked at Ted and replied, "I believe that to be true." As I was speaking, I noticed Ted's hat and said as I pointed, "It appears that your hat has become a casualty of the battle my friend."

"Huh," he uttered as he removed his bowler looking at the neat bullet hole in the front and the exit hole in the back. He put a finger through the front hole and said, "Damnation! This is an expensive hat."

Robert chuckled and said, "Oh, I imagine it was. Never mind that your head was in it when it happened."

Ted put his hat back on his head and tapped it down. He said angrily, "If it hit my head, it would not have done any damage! This bowler cost me ten dollars!"

"Lord Almighty son," I said as I turned away laughing. "Ten dollars for a hat?"

We were joined by the others. Our mission now was to vacate the area and return as quickly as we could to town.

Thad took off his hat, wiped at the sweat across his forehead. "Do not fret about this," he said as he waved his hat over the area. "Me and Bill will send a message to our people and have this mess cleaned up." He put his hat back on his head. "Right now, we need to get back to town and find this son of a bitch and finish it."

Mark asked, "Do you think the Major and his men will try anything knowing we are not there?"

I could tell Mark was concerned, as he should be. I said, "He will wait. It is us he wants to kill and we ain't there. Still, we need to make haste."

Long Buffalo said, "I will lead us out. We will be quick so stay close to me."

We retrieved our animals, reloaded our guns and made ready for the return trip. Long Buffalo and Skinner took the lead followed by Bill and Thad, Robert, Jim and Mark, while I brought up the rear with Buster in tow.

As we climbed the small rise to exit the camp I stopped and turned, looking back at the devastation while shaking my head. There was a sadness to it. We had been called to arms by circumstances created by selfish men. Men that had a choice to leave the war and fighting behind, content in the knowledge that they and so many others had given it their all. True, we had lost the fight and carried the shame of our loss when we returned home. But we had returned home where so many others were left on the battlefields across the country.

Even suffering through the degradation of the punishment imposed by our former adversary was no reason to take up arms, rob from those who tried to move on, and kill those that got in their way. We may have lost the war, but not our self-respect and dignity. These men lost it all.

I turned and rode off, pulling my pack mule behind me.

Long Buffalo was true to his word as we made our way out of the wilderness of The Hill Country. Our pace was quick and steady as we navigated the narrow trail, its sharp turns, dips and twists, threatening to unseat rider from horse or cause our mounts to make one misstep causing injury or death.

As we negotiated the tricky trail my thoughts were focused on getting out of the wilderness in one piece and not so much our hasty return and pursuit of the Major. Though I thought of myself as an expert rider, sitting atop a worthy animal, I knew that an obstruction on the trail could spell disaster. Yet, knowing this, we pressed on as the desire to get back to town far outweighed our need for safety in the saddle.

It was tough going.

As we rode along the path branches from the foliage whipped at us with each passing rider, creating another threat. Limbs swung back and forth hitting us, scratching at our animals, smacking us about the face and head, some small and others not so small we had to endure a beating as we plowed through the wilderness of trees and brush. Dodging left and right in the saddle proved futile, sometimes missing one only to be whacked by another close behind.

Both man and animal protested, but we pressed on. Frustration turned to anger as our pace never slowed. Curses were uttered at the forest, the rebels that brought us here, and the Almighty himself as we longed for the openness of the Texas country.

Just as we thought we could endure no more we were free of the trail, back in the open land. We held up and took stock of ourselves and animals, allowing ourselves a moment to dismount and catch our breath.

All of us were covered in bloodied scratches and cuts. Our clothing torn and stained with blood, yet we were alive and free of the wilderness. The horses, also wearing the marks of the journey, were restless, pawing at the ground and shaking their heads. As much as we would have desired to stay put and mend our superficial wounds we mounted up and continued our journey.

Our formation loose and open we pushed our mounts harder now that we were on open ground. Time was short and our desire to return to town was now all consuming. Ignoring our aches and pains we quickened our pace, riding silent in the saddle, each of us sufficiently angered and determined to be the first in town and put a bullet into the black heart of Major Percy Rawlings and his evil partner, Achak.

Time moved along, not slowed nor quickened; we ignored the measured length of our journey as we rode. Our eyes were focused on the trail ahead hoping, willing the town of Fredericksburg to appear on the horizon.

Then, it was there.

The view of the town on the horizon filled our very souls with the joy of having met our goal. Like finishing a job, a task worthy of hard work and dedication, we were filled with a sense of pride as we had endured much to get here.

As we neared, our feeling of fulfillment was replaced with the anxiety that we may be too late. We feared that what we had endured was for naught and the Major and his gang of ruffians had accomplished what they came for and lay in wait for our arrival.

I yelled above the sounds of our horses, "When we get to the edge of town we need to split up and come in from different sides in case they are waiting to ambush us!"

Robert yelled back, "We split up into our original groups. I will come in through town while Wyatt, you come in from this side."

Everyone acknowledged the order.

Buster, try as he might to keep up, was pulling hard against the lead line. I decided it was best to let him go and I cast off the line yelling to the others, "I let the pack mule go! We split up now boys, quicken the pace!"

Robert led his men off to the right to come into the town from the east while I kicked Caliban to the front of our formation and led the others to the west, closest to the jail. Our intent was to come into town, hell bent for leather, in the hopes that our aggressive move would catch those in wait unawares.

I yelled over my shoulder to the others, "Once in town, spread out and surround the jail! Stay mounted and make ready to fight out of the saddle!"

I lost sight of Robert as the town came upon us fast. We neither slowed nor deviated from our path but rode into the center of the street.

I announced our arrival with a loud and boisterous Rebel Yell.

"Woh-who-ey, woh-who-ey, woh-who-ey," I yelled.

Folks that had been out and about froze in their tracks. Fear, uncertainty, and confusion as to our intentions, they gathered up their courage, scattered and sought cover. The streets cleared in a matter of a few seconds as I rode down the middle of the street, passed the jail and circled back.

Skinner took up station in front of the jail while Jim and Ted rode around back, weapons out and at the ready we all searched for a target.

Suddenly the door to the jail opened and Julius stepped out with the shotgun held at the ready, unsure of what was going on. He saw Skinner, then me in our defensive posture and began searching the area for what it was that had raised such a ruckus.

He called out, "What goes Cap'n?"

"The Major is fixin to attack Julius," I answered. "Is Chelsea with you?"

"No sir. She is down at her place."

Damnation, I thought as I turned Caliban around. As I did Robert led his posse into town chasing what few citizens that remained on the street, to seek protection of the indoors.

I yelled and waved with my pistol in hand, "Mark, get Chelsea and get your ass down here now!"

Robert joined me as the others spread out and surrounded the jail, everyone at the ready.

"What do you think," he asked.

I looked around. "I think the sumbitch is here."

Just then Drew came out of Pepper's Place wearing his pistol belt, sporting two pistols, and a shotgun over his shoulder, chewing on his ever-present cigar.

“What goes Wyatt,” he asked as he looked around for the source of the concern.

I said, “Expecting some serious trouble my friend.”

He took the shotgun off his shoulder, smiled around the stogie in his mouth and said, “Good. I have nothing planned for this afternoon.”

I could not help but smile as I watched the small sized man with the strength and determination of a giant take up station on the porch of the saloon.

I looked around, keeping Caliban in motion. Now it was up to the Major to make his move.

We did not have long to wait.

CHAPTER THIRTY-SEVEN

I watched as Mark dismounted in front of his shop, bolt up the stairs and disappear inside. A moment later he returned with Chelsea, who was carrying her double barrel, and the two of them stepped down to the street.

Mark grabbed the reins of his horse, and they started walking towards us looking left and right as they made their way to the jailhouse.

I breathed a sigh of relief, knowing that Chelsea was safe, then saw movement out of the left side of my vision. It was a slight movement at first and I was unsure of seeing anything until I turned my head. It was a man, dressed in plain clothes raising a pistol up, taking aim.

I was about to call out when Mark turned and saw the man across from him aiming the gun. He pushed Chelsea back while trying to pull his revolver, then the man fired.

The bullet struck Mark on the right shoulder turning his body while the shooter cocked his piece and fired a second time sending the bullet into Mark's left hip, knocking him to the ground.

I pulled my Howdah Pistol from the saddle holster just as Chelsea screamed, raised the shotgun to her shoulder, fired both barrels at the same moment the gunman got off his third shot. His bullet struck Chelsea on her left side above the hip while her buckshot caught the killer center mass sending him through a shop window with a thundering crash.

I was about to kick Caliban into action when I heard my name being called from down the street. It was him, Major Rawlings.

He sat atop a horse in the middle of the street, pistol in hand. He called again, "Chambers, I am calling you out!"

"Get ready for hell, you son of a bitch," I yelled as I spurred Caliban on.

It was then the gates of Hell opened, and the street was filled with gunman. They came from between buildings, from inside shops, the cafe and the general store. They were all dressed in plain clothes. Their uniforms cast aside, they blended in with the townsfolk, unseen by us when we came into town. The devils were everywhere.

Robert dismounted and rushed to the aid of Mark and Chelsea while Thad and Bill mixed it with the gunman that came from behind the jail. Ted and Jim rode out front seeking out targets in the confusion as gunfire erupted from all areas around the street.

As I started for the Major a hidden shooter came from the side of Pepper's Place and took aim at me as I rode past. I heard a roar of a shotgun blast, turned my head and saw the gunman go down and Drew stepped closer, shooting the gunman a second time. As I looked back to the front, I caught sight of the big Indian riding right at me.

I looked as the Indian came on, his massive knife raised up high, his scream turned my blood cold. I pulled Caliban back, thinking the attacker was going to collide with me, and tried to turn to meet the assault. Just then I heard a fierce yell, and Long Buffalo rode between us and jumped off his horse while it was still in motion.

It was perfectly timed as Long Buffalo hit the Indian Achak, wrapped his arms around the larger man and took him out of the saddle. They both hit the ground in a cloud of dust and dirt, with Long Buffalo on top.

Long Buffalo rolled off to the side as Achak swung his massive blade, cutting Long Buffalo across the left breast, opening a deep wound. He continued to roll twice more then came up standing and pulled his tomahawk from his belt and charged at the big Indian, ignoring the blood across his chest. The two men hit each other with an audible thud, neither one falling as they locked arms in a deadly struggle for dominance.

I regained control of Caliban just as Long Buffalo brought his knee up to Achak's crotch, causing the other man to disengage and back off as the wind was knocked out of him. It was that moment that Long Buffalo struck the fatal blow.

Raising his tomahawk above his head, Long Buffalo charged in and sunk the curved axe head into the side of Achak's neck, grabbed the Indian's long blade knife from the weakened man's grip and thrust the blade into the black heart of the killer.

Achak stood awkwardly, swaying back and to on unsteady legs, looked at Long Buffalo for a moment then fell over backwards to the ground, the knife and tomahawk still protruding from his neck and chest.

I dismounted and grabbed Long Buffalo just as he sunk to his knees, wounded and exhausted.

He looked at me and said, "Go, get the Major. I will be fine."

I took my neckerchief and held it to his wounded breast, concerned at the severity of the cut. “I will be back for you, my friend.”

I stood and looked, suddenly aware of the battle around me. I mounted up and kicked Caliban back into the fight, looking for the devil in the whirlwind of the action.

All around me shots were traded. I saw Julius on the street as he let loose with both barrels on a gunman sending him over a hitching rail and Skinner, rifle forgotten on the ground, grabbed a desperado out of the saddle and threw him to the ground. He then pulled his knife from his belt and thrust it into the man’s chest.

I moved Caliban in a circle, the Howdah Pistol in my hand as I sought out Major Rawlings. He was nowhere to be seen. I saw Bill and Thad, both wounded, shooting it out with one of the attackers who sought refuge in front of Pepper’s Place. It was Drew who finally finished the gun fight as he walked up behind the man and emptied his Navy Six into the unsuspecting killer.

Robert was with Chelsea and Mark, both laying on the ground, as Robert administered aid to them. They were alive and moving as Robert fussed over the two, then a shot rang out and Robert fell over, clutching his arm.

Shocked I looked for the shooter and found him crouching behind a horse trough. I spurred Caliban and rode right at him, leveling the Howdah Pistol as I neared. The man saw me coming, stood and took careful aim as I neared. I fired the gun, still riding forward, and saw the bullet strike him in the center of his chest. He came off his feet and landed in the horse trough. Only his feet remained dry as he lay dead in the water.

I turned back around as Robert came up to one knee and waved, letting me know that he was okay. I turned back looking for the Major.

It was then that Ted came riding by his expensive bowler hat missing, as he too sought out the remaining gunmen. As he passed me, a bad guy rode out into the center of the street, gun in hand and spurred his horse at Ted. The two of them rode at each other at a full gallop.

Ted filled his hand with one of his two nickel plated pistols and started shooting as he rode straight at the fella. The other, also shooting, neither deviated nor slowed as the distance between the two closed.

Ted suddenly pulled up, took careful aim and shot the man out of his saddle. Before the gunman hit the ground Ted had holstered his pistol and pulled the second one, still in the fight.

Suddenly it was quiet.

A warm breeze came through kicking up the dust of the street as I looked around, searching for that one and only person that deserved the business end of my pistols. The one man, the cause of all this grief and heartache was nowhere to be seen.

Mark and Chelsea lay in the street, wounded and bleeding. Robert knelt beside them, pistol in hand not yet willing to give up the fight. Bill and Thad were helping each other as they limped to the stairs of Pepper's Place, Drew coming over to offer aid.

I looked back to the jail and saw Julius, Skinner and Jim looking for more bad guys to show themselves, then I watched Long Buffalo, clutching his bleeding breast, as he stood over the lifeless form of Achak.

The bodies of Major Rawlings' soldiers lay in the street, the last of the holdouts, killed in a battle of their choosing. Killed without honor, killed without the recognition of fellow soldiers, killed as common thieves and murderers to eventually lay in an unmarked common grave.

Ted yelled out, "Where are you Rawlings, you son of a bitch!" His horse, equally agitated danced around in a tight circle. "Show yourself you coward!"

"I reckon he lit out," I yelled over to Ted. "We must tend to the wounded, get the Doc out here."

It was then I heard him. Many a time I had used the Rebel Yell to unsettle an enemy as we charged into the fray. His yell, equally unsettling, echoed off the buildings and through the street, thus making his location impossible to pinpoint.

Behind me I heard a charging horse and turned, pistol at the ready and saw Major Rawlings as he sped past me, not but a few feet away. I fired the Howdah pistol at the same instant Caliban bucked at the charging horse. I missed.

Rawlings rode into the street, turned west and high-tailed it to the edge of the town, trying to make his escape. He passed Jim and Skinner as they tried to get a shot off from the ground. Rawlings pulled his pistol, fired twice hitting both Skinner and Jim and continued past.

Julius ran from the jailhouse steps while bringing the shotgun up to his shoulder. As the Major passed, Julius fired twice. The Major never slowed and was last seen whipping his animal out into the wilderness.

I pulled my Walker and prepared to give chase when I looked at the aftermath of the fight. My friends were all injured and in need of help, the Major will have to wait. I holstered my pistol and dismounted.

I waved at Ted, "Get the Doc out here. We need help."

Ted dismounted and ran to fetch Doc Averbeck and put the sawbones to work while I ran to Jim and Skinner as both men were on the ground.

I knelt on the ground and looked to Skinner first. His wound was in the upper left leg, the bullet still there but in the fatty part of the leg.

I said, "We will need to get that out. Put your finger in it Skinner, slow the bleeding."

I moved on to Jim who was on his back, resting on his elbows. He smiled and said, "Sumbitch got me in the leg too. He cannot shoot worth a damn."

I looked at his wound, also in the left leg but lower and clean through the calf. I said, "You got a clean one Jim. Tie something around it for now."

Drew and Julius joined us, keeping the vigil with their guns at the ready.

Drew said, "I think Julius got him. There is some blood in the street where that fella rode by."

"Do not know how I missed," Julius said.

Ted called to us from the other side of the street. "I need some help gettin these two inside, Doc is prepping his surgery."

"Julius, you come with me. Drew if you would stay with these fellas I will be back directly."

We ran over to Ted as he was preparing to lift Mark off the ground. Julius pushed past me and bent down, picking up Chelsea in his powerful arms. She was white as a ghost, bordering on passing out as she leaned into Julius's chest.

Julius said, "Hang on Miss Chelsea. I got you. We get you help here directly so you hang on Miss."

She did not respond, only rested her head against Julius, her eyes half open.

I knelt at Mark's head. He too lost a lot of blood. I said, "Hang on Mark, we got you."

He looked up at me and said, "Take care of Chelsea, Wyatt. Never mind me."

Ted looked at Mark's wounds and said, "Now you just hush. We will take care of both of you." Ted looked at me. "We need a litter or some such to move him, Wyatt. The bullet is in his hip, and we may worsen it by moving him."

I looked around for something, anything that could be used as a litter.

"Wait here," I said as I rose. "I see something we could use."

I ran across the street, up the stairs to the boardwalk and stopped before the closed door of the cafe. I took a quick look at the door, planted my feet squarely on the deck, raised my right leg and planted the heel of my boot against the door on the hinged side. The force of the kick pushed the bottom of the door away from the frame. I then threw the weight of my shoulder hard against the upper half breaking it free of the hinge. The door fell to the floor.

Inside was the cafe's owner, who's name escapes me as I rarely have eaten there, stood in shock as I walked over the threshold.

"Just what in the hell do you think you are doin, Marshal," he uttered.

I bent down a picked up the door and said, "Do not mind me mister. I will have this back to you in no time."

I dragged the door outside and down to the street while the cafe owner stood in the doorway, utterly confused.

Ted came over and helped me lay the door down next to Mark, pushing it close to his body. The object was to slide him over to the flat surface of the door, pick up the door and bring him inside.

I knelt at Mark's head while Ted took the feet. I said, "Okay Mark. This is probably gonna hurt like hell, but we got no choice."

Mark nodded.

I gently crossed Mark's arms over his chest, causing him to moan and grit his teeth when I moved his wounded shoulder then I grabbed at his shirt around the back of the collar and looked to Ted.

I said, "On the three count Ted, we slide him over to the door."

Ted grasped his feet around the ankles and said, "Ready."

"One, two...three, slide."

Mark let out a grunt as he mashed his teeth against the pain. It was over in a second and Mark was on the makeshift litter.

He was breathing heavily as he said, "Well, that was not too bad."

"Up we go," I said as we lifted him off the ground, bringing yet another moan from Mark.

Robert stood by us as we maneuvered Mark and the litter through the door to Doc's office. The easy part done in coming through the door, we now faced the difficult task of getting both man and litter up the narrow stairs.

As we were muscling our load up the stairs I said, "Why in the hell does Doc have his surgery on the second floor?"

Ted said between his grunts, "When this is over, I will be sure to bring it up to him."

We had finally made it up the stairs and laid both door and Mark on one of the beds. When Doc got around to Mark, he will have to do so while he was laid out on the cafe door.

I looked around the room and saw Hy at the far side working over Chelsea. I wanted to lend a hand, but medicine was not something I had experience with, so I stood by dumbly, wishing there was something I could do.

Pepper came charging up the stairs and stopped, looking about taking it all in. She came over and hugged me, then Robert.

She said, "How bad is Miss Chelsea?"

I said, "Doc is with her now, it ain't good."

Pepper looked to the back of the room as a look of determination came over her freckled face. She marched to the back of the room and stood at Chelsea's feet and asked, "How can I help Doc?"

Doc Averbeck, hands covered in blood while he grasped at his surgical tools said, "Come over here to my left and hand me my instruments as I call for them and help me with the bleeding." He looked over his shoulder and addressed us. "You boys do what you can with the others till I get to them. She is the worst and needs my attention right now. And do not bother me any!"

Robert sat down next to Mark while Ted cut away Mark's clothing from the wounded areas and together, we applied bandages and spoke reassuring words to him as his wife went under the knife.

Drew and Julius brought the rest of our wounded up the stairs, Jim and Skinner, Bill, Thad and Long Buffalo. We sat them around Mark's table as we tended to their wounds as best we could, with our battlefield experience.

I said, "Drew, I want you to go find the sheriff. If he is sober, I want protection around this building." I looked at Julius who was watching the Doc at work, concern clearly on his face. "Julius, I want you out front with the shotgun. Anyone tries to get at us, kill 'em."

He picked up his shotgun and said, "Yes sir, Cap'n."

Ted stepped over, wiping blood off his hands. He asked, "What do we do about Major Rawlings?"

I looked around the surgery. My friends, broken and bleeding but far from defeated all looked at me as Ted posed the question.

I said, "We will tend to everyone and get them on the mend."

Ted raised an eyebrow at my answer. "Of course we will Wyatt. But the question still stands. What about Rawlings?"

Bill said, "Wyatt, do not concern yourself with us. The Doc here will take care of these scratches and cuts." He looked over at Doc who diligently worked on Chelsea. "He will take care of her too."

Mark looked up from his litter; face covered in sweat. "Wyatt," he said, "you find that bastard and make him pay for what he has done!"

Ted asked again, "Wyatt, what do you want to do?"

I inhaled deeply and let it out. "I want to track him down and cut out his black heart."

CHAPTER THIRTY-EIGHT

I looked to the back of the room. Doc and Pepper, their hands dripping with the blood of Chelsea as they worked diligently to save her life. Speaking to each other in hushed tones, Pepper handed Doc his surgical tools as he never moved his gaze away from the wounded area. Blood-soaked rags piled high around Doc's feet as Pepper pulled each one away from the open wound, cast them to the floor and replaced it with a fresh one.

I looked at Ted and said, "C'mon. We got someone to kill."

"Right behind you Wyatt," he responded as we walked to the stairs.

I turned back and addressed Robert, "Do not know how long we will be gone but we will not return till this sumbitch is rotting on the desert floor."

Robert, holding a bloodied rag to his wounded arm said, "You do what needs to be done my friend. We will be here."

We stepped outside on the porch. Julius was standing at the head of the stairs, shotgun at the ready, watching the activity as folks began to venture out onto the street.

Little by little, in ones and twos, the townsfolk came out to view the carnage left behind from the street fight. Some stood over the dead, crossed themselves and prayed, for reasons beyond my understanding, while others moved around looking at the dead gunman, quietly talking among themselves.

Try as we might, we had been unable keep the fight from the town. The Major and his ruffians saw to that and gave us no choice but to engage them on the street. Perhaps in the hope that they could seek cover among the populous, being the cowards that they were, or maybe they hoped to bring some of the townsfolk down forcing us to be cautious in our response. Whatever the reason, they thought wrongly, and it cost them their lives. They were dead, the townsfolk spared, and the battle was over.

Yet, the cost had been tremendous.

Just then Drew came up, shotgun over his shoulder, cigar in his mouth, he paused as he came up the stairs.

He said, "Sheriff ain't around Wyatt. Folks say he is out serving papers or some such."

I nodded as I watched the increased activity on the street. Mister Kramer, the town's undertaker, moved among the dead, looking at each one in turn with a practiced eye. He looked at me and merely nodded his head and tipped his stovepipe hat. He understood what needed to be done. There were no words nor contracts to be negotiated this time. They were dead and he would see to the disposition of the bodies, and we would foot the bill.

I said, "Drew, would you stand watch with Julius while me and Ted make ready to depart?"

Drew took the cigar out of his mouth. "You aim to chase that sumbitch down?"

Ted answered, "We do."

Julius took his attention away from the street and looked at me. "I want to come with you Cap'n, but I know I am needed here. I will watch over everybody while you and Mister Ted is gone." He stepped closer, a fierce anger in his eyes. "You jus kill that man for he can hurt anyone else Cap'n. You kill him twice and cut out his heart so he cannot do it no more."

Drew stood next to Julius, dwarfed by the larger man said, "No worries, Wyatt. I wish I was goin' along but me and Julius got things covered here. You boys just git it done."

For a moment I felt the emotion of the day well up in me. I cleared my throat and said hoarsely, "Me and Ted will find him and make him pay."

Ted said. "Yea damn right we will!"

We stepped off the porch and made our way to the jail to retrieve our mounts and make ready for the chase. We walked among the people of our town as they stepped aside to let us pass. No one spoke, some looked away, others nodded their heads knowing that we had done our best in protecting the town, and the people from these cowardly men. They knew that it had cost us dearly in winning the fight and let us be to continue in our jobs as lawmen.

From behind us a man called out. We stopped and turned. He was someone I had seen in town before. A man I had exchanged greetings with, daily pleasantries. His name was unknown to me, but his face was familiar.

He said, "Marshal. You do what needs to be done. We will watch over your friends. We will take care of them for you Marshal, you can count on it sir."

I looked around as the many faces stopped what they were doing and looked at us, the silence broken by the wind. Men and women alike nodded their heads in agreement as they focused on us.

I said, "We are obliged to you folks for that."

It was all I could say as I turned away, tears showing themselves in my eyes. I had not expected this and quickly wiped the betrayal from my eyes.

Ted said softly as we walked, "Good folks you have in this town. Make a fella want to set roots down and be part of it."

I looked at Ted and smiled. "You are more than welcome my friend. I would like that."

We found our mounts and walked them down to the jailhouse, tying them off on the hitching rail. Ted had found his bowler hat, inspected it for additional holes and, satisfied put it squarely on his head.

As we made our way up the steps I took one last look at the town. The folks were helping Kramer in his duties, and a wagon arrived to collect the dead. By the end of the day, little evidence will remain of the terrible fight, except in the memories of those who witnessed the gun battle, and those that had taken part.

For some, I am certain, those memories shared will take on a life of their own. It will become epic in its retelling, mixing fact with fancy, imagination with glory, and truth with lies. Those that survived will be hailed as heroes or cursed as villains. The more the story is told a bit of the truth will be cast aside, lost through time, and replaced with the teller's own notions.

For us, the ones that pulled the trigger, stood our ground in the dusty street of the town, faced down an enemy bent on our destruction, it will be yet another memory to be pushed down into the darkness of our thoughts along with so many others. It was what we did, what we were called upon to do, but not who we were.

Such was my thoughts as I went about gathering up ball and powder, food, and water. Stuffing both my possibles bag and saddle bags for a journey of unknown duration or destination. We were going to hunt down a demon and hold it accountable for the evils perpetrated on innocent folks. This is who we were.

I sat at the table as I spread the map out and began reloading my pistols. We had no notion as to where the Major went or where we were to pursue him. He lit out west, that we knew.

Ted came over and joined me at the table, putting both his pistols down as he too reloaded fresh for the journey.

I said, "We do not know where he is going."

Ted, pistol in hand, stuffed another premade paper cartridge down into an empty chamber, pushing it down with the loading lever and plunger all the while looking at the map. He said, "Well he went west, that is certain." He leaned in closer, studying the map and asked, "Anything of importance west of here?"

I searched the map as my eyes followed west of town out into the wilderness. I said, "There is plenty west but his choices to hold up will be few. He cannot turn northwest and head that way. The army has reoccupied all those forts, save one."

Ted added, "He cannot take a chance running across a patrol through there. I am sure the boys have gotten through to Fort Mason to warn the soldiers."

I nodded. "I am sure he will not go that way." I thought for a moment then said, "I think he will go deeper into the wilderness. He will continue to travel west cause it is the safest bet, and he will not return to his camp knowing we destroyed it. I believe he is gonna meet up with his brother in the western wilderness."

"The preacher man," Ted asked. "How do you know this?"

"When we sprung Long Buffalo free from the jail at Fort Mason, he told us of seeing the preacher heading southwest in his wagon and we know he did not show up at the rebel camp, nor did we see him on our return." I sat back. "No, he is going west."

Ted looked closer at the area west of town. "Damnation. There is nothing out there Wyatt." He paused then asked, "You said save one. What fort is that?"

I said, "There is one place he might go, Fort McKavett is out there."

Ted looked at me and asked, "Has the army reoccupied it?"

I shook my head. "Not yet. There are plans to send a force out there and do so but last I heard the only thing out there are squatters, folks moving further west."

"How far out there is it," Ted asked.

I sighed. "It is out there a ways. A bit over a hundred miles as the crow flies."

Ted stood, grabbed his pistols, and spun them on his hands, returning them to his holsters in one quick, smooth motion. He said, "We best be gettin' to flappin' our wings then pard."

I smiled and looked up, "By God sir, you are a Son of the South."

We gathered up our gear and made our way outside. The sun was hot as the day was closing, usual for this time of year, and one that will cause us great concern. There had been little to no rain of late and as such our watering holes along the trail will be few and far between. A concern it was but one that will not stop us in our pursuit. We knew this and took extra canteens and several Bota Bags full of water for the journey.

We mounted up and turned our horses back to the Doc's place to let them know that we were off to chase down the blackguard Rawlings and possibly his brother. Also, not knowing the duration of our journey we needed to know how our friends were doing at present as we will not get any news in the wilderness.

We pulled up just as Doc came out of the door, wiping his bloodied hands with a rag. His face, neutral, his stare distant and vacant he looked to be somewheres else.

I remained in the saddle and asked, "How is Chelsea Doc?"

He looked up suddenly, showing no recognition at first, breathed in deeply then said, "I believe she is going to make it Wyatt. I stopped the bleeding and got the ball out. She needs to rest." He shook his head and cast his look down. "She lost a lot of blood," he muttered.

Ted asked, "And Mark, the others?"

Hy looked up and sighed heavily. "Mark may have a busted hip. I can get the ball out easy enough. Long Buffalo will need to be stitched up." He waved his hand behind him still clutching the bloodied rag and said, "The others I can fix up. I just needed to take the air. Pepper is getting Mark ready."

I nodded, unsure of what to say. Doc was exhausted; I was exhausted. I managed to say, "We will be off then to find Rawlings. Thanks for what you are doin' Doc. We are obliged to you and Pepper."

Hy nodded his head and wiped at his hands with the rag, staring at the ground.

I motioned to Ted and turned Caliban back to the street and started our journey west.

When we were in the middle of the street Doc called out to us, the anger and desperation clearly heard in his voice and his words.

"You find him Wyatt," he yelled. "You find him, and you kill him! You kill that son of a bitch, do you hear me son? You kill him!"

We stopped and turned back looking at the sawbones standing on the porch, clutching at the railing with both hands as he leaned out, Julius and Drew standing behind him.

"You kill him Wyatt," he said once more.

Ted said, "We aim to do just that Doc. Rest assured we will get it done."

We turned our horses west and began to make our way out of town.

Most of the dead had been removed from the street, the wagon, loaded down with its gruesome cargo was in front of Pepper's Place as the last of the bodies were unceremoniously tossed in the back, stacked one on top the other like so much wood. Mister Kramer looked up from his task and saw us. He motioned to us, and we stopped, waited for the tall lanky man to walk over.

As he neared, I asked, "What is it we can do for you Mister Kramer?"

He took his stovepipe hat off and held it to his chest as he spoke. "Wyatt, I understand what it is that is required of me and our agreement of past dealings. I have but one exception that I feel I must burden you with."

I raised an eyebrow in curiosity and asked, "That being?"

Kramer said angrily, "It is the Indian, sir. What am I to do with the Godless heathen that is responsible for such heinous crimes against God fearing Christian folk? I do not bury heathen Indians sir."

I sighed and cast a questioning look at Ted. "What do you say my friend? What is he to do with the Godless heathen Indian?"

Ted leaned back and looked up to the sky as he spoke. "God fearing Christian folk," he repeated. "Well, those he killed may have been God fearing but I am uncertain that they lived anything of a Christian life." He lowered his head and looked at Mister Kramer. "That being said, Mister Undertaker, I suggest you bring the matter up to Mister Long Buffalo, our dear, close friend. He being an Indian may have a notion as to what to do with Godless heathens as it is out of our jurisdiction."

Kramer stepped back, nodded and said apologetically, "Oh, yes sir. I will see to it. I am sorry to burden you with such trivial concerns." He took another step back, bowed slightly at the waist and repeated, "I will see to it sir, yes I will."

I watched as the undertaker retreated and resumed his task of collecting those slain in the gun battle. I would guess he was humbled by Ted's instructions, but I could be wrong as feelings such as his run deep and long.

I looked at Ted, smiled, and said, “You handled that well Ted.”

Ted grinned and replied, “Yes, well, sentiments such as his never ceases to amaze me. I have a troublesome time keeping my tongue with such pig ignorance.”

“No, you did good my friend.”

Ted uttered quietly as we kicked our mounts onward, “Grave diggin’ bastard.”

I held my laughter in check as we made our way out of town. Our journey, long or short in time and distance was awaiting us. Our task simple. We were to track and kill a man whose evil heart had caused much grief and heartache, pain, and suffering for reasons that spoke of nothing but hatred and greed.

We had a general idea as to where he was headed, what it was he was going to do, and that is all we knew. Yet, it was not going to slow us in our pursuit, nor will it stop us. Ours was a cause filled with righteous determination. Both Ted and myself were filled with the overwhelming desire to see the task to its conclusion. Either we were going to kill Major Rawlings, or he us. However way it ends, it will be done.

CHAPTER THIRTY-NINE

Leaving the town behind, we made our way into the wilderness. The ground, hard and dusty from the lack of rain would prove difficult for our animals. It had been a long day of travel already and we were asking our mounts to continue with little rest, so we kept a steady yet easy pace, not wishing to push the animals too hard. Not this early in our journey, not yet. We had already asked much of them and we found a comfortable rhythm as we headed west, into the vast openness of the Bexar Territory.

There was no need for us to bring the map along. I had committed it to memory, what little there was depicted on the page. Our journey was going to take us west by northwest some hundred miles, give or take, and hopefully we will find evidence of Rawlings direction along the way. Or find the man.

We rode in a comfortable silence as we both scanned the country before us for unseen dangers or areas that may cause us concern. There were other things to consider in the wilds of the country we traveled through. The lack of water sends man and animal alike in search of watering holes, rivers or streams, anything to provide relief in the arid environment. With the lack of water comes the lack of food which can cause an animal to look upon us as an inviting meal, crazed with thirst, and hunger they might consider an attack where before our presence would only earn us a passing glance.

I broke the silence and said, "Fort McKavett is west by northwest. Reckon the best way for us to travel is west for a spell then turn northwest."

Ted asked, "Any trails leading to the fort?"

I recalled the map and replied, "If there is it has not been well traveled for some time."

Ted looked down at the ground. "Well, we are not gonna see his damn tracks on this trail. Too many have passed before."

I looked down at the ground. He was right. The trail that led west out of town was well used by townsfolk and settlers alike. Much traffic had passed along this route and attempting to distinguish any tracks made by Rawlings would be near impossible.

"Perhaps when we get some distance between us and the town, we can pick up his trail," I said.

Ted leaned forward in his saddle, attempting to get comfortable. He asked, "What lays beyond Fort McKavett?"

I grinned as I thought of the lands beyond the Bexar Territory. "Reckon the edge of Texas," I said.

Ted looked at me for a moment and saw the grin on my face. "Hell Wyatt. You be sure to let me know when we get to the edge of Texas."

I laughed. "If we get to the Rio Pecos, we went too far."

Ted laughed and said, "Well I hope Rawlings does not head off to Mexico. I am well versed in a few languages, but I have not bothered to learn Spanish."

"Well," I began. "Do not look to me. I barely have a command of English."

Ted laughed and again tried to get comfortable in his saddle. Shifting his weight from side to side, standing in the stirrups then sitting back down all the while working his backside into the saddle.

I looked on curiously, knowing what troubled him and finally asked, "Something causing you some discomfort Ted?"

He looked at me, trying to hide the embarrassment at being discovered as if it were some great transgression. He said, "Oh, it is nothing."

I persisted. "No, tell me my friend. What ails you?"

He sighed and said, "I am not used to being in the saddle this long. Got a touch of the cramp."

Knowing that he was slightly embarrassed to admit this to me, or anyone for that matter, I suppressed my laughter. Being an old cavalry trooper, I myself had gone through a spell in my early days where I longed to get out of the saddle, hell, I prayed to get out of the saddle only to be denied and forced to suffer through the long ride.

However, I took pity on my friend, not wishing him discomfort and pulled up and made a show of rubbing my leg.

I said, "I reckon we should walk a bit. I too am growing weary of being in the saddle. It has been a long day."

Ted pulled up passed me and turned his mount. He said, "Do not slow the pursuit on my account Wyatt, I can ride."

I got down off my horse and stepped closer. "Nonsense. The animals could use a break as well. I say we walk until dark, then find a camp. Rawlings will not get too far away, I am sure."

Ted dismounted as I walked up next to him, and we began to lead our animals at a slowed pace. It was best for both man and beast I suppose. No need to kill ourselves this early in the chase. It was not as if I had a notion as to how long our pursuit will last, I was just planning on a long journey knowing that a man like Rawlings was not one to give up the fight easily.

The sun was setting in the west and with it the temperature began to drop allowing us a small measure of comfort.

As we walked, I gave into my curiosity about the man walking beside me and began to ask of his past and of his home.

"Tell me Ted," I began, "do you miss Knoxville? Ever have a notion to return?"

He looked off to the setting sun as he spoke. "Someday perhaps I will."

I sensed a sadness in his short declaration and decided to let it drop.

Ted continued by saying, "Miss Chelsea asked if I was married. I am not, but I was."

I looked at Ted as we continued our trek. "Oh?"

He nodded, still watching the setting sun. "I was. Had a daughter too, three years old." He shook his head and looked at the ground as we walked side by side. "She looked just like her mother, angelic, both of them. Had a nice spread too in a place called Rocky Ford, south of Knoxville in Blount County. Beautiful country it is."

I said, "I did not mean to intrude Ted. You do not need...," he cut me off.

"No, I can talk about it." He paused and added, "Maybe I should talk about it more instead of keeping it to myself."

I merely nodded, remaining silent.

"We farmed a bit, hunted to put food on the table and I had hung my shingle out and helped the folks with legal matters to make ends meet. It was a good life, for a while."

"What happened?" I asked.

He sighed, shrugged his shoulders, and said, "They got the typhus, and both died a day apart. I buried them on the land, burned the house, and wandered around a bit. Then the war came up, and I was all too eager to join up." Again, he shrugged his shoulders. "Had nuthin' else to do."

I stopped walking, sadden by this revelation. I said, "I am sorry for your pain my friend."

He turned and forced a slight grin. "Thanks Wyatt. You would think after all this time it would not bother me any. That is not the case my friend."

I nodded knowing all too well of the continued suffering from loss. Loss of family, loss of friends, and loss of men. Though we carry forward the memories remain, and we try to find a level surface to live our lives.

Ted looked me straight in the eyes and said, "Wyatt, if I do not make it through this, I want to be buried next to my wife and child." He looked around as the sun slowly set casting the land in a pleasant orange glow. "I do not want to rest in this harsh land." He turned back to me and stepped closer. "Will you see to it Wyatt?"

I took a moment, thinking through what was just asked of me. Was it a premonition that made him ask this? It was a great request to make of someone and to make it to me no less.

True, we had developed a bond, a bond born in battle. A bond so great that kin, brothers even, often do not develop such a friendship among their siblings. Ours was a bond born of blood and desperation, a soldier's bond.

To share life at its most extreme created such friendships. Friendships that go beyond the understanding of those that have not experienced such trauma, such anguish and brutality.

I pulled my hand free of my leather gauntlet and extended it to him. I said, "I will my friend if you promise the same. Do not leave me out here."

He pulled his glove off and grasped my hand firmly. "I will see it done," he said.

I worked my hand back into my glove, took a deep breath and quickly pushed the lingering thoughts from my mind. Now was not the time to dwell on such things.

I said, "While we have some little light, I suggest we set up camp and get some rest. We can start fresh in the morning." I smiled. "What say you, Ted?"

He smiled broadly and said, "My ass, though numb at this point, agrees with you."

We laughed and led our animals off the beaten trail and sought out a suitable location to establish our camp.

Weariness began to set in as we set up our small yet functional camp. We decided that we were safe in having a small fire to cook, gathered some wood, tended the animals, and soon had the coffee pot on the cook-fire.

Our foodstuffs were limited as we did not have either pack mule or horse burdened with panniers on our expedition. We had corn biscuits, hardtack, dried beef and jerky, bacon, raisins and pickles, and beans which we planned on putting in the soaking pot once we came to our first watering hole if it was not dry.

We ate light, sat by the fire, leaning up against our saddles as we drank coffee while I enjoyed my pipe and Ted a cigarette.

Ted looked up at the stars, exhaled a cloud of smoke, and said, "This is one sight that I will never grow tired of."

I looked up. The stars seemed to be a blanket over the land, extending from horizon to horizon in all directions. Ted was correct. I never grew tired of the beauty of the night.

Ted asked, "Do you miss Georgia any?"

"Well, I miss the memories of my home. My father and sister, memories of growing up."

Ted sat up and looked over at me. "Then you have no desire to return? Even if," he paused, "you do not make it through this?"

"Well," I said. "I reckon stayin' here in Texas is good enough for me. I made this my home. I just do not want to be left out in the wilderness without a proper place to rest. Figure my family could come and, maybe, put flowers on my grave."

Ted seemed satisfied with this and sat back. "Get some sleep, I will take first watch."

I pulled my hat down over my eyes, settled back against my saddle and said, "You have no argument from me sir."

The night passed quietly, Ted woke me for my shift of night-hawking and come sunup, I had the pot on the coals, bacon in the pan, and we began to break camp and prepare our horses for the day's journey.

I just finished saddling Caliban, checking over the security of all the equipment we brought along, and turned my attention west.

I asked, "What do you think Ted? Should we continue west?"

Ted finished tying off his gear, looked back at me and said, "This is your country, my friend. I think you have a sound plan, and we should stick to it."

"Then west we shall go," I said as I mounted up. "Let us see what the day brings before we change our direction of travel."

Ted mounted his Appaloosa and turned him west, holding him still for the moment. He said, "Maybe we will find something of the Major today. Surely, he too rested during the night."

"Maybe," I said as we headed out to the trail.

The morning sun was at our backs, climbing in the sky as the temperature began to rise. It was a cloudless morning, no wind, and no indications of any change other than hotter temperatures.

In this part of the country, I had learned that the weather could change without warning nor indication that it was going to be anything other than hot. This time of year, normally brought nothing but drought and misery for those caught out of doors.

Like us.

Still, one could always hope for rain, a blessed relief from the stifling heat of summer. But rain during a drought also brought the danger of flooding. Where once there was no river, the rains could bring a fast-moving wall of water destroying everything in its path, following the path of least resistance, unable to flow into the ground. Flowing across the hardened earth that was unable to absorb the massive amount of water suddenly falling on the ground made for difficult if not impossible travel. One just had to seek out higher ground and wait.

But it did not look as if that would be a concern for us this day. It was going to be hot.

We made our way along the trail, seeking out signs of recent travelers, more especially our elusive Major Rawlings. We studied the ground for anything that may tell us we were on the correct path in our pursuit. Anything to tell us we were correct in our assumptions as to his destination, his plans and objective.

The day wore on. The temperature grew hotter; the air dry, unmoving as we pressed on. Our determination only grew stronger with each passing mile as did our anger. Our anger soon motivated us to continue the chase as we spoke of what miseries we would inflict on the blackguard once we found him.

It was passed mid-day when we came upon what was a watering hole that we found the reassurance we so desired.

The hole, showing evidence of once having been full of water, was nothing more than a dried-up depression in the ground. It had been without water for some time as the ground was hard and cracked. The dried carcass of some small animal, fox or coyote, lay dead at the edge of the pit, and did nothing to reassure us of our future travels.

We pulled up and looked at the emptiness.

I said, "Ain't gonna water down the beans from this hole in the ground."

Ted snickered. "I do not know if that is a good thing or a bad thing Wyatt."

I turned to Ted to respond when I took notice of something over his shoulder. I pointed and said, "Look at that."

Ted turned away from me and said, "I do not see what you are..." He stopped. Then asked, "Is that a swarm of flies?"

Not ten or twelve feet beside him was a small black cloud a few inches above the ground. Its shape, one moment circular, then oval, small then large was moving, yet it remained over the same spot on the ground.

We both dismounted and stepped the short distance to the oddity.

"Blow flies," I said, "Hundreds of 'em."

Ted knelt, removed his bowler hat, and shooed them away, revealing a rag, covered in blood. He continued to shoo the flies away as he reached over and picked it up for closer examination. He stood.

Holding it high, he said, "It is a bloodied rag." He turned it over in his hand. "No, it is a field dressing, and the blood is still fresh enough to attract the flies."

I stepped closer. "Julius fired two barrels of buckshot as Rawlings made his escape. I reckon he hit him." I pointed at the bandage. "This must be his, it is too fresh, and it is an army issued field dressing. I recognize it."

Ted, still holding the dressing, looked around. "You do not suppose the Yankees are out and about here, do you? Maybe one of them left this."

I too looked around. The landscape had flattened out, and one could see for miles. There was no dust, no movement on any horizon, nothing.

I said, "I do not believe that is the case. We would have seen evidence of a patrol in the area."

Ted said, "Yea, that is true."

I looked back at Ted, smiled, and said, "Yankees, really?"

Ted shrugged his shoulders, grinned, and replied, "Old habits."

I laughed, shook my head, and said, "As I said before. You can take the boy out of the south."

Ted tossed the bloodied bandage aside, letting the flies finish the job. "Well, I guess we are on the right track." He looked off in the distance. "How far ahead do you think he is?"

I looked back at the cast-off field dressing. The flies had quickly rediscovered their missing treasure and attacked it in force. "I would guess he ain't but a few hours ahead of us. He is wounded which means he will be moving slower." I waved my arm over the dried-up watering hole. "He may be out of water."

Ted walked back to his horse, grabbed the reins, and said, "Then we should mount up. I did not come this far out into the wilderness to let that evil bastard bleed out nor die of thirst." He mounted his horse and looked at me, a renewed determination in his eyes.

I said, "Right. He will die by our hand and our hand alone. Satan can have him when we are done!"

CHAPTER FORTY

We resumed our trek out into the flatlands of West Texas, the hills behind us now, and the expanse of the Bexar Territory lay before us. We continued our steady pace, fighting the urge to quicken our pursuit knowing that the next watering hole may be another dried up depression in the ground, and we dare not risk it.

This will be the most taxing part of our journey. Though I had never traveled this area myself, I was aware of the difficulties we were to face, having talked with Skinner Stevens about the range beyond our town and Bexar Territory in particular. The vastness of the territory beyond the horizon; the desolation for hundreds of miles seemed impassable.

Our course was to take us just inside the edge of the territory before we would turn north by northwest and up to Fort McKavett, and hopefully there we would find the Major.

Though the army did not yet occupy Fort McKavett, it served as a stopping point for many a settler heading west. Its buildings, though in disrepair, provided shelter from the elements, and more importantly, it was near the San Saba River, a ready source of water.

Ted broke the silence and asked, "How far to the fort yet?"

I gave it some thought before I answered. Through years of traveling on horseback both during and after the war a good cavalry trooper can easily judge distance traveled, distance yet to travel as well as the pace of travel. Though some would say it was nothing but a guess, I liked to think it was an educated guess, based on experience.

I said, "Reckon at least another two-day ride to the fort, could be three at this pace. We are about one third of the way." I looked ahead. "Might ought to adjust our course and take a direct line to McKavett."

Slowly we steered to the desired direction and continued our steady, almost frustrating pace of march.

"I take it there is a good source of water there," Ted asked.

I nodded my head, took off my hat, and wiped the sweat from my brow with my neckerchief. "The San Saba is close by," I said adding, "If it has not dried up in this damn drought."

Ted too removed his bowler hat and wiped his brow, then the inside hatband. He lingered at the bullet holes in his hat, frowned, placed it back on his head then said, "Times such as these I do miss the green of Tennessee."

I said, "The green of South Georgia."

Ted leaned forward, then back stretching out his sore muscles. "Yes sir," he said. "Very green." He looked around. "Still, there is beauty in this land if you look."

I grinned, "Thinking of relocating Ted?"

He looked at me and laughed. "Maybe I am Wyatt. Thinking of all these settlers coming west looking for a fresh start. This will be a wonderful place when it is settled. Folks everywhere, carving out a piece of life from this land."

"My Lord," I said. "You are thinking of relocating." Then I asked, "Thinking of giving up on the Pinkertons?"

He looked down at his badge reflecting the bright sun. "Maybe put my law degree to some use instead of chasing bad guys across the country."

I found his notion agreeable and said so. "That sounds like a fine idea. You could hang your shingle in Fredericksburg. Robert and me could bring in the desperados and you could defend them before Judge DuBose"

"Oh Lordy," he uttered, shaking his head. "I fear that arguing a case before Judge Dubose will be a difficult task at best."

I found this statement to be true, having been in his court many a time with our prisoners. I said, "He is tough, but fair."

Ted said, "I have heard about his temperament behind the bench." He turned to me and asked, "Is it true he threw his gavel at a defense attorney?"

I laughed, recalling the incident as it had happened with a degenerate that we brought before him. "That is only because the attorney for the miscreant was dumber than a bag of hammers and told Judge DuBose to go do it with his horse."

"You must be joking?"

I shook my head. "I am not." I laughed as I recalled the incident. "This fella kept objecting to everything that was being said and got mad cause the Judge kept over-ruling him. Then Judge DuBose told the fella to shut up and told me to gag him if he objects one more time."

"And that is when he told the Judge to do it with his horse," Ted asked.

I nodded. "It is. After the trial, the judge sentenced both the prisoner and the lawyer. The prisoner got ten years, and the lawyer got ninety days."

Ted shook his head and laughed heartily. "Perhaps," he began, "I will stay with the Pinkertons. It may be a safer vocation."

I said, "I think you would make a fine attorney for the town. You should give it some thought." I added, "Course, you would have to get a different hat. A city hat does not do much good out here."

Ted looked at me, then rolled his eyes up to his hat and laughed. He shrugged his shoulders and said, "I will do that Wyatt." He leaned over. "The hat first."

We pressed on as the day grew hotter. There was no breeze to move the air and the heat radiated across the barren landscape. The further one looked, the more distorted the image as the heat shimmer looked to be a wall before us. Impassable, menacing, threatening our continued journey into the territory.

We decided to walk our mounts for a bit to rest their backs, and our rumps. While we walked, I took a drink from the canteen and handed it to Ted. Then, with one of the Bota Bags we watered our animals being careful not to let them consume too much too soon. We still had a great distance to travel and figuring that whatever watering hole we were to come upon would be dry. Should it have some water, then we would be blessed. If not, we would continue to our destination and the cool waters of the San Saba.

The sun shone over our left shoulders reflecting the heat as it radiated upwards. Like walking through a fat filled frying pan. Instead of the inviting sounds of sizzling meat from that frying pan, there were only the sounds of our feet and those of our horses as we walked across the hard packed surface.

We stepped among the underbrush, cacti, scrub brush, small and low to the ground, stunted from further growth from the lack of water. The dust, a fine powder, kicked up as we walked and stayed around our feet as there was no breeze to bring it any higher. A blessing, slight as it were, because the dirt did not occupy our already dry mouths.

"Lord Almighty Damn," I uttered. "Hard to imagine anything living out here."

Ted stopped walking, brought his hand up to shade his eyes from the blazing sun and said, "Thought I saw something off in the distance."

I looked off in the direction he was looking. The heat shimmer, distorting the view, did not help in distinguishing anything of importance or concern. I saw nothing.

Ted dropped his arm. "Oh, it was nothing. Just the heat."

I continued to look out before us as I spoke, "Well, perhaps it was the sun reflecting..." I stopped speaking. I too saw something off in the distance.

Ted stepped closer and said, "There it is again. Looks to be a reflection. Something shinning off the sun."

"We best mount up and see," I said as I walked to the side of Caliban. "Could be something, could be nothing."

Ted mounted up and said, "Only one way to find out."

We quickened our pace, interested in the oddity we saw but not so as to cast our caution aside and ride hard and fast into what could be danger.

We stayed abreast as we rode closer to the area. The reflection, whatever it was, stayed steady and was more noticeable as we neared, yet nothing else could be seen through the wall of heat.

Ted pushed back his coat to allow easy access to his pistols and said, "May I suggest we split up and come at it from different sides."

I unlashed my Walker. "Good idea. I will go right."

With no further discussion, we split up. I went right while Ted went left. We would circle around and come at the anomaly from two sides ready to engage or render assistance, whatever circumstances dictated.

Now adjacent I turned Caliban and headed directly at the shimmering object, still some distance off. As I neared, its luster, still moving about, seemed to diminish in its intensity, grow faint. Its movements were without reason, moving from left to right, back again, staying stationary, only to move again. The distortions from the rising heat kept the object out of focus.

Closer now, there seemed to be a dark mass around the reflection. It still moved about, without sense nor direction, aimless. The reflection grew dim then became two, then three smaller lights as the dark mass grew larger.

I pulled up and uttered aloud, "My God, it is a horse."

I pulled my Walker Colt free of the holster, cocked the large pistol, and kicked Caliban forward. It was a horse, its harness fixtures reflecting off the bright sun.

The horse was without a rider.

I came upon the riderless animal just as Ted came in from the opposite side. Without speaking, we knew what needed to be done. We turned our mounts in circles, moving out in different directions, scanning the ground, looking for the rider of the horse.

Our search brought us out a great distance from the animal, again we were on opposite sides of the riderless horse. Nothing, no rider could be found.

I holstered the Walker and rode back to the horse meeting Ted where we both dismounted and approached the beast.

Cautiously I removed my hat, held it away from my body, extended my other hand and made soft cooing sounds as I approached the stallion from the left side. He was nervous, frightened, and looked to be hurt, repeatedly lifting his left foreleg off the ground.

Slowly I reached for his harness, rubbed his nose, and settled him down.

Ted came in slowly. He said, "Poor animal is done in."

Ted bent down and examined the horse while I whispered softly to the animal, stroking his head.

Ted stood, the look on his face said it all. "He has a busted cannon bone Wyatt. Poor fella is done in." He walked around the right side of the beast, continuing his examination.

I nodded as I looked over the animal. He was in poor shape to say the least, ridden hard and abused, broken leg, breathing heavily and obviously in pain.

Ted said, "There is blood on the saddle."

I came around and looked as Ted showed his gloved hand. It was bloody as was the saddle.

"It was his animal," I declared.

Ted looked around. "Then where in the hell is he? Did he set off on foot?"

I returned to the head of the horse and stroked his neck. I said, "I reckon we should look for sign. In the meantime, would you collect up our horses Ted."

Ted came around, stroked the lame horse and said softly, "Sure thing Wyatt."

As Ted gathered our mounts and led them away, I stepped in front of the horse and looked into the animal's eyes while I looped the reins around his head to keep him steady. I spoke softly as I worked.

"Sorry fella. I will not let you suffer in this awful condition," I said as I held fast to the reins with one hand while pulling my pistol with the other.

I brought the gun up slowly to his head and cocked the revolver, pressing the barrel to the center of his head, just above the eyes. He did not move nor faulter. He just looked at me. I believe he understood what needed to be done.

I pulled the trigger.

I walked over to where Ted had moved our animals and took the reins from him as I holstered my pistol. I said nothing as I mounted up. There was no need to discuss what just occurred; it had to be done. It was just one more reason for us to hate the man we pursued.

Ted said as he pointed to the ground, "Looks like he is on foot. Tracks lead off toward the direction you figured Wyatt."

I looked down and clearly saw the footprints in the dirt. It would not be long now.

"There is something else," Ted said.

"Oh?"

He pointed to our left. "Wagon tracks over there. Two horses pulling a wagon and an out-rider, single mount."

We moved our horses to the area he pointed to, and I dismounted. I saw two distinct ruts in the soil and two sets of horse tracks through the center of the ruts. I also noticed horse shit on the ground. I walked over and knelt next to the droppings.

I reached down and picked one of the horse apples up. It was not fresh, but it had not been present too long as the brutal sun was just now baking and drying it out.

I cast it aside and said, "It is not more than a day old. Maybe early this morning." I stood and looked off in the distance. "Do you reckon it could be his brother," I asked.

Ted said, "It could be." He pointed to the other tracks of the single rider. "That means we have another gun hand to deal with when we catch them."

I examined the wagon tracks again. Something was not right as I looked hard at the ruts in the ground. I stepped between the two lines in the dirt, faced the direction of travel and extended my arms keeping them parallel to the ground. That was what bothered me.

I said as I turned back to Ted, "It is not his brother. This wagon is too narrow."

Ted asked, "How can you be sure of that?"

I grinned as I looked up at Ted. "I have this knack of sorts to remember things in all its detail. I remember the preacher's wagon. It was unusually wide with thick wheels to support the added weight."

"You mean like a freight wagon?"

I looked back to the direction of travel and said, "Something like that. It was definitely a custom job to be sure. That church wagon of his was built from the axels up to be a church wagon."

Ted looked off in the distance then said with a tone of urgency in his voice. "Oh, good Lord, settlers!"

I turned to Ted and we locked eyes. We were thinking the same thing as I quickly mounted up, and we kicked our horses back on the trail.

We got back on our course, both of us ready to pull our pistols and engage should we come across our adversary. Our thoughts were such that Rawlings had either joined up with the small group of settlers heading west, or worse.

We quickened our pace as our eyes scanned the area in front of us. Our hopes were such that we would come across the Major while still on foot. Then it was a simple matter of finishing our job and going home.

But it was not to be.

We were not long on the trail when we saw, off in the distance, the distinct image of black, long winged birds circling above the ground. There were six of them, slowly moving in a tight circle, riding the air currents, floating on the rising heat. It was the worst site one could see while out in the wilderness.

Without a word we kicked our mounts into a gallop towards the kettle of Turkey Buzzards, knowing that there was more than likely a wake of the birds on the ground as well.

Again, the heat shimmer distorted our view as we neared. What we saw through the waving reflections of rising heat was troublesome. The distorted image of a wagon, unmoving with the dark silhouettes on the ground in front of it. The closer we got, the more distinct the shapes became until there was no mistaking what lay before us.

The wagon, horseless and unmoving, the cover pulled back revealing the support ribs like the skin of a large beast peeled back exposing the innards to the outside world. The figure of a body, that of a woman was clear to be seen as she was half in, half out of the wagon seat. Her long hair hanging down, touching the sunbaked ground. Her blue dress torn and covered most of her body as she hung in the awkward position, lifeless.

We pulled up and stared at the scene before us.

The two horses, still in their harness, lay lifeless in front of the wagon. A small wake of Vultures sitting atop them like some terrible guard protecting their property waiting for the feast.

To the right we saw a prone figure, that of a man, hat less, arms stretched out before him as if he were running to the wagon as he was felled. Blood, dark brown, stained the dirt around his body.

Then we saw a boy some distance away from the wagon, face down, blood stains on his back. He looked to be running away when he too was killed. Shot in cold blood, gunned down, murdered.

We said nothing.

We knew they were all dead. There was no need for us to rush into the killing field to check for survivors, there were none. We just sat our horses and looked, uncomprehending the evil that swept upon this family of innocent settlers.

Ted pulled his rifle from the scabbard and brought it to his shoulder, taking aim at one of the vultures that sat proudly atop the carcass of one of the dead horses. He fired, and the others took flight, as he returned his rifle to the scabbard without an utterance, a curse or pronouncement.

I dismounted and led Caliban into the killing field and said over my shoulder, "I will find a shovel."

CHAPTER FORTY-ONE

As we walked through the carnage, our minds, through years of conditioning and experience, reconstructed the scene. It was not difficult as we saw in our mind's eye what had happened, the events and circumstances that took this family to a violent end.

Either Major Rawlings had found them, or they found him. Regardless, it was a death sentence for the poor unsuspecting settlers as they met the man. Perhaps general pleasantries were exchanged, or they showed a Christian compassion for a wounded man walking through the wilderness and attempted aid and comfort. Or, maybe, the wickedness in Rawlings was to just walk into their camp and gun them down without a word spoken.

However it began, the woman was first. She was still seated on the wagon's seat; jerk lines still in her hands when the bullet tore through her chest. She fell out to the side; her leg twisted under the seat spring, leaving her hanging upside down half in and half out of the wagon.

The man was next. He was the outrider we knew of. He probably heard the shot and rode forward, then dismounted and ran to aid his fallen wife. He too was shot in the chest. One bullet, down he went as he tried to help his woman.

The boy, witness to the shooting of his parents, frightened and now alone ran off out into the wilderness. Too young to fight, he chose to run and hide in the hopes of finding safety. He was shot in the back as he tried to flee.

Then, for whatever reason, he killed the horses. One shot each in the head, keeping the man's horse.

As we moved the body of the man to the freshly dug grave, I took notice that he was without pistol. It was foolish not to be heeled when traveling through the openness of the country. Perhaps he had a rifle in his scabbard, which meant that in addition to the missing horse, Rawlings may have gotten another gun.

We searched through the wagon in the hopes of identifying the family we were burying. Something to notify any other living family members of their demise or find out from where they had traveled. Even a name to put on a grave marker.

It was in a wood box that we found the answers we sought. It was not overly large but sizable enough to hold the man's pistol, a small bag of gold coin and what looked to be family papers.

I handed the papers to Ted as I stood in the back of the wagon, holding the pistol while I looked at the man resting next to his wife and son in the freshly dug grave. I shook my head, pulled the army revolver free of its holster and stuck it in my belt, tossing the holster away.

Ted, thumbing through the stack of papers, said, "We need to finish burying these folks then I will go through this for a name. It is getting late and I do not want those damn birds coming back."

I jumped off the wagon and said, "Right, let us finish this task and figure what we do next."

Ted rolled the papers up and stuck them in his shirt saying, "Easy, we find Rawlings and kill him."

We took one last look at the family as they lay in the grave. I took a tarpaulin and covered them as Ted began to shovel the freshly dug up earth back into the grave, moving the large pile a bit at a time until they were covered, and the dirt created a mound.

We then began to gather rocks, large and small and piled them atop the mound in the hope that it would prevent a scavenger beast of the wilderness from digging them up.

As the sun reached the western horizon, we had completed our task, and we just stood at the foot of the grave silent, staring down at the pile of rocks and dirt. There were no words to speak, no prayers to recite nor hymns to sing that would have made a difference to us.

We were chasing a great evil and until we completed our terrible task, we had no words of comfort to share, no goodness to embrace, just a burning in our hearts to kill the man responsible.

I tossed the shovel aside and began to walk away saying, "We might as well set up camp close by. Ain't no sense venturing out tonight."

"Right," Ted said as he fell in behind me.

We led our animals off a distance, out of sight of the wagon knowing that the dead horses would soon attract critters looking for an easy meal. Once they found them, the worst place to be was near as they feasted on the dead carcasses. With the drought of the desert, starvation was thrust upon the animals of the wild, making them dangerous.

We found a spot, ground tied the horses and began to set up camp for a light meal, discussion on our continued pursuit of the Devil Major, and some much-needed rest.

I was unsaddling Caliban and watching Ted as he sat on a large rock, thumbing through the stack a paper we had found in the wood box, spectacles perched on his nose. The papers, of varying sizes, were all that was left to tell us who they were. Their lives had been reduced to a stack of mismatched documents that may or may not tell a story of the family we had just buried.

It did not seem right nor fair. Having spent time in this world, long or short in its duration, a person deserves to leave something behind to let others know they were there. That they had accomplished something, anything. They may not have been famous or well known to others, but they had made a family and perhaps that was more important than fame or riches. They deserved a name.

Ted jumped up from the rock suddenly and yelled, "Lord Almighty Damn, Wyatt! There is another child!"

I froze, holding the saddle in both hands. "What in the hell do you mean, Ted?"

He held up a piece of paper, a letter and said, "It is a letter from the man's mother. Their name is Harrison." He brought the paper closer to his face and read aloud. "Matthew, my dear boy, I am glad that you, Sally, Elizabeth, and Matt Junior are heading out to Texas to find you a life. The children deserve a fresh start." Ted dropped his arms and looked at me over his glasses. "Wyatt, there were four of them in the wagon!"

I dropped the saddle and ran back in the direction of the wagon, Ted on my heels.

We raced to the wagon, urgency in our movement as our thoughts went through the many possibilities. Did the child escape and is now alone, wandering through the desert? Did Rawlings track her down and murder her as he did the other members of the Harrison family? Did he kidnap her for some devious plan or reason? Was there even a child, were we mistaken?

The cactus grabbed at our legs, tore our pants as we ran through the underbrush ignoring the many scratches and scrapes. We hurried to beat the setting sun, and the much-needed light should we have to begin a search.

We came upon the wagon and halted in our tracks. There was enough light remaining for us to see the unthinkable. They were everywhere. They were circling the dead horses, attacking in groups, driven mad from hunger they fought each other for the prize of a mouthful of dead flesh. Their yips and cries rang out all around us as they threw caution aside in the hopes of something to eat.

The coyotes were massed around the wagon, dozens of them, crazed and aggressive. Their fear being replaced by the madness of hunger, they would normally give a man a wide path, now they cared not. They were starving and our presence only came as an unwanted distraction if not a nuisance.

I drew my Walker and said, "Keep them off me Ted while I make for the wagon."

Ted pulled both of his pistols. "What is your plan," he asked.

I answered as I made my way to the wagon. "I saw a chest of drawers in the back of the wagon. We must make certain that they traveled with the girl. If I find her clothes, then we search for her."

Ted pushed out in front of me, pistols at the ready. "I will clear a path for you."

As we moved closer, the coyotes took notice of us and quickly viewed us as a threat to their meal. Two of them, teeth bared, came at Ted. He fired, one shot from his right, one from his left as both animals yipped then fell dead. The others backed off as we neared but still the way to the wagon was blocked. Ted fired again.

The path cleared, Ted yelled over his shoulder to me, "Git you ass up there Wyatt, I have them here."

I ran forward and jumped into the wagon. Pushing aside various household items, a chair, which I tossed out of the wagon, I made my way to the front and found the chest of drawers I had seen earlier.

It was nothing fancy; nothing that would have been handed down through generations. It was simple, usable, well-made, and sturdy. It had five drawers of decent size to hold one's clothes with brass knobs at either end on the front. I yanked open the top drawer and began tossing out articles of clothing.

It was all men's clothing. A couple of shirts, pants, an extra set of undergarments, and a sleep shirt. I emptied the drawer as two more shots rang out. I had been so engrossed in my task that I had forgotten about our animal adversaries circling the wagon.

Ted moved passed me in search of more targets. He said, “Do not mean to rush you Wyatt but these critters are gettin’ a bit angry at us for disrupting their supper.”

I said nothing as I yanked open the second drawer. I grabbed the top article of clothing. It was a simple dress. I unfolded it with shaking hands and held it up. It was for a grown woman, not a child. I tossed it aside and quickly went through the remaining garments. Again, there was nothing that spoke of a small girl.

I slammed the drawer closed as another shot rang out followed by the cry of a dying animal.

I inhaled deeply as I grabbed the two brass knobs of the third drawer and yanked it open. Even in the fading light I took notice of the care that was taken in folding of the items in the drawer. On the left was a white dress shirt, pressed and folded on top of a black suit jacket. Next to it was a bright, colorful dress, again folded with care. On the far-right side there was a pair of men’s dress shoes and a pair of lady's shoes. Their Sunday go to meetin’ clothes. I suddenly felt terribly sad. These clothes were given a special drawer, folded with love and the expectation of attending yet another Sunday service.

Two more shots. Ted yelled, “Find anything Wyatt?”

I came back to the present, shook my head and said, “Not yet.”

I slowly closed the third drawer and pulled open the fourth. My heart sank as I looked down at the neatly folded dresses of a little girl.

One more shot. “Do not mean to sound the alarm Wyatt,” Ted began as he sent off a another shot, “but I am running short of bullets my friend.”

Without a word I pulled my Walker and jumped off the wagon. Immediately, a miserable looking coyote, ribs protruding from his sides came at me. I raised the Colt and fired. The bullet struck him on the side and rolled him over multiple times, settling in a cloud of dust.

Ted joined me. “What did you find?”

We began stepping away from the wagon, remaining diligent as we prepared to fight our way out of the area.

I said, “They had a little girl with them.” I looked around then asked, “Where did we find the little boy?”

Ted pointed with one of his pistols. “Over there. What do you figure?”

Keeping my pistol out in front of me, I began to walk over to the spot where we found the youngster. “It is just a guess on my part but maybe his big sister was leading the boy to safety when Rawlings killed him.”

“Makes sense to me,” Ted said as he faced the angry coyotes coming up behind us.

We came to the spot where the boy had fallen, and I searched the ground for something that could tell me a story. Footprints, scraps of clothing, anything that could set us off in the right direction to find the girl.

As I was searching the ground around my feet I asked, “How many shots do you have left?”

Ted had one pistol holstered while he held up the other. He smiled and said, “One shot.”

I handed him my Walker and said, “I have four.”

Ted accepted the pistol and hefted it in his free hand. “Lord but this thing is heavy.”

I looked down and noticed two parallel marks on the ground and knelt beside them as I saw the story unfold before me. The lines in the dirt were drag marks next to a set of footprints, larger than the boy's feet but still those of a child. I followed the tracks back towards the wagon. There it was. Two sets of prints, side by side. I saw in my mind what happened.

They were running to safety. Somewhere, anywhere but here. They just saw their parents gunned down. The sister was leading her younger brother away from the man with the gun. They were holding hands. Fear gripped them both as they ran off into the wilderness together. Then, the boy was shot, he fell, the sister kept running, probably not yet knowing her sibling had been shot. She must have dragged the boy along before she realized what had happened.

I followed the tracks back to where we found the boy. Her prints, toes turned back to the fallen child had circled the prone figure. She must have dragged him a bit more, pleading, crying out for him to get up, only to understand that the badman had killed him too.

She ran.

The tracks kept going away from the wagon as I followed them, bent over as I traveled with her away from the badman, away from the danger.

Ted fired off a shot, holstered his piece and said over his shoulder, “Down to your four shots, I hope you picked up a trail.”

I kept walking bent over, traveling with the girl farther out into the wilderness; she was alone, frightened and unsure of what to do she kept running. I was with her now as I quickened my pace and followed the small footprints in the dirt, Ted watching my back.

Another shot as Ted fell another wild animal.

Shortly after the last shot, Ted announced, "I think we are safe for the time being. Their attention is back to the dead horses."

I stopped, stood erect and said, "Stay put Ted. I have something."

Ted nodded and kept a sharp eye out for any animal that favored us over the dead horse flesh as I made my way slowly ahead of him.

Here the story changed. Where a little girl was running away from danger, danger came for her. Horse tracks came in from the right of the girl's footprints. The animal was shod which could mean it was the father's horse now in the possession of Rawlings. He rode up on the little girl; the tracks told me that. He circled her, like a cowhand might corner a steer or horse.

I walked a bit further and picked up the animal tracks heading west, but no footprints were to be found, so I returned to the meeting spot of the little girl and the horse.

I searched the ground and found what I thought was a piece of garment under some brush. When I reached under the scrub, I pulled out a doll. It was a rag doll.

I held it up to Ted. "The son of a bitch took the girl."

Ted stepped forward, handed the Walker back to me, and took the doll from my hand. He turned it over in his hands, examining it closely. Sadness passed over his face as I looked at him. Did it bring back memories of his lost child, or was it sadness for the stolen girl, taken by a murderous villain?

He said nothing as he handed the rag doll back to me.

I said, "Reckon we should mount up and track him down."

Ted said through clench teeth, "I am gonna load all twelve chambers of my pistols. I aim to fill that evil bastard full of lead!"

I looked out in the direction the Major went. "He lit off directly west. Gonna be hard tracking him at night if he ain't goin' to Fort McKavett."

Ted began to walk back towards our horses. "I do not care where he is going. We have got to get that little girl."

Chapter Forty-Two

It was dark when we came upon our mounts yet quickly set about saddling them to return to the trail. Once that task was completed, both Ted and myself reloaded our pistols, checked our rifles, passed a canteen between us, and watered the horses. One final check and we were ready to continue our pursuit.

I mounted up, settled into the saddle and said, "We pick up his trail and follow it best we can during the night. He might be headed elsewheres trying to steer clear of folks for a time."

Ted asked, "You think he might not be going to McKavett?"

I said, "He may try and meet up with his brother. What his intentions are with the girl is beyond my thinking."

Ted settled into his saddle. "Matters not, he and his brother are dead men."

Without another word, we returned to the spot where we found his trail. With the aid of the moon lighting the area, we were fortunate to follow his tracks, but at a slow and frustrating pace, often causing us to lean out of the saddle, or to dismount to ensure we were still on the right track.

Hunger, thirst and weariness began to take hold of us as we pressed on through the night, adjusting our course to follow the tracks

Ted said, "We are heading more to the west than northwest."

"Reckon, he and his brother have a special place set up to meet. Away from folks," I said.

Ted's sadness had passed, as did his anger as we both began to settle in for what could be a long ride, a long pursuit or a frustrating end. Often times we, as professional soldiers, force our emotions away from the present to concentrate on the job at hand. Emotions could cloud one's judgment to act on the task required, thus bringing about failure.

We wanted the man dead, that was certain, all emotions aside, we wanted to do it, and a part of us did not want to be cheated out of sending the man to hell. We were not killers, those that took pleasure in taking a life; we were not such men. We felt that Rawlings, and the misery he caused, gave us the right to be the ones who would end his reign of terror.

Being one raised in a Christian background, well versed in the Bible and its teachings, I often questioned my feelings as well as my actions in the past and those yet acted upon. Was I to be judged and held responsible for my actions? Was my desire to kill an evil man just as bad as the man I so wished dead? Did the fact that I took no pleasure in taking a life exempt me from judgement?

I could go round and around, argue both the pros and cons of such matters. And, I have done so over the past few years, yet I continue in my duties and struggle with my conscience on occasion.

Ted interrupted my reflective mood and asked, "Wyatt. Do you ever think of the moral conflict of what we do?"

I pulled up and stared at my riding mate. Could this man read my very thoughts?

Ted pulled up and turned around in his saddle. "What is it, Wyatt?"

I smiled and thought to myself that no, he could not read my thoughts. We were two like-minded men that pondered the same moral dilemmas since we were called upon to make such choices.

I said, "I was just thinking the same my friend. Are we wrong in wanting to put a stop to this evil man with such eagerness?" I spurred Caliban forward. "I am sure you have given this some thought."

Ted fell in beside me as we continued. He said, "Not so much as putting a stop to him as taking a certain pleasure in doing it."

I nodded. "Like filling him full of lead?"

Ted laughed then said, "Like filling him full of lead, yes." He paused and became thoughtful for a moment then continued. "I cannot say I have ever taken pleasure in killing a man. No sir, I have not. Truth be told I do not much care for it Wyatt."

I said, "Nor do I. It just seems like it needs to be done and sometimes it just feels wrong."

Ted pursed his lips; his eyes narrowed. "I kinda gave up on thinking about the right and wrong of pullin' the trigger on a man." He sighed, then continued. "I am not a religious man Wyatt, but I was raised in the church, and I do know my Bible," he said as he leaned forward in his saddle and he looked up at the evening sky. "I recall a verse from Proverbs that begins, 'rescue those being led away to death'. Then it goes on to warn of the consequences of doing nothing."

I was beginning to shake off my slight crisis of conscience. Perhaps I just needed reassurances, though I do not know why I was feeling such as I was. Ted's words reminded me of the need for men like us. I was feeling better.

I said, "Evil prevails when good men do nothing."

"Very true Wyatt. Very true indeed." He looked at me. "Having second thoughts of killing Rawlings?"

I shook my head. "I am not. I sometimes grow weary of pullin' my pistol."

Ted nodded. He said, "I do know that feeling. By wars end I thought of throwing my guns down and walking away from it all."

"I did," I said.

Ted again looked at me. "What did you do?"

I shrugged my shoulders and answered. "I left Georgia and came out here and wandered around for a spell. Near a year to be honest. Then I met Robert and we sort of fell into this law business."

Ted began nodding his head. "That would explain the references the Judge made when I first came on this case. He kept saying things like saddle tramps and such when talking about you and Robert. Kinda confused me cause he got angry when he said it."

I laughed at the reference. "Well, we were near that. We just had a means of support to keep us from turning to the wrong side of the law."

Ted asked, "What means did you have?"

I let out a slight laugh and said, "Poker."

Now Ted laughed then said, "Well my friend. When this is over, we will have to see just how good you are."

I looked at Ted. "Bit of a cardsharp, are you?"

"Not so much," he responded. "I just get a feeling when I play. I have done well in a few games."

"I will keep that in mind Ted."

We rode on, slowing our pace to check for sign, making certain we were on Rawlings' trail. He was heading west now, Fort McKavett somewhere to the northwest, out of reach. His plans, unknown to us, did not seem to include a stop at the old fort. We only surmised that he was going to meet his brother, open the safe and split up the loot they had taken over time.

Through all the recent gun battles, fights, tracking, searching, and riding I had forgotten about the reason we had gotten involved in this matter.

The safe, having never laid eyes on the damn thing myself, was no longer a concern. Be that as it may, I would like to see it at least once before all this is over. Maybe, run my hands over it and see for myself that it does exist. Other than that, I no longer cared about the Italian made iron box and the money it contained. Perhaps, if it is large enough, we can bury the Major in it or at least seal his black heart within and destroy the key.

I looked up at the stars wondering for the first time since we departed what time it was. Still evening, early morning, I had no idea, nor did I care to know. Our progress was not measured by the hands of a time piece, nor the position of the sun but by the distance between us and our quarry and our ability to close that distance.

As I dropped my head, I began turning it from side to side working the stiffness out when something on the ground to my right caught my eye. It was just a flash, a momentary sight of an anomaly that seemed out of place. At first my mind did not acknowledge what my eyes had seen and was about to dismiss it when I pulled up and sat my horse for a moment.

Ted pulled up and turned. "What is it," he asked.

I looked over my right shoulder and searched the ground behind me. "I thought I saw something on the ground back there," I said as I dismounted.

I walked back and slowly scanned the area, taking care not to step on whatever it was I saw, or thought I saw.

Ted said, "Let me know if you need help with anything."

I nodded and continued searching the ground, left, then right, forward then left again, stepping slowly as my head remained in motion. Then I saw it.

I moved off to the left and bent down, picking up what caught my eye. It was a bloodied bandage; its white edges stood out against the darkened ground.

I held it up and turned back to Ted. "It is another field dressing."

Ted walked over to me and examined it closely as I turned the large bandage in my hand. He said, "Well, the bastard had not bled out yet which means we still have a chance at killin' him."

Ted looked around and stepped off beyond where I found the bandage. Not but a few feet from me he bent down and retrieved something from the ground. His back to me he held it up.

I asked, "Whatcha got there Ted?"

He turned back to me and said, “It is a canteen.” He shook it and tossed it to me. “Empty.”

I caught it and turned it over in my hands. It was a Bullseye tin canteen covered in a colorful wool of red and green stripes. Its stopper, hanging from a cord, was out and the strap was broken. I up ended it and shook.

“Damn sure is empty,” I said as I tossed it away.

Ted joined me and asked, “How fresh was that blood?”

I looked down at the ground where I had tossed the dressing. Come sunup, the Blowflies were sure to have a feast. I looked up and said, “Fresh enough that we are close for sure and for certain.” I looked down at the bandage. “I am surprised the smell of fresh blood had not attracted coyotes.”

Ted showed concern on his face. “Think he still has the girl?”

I sighed. “Well, I reckon he does. We had not seen anything to tell us different.”

He nodded. “Yea. We best be gettin’ back on the trail.”

We mounted up and continued our pursuit, heading deeper into the Bexar Territory.

Ted asked, “What time you reckon it is?”

“Mornin’ sometime I suppose.”

Ted looked at me, grinned and said, “Forgot to wind your watch I see.”

I said, “As did you.”

“That I did,” he said. “Just did not see the need for it.” He looked back over his shoulder. “Sun should be up in a couple of hours, and we can quicken our pace.”

I said, “We could use a watering hole too.”

“So could Rawlings,” Ted said.

“Then let us not dawdle,” I said as I picked up the pace.

We rode on, confident in our direction, confident that we will soon overtake Rawlings and hopefully save the child he had taken. Once we were sure of her safety, we will deal with the man himself.

The horizon behind us began to brighten as the nighttime sky surrendered to the sunrise and cast an orange yellow shadow over the ground. The terrain was much like it was when the sun retired the previous day; the only exception was the mesquite grew a bit taller and was more in abundance.

To the south, hills could be seen in the distance as I recalled the map we elected not to bring. It mattered not as we were no longer going to a specific place, and I knew our general location. We were in pursuit of a man that had a specific place to journey to. If the map had shown watering holes or locations of small settlements, we would have brought the paper graphic along. But, out here, there were no such settlements. Only desolation.

As we pressed on, I would look down and see the tracks left by the Major's horse. The marks told me that he was also moving at a slow pace as the prints in the dirt were close together. Should I see a change, that being a lengthening of the tracks, then the Major quickened his pace, and we would also pick up the pace.

I felt confident that we would soon come upon our quarry and offered Ted a suggestion.

I said, "What say we walk the horses for a spell before it gets too damn hot."

Ted pulled up and dismounted before he spoke. "I thought you would never suggest it," he said then laughed.

We walked along and passed a canteen between us, taking small sips, water now a concern as we had yet to come upon a watering hole.

I looked out over the country before us and shook my head. "We best find a source of water soon. Not much left."

Ted asked, "This river you spoke of by Fort McKavett. Does it come down this far south?"

I shook my head. "I do not believe it does. The San Saba is north of us and a couple of rivers south of us near the mountains. Couple of days ride in either direction I am afraid."

Ted hung the canteen back on his horse. "Well, hell. We seem to be splittin' it right down the center."

"Not us, my friend," I said. "That good for nuthin' degenerate we are chasing picked our route of march."

Ted took his bowler off and wiped his forehead with the back of his arm. "Then there is another reason for me to hate the man."

As he was putting his hat back on his head, he stopped and looked to his left. Then, without a word, he handed me the reins to his Appaloosa and stepped off.

I watched him closely as he stopped a few feet away and began looking at the ground. He looked left, right, turned in a tight circle, stepped off then knelt, examining the ground.

Suddenly he stood, looked off to the west and said, "Horses. Near as I can figure about eight of them. All unshod."

I looked west and uttered, "Comanche."

Ted bent over and picked up a broken prickly pear cactus and looked it over. He said, "Fresh. It has not dried out yet." He tossed it aside. "They are just ahead of us, Wyatt."

I pulled my Walker from the holster, halfcocked it and rotated the cylinder, checking the action. Putting it back in the holster, I went to my saddle and pulled the Howdah Pistol, broke it open, and checked the shells. Satisfied, I pulled my Colt rifle free of the scabbard and repeated the check of the gun.

I looked over as Ted had just completed his checks. He looked back at me, nodded, and mounted up.

I mounted up and said, "We pick up the pace and be ready for anything. I believe they may be tracking Rawlings. I think we should keep our distance for now, sneak in behind them and see what transpires."

Ted settled himself in his saddle. "As long as they do not hurt the little girl."

"That goes without sayin'," I said.

Then Ted pointed to himself with his finger and added sternly, "And I get to kill Rawlings."

"You can kill him," I reassured him. "Now, c'mon."

Since the two sets of tracks, Rawlings on the right and the Comanches on the left, were so close we split the middle and kicked our mounts into a trot keeping a close eye both in front of us and to the flanks.

I would say our pace was moderate and not too taxing on our animals for the moment. Our hope was such that the Comanche would meet up with Rawlings in short order, and we would not wear our animals down until that time. We still had to consider our return trip.

An hour or so into our pursuit the tracks joined as it would seem the Comanche fell in directly behind Rawlings and us behind the Comanche. Still, we had seen nothing of either party.

I was beginning to question our decision to pursue when I spied in the distance a small cloud of dust rising into the air. I pointed this out to Ted as we both fought the urge to quicken our pace. Experience dictated that we err on the side of caution in our approach. We did not want to join the fray without a knowledge of the belligerents or a lay of the land.

Ted said, "May I suggest that we seek cover and approach on foot. We have no idea what is ahead of us."

I pointed and said, “To the left in those mesquites. There is enough for us to make our approach safely as it runs right up to the dust cloud.”

We found ourselves in among the mesquites and dismounted, tied our horses off, grabbed up our extra weapons and stepped out of the brush. We looked over the area with a practiced eye, satisfied that our horses were well hidden; we struck out to scout ahead.

CHAPTER FORTY-THREE

Keeping low, I moved forward, sliding in and out of the high growing mesquite. Its unique growth, some tall and straight while others low to the ground grew out instead of up and provided plenty of cover as we made our way closer.

As we moved in and out of the trees, I took notice of its green foliage. Looking more like a vine than a broad leaf, it produced a long thin seedpod that hung down and brushed against my face, often knocking my hat off, as I moved in and out and around the many low hanging branches.

The closer we got to the rising dust the sounds of its cause became apparent. We still could not see as the mesquite blocked our view but from what we heard, we could surmise what was going on by the sounds of horse hooves striking the hard ground.

We then heard the Indians yelling, whooping and the occasional voice yelling in English. We were not close enough yet to distinguish any one voice, let alone what was being said, so we moved closer.

Ted moved up next to me as we came to a spot that provided concealment yet allowed us to observe what was happening. On the other side of the mesquite we were crouched behind, we saw a clearing. Our view was such that we saw everything within the area. The Comanche, all on well cared for strong ponies, were moving in tight circles in the clearing, each armed with a long war lance, bow over their shoulders and arrow quivers across their backs.

The war party commanded our attention as we assessed their strength and intentions. Then we focused on the recipients of their scorn.

At the edge of the clearing was the large church wagon I had seen back in Fredericksburg. The two horses, agitated at the aggressive Indians, danced in their harnesses and pulled against their restraints while a single mount, saddled and tied off on the side of the wagon was pulling against his reins, frightened and worn out from a long ride.

The dust momentarily cleared enough for us to see what the Comanches were yelling at.

In the center was a makeshift fire pit of rock formed in a circle. Kneeling with arms raised were Rawlings and his preacher brother, Adrian Tremellius. Scared, heads lowered, arms waving back and forth held high; they were pleading for their lives.

I leaned closer to Ted and said softly, "Do you see the girl?"

He shook his head.

I looked around the campsite, praying for the dust to clear and show me the child.

Just then Ted grabbed my arm with such force I near cried out. He pointed at the back of the church wagon.

The dust had parted revealing the open door to the church. On the bottom side of the threshold was a small white face with unruly brown hair falling over her eyes. She was peeking out watching the dramatic show of force take place. The fear clearly on her face. I became excited and wanted to yell for her to run. To run to us and safety. But she retreated inside and the door closed.

I turned to Ted. "Do we take out the Indians and grab the girl?"

Ted held up his hand then pointed into the camp. I turned and looked. The Comanches had settled down and formed a circle around the two men, their war lances pointed at the cowering figures in the dirt. One of the Indians began yelling in Comanche and gesturing with his war lance at the Major.

Ted leaned closer and said quietly, "He says he is taking the horses. Should they try and stop them they will die a terrible death and be left for the animals of the desert to feast on their innards and drag away their bones."

There was more yelling from the squad of warriors. The leader continued addressing the Major while Ted translated for my benefit.

Ted said, "He says his name is War Hawk and he will kill the white man if he keeps invading his land." Ted paused as he listened. "He just told his warriors to take the horses, they are leaving."

I breathed a sigh of relief. We were not going to engage the Comanche warriors after all. Taking on the Major and his preacher brother, thus saving the girl was enough for the two of us to handle. But, taking on eight Comanche warriors on horseback was foolish, if not downright dumb.

The Indians gathered up their prizes, raised a bit of Cane and made a quick exit from the area leaving Rawlings and his brother still kneeling on the ground, but alive.

I said, “We go back and get our mounts then return and finish this.” I gestured to the camp with my hand. “They ain’t goin’ anywhere. I say we ride in nice and slow from this side using the church wagon as cover. We come in, guns out and ready. What say you, Ted?”

Ted smiled and replied, “What the hell are we doing here gabbing about it? C’mon.”

We quickly, yet quietly departed the area using the same path we came in. On our return walk we both fought the urge to run back to the horses, excited at the prospect of saving the girl and sending Rawlings on his way to hell. The Comanche were still in the area, and we did not wish to fall victim to an already angry group of warriors.

We got back to our horses and, without a word, mounted up. I made a show of checking my equipment as I settled in the saddle. My purpose was simple yet intentional. Prior to battle I would force myself to take a moment with something mundane, useless even, just to provide a distraction and steady my nerves, slow my heart, and clear my head.

I looked at Ted and saw he too was checking over his equipment. I smiled.

I said, “Reckon this is it my friend.”

He nodded. “It is. Time to finish this.”

“Fall in behind me and I will bring us to the blind side of the church. Then you go right and I go left, and we meet at the fire pit,” I said.

He smiled and said, “Tis a fine plan, Wyatt.” He motioned with his hand and a slight bow of the head. “After you sir.”

I tipped my hat and turned Caliban back in the direction of the clearing.

If it was not for the task at hand, it would feel like a leisurely ride on horseback among the mesquite on a summer day. The pace was slow, even and unhurried. Turning left then right, moving through the shade while a slight breeze kicked up seemed pleasant and relaxing. It was nothing of the sort.

My heart was racing. I thought it was going to come out of my chest as I struggled to keep from kicking Caliban into a gallop and storm the camp, guns blazing away without word nor pronouncement of our intentions. Just ride in, kill them both, grab the girl and return home.

We were not going to do that. If I was leading a patrol on a sneak attack against an enemy's position, that would be expected. Soldiers fought in such an aggressive manner. Soldiers defended and prepared for such attacks.

Ours was a different kind of assault. We were lawmen sworn to uphold the law and protect those that could not protect themselves. We would ride into their camp, slowly and deliberately, and do our jobs.

I pulled up and sat my horse as Ted moved in beside me. We were on the edge of the brush, still concealed, looking into the camp. Both men were at the fire pit. The Major was seated on a wooden chair, no doubt taken from the church, while his brother tended to his wounded arm, a small table next to him with bloodied bandages and his over-sized Bible. They were speaking to each other.

I motioned to Ted that we would move left and come out of the brush next to the church wagon. This way neither of the two men will observe us as we came into the clearing.

Once in position I looked at Ted, smiled and nodded my head as he pulled one of his nickel-plated revolvers and I the Howdah Pistol.

I turned Caliban slightly to the left, and I moved around the front of the wagon. One quick glance over my shoulder, and I watched as Ted went off to the right, behind the wagon.

Slowly I came out into the open, around the now empty harnesses, and behind the preacher man. He was bent forward as he worked on his brother's wounded arm, blocking his view as I neared. I looked over and saw Ted, his pistol pointed at the two, move closer to the fire pit.

I pulled up, held the large pistol up, and cocked both hammers back with an audible click.

Brother Adrian stopped his work and stood straight only casting a glance over his left shoulder when Ted cocked the hammer back on his pistol.

I said, "Howdy boys. Having a bit of trouble?"

The preacher spun around as the Major jumped out of his chair. They both froze as I leveled the massive double barrel pistol at them.

Ted said, "I would not try anything boys. We will surely kill you where you stand."

Rawlings, the rage on his face was plain as day as his eyes grew wide, and he turned a bright red. He began to shake as his hands closed into tight fists. Through clenched teeth in a voice that was more animal than man he said, "Chambers!"

My voice was surprisingly calm as I said, "That is correct you son of a bitch. Now you and your brother will answer for your misdeeds and evil ways."

Ted said, "We aim to kill you both, so make your peace now."

Brother Adrian, still decked out in his black cossack, dirty and disheveled, looked at me with eyes equally black and soul-less as he became visibly agitated and frightened. He held up both hands, palms out as if pleading with us would make amends.

His voice cracked as he spoke. "Now surely gentlemen you cannot hold me accountable for any misdeeds or the evilness that so accompanies it? I am a man of God, Brothers."

I said, "Shut you damn mouth boy! We came to save the girl!"

He dropped his arms to his side and cocked his head. He said, "We know of no girl Marshal." He stepped closer to me. "What girl do you speak of?"

Ted dismounted and stepped closer to the two men and pulled his second pistol. "Do not try to lie you bastard." He addressed me while keeping his attention on the two men. "Go and get her Wyatt. I got these two covered."

I said, "First I am gonna check them for weapons. Keep your pistols on them Ted."

I slid the Howdah Pistol in my gun belt, dismounted and stepped over to the preacher man. With my left hand I grabbed him by the back of the neck, held him tight while I patted him around the chest, under the arms and around the waist. I made sure I was rough and hard in my search. As my hand made its way around his body, each pat; each slap was more like a punch as the sound of the impact resonated loudly, like a deep echo in his chest.

The only item that came out of the search was a small leather pouch tied around his neck, which I removed.

Ted asked, "Whatcha got there Wyatt?"

I stepped back and opened the sack and looked inside. I said, "Gold coin." I reached in and withdrew a five dollar gold piece, the one I had stupidly given over as a donation and held it up between two of my fingers so that the preacher man could see.

I looked at the man's dark eyes, pale face and said, "I will be takin' this back."

He said defiantly, "As you wish Marshal."

I tossed the leather sack on the small field table where it landed on the large leather-bound Bible. I stared at it for a moment as the hypocrisy of the preacher and his church struck me. I closed my left hand into a tight fist and back handed him across the jaw, sending him to the ground.

Rawlings made a move towards his brother, and Ted stepped closer, extending his pistol laden hands forward.

He said, "Stand fast you son of a bitch!"

I looked on and saw fear come over the Major's face. He knew, as did I, that Ted meant business.

I stepped around the fire pit to Rawlings and said, "Raise your hands."

He replied, "I am wounded. I can only raise the one."

I took in his appearance and recalled our first meeting at the jail. He was a strong arrogant man with all the answers, confident in his plans and in charge of his destiny. His hair and mustache well groomed. Now I looked upon a broken, disheveled man, filthy and bleeding through the bandages on his right arm and shoulder. His future now in our hands.

I grabbed him in the same manner I had grabbed his brother and forcibly patted him down while fighting the urge to strangle the life out of him. When I was done, I shoved him away.

Turning to Ted I said, "I will go and get the little girl."

"I got you covered pard," he said as he circled around the fire pit, one pistol pointed at the Major and the other at the unconscious form of his brother on the ground.

I turned my back on them and walked to the rear of the church wagon. My heart began to race as I neared the three steps that led inside. Questions flooded my mind with each step. Was the girl still alive since we last saw her? What misdeeds have been put upon the child? What has this traumatic event done to her?

I shook my head and cleared my mind as I lifted my leg to the first step, the second step, then, with a shaking hand I reached for the door handle. I paused.

"Ah hell," I uttered as I forced my hand to open the door.

The inside was dark, musty, and uncomfortably hot. Blankets had been hung over the stain glass windows to block out the sun, though some of the sun's rays had sneaked through sending beams of light throughout the interior of the small chapel.

Here and there the rays of light, thin and narrow lit small areas of the interior. I looked around the small enclosure. The chairs, once in neat orderly rows, were cast about. Some still standing, others laying on their sides or piled in a disorderly manner. At the front was the lectern. A single beam of light shone on the gold cross stitched into the dark velvet.

I stood at the open door and called out. "Hello. Elizabeth, are you in here?"

Silence.

I stepped deeper inside and said, "Elizabeth Harrison. I am Deputy Marshal Wyatt Chambers. I have come to take you away from here darlin'."

Still, nothing.

I took another step. "Elizabeth honey. You need not be afraid. I am here to help you."

It was then that I heard a muffled moan. So slight, so quiet that I turned my head, closed my eyes, willing the sound to repeat itself.

I heard it again, turned my head and looked at the lectern. I said, "Darlin', I am going to come in. Can you show me where you are hiding? I promise, I will not let anything more happen to you."

I saw movement in front of me. A small foot in a tattered shoe, then a thin leg followed by a hand at the top of the box. Little by little, a small girl appeared before me. Her face, caked with dirt, showed frightened eyes.

I smiled and took off my hat. "Hey there, darlin'. My name is Wyatt. Are you Elizabeth?"

She gripped the top of the lectern with both hands, her head looking over the top as she kept the box between us. She nodded her head.

I took a step closer and said, "I have come to take you to safety sweetheart. You need not be afraid." I held out my hand. "Do you want to come with me?"

Again, she nodded.

I took two more steps, my hand, palm up extended out in front of me. "Take my hand little darlin' and we will get out of here."

She slowly came out from behind the lectern. Her dress, dirty and torn, hung loosely over her small frame. Her hair was equally dirty; unkept fell to her shoulders and across her face. She paused and looked around, her eyes seeking out hidden dangers in the shadows.

I encouraged the child forward with a wave of my hand.

Her steps, cautious and unsure, moved her closer to me as she extended her hand, reaching out to mine. Her fingers inches from mine were shaking.

I leaned forward as our fingertips touched. My rough, calloused hand touching the softness of the child's hand, I grasped hers in mine and gave it a reassuring squeeze.

Chapter Forty-Four

I held the small hand in mine as I knelt in front of her. Slowly I reached up to her face and brushed the hair away. Her brown eyes wide, fearful as she looked at me.

I gave her a reassuring smile. "What say we get out of here and take you someplace safe."

Her lips moved as a sound came out.

I put my ear closer to the small mouth and asked softly, "Did you say something honey?"

She nodded her head and said softly, "But the Indians are out there."

I grinned and tried to make light of her concerns. "No worries, darlin'. Me and my friend chased them off. They were plenty scared when we rode up."

She looked down at her feet and whispered, "What about the bad men?"

Again, I attempted to put her fears to rest. I said, "My friend has them taken care of. They ain't gonna hurt you none sweetheart. I promise."

She looked at me. "You promise?"

I stood, keeping a firm grasp on her tiny hand. "I promise darlin'." I looked over my shoulder then said, "When you are ready, we can go."

She nodded her head, and I led her to the door.

I leaned out and said, "We are comin' out, Ted. I have Elizabeth."

Ted replied, "Thank God! Come ahead pard."

There was a tug at my hand, and I looked down at the child and asked, "You ready Elizabeth?"

She looked up at me and said, "Lizzie. Only grandma calls me Elizabeth."

I could not help but smile. "Okay, Lizzie. What say we go outside so I can introduce you proper to my friend."

"Okay, Wyatt," she said as she made for the door.

I went out first and stepped down, turned around and reached for Lizzie as she held her arms out to me. As I lifted her, she fell into my arms and wrapped herself tightly around me and squeezed. I put my arms around her and gave her a reassuring hug.

I whispered, "It will be fine now, child. I will protect you."

I carried her around the side of the wagon. Ted was standing near the Major and his preacher brother, who had recovered his senses.

I said, "Ted. This here is Elizabeth, but she goes by Lizzie."

Ted turned, keeping his pistols trained on the two men, and nodded his head in a gentlemanly fashion. He said, "It is a pleasure to meet you young lady."

Lizzie looked over at Ted, then back to me as if I needed to confirm what Ted had just said.

"That big fella with the shiny pistols is my friend Ted," I told her.

She looked back at him a gave him a slight wave of her hand.

I walked over to the front of the wagon, leaned down and planted Lizzie on her feet, then knelt before her. I said, "No we have some business to tend to with these bad fellas, so you just stay here. Once we finish, we will head for Fredericksburg."

Lizzie grabbed hold of me and said, "Please stay with me Wyatt. I am scared."

I held her arms and leaned a bit closer. "I promised to protect you darlin', and I aim to do just that. But I have some things to take care of first."

She inhaled, nodded her head and said, "Okay Wyatt. Please be quick."

I found another chair and set it up for her. "I will be back directly."

As I turned to face our two prisoners, I saw that the preacher had retrieved his Bible from the table and was clutching it to his breast. Suddenly a deep penetrating cold came over me as I felt something was amiss. I turned and looked at Ted.

Standing next to his Appaloosa, guns pointed at Rawlings and the preacher, Ted returned my look and smiled. As he turned back everything seemed to slow down. It was then that it all went to hell.

Suddenly, Ted yelled out, "Gun!"

I instinctively reached for my Walker as I backed up to Lizzie to shield her, not knowing where the threat was. Shots rang out as I pulled my pistol. Ted fired off a round as two more shots sounded, then a third. I turned with my pistol and saw the preacher man had produced a handgun and got off three shots at Ted and turned to me.

I reached behind me and pushed the child off the chair while bringing my revolver up. I fired off one round at Brother Adrian, the bullet striking him in the gut, sending him to the ground. He tried to raise his pistol to get off another shot when I sent the second ball into his head.

The Major tried to reach for his brother's pistol. I fired again, hitting him in the leg, sending him down on one knee. I cocked the Colt and drew a bead on the man's head when he looked up at me with eyes filled with hatred and rage.

Through gritted teeth of pain and anger, he said, "Do it. Kill me."

My finger started to pull on the trigger. Just the slightest bit of pressure would end this all right here, right now. Just a slight jerk of my index finger and Major Rawlings would be no more.

I lowered my revolver. "No," I said, "not yet."

I holstered the Walker Colt and looked over at Ted. His back was to me as he was standing over his horse, looking down at the dead animal. A victim of an errant shot from the now dead preacher man. Ted slowly turned back to me.

My blood froze as I gazed upon my friend. The front of his shirt was a deep crimson, growing larger, soaking the green fabric. As the blood flowed over his shirt, the color left his face, and his strength failed him as he tried to walk toward me. His last act was to holster his pistols, then he fell to the ground.

I rushed over to him, rolled him over ever so carefully and pulled him close to me. His mouth moved as he tried to speak. He coughed once, turned his head and died.

I looked into the face of my friend, reached up with a shaking hand and closed his eyelids over what once were eyes that reflected a colorful soul. As I pulled my hand away, I lowered my head and closed my eyes tightly as the tears threatened to escape, to betray me once again. I gritted my teeth and fought against the emotions that begged to escape, pleaded for release.

I gave in, raised my head up and screamed, "No...no...Nooo!"

I do not know how long I knelt there holding my friend in my arms. Hours, minutes, I do not know. I only know that I found Lizzie kneeling next to me, her little arms wrapped around mine while she leaned her head against my chest, squeezing with all her might.

I looked over the fire pit and saw the body of the preacher. Off to the right, where he fell, was Rawlings. He was trying to tie a bandage around his wounded leg. He looked up at me, fearful, sharp quick motions of his head as he looked around for a safe haven. A place to hide knowing that he was going to incur my wrath.

I released the hold on my friend and lowered him to the ground. Taking Lizzie in my arms, I stood and walked back to the chair and set her down.

I asked, "Are you okay sweetheart?"

She nodded her head.

I said, "You sit tight here, Lizzie. I have matters to tend to before we can leave." I walked over to Caliban, unhurt, and brought him back to Lizzie. "Will you watch over my horse while I get things ready?"

She stood and extended her hand to Caliban. He lowered his head as he stepped into it. She lovingly rubbed him and asked, "What is his name?"

"Caliban."

She stepped closer to him as he accepted her affections. "Funny name."

I smiled. "Yes, I reckon it is."

Then Lizzie looked at me and said softly, "I am sorry about Ted." She then looked past me at the sitting form of the Major. "Are you gonna make him pay Wyatt? For what he done to your friend and my ma and pa and little brother?"

I followed her gaze and thought to myself. It was a shame that a little girl had been forced into a world such as this and now held feelings of retribution.

I sighed. "He will pay darlin'. Know that I will make him pay." I turned back to her. "Now, you mind Caliban while I make things ready for us to leave this place."

She seemed content with the job I had given her as I walked around the camp looking at what was left. I began to plan our exit, examine what I had available to make it so. I made mental notes of what needed to be done. Water, food, build a travois, care for Ted and lastly, take care of the Major.

I found some rope and cut a three-foot length and walked over to the Major. I rolled him over and tied his arms behind his back at the elbows. Though he cried out in pain, I ignored his pleas for mercy as I did for his requests for water. As I walked away, I picked up the preacher's pistol and Bible. When I opened the cover of the book, I saw it had been hollowed out to secret the pistol I held in my other hand. I threw them both away.

Then I set about building the travois. Remembering my promise to Ted, I had no intention of leaving him out here in this inhospitable land.

Using wood I pulled off the church wagon, and rope that I had cut, in a short time I had fashioned a suitable yet sturdy device to carry my friend home.

Keeping one eye on the Major, I went through the church wagon and the camp gathering up any food and water I could find, extra saddle bags and rope. Once I collected all the canteens and bota bags I came across, I consolidated them into one canteen and two bota bags. Looking at the collection, it did not take me but a moment to realize we did not have enough water for the return journey.

I paused and looked out over the wilderness that surrounded us. We could travel north and try and find Fort McKavett or go south to the mountains in search of water. Either way presented its own problems. I had no idea exactly where McKavett was located, and we could easily miss it in our travels and wander further out into the frontier. Going south in search of water was just as risky as I had no knowledge of the territory and again, we would wander through the mountains only to die of thirst.

Then there was also the Comanche that roamed the area to the south. The prospect of being cornered or captured by a hostile band of Indians was more fearful to me than dying lost in the wilderness. They would surely make our last moments on earth miserable.

I decided we would take our chances and head straight back to Fredericksburg. We would have to ration our water and do most of our traveling at night. I felt that of the three choices, Fredericksburg was the most sound.

I then turned my attention to Ted. I had grabbed the blankets from inside the wagon with the intent of wrapping my friend in them while he rested on the travois. While I was tending to this matter, Rawlings began his pleadings for mercy.

He said in a gravelly voice that spoke of thirst, "I sure could use some water, Wyatt. You cannot let me die of thirst. I also need a doctor." He looked around. "You could lay me out on the travois, and we should be able to make it to town. I will go peaceable Wyatt, I will."

I laid out four lines of rope then laid one of the blankets on top next to Ted's body. Then, I rolled him over, face down, onto the blanket and laid his arms out to his sides, removing his pistol belt.

Rawlings said, "You could take me back to town and get me fixed up proper Wyatt. If you do that, I will give you half the money I got." He paused. "How'd that be? We could split the money. I will take my share and disappear Wyatt. You will never see me again. I swear it."

Then I folded the blanket over both sides' lengthwise, then over his head and feet. Taking a second blanket, I folded it in half down the length and laid this over his back, head to toe.

The Major was becoming agitated. He said angrily, “Come now Wyatt! This was not personal. This is war! We could have won if Lee had not quit the field when he did. You know that.” He pulled against his restraints, crying out in pain. “This is inhumane treatment.”

Starting at the shoulders, I tied off each section of rope finishing at the feet. Once complete, I gently rolled Ted over on his back and looked at the covered body that was once my friend. I laid a hand on his head as I thought of the short time we had known each other yet had become close friends.

“Now listen Wyatt,” the Major continued. “You cannot treat me in this manner. I am a superior officer Captain Chambers.” He struggled against his restraints. “And as such I order you to release me this minute.”

I picked up Ted’s bowler, stood and walked past the Major to Lizzie as she tended Caliban. I handed her the hat and smiled when she put it on her head against the sun.

Rawlings looked over, evil in his eyes. “You cannot ignore me Chambers. You are a lawman of the courts, and you must take me in.” He looked at me. “Damnation, do you hear me man!”

I returned his stare then shifted my gaze to the perimeter of the camp. I looked from tree to tree, cactus to shrub as an idea formed in my mind. It came together and the proper place was selected.

I grabbed an empty saddle bag and walked over to the fire pit, stepping over the body of the dead preacher man and stood before Rawlings. I bent over and ripped open his filthy jacket and shirt, exposing his chest. It was just as I suspected.

He said in a quivering voice, “Wha...what is it you want Wyatt?”

I saw the leather cord around his neck and pulled hard in the hopes that I would be inflicting more pain as I took two brass keys from under his shirt.

Rawlings yelled out as the leather cord broke. He said, “Yes Wyatt. The keys to the safe. All the money is in there. We can split it, Wyatt.”

I held the two oddly shaped keys in my hand and studied them.

The Major said, “I know how the safe opens Wyatt. There is a trick in doing it. Help me up and I will open it for you.”

I turned away and walked to the wagon and up the stairs.

Inside the sun illuminated the interior as I had taken the blankets down during my preparations. While doing so I intentionally ignored the lectern and what I knew was beneath the cloth covering.

My original plans were to leave it and set the wagon on fire when we departed. After some thought I realized, though satisfying as it would be, there are folks back home that were hoping to see the money again. I stood there and looked at it with only mild curiosity.

I reached over and pulled the covering away, casting it aside.

Perhaps I was expecting something a bit more ostentatious instead of what I saw. With all the talk, with the admiration of its previous owner I would have thought it was something more than a simple black box with huge rivets, like knobs all over the front and sides. The only item that stood out on the box was two oddly shaped holes surrounded by a brass face. I assumed these were keyholes.

Remembering the instructions from the bank manager, I looked at each of the two keys and matched them up to the appropriate hole. Then I closed my eyes as I recalled the demonstration the manager had given us on opening the iron box.

I reached out and began the sequence by turning the top key to the left until it met resistance. Then I turned the bottom key to the right until there was an audible click as one of the locks was released. Returning to the top key, I continued to turn it to the left until it gave off a loud click. That being the second lock, bringing me back to the bottom key and the final locking mechanism.

Turning it again to the right there was slight resistance then a loud metal click as the dead bolts were thrown free of the door. I pulled it open.

There it was. All the money we had been seeking. Leather bags of gold from the bank and folding money from the federal payroll. But as I looked, I found more money than we had originally sought. For us, the money from the bank in Castroville and the Federal payroll was all we knew of. The safe was filled with money and sacks of gold coins.

I shrugged and began to fill the saddle bags. In short order, the bags were filled to the point of bursting the seams of the fine tooled leather. I could not close them as both coin and paper money spilled out. I would need another set of saddle bags.

I carried the stolen loot outside, happy to be out of the confines of the wagon. I walked around to the front making certain that Rawlings saw what it was I was carrying.

Shock was clearly heard in his voice as he yelled, "How did you do that? How did you get into the safe?" He tried to stand, only to fall over to his side. "You cannot take that Wyatt! That is my money, you cannot have it!"

I set the heavy bags down and began spreading the load between two sets of saddlebags. As I was doing so, another concern presented itself with the weight of the money and coin.

Rawlings began his pleadings once more. "You must not leave me with no money Wyatt. That is my money!"

I began figuring the weight that Caliban will carry. With the added saddlebags, Lizzie and the travois through the wilderness on rationed water, my weight would be too much of a burden on my mount. I will have to walk us out of the frontier.

I led Caliban over to Ted's body and began attaching the travois, all the while Rawlings' ravings became more enraged.

"You no good son of a bitch, Chambers," he yelled. "I hope you rot in hell! You and that girl! I hope you die in the wilderness! I hope the Indians take your stinking scalp you bastard!"

I rolled Ted over onto the travois, secured the saddlebags of money behind the saddle and took one last look around.

Lizzie came up to me and grabbed my hand. She asked, "What about him?"

I picked her up and put her in the saddle. "Reckon I will take care of that right now."

CHAPTER FORTY-FIVE

I rested my hand on her leg as I looked back at the camp. I had already picked out the spot, gathered what I would require to carrying out this much needed task so now it was a matter of finishing it.

I patted Lizzie's leg and said, "Stay put darlin'. I will be back directly."

I walked back into the camp, past the Major and picked up the chair that had fallen over when the ruckus began. The Major, sitting in an awkward position on the ground next to his dead brother, arms still bound tightly, watched me intently as I walked past him to the opposite side of the camp, stopping under a high-growing tree.

He said, "What are you going to do Wyatt?"

I turned back and walked up behind Rawlings who was trying, unsuccessfully to turn around and face me. I reached down and grabbed him by the back of the jacket collar and dragged him towards the chair. Try as he might with his thrashing about; he was no match for my strength born of vengeance.

He yelled, "What the hell are you doing? You cannot do this to me! I refuse to be treated in such a manner!

I pulled even more, my resolve, feeding my anger as I dragged him across the hard-packed ground to the chair. His legs struck out against the ground as he tried to gain a foothold, kicking up more dust. He bowed his back, twisted his head, and shook his shoulders as he fought against me only succeeding in inflicting more pain upon himself.

He cried out, "Unhand me you son of a bitch!"

I came up to the chair and released my grip on his collar. Before he could regain any comfortable position, I bent forward wrapped my arms around his chest from behind, lifted him off the ground and sat him down hard in the chair. He cried out in pain.

I stepped around and faced him, putting my hand on my Walker Colt, stroking the bone handle pistol grip as I looked him in the eyes.

He looked down at my hand then back at my face. His voice cracked with emotion as he spoke again. "So, that is your plan. You are to execute me by firing squad." He shook his head and puffed out his chest defiantly as he said, "You will give me a soldier's death, is that it?"

I turned away and walked back to the wagon.

I stopped at the front wheel, bent over and retrieved the coiled rope I had set there earlier. As I held one end in my hand, I looked at the tree the Major sat beneath, then back at the coiled rope in my hand. Satisfied that I had the proper length, I dropped the rope on the ground, keeping one end in my hand and, leaned back against the spoked wheel and set to work.

Rawlings called out, "What are you waiting for Chambers? Do you think I will plead and beg if you prolong this?" He turned his head and spit on the ground. "I will not give you the satisfaction you bastard!"

I formed a loop in the rope by bringing the end up and held it against the length of rope, made a smaller loop at the top, leaving a long tail hanging down. Reaching behind me, I felt along the axel of the wheel and grabbed a handful of grease. With the grease I rubbed the two joining lengths of rope. Satisfied, I wiped off the excess on the top of the wheel.

Rawlings again called to me. "What are you doing. Shoot me and be done with it!"

With the tail end of the rope, I began wrapping it around the two joined lengths, starting at the bottom, repeating this until I created seven looped knots up the length, stopping at the smaller loop at the top. Taking the tail, I fished it through the smaller loop then pulled one end of the larger, lower loop until the smaller loop collapsed and captured the tail.

I held it up, almost admiring my handiwork. This being only the second time I had tied such a knot, I was satisfied in knowing that it would work, as it did the other time.

I gathered up the coil of rope, threw it over my shoulder and walked back to the Major, holding the large, knotted loop in plain view.

As I neared Rawlings looked hard at what I was carrying. He squinted his eyes against the sun, trying to discern what I held in front of me. The closer I got to the vile man the more he understood what his final fate would be.

Eyes wide, fear clearly on his face he cried, "No! No!" He began to rock back and forth in the chair. "You cannot do this! I will not hang! You cannot hang me!"

I stopped in front of him; the noose dangled from my hand, swinging freely from side to side.

He looked up with pleading eyes. He said, "Please Wyatt. I beg you not to hang me. Shoot me. Give me the honor of being shot as a soldier Wyatt. I implore you."

I reached out, dropped the open loop of the noose around his neck, and pulled. Before he could react, I threw the coiled section of rope over a thick limb of the tree above me, caught the rope as it came back down and took up the slack.

Rawlings' head was forced at an awkward angle as I maintained the pressure on the rope. With my free arm I grabbed the man around his upper body and together with the rope I lifted him off the seat to the standing position, balancing precariously from side to side standing on the flimsy chair.

I kept pulling on the rope so he would not fall free of the chair as he thrashed back and forth trying to escape his bonds. I walked it back to the base of the tree where I looped it around the trunk several times then tied it off, leaving just a hint of slack in the line.

Again, I stood back and looked over my handiwork.

Rawlings, trying desperately to maintain his footing on the rickety chair, ceased thrashing about realizing this would only hasten the outcome. His head, pulled to the side by the tightness of the knot and rope, made him gag and cough as he sucked in the air.

He said between gasps of breath, "I beg you Wyatt, do not hang me." He coughed. "Please Wyatt."

I stood in front of him, looked at his contorted face, shook my head, and walked away.

He called to me. "Where are you going? You cannot leave me here!" He coughed repeatedly yet continued to plead for mercy. "I beg of you Wyatt, please cut me down."

I joined Lizzie, reached up and took her hand in mine. I asked, "Are you ready to go darlin'?"

She looked over her shoulder at the Major then back at me. She adjusted the Bowler hat and said, "I am ready Wyatt."

I took the reins and led Caliban, Lizzie, and Ted into the wilderness. Behind me I heard the Major's screams and pleadings.

"You son of a bitch! You cannot just leave me here hanging! I cannot stand forever on this chair! Come back here you bastard!"

We walked at an easy pace. It was going to be a long, hard journey. Behind us the Major's pleas grew faint as the distance between us increased. Before long, we heard nothing but the wind.

The land stretched out before us as my mind went through the possibilities of making the journey back to Fredericksburg. Short on water, only one horse and little food the odds were certainly not with us, yet; we had to try.

I took this time to get to know my riding companion on this latest expedition. I looked over my shoulder at the young child. She was a beautiful girl under all that dirt and grime. Her small hands held onto the saddle horn as her body moved with the motion of the horse.

I asked, "Where are you from Lizzie?"

She said, "We were from Tennessee. Chattanooga way. Pa wanted to give us a fresh start here in Texas with the war ruinin' everything back home."

I nodded. "That is what brought me to Texas. I hail from Georgia."

She asked, "Did you fight in the war Wyatt?"

"I did. I was a cavalry officer under General Stuart." I turned back to her and said, "I fought for the south."

"As did my Pa," she said. "Do not know who he was with." She paused then asked, "What will happen to that bad man Wyatt?"

I sighed. "Do you really want to know?"

She said, "I do."

I looked back at her again and asked, "How old are you darlin'?"

She sat a bit higher in the saddle and said, "I am eight years old, fixin' to be nine."

"You are rather inquisitive for eight years," I said.

She stood her ground and asked again, "What will happen to him?"

Again, I sighed, then said, "He will grow tired of standing and fall off the chair, or the animals will get him when the sun goes down. Either way he is as good as dead."

She was silent for a moment. I suppose she was mulling this over, and once more I found sadness in this line of questioning. She was eight years old and forced to accept a situation that may have just robbed her of her childhood.

Youngsters should be concerned with the simple things in life. The pleasures of playing with friends and school chums. Suffering through the pains of book learning and dictatorial schoolmarms, learning to read and write while creating memories of family and fun. Not concerns about losing your family and what is to become of those that caused such suffering.

She said, "I am okay with what you done Wyatt. I thought you were goin' to shoot him at first. But, you done right."

"I am glad you think so," I said.

She immediately asked, "What troubles you, Wyatt? I can tell you are bothered by the way you talk. My Pa used to do that at times."

"How did you get to be so smart Lizzie?"

She giggled then said sadly, "My Pa used to say that to me." Then she grew quiet.

I stopped walking and turned back to her. She was crying softly. Her head hung down as she wiped the tears from her face. I reached up to her, and she fell into my arms, wrapped arms and legs around me, and cried into my chest. I held her tight, whispering in her ear that it was okay to cry. Let it out, darlin', let it out, I thought.

She looked up at me. The tears had fallen down her dirty face showing the clean white skin of a child. She asked, "What is to become of me?"

I took my neckerchief and wiped the tears while cleaning the dirt away. I said, "I will get you back to Fredericksburg then we will reach out to your grandmother. Have no fears darlin'. I will not let anything bad happen to you anymore."

She wiped at her eyes and inhaled. "What happened to my ma and pa and baby brother after they was shot?"

I gritted my teeth as I wished a miserable death upon Rawlings for what he has done to this child. I said, "Me and Ted buried them proper sweetheart. Real respectful like."

She sniffed, wiped her eyes again and asked, "Will you take me there someday?"

"I will. I promise."

She hugged me long and hard, kissed me on the cheek and said, "We best be goin, Wyatt."

I could not help but smile as I put her back on the horse.

I grabbed the reins and resumed our trek through the wilderness feeling a bit better than when we left. Though our chances were slim, they were not impossible. I looked up at her in the saddle. Once again, she adjusted the bowler hat.

She asked, "Why does this hat have two holes in it Wyatt?"

I said, "Ted was with me when we got in a fight with some bad men, and a fella tried to shoot him in the head and missed."

She took the hat off, looked at the holes, and whistled. "The fella did not miss too much."

I chuckled when I said, "Ted thought the same thing."

Lizzie put the hat back on her head, adjusted it then asked, "What was your friend like?"

"Well," I began, "he was a strong man. Smart, like you. Always thought tomorrow will be better and never gave up."

Lizzie was thoughtful for a moment then said, "Then I will wear his hat forever and ever."

I looked over my shoulder and said, "He would like that, Lizzie. He really would."

We fell silent, talked out for the moment I suppose. It was not an awkward nor uncomfortable silence, just one of reflection. I thought of Ted while, I am certain; she thought of her family. It was best to remember those departed with fond memories and not dwell on the way they met their end.

I reached back for the canteen and passed it up to Lizzie saying, "Just enough to get the dryness out of your mouth darlin'."

She took a swig and handed it back. "Just enough," she said with a smile.

I took a swig and returned the canteen to the saddle horn. Taking the bota bag, I stopped and gave Caliban some water taking note as to how much we had left. Try as I might, I could not figure a way to ration our water for the journey.

Near as I could figure, we should make Fredericksburg in five to seven days. Any way I figured it, we did not have enough water for the trip. Food could be gotten along the way. I could shoot a rabbit, a coyote even to give us food. But water was something I could not find in this desolate place. I had heard that a man could go three days, sometimes as many as five without water. But what would that be like as we tried to walk out of the wilderness?

I pushed these thoughts out of my mind. We will cross that bridge when and if we get to it. At this moment my only concern needed to be putting one foot in front of the other and walking out of this unforgiving place.

Lizzie asked, "Are you married Wyatt?"

"I am not. But I have a girl. Her name is Arabella, and we plan on getting married one day."

"Is she in Fredericksburg waitin' for you," she asked.

I thought of Arabella's beautiful face as I answered. "No, she lives in Kentucky. When the time is right, she will join me down here."

"I bet she is pretty."

I laughed. "She is very pretty."

Quietly, almost to herself Lizzie said, "My ma was pretty."

I looked over my shoulder at the young girl. She wiped at her eyes quickly, shook her head as if she was shaking out the creeping emotions of sadness and looked out over the horizon.

She said, "Reckon the sun will be goin' down soon."

"Yep," I said.

Until then, we walked while the sun hit our backs feeling like the heat of a fire. There was no escape from the misery of the burning sun that cooked the very ground we trod.

My footfalls were loud as the hardened heels of my boots struck the hard surface, kicking up clouds of dust. Like walking on stone, punishing my feet with each step. The vegetation becoming sparse, making way for more dirt and sand.

This section of land we had traveled at night when we searched for the girl. It was uninviting, threatening, and terrible. Everywhere I looked seemed the same as what lay before me. The heat shimmers rising to the sky distorted the distant view of the horizon. Be it straight, left or right, it was the same. Desolation.

CHAPTER FORTY-SIX

The night was upon us now as we continued our journey through the wilderness. One step, then another I led Caliban, Lizzie, and Ted deeper into the darkness as I willed my tired legs to stay in motion. One step, then another as I called upon my strength to keep moving.

I tried to recall the last time I slept as the past events played out in my mind. My time piece long forgotten as the hours and days were no longer measured by the hands of a watch, but by the singular scrapes and fights, we had endured. From the moment the desperadoes tried to take us after leaving Kerrville, the first gunfight in the street, the discovery of the rebel camp and its destruction, to the final street fight leading to the chase. When had I lay my head to rest?

Up until now, I had been charged by the energy of hunting down the Major and his brother, always in pursuit of something or someone. Now, having left the Major and his brother behind, so goes the energy that had fueled my body. Like coming to the end of a great quest, a long endeavor, it was over.

Yet, as I looked out through the darkness, I knew that my quest was not, in fact, at an end. Perhaps this will be the most dangerous, the most demanding and difficult task I was to face in this strange adventure.

I looked over my shoulder as my feet, the heels striking the hard ground, stepped out, one foot in front of the other. The child was asleep, head down, moving with the motion of the horse as he too stepped out. His hooves striking the rock-like ground, one in front of the other, determined to continue through the night.

Looking at the girl, I thought of the responsibility that had been thrust upon me. The safeguarding of this child now seemed to be greater than all that had transpired thus far. Whereas myself and my friends had gone up against a great evil, ready to accept the danger, this innocent child had made no such choice nor decision to take part in this horrendous endeavor. She had been unwillingly thrown into it, losing all she had, and perhaps all she would ever have.

I returned my gaze forward as I mulled over this dilemma before me. Though the choice was clear to me and without question nor concern, I still tossed it around in my head. But I knew I would protect this child with my life. I will make certain that she makes it to safety, come hell or high water. I will make it so.

High water, I thought with a grin on my face. Hardly an expression that is fitting for this place. Hell? Well, of course this was hell. How could it not be? Those that traveled through this inhospitable region were faced with two outcomes, and only two. Life, or death. To die in this living hell, I reasoned, would be to condemn your soul to wander around with the burden of living the torment for all eternity. To survive gave you the bragging rights to say that you had walked through hell and came out the other side.

"And that is what we are gonna do," I uttered aloud.

Where my shoulders drooped, they now picked up. Where my back was bent, I now stood taller and straighter. My steps now became more forceful, confident, like my days of marching at VMI. I was a soldier once more and as such will conduct myself accordingly. I was going to walk us out of this God-Forsaken place.

Behind me Lizzie said, "Wyatt. I would like to walk with you a spell. I cannot feel my backside."

I stopped and turned to her. "Sure thing darlin'," I said as I picked her out of the saddle and set her down. "You sure you want to walk a bit?"

She reached up and put her small hand in mine. "I am sure Wyatt."

I asked, "How about a drink first?"

She smiled and said, "Only enough to take the dryness out of my mouth."

I handed her the canteen, taking note of how little remained in the vessel. I said, "That is right Lizzie."

She took a small swig and handed it back. I shook it once, replaced the stopper, and hung it back on the saddle.

She looked up at me, clearly puzzled. "Ain't you gonna have a drink?"

I smiled, feeling the dryness of my lips. "Nah, I am fine. I had a drink while you were sleeping."

"I think you might be tellin' me a tale," she said as she took my hand.

I gave her tiny hand a reassuring squeeze and, taking up the reins, began to resume our trek, though with shorter steps.

We walked in silence, hand in hand, stepping around the many ground obstructions. Scrub brush, prickly pear cactus, low growing mesquite, and rocks. The ground, flat and never-ending, differed from the black star strewn sky above. One held the desperation of a harsh, unpleasing environment. The other showed hope and beauty.

I used these stars to navigate and keep our course in an easterly direction. By no means an expert at navigating by the stars, I was still well versed in knowing the cardinal directions by seeking out specific stars and constellations.

As I was looking at the stars, I caught a quick motion in front of us. Lizzie too had seen it as I heard her catch her breath and stop in her tracks.

She gripped my hand tightly and leaned into my leg. "I saw something run in front of us Wyatt," she whispered.

I put my hand on my pistol and said, "I saw it too darlin'. Probably a coyote."

"Will they attack us," she asked.

I thought of the early evening when Ted and myself fought our way through the large pack of coyotes, driven mad by thirst and hunger. I took a deep breath and said, "No Lizzie. They are just curious."

Then, a second animal ran in front of us as Caliban became nervous, pulling against the reins.

Lizzie said, "Wish I had my Pa's pistol."

Never taking my eyes away from our surroundings I asked, "Your Pa teach you how to shoot?"

Lizzie's head was in constant motion, looking left then right as she answered. "I used to go hunting with him back in Tennessee. I can shoot real good too."

"That a fact," I uttered while searching for the unseen danger.

I turned, picked Lizzie up, and put her back in the saddle. I said, "You stay up here Lizzie." I pulled my pistol. "We best be movin' on."

I picked up the pace, reins in one hand, the Walker Colt in the other as we continued our march. My eyes seeking out the danger in the darkness, my pistol following my line of sight. Finger on the trigger, thumb resting atop the hammer, I was ready to engage the enemy as I continued leading us eastward.

As we walked, the sounds of the night became desperate as the hungry animals called out. Yips and cries were heard all around us, yet they did not come closer. They voiced their hunger, their despair as they shadowed our path. I knew it was only a matter of time before one of them would brave an assault in the hopes of winning out to soothe the aches and pains of an empty belly. This, I hoped, would happen.

Lizzie cried out and yelled, "Over there Wyatt! I saw one of them."

I looked to the left, where she was pointing and stopped.

His eyes reflected the dim light of the stars, giving him a sinister look. His mouth was open, tongue hanging to the side as he bared his teeth, slowly coming near.

As the animal began to sink forward in his stance, I knew he was going to attack. I raised the pistol and said, "Cover your ears darlin'."

I pulled the trigger, sending the forty-four caliber ball into the coyote's face. The force of the impact sent his body backwards, spraying the ground with bone, flesh, and blood. It was just what we needed to make our escape.

Our walk had now turned into a near run as I pulled the reins. Behind us, in the darkness, we heard the sounds of the other animals tearing into the dead coyote. The sound of nature at its most extreme sent a chill down my back.

How far we had gone or how long I kept up the difficult pace is unknown to me. I just kept going, willing the distance between us and the carnage behind to increase with each step. The greater the distance, the better.

After some time, I slowed then stopped, trying to catch my breath. I was winded and surmised I had run a mile, perhaps more.

Lizzie asked, "Do you think it is safe now?"

I looked around, hand on my pistol. "I believe it is darlin'."

Lizzie swung her leg over the saddle and lowered herself to the ground. She came over and hugged me.

I said, "Do not worry Lizzie. I will get us out of here."

She released her grip on me, took my hand and said, "I know you will Wyatt." She looked out into the darkness. "I think we should keep going."

I could not help but admire this young lady. I asked, "How did you get to be so tough?"

She adjusted the bowler hat with her free hand. "I reckon it was Pa. After he came back from the war, Ma said he was different. He taught us all kinda new things."

I smiled, knowing how her father had changed. Those of us that returned to our homes after four bitter years of fighting came back changed men. Not all of us for the wiser, and not all of us for the better.

We walked through the night, keeping our guard, aware of our surroundings should the wildlife mount another attack against us.

In front of us, the sky began to lighten as the morning sun showed itself. The sky turned red and orange that reminded me of the colors of fire on a dark night. On any other occasion, it would be a vision to admire. Not so for us. It was a dreadful reminder that with its beauty came the harshness of the day. The stifling heat with the brutality of the sun would steal our strength, beat us down until we fell.

I stopped, looked around and uttered, "Damnation."

Lizzie looked up at me and asked, "What is it, Wyatt?"

I said as I looked down at her, "I reckon we need to find someplace to take shelter from the sun."

Lizzie released my hand and went to the canteen hanging from the saddle. She said, "Wyatt, your lips are cracked and dry. You need water."

I sighed. "Well, maybe just a swallow."

She handed me the canteen and stood with her arms crossed over her small chest. The look on her face was one of both concern and determination. I knew it would be a useless gesture on my part to argue with her. Again, I had to admire this strong-willed young lady.

I took a small swig of the warm water, licking my dry cracked lips when I finished. We were down to a quarter of a canteen and one bota bag.

I said, "Give Caliban some of the water from the bota bag Lizzie."

She followed my directions then returned both the bota bag and canteen to the saddle.

I looked around again in the morning light, already feeling the rise in the temperature. I had brought some of the rope and a few tarpaulins taken from the church wagon to rig up a shelter against the sun. It was now just a matter of finding the right spot.

Seeing one off in the distance, I pointed and said, "Over there by those rocks and mesquite, I think I can rig up a shelter for the day."

I led the way, my tired legs, and sore feet protesting with every step. I kept telling myself that rest would come soon enough. I just needed to keep going as I leaned forward as I walked.

The rock formation was not high, perhaps a few feet above the ground. What made its location and position ideal was the direction the formation of rock and brush was facing. Long and narrow, it went from north to south, enabling me to string up the covering to keep us out of the sun for the entire day. Its height was just so that we would be in the shadow of the rock as well as the shadow of the tarpaulin strung above as the sun made its way across the cloudless sky.

In short order, I had strung up the overhead cover, unburdened Caliban, and moved him into the shadow of a large mesquite, laid out my bed roll and sat in the shaded area with Lizzie.

I said, "Before it becomes unbearably hot, we should eat a little somethin' to keep up our strength."

She asked, "What have we to eat?"

I grinned as I attempted to make light of our depleted stores. "Well, my dear one. We have the finest in Texas beef. Cut and dried to perfection."

She leaned forward and looked into the sack. "Reckon it will have to do."

I handed her a strip. "I am afraid the hardtack and salt pork will do nothing for our thirst. Should we find some water we will have it then."

She took the jerky, bit into it, and smiled. She said, "Best jerky I had all day, Wyatt."

I could not help but laugh. Even with the annoyance of cracked dry lips it struck me funny.

We ate in silence, savoring the meager meal, only washing it down with a swig of water, which was now dangerously low. I figured on having just one more day of water then our position would become perilous at best. We still had many miles yet to travel.

Leaning back against my saddle, I tried to get comfortable. I took off my pistol belt and laid it by my side. I was still wearing my vest, though tattered and torn now, so I removed the derringer pistol from the front pocket and took it off.

Lizzie looked at the small handgun and asked, "What kinda gun is that?"

I held up the two barreled pistol and said, "It is a Remington forty-one caliber derringer." I pointed to my Walker Colt and said, "Unlike the cap and ball of that big pistol this takes a small metal cartridge."

I broke open the breech, rotated the barrel up and removed one of the short cartridges. I then began to demonstrate to Lizzie the basic operation of the handgun, teaching her how to load it, unload it and how to cock the hammer.

She said, "That is easy enough." She grinned and said, "Bet I could shoot it."

I was thoughtful for a moment. This young girl who had lost everything, including her childhood in a matter of days, was now expressing a desire to learn the use of a pistol. What a cruel turn of events I mused.

I said, "Your Daddy did teach you to shoot."

"That he did," she responded.

I sighed and leaned forward, handing her the derringer. "Well, what say we have another lesson? I could always use a hand to back me up in troubled times."

She took the small frame pistol and stood. "Okay Wyatt."

I crawled out from the shaded cover, stretched my sore back for a moment, and looked for a target.

I pointed to a prickly pear cactus some ten feet distant and said, "It works like your Daddy's pistol. You cock the hammer for each shot. Only difference is you only have two bullets in this gun."

She stepped next to me and brought the pistol up.

I said, "You will have to get a few feet closer darlin'. It does not have the same range as your Daddy's revolver."

She stepped up to within five feet, raised the pistol and said, "That one pad sticking out on the side."

I watched as she used both hands, cocked the hammer back with her thumb, and slowly exhaled. I could tell, even before she fired, that her Pa had taught her well.

She squeezed the trigger; the hammer fell, and the gun fired with a loud crack. The prickly pear cactus pad snapped back and fell to the ground.

I stepped over and picked up the pad, holding it up to my eye. The hole was directly in the center. I lowered my hand and whistled.

I said, "That was some good shootin'."

Lizzie was grinning from ear to ear. She said, "Tol ya, my Pa taught me."

Despite the misery of our situation at present I decided to have some fun with her. I said, "You were just lucky. I bet you a shiny five-dollar gold piece you cannot do that again."

She said, "I ain't got a gold piece. But I can do it again."

I playfully put my hands on my hips, cocked my head to the side, closed one eye and said, "I reckon I can trust you. You are good for it."

She giggled and said, "Okay. How about that cactus pad sticking out on the top?"

I looked over my shoulder, identified the target in question then suddenly uttered, "I reckon I need to get out of the way."

Once I joined her, she again took aim and cocked the hammer. The pistol shot cracked and the cactus pad fell to the ground. I stood there shaking my head.

She looked up at me and said with a giggle, "You owe me a shiny new five-dollar gold piece."

I looked down at her and said, "I did not say anything about it being new."

We returned to the comfort of the shelter. Before I sat, I fished the five-dollar gold piece out of my vest and handed it to Lizzie. I told her, "Here you are darlin'. I lost fair and square."

She took the large coin and held out the pistol to me.

I said, "You can keep that too. You have a right to defend yourself out here Lizzie." Again, I reached for my vest and handed her two fresh cartridges. "You best reload it."

I watched her as she removed and discarded the spent shell casings, then load the two cartridges into the breech, close it, then secured it with the loading lever. I nodded in approval and took a seat against my saddle.

Pulling my hat down over my eyes I said, "Reckon we should get some rest Lizzie."

I began to drift off when I felt her little body slip under my arm and snuggle close into my chest. I raised my hat, looked down at the top of her head, and wrapped my arm around her.

We were soon asleep.

CHAPTER FORTY-SEVEN

How long had we been traipsing through the wilderness? The days now became confused as did the nights. Near as I could figure we had been walking four days now. My confident steps had become more of a shuffle than a walk. Slowly dragging my feet across the hard-packed ground as the days gave way to night, and the night gave way to days; it mattered not. We had to keep going.

The water, long since consumed, was but a memory as was the food. We had supplemented our thirst and nourishment with the ever-present prickly pear cactus. Its sweet flavor was unique, and its moisture welcomed to our dry mouths and empty stomachs. But it was not enough to combat the oppressive heat and the energy expelled on our journey.

We were barely alive as we made our way through the land.

It was night now as I shuffled along. The past few days I had tried to display a confident outlook, free of concern for Lizzie's sake. She would often question our route of march, our distance yet to travel, our need for water and food. The concern clearly in her voice, in her words. She was not one to complain nor call into question my competence in getting us back to civilization. Rather, it was questions for her own understanding. In fact, during times of rest or when I was preparing another cactus pad for our meal, she would help by gathering the fruit and tending to Caliban. She was a strong-willed youngster, sharing in the burdens of the journey.

I looked over my shoulder at her as I shuffled along. Her head hung down, the bowler hat covering her face, her small hands gripping the saddle horn; she was asleep.

Across her shoulder, bouncing with the motion of the horse, hanging across her side, was the small possibles bag for my pipe and tobacco. I had given it to her to keep her five-dollar gold piece, pistol and cartridges. It hung across her chest, over her torn and tattered dress. The once white fabric with hints of blue flowers was covered with the dirt and dust of this damnable place. I suppose I too was a sight.

I sighed and turned back to the direction of travel. Out there, somewhere was the town of Fredericksburg, Texas. Perhaps, just beyond the horizon. Surely one more day, we will arrive. Just one more day in this hell. Yes, we could do that. One more day of this torture and we will walk into town, straight to the cafe for a thick steak and a pitcher of cool water. No more cactus pads. Yes, sir, just one more day.

I reached up and touched my dry, cracked lips. They seem swollen now, painful, making it difficult to talk. My tongue, dry and rough, was thick, causing me difficulties when trying to eat. The only relief came when I sucked on the cactus pad. But it was not enough.

Ah, hell, who was I kidding? We were dying.

I looked out over the dark horizon. The weight of our situation was becoming unbearable, and I stopped and looked up at the stars. I wanted to scream, to yell and shake my fist at the Almighty. I wanted Him to tell me why He had forsaken us. Why is He going to leave us in this place to die? Why has He turned his back on us, ignored us and condemned us to this place?

Suddenly, I felt lightheaded and fell to my knees and hung my head, my arms limp at my side as I felt the last of my energy drain away. Was this how it was to end? I fell forward on my hands, my breath, short and raspy. Blackness surrounded me.

Suddenly, out of this void I heard a voice. Faint at first, like a whisper almost, yet it was familiar to me. I felt my body moving, shaking back and too. What is it? What is this rocking motion I feel?

Then my head cleared and I heard the words as they were spoken to me.

"Get up Wyatt! You cannot give up," she said.

I turned my head and saw the dirty, yet angelic face of Lizzie. She was pushing on my back repeatedly trying to get me to my feet.

She yelled, "Get up Wyatt! You cannot die and leave me alone!" Her little hands became fists, striking me on the back. Over and over again, she lashed out at me. "You promised me Wyatt! Do not leave me out here alone...please Wyatt!"

She began to cry all the while striking, lashing out at me.

I pushed myself up and sat as I reached out to her. I wrapped my arms around her little body, pulled her to me and held onto her as she sobbed against my neck.

I tried to speak. The words, hoarse past my dry tongue. "I am not going to die on you little one." I cleared my throat and coughed as I tried to reassure her. "I just tripped darlin'. I am okay now."

She pushed away from me and said between sobs, “You best get on your feet.”

I nodded. “Help me up Lizzie.”

I made a show of accepting her assistance as I got back to my feet. I inhaled deeply and looked up at the heavens. I said in defiance, “I ain’t dead yet.”

I looked down at the child, grateful to have her by my side. I said, “Thank you Lizzie.”

She took my hand and said, “I am sorry I hit you, Wyatt. I was scared you was gonna leave me.”

I smiled through my cracked swollen lips. “I made you a promise darlin’. I ain’t goin’ anywhere.” I looked east as the sun began to show itself. “Reckon we should keep goin’ for a spell, then find some shelter.”

We walked hand in hand toward the rising sun. My resolve had been renewed as had my stubborn determination. I would fulfill my promise to both Lizzie and Ted.

As the sun rose, so did the temperature. It was time to seek shelter from the coming heat and rest our weary bodies. I kept telling myself, just one more day and we would be home.

I found a suitable spot and strung our cover. Though not as quickly as I had done in the previous days, and perhaps not as efficient, it would do for our needs. I made a quick inspection of the camp then we unburdened Caliban and moved him under a shelter I had rigged to keep him in the shade.

Lizzie began to gather our prickly pear cactus, and I joined her under the shelter. Taking my knife, I began to cut away the spines then, making a lengthwise cut I peeled off the skin.

As I was preparing another of the pads, I felt as though we were being watched. Like the feelings I had before our many street fights, I trusted this feeling. I dropped the pad and crawled out from under the tarpaulin still clutching the knife.

He sat atop his pony. He was tall, muscular, with a fierce look upon his dark face. His long black hair hung around his shoulders with a single feather hanging off to the side. He gripped a long war lance, pointing skyward, two black tipped white feathers hung from the spearhead. Around his neck hung a colorful beaded necklace, bedecked with small feathers over his bare chest.

It was the Indian, War Hawk.

I dropped the knife and put my hand on my pistol. He raised the war lance and pointed it at me, ready for the attack. I went no further.

Lizzie came out of the shelter, gasped audibly, then stood close by my side. In her hand was the Remington derringer. We stood together looking at the warrior, motionless.

He began to speak, to yell. He motioned at us with his war lance. He was animated as he spoke unfamiliar words to us. Occasionally thrusting his war lance in our direction as he spoke in his native tongue. I was mesmerized by his passion.

Then he fell silent and just looked at us.

Lizzie leaned against my left leg, knowing that I needed my right hand to pull the Walker pistol.

Quietly I said, "Darlin', get behind me."

She slowly moved, hugging my leg as the warrior watched intently.

My hand rested on the pistol grip of the revolver as I locked eyes with the Indian. I wanted to convey a firm message that I was ready for a fight.

He returned my stare then quickly looked over his shoulder to the east. He looked back at me and made a sort of growling noise through clenched teeth.

Pointing his war lance in our direction again, he yelled, raised the long weapon and thrust the knife-like end in the ground. Holding the reins of his pony, he again spoke through clenched teeth, then smacked the animal and rode off, leaving the war lance sticking out of the ground like some tall limbless tree.

I staggered over to the lance, grabbed it with both hands, and leaned against it for support as I tried to catch my breath. My heart was racing as I leaned heavily against the weapon, hanging onto it to keep from falling to my knees.

I pulled the war lance free, held it up and screamed at the top of my lungs. My anger consumed my very being. I dropped to my knees, still clutching the spear. How many more trials must we endure? When will this nightmare end, and how?

I threw the weapon aside as Lizzie came up and wrapped her arms around my neck. She said, "It was that Indian from the wagon Wyatt." She leaned against me, then asked, "What did he want?"

I shook my head and said, "I do not know darlin'. I just do not know."

I lifted my head and looked out to the east. My eyes, tired and burning were trying to focus on an image off in the distance. It was difficult to discern as I tried to focus through the rising heat shimmers.

I pointed and asked Lizzie, "What is that I spy off to the east?"

She looked, rubbed her eyes then said, "It looks to be a dust cloud."

I coughed and tried to clear my dry throat. "A dust cloud," I repeated. "A dust cloud."

Just then Lizzie said with alarm, "Wyatt, I think I see a rider out there." She rubbed her eyes again. "Oh Lord, the Indian is coming back!"

Still on my knees I grabbed Lizzie with one hand as I pulled my pistol with the other and said, "Get behind me."

She stood behind me as I raised the revolver up and tried to hold it steady. Suddenly its weight was more than my weakened arm could hold. Try as I might I could not keep the pistol centered on the growing mass of man and horse as they came closer. The pistol danced in my hand from side to side, up and down.

I looked at the approaching man, blinking my burning eyes as I tried to focus. The image was a blur, hazy at best. How was I to shoot if I could not see clearly? I willed my eyes to see as the image grew large.

Lizzie stepped around from behind me and held her pistol out with both hands, pointing at the incoming rider.

She said, "It is not the Indian Wyatt." She kept the pistol raised and called out. "That be far enough mister!"

I tried to focus on the image. It was not the Indian as far as my tired eyes could see. He was a large man, dark of skin atop an equally large animal. His hat obscured his face. He pulled up and sat his horse.

I tried to speak but the words failed to make it passed my dry tongue, cracked and swollen lips. Instead, I tried to keep the Walker Colt from falling free of my grip and pointed the pistol at the unknown rider.

Lizzie yelled, "What do you want, mister? Are you with that Indian?"

I watched as the giant of a man dismounted and held up his hands. "Now missy, I aim to do you no harm," he responded.

I shook my head. I must have slipped into a state of delirium as the voice rang familiar to me. I tried to speak but only coughed. I fell forward on my right elbow, still trying to keep the pistol on the man.

Lizzie asked, "Who might you be mister?"

He stepped a bit closer, lowered his arms and said, "Cap'n. Is that you?"

I squinted my eyes and finally saw the clear image of the man. I managed to utter, "Julius." Then I fell forward to the ground. "Julius," I repeated as I rolled to my side.

I watched as he cautiously came forward with his hands held out to the sides. Lizzie kept her pistol on him as she kept looking from the large man to me, uncertain as to what was going to transpire.

I managed to say with a rough voice, "It is okay darlin', he is my friend."

She lowered the pistol and dropped to her knees. "Oh, thank you Lord," she whispered.

Julius came over and knelt beside me. He wore a large brimmed, low crown hat against the sun and a pistol around his waist. It was the first time I had seen him so attired. I could not help but smile.

He said, "Lord have mercy Cap'n. You look near death." With a shaking hand he rested it on my shoulder saying, "I will get the others over here."

I felt the last of my strength leaving me, my throat raw and sore but managed to ask, "The others?"

"Yes sir," he said as he rose. "All of us has been lookin' for you the past three days. We got the army with us too."

I smiled and said, "The army. How 'bout that."

Lizzie leaned against me as Julius stepped away. I put my arm around her and pulled her close. I said softly, "We are safe now darlin'. We have the army with us."

She nodded, draped an arm over me, and rested her head on my shoulder. She said, "Thank you Wyatt."

Julius began to shout, "Over here! I found them!" Taking his pistol from the holster, he began firing shots into the air. "I found them! Over here! Come quick!"

As quickly as he left us, he returned with a canteen and knelt next to us. He offered it to Lizzie first saying, "Not too fast now missy, not too fast."

Julius helped me sit up as he gave me the canteen. I took a drink, fighting the urge to swallow the entire contents. I handed it back to Lizzie with shaking hands.

I said, "How is it that you are here my friend?"

Julius said, "Once the Doc fixed everyone up, we decided to head out and join up with you. Figured you might need some help." He looked around then asked, "Where is Mister Ted?"

I looked over my shoulder where Caliban was under shelter. I said sadly, "He did not make it. I have him on a travois."

Julius hung his head. "Oh, damnation. And the Major?"

I looked back to the west and said, "He and his brother are out there. Food for the beasts of the wild and those wretched birds."

In the distance, I heard the sound of horses approaching.

Julius looked up and nodded. "Good." He looked at my companion and asked in a soft voice, "And who might this be?"

"Her name is Elizabeth, but she goes by Lizzie," I said.

Julius extended his massive hand and said, "Pleased to meet you, Miss Lizzie. Folks call me Julius."

She reached out and took his hand, hers disappearing in his. "Are you a lawman like Wyatt?"

Before he could answer, I said, "Yes, he is Lizzie. The best of us." I looked back at Julius and asked hoarsely, "Who all is out here with you?"

Julius said, "Well, Sergeant Major Robert, Drew, Mister Thad and Bill, Mister Skinner and Long Buffalo. Marshal Sweeny." He paused. "It were Marshal Sweeny that got the army to come along."

I took another swig of water and handed the canteen back to Lizzie. "How did Jim get the army to come along?"

Julius said, "Well, they came in lookin' for the fellas that busted up the two soldiers and took Long Buffalo." Julius smiled. "Marshal Sweeny told the army captain they should have been shot for what they done to Long Buffalo. After some more words the army left some soldiers behind to guard the town, and the rest came lookin' for you."

I then asked, "What of Mark and Chelsea?"

Julius smiled again and said, "They are gonna be just fine. Doc did real good fixin' them up."

Behind us the sound of many a horse grew louder. The dust that they kicked up enveloped them as they neared. It was a reassuring sound, one that not only brought back memories but also spoke of our salvation.

Lizzie passed the canteen back to me and said, "The blue coats are comin'."

I laughed at her remark, knowing that she had heard such a phrase from her father. "Now do not be too judgmental of these soldiers, Lizzie. They are here to save us," I said.

Still seated, I turned and watched their approach. Out front there were two men. One uniformed in blue, the other dressed in the familiar attire of my friend Robert. I tried to suppress my smile, as my lips hurt like the dickens, but failed. I took the inconvenience of the throbbing pain knowing that my friends had found us and we were going home.

Chapter Forty-Eight

I stood on the balcony of the Grand Hotel watching the comings and goings of the folks of San Antonio. Here and there they came and went in pursuit of their daily needs and desires. From shopping for a new hat, clothes, or food to put on the table, they came and they went.

I pulled on the rich Virginian shag in my pipe as I toyed with my new hat. I rolled it around in my hands studying the fine stitching, the intricate hand-woven band that circled the flat crown. The light brown of the fabric and the wide brim was just what was required against the Texas sun. I stroked the two black tipped white feathers attached to the hat band as I put the hat on my head and exhaled the fulfilling smoke.

It just was not the same as my old cavalry hat. I repositioned the hat trying in vain to find a comfortable location on my noggin. It was my size, and the fella that sold it to me said it spoke of a dignified authority, whatever the hell that meant. It just did not feel correct.

I heard the door open behind me and turned around. I knew it would be Mister Amon Seltzer, private secretary to Judge Johnathon Hayward DuBose, my boss.

He was just as I remembered him from our first encounter. Small, short in fact, slight of frame and a nervous little fellow. His black hair neatly parted down the middle, pasted down with a fragrant pomade. His spectacles, small and oval enlarged his blue eyes. One might find his appearance comical or amusing thinking that he was faint of heart, frightened of everything. But I knew different.

What he lacked in looks and size he made up with a forceful personality. He was a man of precise thinking and sound decisions, and it was no wonder as to why the Judge had employed him as his second.

He raised his fist to his mouth and cleared his throat. With a slight German accent he said, "Marshal Chambers, the Judge will see you now."

I took the pipe from my mouth, exhaled and said, "That is fine Mister Seltzer. Thank you."

I tapped the pipe against the palm of my hand, intentionally taking my time. I looked at my pocket watch, ten in the a.m. I had waited for the last hour for the Judge to adjourn his court and meet me here, as planned. I had spent the hour trying to figure out what it was I wanted to say and the manner in which I was to say it. I sighed, put my pipe in the pocket of my new frock coat, adjusted my pistol belt, and made for the door.

Again, Mister Seltzer cleared his throat. I stopped and faced the small man.

He said, "I just wanted to say Marshal, that I am very appreciative of the fine work you and Marshal Barton had done on this extraordinary case. You sir, are to be commended."

I grinned. This was the first time Seltzer had broke character and acknowledged events on a personal level. For him, it was always the letter of the law. Everything is all neat and tidy and in its place.

I said, "Thank you Mister Seltzer. But it was not just the two of us. So many gave to bring this to an end." I paused. "Some gave everything."

He produced a white handkerchief, removed his glasses, and began nervously cleaning each lens. He said, "Yes, of course." He put his glasses on and continued. "May I say it is tragic that you lost your friend and the young lady lost her family."

I patted his shoulder and said, "I appreciate that Mister Seltzer." I looked to the glass doors of the balcony. "What say we go meet the Judge."

I followed Mister Seltzer through the winding hallways of the hotel. My footfalls were silent as I walked the red carpeted floors in my new boots. I took notice that the wallpaper was new. Its mixture of gold, red and black stripes ran from floor to ceiling. Since my last visit it seems like the old place was getting fixed up.

In no time we had reached the door to the Judge's room. I looked up and down the hallway thinking that perhaps he had taken a different room; it was unfamiliar to me. He was known to frequent this establishment when in town and always stayed in the same spacious quarters. It mattered not as I shrugged my shoulders and waited to be announced.

Seltzer knocked on the door, waited a moment, opened it, and stepped inside.

He stood away from the door and said, "Marshal Chambers, sir."

I stepped into the large well-appointed room, hat in hand and looked straight ahead as if I were reporting to the commandant of VMI. Old habits will always show themselves when you least expect it, and for some unknown reason I was nervous, and as such, fell back on old ways.

"Thank you, Amon," came the unseen voice. "That will be all for now."

From an adjoining room Judge DuBose came into the common area of the apartment and stood in the center of the room, wiping his hands with a small towel.

He said, "For goodness' sake my boy, relax." He tossed the towel aside. "You look as though you have been called before a court-martial or something."

I relaxed my shoulders and dropped my arms to the side as I looked at the old family friend and Federal Jurist for Texas. His thick wavy hair showed a few new patches of gray and stood out against his black frock coat and white shirt. He looked a bit thin since we last saw each other. But otherwise, everything about his person was as it should be. Especially his deep penetrating eyes.

He stepped forward and extended his hand. "My God son, I am glad to see you safe." He took my hand in both of his and held firm. "This has been such a terrible occurrence my boy. Terrible, simply terrible."

I said, "Yes sir. It certainly was."

He released my hand, put his long arm over my shoulder and led me to a settee in the center of the room.

"Sit my boy. Please sit."

I sat, my back ridged and straight, still holding my hat. I said, "Thank you sir."

He sat next to me, rested his hand on my knee and said, "Damnation boy. Will you relax."

I exhaled, tossed my hat on the low table in front of me, and sat back against the soft cushion.

He looked over at my hat and asked, "New hat?"

"Yes, sir. It is," I responded.

He laughed. "Never thought you would get rid of that old cavalry hat of yours." He looked me over. "New duds as well I see."

I said, "Yes sir. My other clothes did not hold up too well here of late."

He became thoughtful for a moment then said, "No, I expect they would not after what you have been through." He stood, placed his hands behind his back, and began pacing the floor. He stopped and turned to me. "I have spoken with the others involved in this terrible affair, Wyatt. I would like to hear what you have to say, but I fear there is something else on your mind."

I looked up at him. His eyes were not unlike those of my father. Eyes that were either accusatory or sympathetic. I was unsure as to which eyes I beheld.

"Where is your Marshal's badge, Wyatt," he asked.

I reached into my vest pocket, looked at the gold shield, and ran my thumb over the engraved letters, and the fancy scroll work about the edges then promptly tossed it on my hat.

The Judge reached down, picked it up and looked at it, remaining silent for a moment then turned his back to me as he pocketed the tin.

He turned back around and said, "I fear there is something you wish to confess to me son." He sat down in a richly upholstered wing back chair facing me, crossed one of his long legs over the other and said firmly, "Out with it son."

I inhaled deeply and said, "I am afraid Judge that I have violated my oath and your trust."

He continued to look at me and said, "Go on."

At this time, I leaned forward, rested my elbows on my knees, and I began to tell him the tale of what I felt was an ugly, if not dark affair. I spoke of our journey south when first called upon to investigate the robbery. I told him of our return trip, gun battles, and street fights. The killings, the rebel camp, and my part in its destruction. The street fights we failed to keep out of our town and the wounding of my friends.

I left nothing out. I spoke of the anger and despair, the dangers, the failures and the terrible feelings of revenge against those we were sworn to bring in to face justice.

I paused and looked over at the judge, expecting a condemning stare, a look of disappointment even. I got nothing.

He leaned forward and said softly, "Continue."

I waited a moment as I gathered the remaining thoughts I had of this sad situation. It was then that I came to the pursuit into the wilderness, out to the frontier, and the dilemma I suffered from. I told him of Ted and our desires of revenge and our plans to carry these plans to the end. Again, I left nothing out as I told him of the child's abduction and our anger at finding the family slaughtered in the wilderness. I spoke of our continued chase through the frontier until the guilty were found, and they had been apprehended. I then went into the shoot out and the death of my friend. After that, I stopped talking.

The Judge was silent for a moment. Again, he leaned forward in his chair and asked, "What happened to Major Rawlings?"

I sat back and said in a neutral tone, "I hung him."

The Judge said nothing. He slowly uncrossed his legs and pushed himself out of the chair and began pacing around the room once more. From one side of the room to the other, hands behind his back as he would occasionally look up at the ceiling, then back to the floor. He paced.

Suddenly he stopped and turned to me. He asked, "Do you regret hanging this man?"

I looked at the Judge, unblinking and said, "Not one damn bit."

The Judge stepped behind the wing back chair and rested his hands on the top, lightly stroking the thick upholstery with his long fingers. He asked, "Then what is the problem son?"

I looked at him in surprise. I said, "I was sworn to bring him in. I violated my oath and your trust."

He lifted a hand to his chin and thoughtfully rubbed it. "Oh yes. There is that." He stepped around the chair and sat down. He said as he leaned closer, "Well, do not do it again."

My surprise turned into shock. I could not think of anything to say. I sat there befuddled by this. I had been beating myself up since our return, feeling as though I had failed my position as Marshal and the Judge by giving into my feelings of revenge. I did not care a damn for doing it to the villain; he deserved what he got, and I would do it again under the circumstances.

The Judge stood and came around the table and sat next to me. His tone changed as did his demeanor when he began, "Wyatt, in all my years on the bench. Through all these troubled times of war, the unsteady peace and the rebuilding of a nation I have never heard of such an occurrence."

He stood as his outstretched hand waved about the room as he paced. "The absolute evil this man brought down on innocent folks in this, and other states speaks of a man beyond redemption." He smacked a tight fist against his open palm. "By God sir, it was if Satan himself fell upon the people. He had to be stopped." He turned back to me, his voice getting louder, more passionate as he continued. "You, Robert and all the others were thrown against him and his kind to stop him, and, by the Grace of God you did sir!"

He sat next to me again and took a moment to catch his breath.

He looked up and said, "Having said that. I understand the guilt you have carried for your actions." He paused and grinned as he looked at me. "I used to think that the law was black and white. It was either right or wrong, Wyatt. But that is not always the case, nor is it suited for what we have been presented with in these troubled times as we combat an evil beset upon the people."

He stood and turned back to me. Reaching into his pocket he removed the gold shield and said, "I believe this belongs to you, Marshal Chambers."

I stood and faced him. "Yes sir. I believe it does."

His smile was broad as he leaned over and pinned it on my vest. He said, "We will speak no more of this Wyatt."

I returned his smile, nodded and said, "Yes sir."

He inhaled deeply and asked, "Now. What are your plans? Robert mentioned something to me about a trip."

I said, "I made a promise to Ted that I will take him back to his home and bury him next to his wife and child on their old homestead in Tennessee."

He nodded. "And what of the child, Elizabeth?"

"I have sent a wire to her grandmother informing her of the loss of the family," I said. "I also offered to bring Mrs. Harrison back to settle in Texas and that she will have plenty of help in raising the child."

"Oh? And what did she say?"

I smiled and said, "She asked me how soon we could make it out there to pick her up."

The Judge said, "Very noble of you Wyatt. Who will make the journey and when will you depart?"

I said, "Myself and Robert along with Marshal Sweeny, Sheriff W.B.D. Burns and Sheriff Thadius Polehouse." I lowered my voice and added, "We all feel as if we lost a brother."

The Judge nodded. "I understand. They are all fine lawmen. You keep good company Wyatt."

I said, "Mark and Chelsea are not in any condition to make the journey so they will stay behind and care for Lizzie in our absence." I added, "I took the liberty of deputizing Long Buffalo and Skinner Stevens to mind the store while we are gone. Julius will keep them in line."

Again, the Judge smiled and said, "Such a cast of characters in this affair. I will have the Marshal keep an eye on things if need be. How long do you believe the trip to take?"

I said, "I figure two months at least, and we leave the day after tomorrow."

He said, "I should like to see everyone before you depart. Where are you staying?"

"We are all staying with Miss Gwendoline and her father."

He raised an eyebrow when he asked, "Is Miss Arabella in town?"

I felt my face flush and said, "She is. She made the journey while I was recuperating at the Doc's."

The Judge put his arm over my shoulder. "Then tell the ladies I will be around for dinner this evening. I very much want you all to regale me with the tales of this misadventure." He held up a warning finger. "All except for the end. That is between us my boy."

I bent over and grabbed my hat saying, "I will let the ladies know Judge."

Judge DuBose extended his hand and said, "I will be there about five o'clock. I know where the house is."

I shook his hand, put on my hat, and stepped to the door.

As I turned back, the Judge said, "Now that new hat speaks of a dignified authority, Wyatt. I like it."

I grinned, opened the door and said, "Yes sir."

I walked down the hallway seeking the stairs and my exit. I felt so much better since I had unburdened my guilt in my failings. I did not want to embarrass nor break the bond of trust that existed between the Judge and myself. Just like the trust I had with my friends. For me, it was sacred, as it was for them.

I found the staircase and again took notice of the fresh new carpet as I made my way to the lobby, stopping at the foot of the stairs. I turned to the desk to acknowledge the clerk and smiled at the man behind the counter.

I stepped over and extended my hand. "Hello Anthony. So good to see you again."

The middle-aged man in his string tie and white pressed shirt looked up from the ledger and smiled. He reached out with both hands and took mine in a firm grasp.

He said excitedly, "My goodness, Marshal Chambers. So wonderful to see you again."

I recalled the pleasant interaction we had when we first met the hotel employee. We had been thrust into a world unknown to us, and he had taken us through it, never complaining and always helpful.

He asked, "How are you and Marshal Barton?"

I said, "We are well. How are you and yours my friend?"

He said, "Oh fine sir. Very well." He lowered his voice and said, "I heard about that recent trouble you had out in Fredericksburg." He began shaking his head. "Terrible, just terrible. I am glad you came through it all okay."

I did not bother to press him on the details of the stories he may have heard. I am certain that what he has heard was far from the truth as it usually was. No matter. We chatted for a spell, then I bid him farewell and made for the exit.

Out on the street I looked around then set off to our temporary lodgings and the company of my friends. It was a bit of a walk from the hotel but one that I took pleasure in.

My journey was just beginning, and I took the time to break in my new boots.

About the Author

Having served in both the United States Army and Air Force, Steven McKain retired from military service and lives in Richmond Hill, Georgia, with his wife. Together, they travel the country, spending time in Texas with their children and grandchildren while searching for more stories to share.

www.ingramcontent.com/pod-product-compliance
Lightning Source LLC
LaVergne TN
LVHW041140150826
845673LV00001B/54

9798998564727